ANDERSEN LIGHT

A META-NORMAL NOVEL

TANYA D. DAWSON

12/14/2021
Dear Helton familia,
Keep shining your bright
lights in this world!
Que tu luz siga
brillando.
With love & gratitude,
♡ Tanya D. Dawson

EMPOWER
P R E S S

TANYA D. DAWSON

ANDERSEN LIGHT

A META-NORMAL NOVEL

Cover Design by Mibl Art

An Imprint for GracePoint Publishing (www.GracePointPublishing.com)
GracePoint Matrix, LLC
624 S. Cascade Ave
Suite 201
Colorado Springs, CO 80903
www.GracePointMatrix.com
Email: Admin@GracePointMatrix.com
SAN # 991-6032

Library of Congress Control Number: 2021915707
ISBN-13: (Paperback) – 978-1-951694-76-0
eISBN: (eBook) - 978-1-951694-75-3

Books may be purchased for educational, business, or sales promotional use.
For bulk order requests and price schedule contact:
Orders@GracePointPublishing.com

CONTENTS

FROM THE PUBLISHER

For more great books, visit Empower Press online at https://
gracepointpublishing.com/empower-press/

For Paula,
and all those endeavoring to
become who you are.

CHAPTER ONE

STARKTON

Georgie tucked into the cozy crook of Dad's old willow tree, knees to chin. Leaf shadows danced along her arms and legs as afternoon sunlight trickled through narrow leaves. Summer's lingering scent and light breeze whispered and swished through the willow's cascading branches. The rhythm comforted—just what a girl needed after having her life whacked out of orbit.

She could pinch herself. Georgie was out west in Mystic Creek, Oregon now. Even here, safe with Dad and his gigantic tree, her body tensed with the memory of Starkton. Should she have said or done something earlier? Nope, not with the threat against Mom. Georgie hadn't been heroic or anything. She'd done what she had to. Anybody would have. Thank God her family didn't live in Starkton anymore.

Mom had wanted to start over with a clean slate after her divorce from Dad. She shook the hell out of the cosmic Etch A Sketch and they'd landed in Starkton. It wasn't just about what happened there. Anyone with half a brain could have seen what it was like. Even its air felt empty, with no scent or promise.

Georgie had lived there with her mother, two younger sibling units, and stepfather—a new and most unwelcome addition—until, in a slow, steady descent, life tipped over and exploded. Hooks grabbed at her insides even now as she reflected on the day she'd come home from school to discover her sister literally cornered by their creepy stepfather. She squeezed her eyes shut to keep from even thinking about Starkton.

Of course it didn't work, but she could find relief in the memory of its blandness. As its name insinuated, Starkton was a place built for function, not for fun. It didn't inspire thoughts of magic or spark spontaneous bouts of creativity. It left Georgie wanting—what, she didn't exactly know, but the blankness caused her soul to search, like a ship's captain forever scanning the horizon.

She imagined how the area they lived in resembled a rectangle, as if someone had drawn faint lines of a giant football field and divided it into a neighborhood. Situated on the county road she used to run on, each house had its own rectangular yard and identical concrete sidewalk.

Their yard was empty except for the stubby grass and a patch of flowers her mom kept to console her inner artist. Marigolds punched through the rocky dirt as if to laugh and flip off the starkness. They were miniature miracles, bursts of color growing in spite of some unspoken rule, urged into being by Mom's love of them.

The Braun family lived in the first rectangle. Mrs. Braun spent most of her time keeping a lookout, yelling at the two Braun children to, "get down, be quiet, or to go to your room." Georgie lived next door in the second lot with Mom, a.k.a. Mary, her sister Rose, brother Bill, and their stepfather.

His name was Jack, Jackass to Georgie. When Mom wasn't home he often walked around the house and yard proclaiming to Georgie, Bill, and Rose how he was king of the kingdom and all he surveyed. His favorite oversized and overstuffed chair in the living room was off limits. The three of them called it the king's chair. When they were younger, like last winter, they warned each other not to sit in it as they bounced on it like a mini trampoline. That was before.

At nearly fifteen, Georgie took charge of lightening the weird atmosphere for Bill and Rose. She introduced the table setting game in which they placed the biggest king-sized utensils at Jack's place, like extra-large serving spoons and barbecue forks. Depending on the menu, he might also get a mixing bowl and supersized drink tumbler. The sport didn't last long since Mom got angry and made them change out their hard-played work. Mom didn't get it.

Jack's walks around his kingdom and declarations of royalty came to almost seem normal. They'd hear him coming by the thud, thud, thud of his massive feet lumbering under the weight of his tall frame. Times when he wore only underwear never seemed normal. He'd hook his thumb deep into the waistband of his tighty whities, stare off into the distance, no doubt gloating over his imagined realm, and with a loud and booming voice announce, "Your mother is a lucky woman." He'd leer and pause for dramatic effect, "And you will be too, Georgie." She cringed and wondered what he meant, but didn't ask. He said lots of other things. No way she'd ask about those either. His standard, unveiled threat followed, "But that is our little secret. It'll stay that way if you love your mother." A sickening feeling moved from her throat way down into her gut somewhere, even before his foul expression forced eye contact.

Ordinarily upbeat and outgoing, at first she didn't notice how her stomach tightened in fear or how she held her breath whenever he was around, as if either would make her less noticeable or make him go away. Bill and Rose mirrored her. They, too, held their breath, and their wooden faces reflected the fear and dread Georgie wished they didn't feel. She'd roll her eyes for Bill and Rose as if to say, "What an idiot." It was enough to breathe again. They could laugh later.

Running the country road adjacent to her neighborhood rectangle almost cleared Georgie's head. Most days she ran through tears and clenched teeth. She was getting fast, very fast, but not enough to shake the Jackass muck.

Sleep produced unusual dreams visited by a tall stranger whose entire body exuded a bright gold and white glow. The two of them dangled their legs from a bridge and watched water race toward its destination while they talked about her life. The dreams became instructive. Under his watchful eyes she created a sword, its blade of light, hilt and scabbard sparkling with jewels of ocean hues. She practiced making the blade flame into a huge, brilliant blaze. How did it not burn her? "Your sword has powerful protective qualities. It will never harm you," he assured her. The sword hovered next to her bed at night in the bedroom she shared with Bill and Rose. She visualized blazing sword clones hovering near their bunkbed, and over Mom as she slept.

While awake she imagined her sword ablaze in a protective stance. She added a force field, like the one they put around the spaceship from her favorite TV show. If it wasn't for the certainty of the stranger, she doubted she'd believe any of it would work. It didn't stop Jack from being a jackass, but he didn't touch them. *We are safe*, she repeated silently, and pictured him repelled by the flaming sword and force field. *We are safe.*

Jack focused his lewd behavior and overt innuendos at Georgie. He wandered away after he appeared convinced she got his message. *Yeah, I got you, Jackass. Loud and clear.* She made new faces so Bill and Rose would breathe.

Then came the dreams of him standing over her bed, watching her—at least she hoped they were dreams.

ON THE BUS ride home from school Georgie forced herself to think against the white noise of voices, electronic devices, and the mudslide of her own emotions. Outside the window the sky was gray and cloudless with nothing on which to fix her attention.

Most of last night was sleepless with a lot of tossing about, like most other nights. Amid the quiet of Bill and Rose breathing, she'd deliberated. As usual, she struggled to figure out what to do about the pervert. Just the thought of him made her want to hurl. He was obscene, but hadn't actually touched any of them. What if touching was his next move? It wasn't unimaginable to her. His thumb-in-the-waistband act was more animated these days, as were his spouts of greatness. What if the lewd rantings, gestures, and threats turned into something more? They were scared every time he was around. The scumbag had threatened to hurt their mother if they said anything. *Really? Would he? How?* Georgie couldn't take the chance.

Why hadn't Mom noticed how tense they were around him? Maybe she was fooled by the grim smiles they clamped on their kid faces so she wouldn't know. Or maybe she assumed they were well-behaved. That was a laugh. Bill always schemed, not like Georgie blamed him. But then she caught him hunched over Jack-wad's underwear drawer, a toy bucket filled with dirt in one hand, plastic shovel in the other.

"Bill! Stop! Step away! Just what we need—to make the psycho more psycho." Her warning startled him. His bucket tipped the dirt onto the carpet.

"I'm sorry, Georgie. I just wanted to . . ."

"Get him back?"

"Yeah."

"I get it. But we can't. Not yet. Who knows what he'd do if he found dirt in his underwear? Best not to find out. Don't worry, I'll get the vacuum. Go hang with Rose."

The bus's white noise got noisier. Georgie crossed her arms into herself. They couldn't live like this any longer. But what could she say anyway, since he hadn't technically touched them, only threatened? She had no proof, just their side of the story, children's stories, doomed to be categorized as make-believe, a childish rebellion against the institution of step-fatherhood. What if she didn't get the credence the situation required? She'd learned kids' words didn't carry the same weight as an adult's. It was crap. Maybe when she was seventeen. . . . Being young didn't equate to being stupid, hello!

Then came the strange recurring dream where Bill flew around like a bat, shrieking, "Rose, Rose, Rose!" and Rose stood straight as a board, like a ghostly pillar while a wide, gray ribbon wrapped itself around her. Jack morphed into a goat with sharp horns raking and eating away at the ribbon as it wound round and round Rose. The room closed in as he sucked at the air through his leering mouth and flaring nostrils. A tug around Georgie's ankles almost pulled her over. She glanced down. Inseams of her jeans stitched themselves together, tighter and tighter. She tottered and gasped, "Oh my God!" Her flaming sword materialized in her hand. She took aim and swung the blade to sever the stitching and turned to Rose. The blazing sword flew out of Georgie's hand and insinuated itself midair between Rose and the jackass-goat. Goat-Jack bleated loudly and ran away as the ribbon slipped from Rose. It was a seriously weird dream, but even weirder, she'd have it again and again.

She woke up in a panic from another repeat of the dream. There was no getting around it. Her inner self called for action. Georgie sat on the edge of the bed and stared into the grainy dark. If it wasn't for the threat against Mom, she'd call Dad. *The whole thing was B.S. To hell with it!* She'd take the bluff and call anyway. Tonight.

Georgie jostled back to reality as the bus stopped at her rectangle. Bill and Rose would be home already. Mom would still be at work. If the crazed mutant was late they'd have some time to themselves today. Up the steps and through the door, she checked the living room. The television was off. The kitchen was empty. An odd tingling passed over her scalp. Something besides the TV was off. It was too quiet. *They must be in our room.* She headed down the hallway.

She gasped and stopped in her tracks. Jackass was already home. The sight slugged her gut. Solely in his underwear, he had

Rose pinned against the back door. Her face nosed into the tiny corner between the door and the door jamb. His arms hung motionless at his sides, but he stood right up against her, a hair's breadth suspended between them. Rose was trapped. Bill held back inside the bathroom doorway, his head twisted toward Rose and their stepfather. Bill turned as Georgie neared, a finger to her lips. Steel clarity kicked in. Nausea turned to momentum and clenched hands into tight fists. In the split-second it took for her to assess the scene, she projected a protective force field around Rose. Her flaming sword hovered in the tight space between Rose and Jack. Georgie crept forward until she was an arm's length away from them. Was that her voice? Each word slammed out in deep rage, "Leave. Her. Alone!" She willed Jackass to freeze in place.

He said nothing. He didn't move.

"Rose, are you okay?" Georgie asked, her voice tight. Rose didn't answer or move. "Leave her alone!" she yelled again. No response. Bill moved somewhere behind her. He was too close.

"Bill," she turned to her brother. His face was pale and locked in fear. She placed her hand on his shoulder. "Run to the Brauns' house and tell them what's happening!" Bill nodded slowly, then raced away.

Georgie ran to the front door and bolted out of the house in a blur. *Did Jack suspect she'd contemplated calling Dad? Is that why he had cornered Rose? She hadn't told a soul. Did he read her mind? Duh. People can't really do that.* Emotions blocked her mind from registering her speed, only that the back door was locked. Georgie banged on it with her fists and fought back the panic. "Let her go!" she shouted through the door. *If he touches her, I swear . . .*

Having dashed back around and into the house, she slid to a stop near Rose and the perv. Neither had moved. *Okay, deep breath.* "Rose," she said, her tone measured and even, "unlock the door." He stirred. "Leave her alone!" she roared, and rushed to the front door and back outside. In a whoosh of movement, Georgie sped around the house in seconds, heart racing from fear, throat dry. She pounded on the back door until her hands smarted and throbbed. The lock moved. Rose must have moved her hands in place to twist it. Georgie wrenched the door open and grabbed Rose's hand. "Run!"

Georgie glanced back to see Jackass move, trance-like, outside. She pulled Rose to keep up, until they arrived at the front door. "Lock this door, Rose!" Georgie hurried down the hall to the back door. It was agape. Jack stood in the yard and stared back at the house, his arms slack at his sides. *Creepy.* Georgie slammed the door shut, locked it, and rushed to find Rose.

"Are you okay, Rose?" Their eyes locked. "Did he touch you?"

"No." Her voice quaked. "He just stood there. I was afraid to move." Tears rained down her young sister's cheeks.

She swallowed hard, stifled her own tears and led Rose to the couch. Gently, she held Rose's shoulders with both hands and looked her over for signs of trauma. "We're okay, Rose." *On the outside.* Georgie kneeled on the couch cushions and leaned toward the window. Jack had roamed to where the front yard met gravel road. *What!* She took in a sharp breath. Something glinted in his right hand.

Sirens screamed. Her heart leapt. She met Rose's eyes. Mrs. Braun must have called the sheriff. Rose stood on the couch next to her. Two county sheriff cars pulled up. Their flashing lights glanced off the front window and across Jack's chest. A deputy got out of each car.

"Whoa," breathed Rose. Her eyes grew wide. One uniformed deputy pulled out a gun and pointed it at Jack-the-perv while the other positioned herself behind him. The first one yelled, "Drop it!" Something fell to the ground. *Was it Mom's kitchen knife? How'd I miss that?*

The second deputy charged forward and handcuffed him. She steered him toward one of the cruisers while the other deputy picked up the knife and dropped it into a plastic zip bag. Jack's shuffle was slow and silent. He moved like a zombie with his hands behind his back, an officer on either side of him. They situated him into the backseat.

"Look." Rose pointed her small finger at the female deputy coming toward the house.

Georgie opened the door before she knocked and invited the woman in without a word. Sergeant Susan Jensen introduced herself and asked if they were okay. The deputy looked them over, which was okay. *I get that.*

The woman alternately reassured them of their safety and asked questions, like where their mother worked. She took notes the whole time in an official-looking, black leather notepad embossed with the seal of the county sheriff. The sergeant inspected photos and things on shelves in the living room. A radio on her shoulder crackled, "The mother is en route." Moving to the kitchen, she acknowledged the caller, opened the fridge door, and inspected the sink. They moved down the hall. Her gentle questions continued. "This is your room?" The notepad filled while Georgie and Rose gaped at the deputy's uniform, face and hair, gear, boots, and her holstered gun.

"Things look good here." Leather notepad stowed, she handed them each a business card. "You are brave girls. I understand you can take care of things, but please call me if you ever need anything. Anytime. Any reason." She stood. "I'll be right outside."

Georgie perched at the window. Deputy Susan strode to where the other deputy sat behind the wheel. She spoke to him and gave the car's roof two solid pats. It pulled away with Jackass behind a mesh screen, eyes forward, the lights flashing, and siren blaring.

Georgie turned to Rose. "He's gone." They could breathe now. The two sank into the couch and the quiet, except for the ticking of a clock and their own breathing.

"Come on, Rose. Let's go wash up." They washed the residue of Jack from their faces, hands, and as much arm as they could get into the sink.

Bill, back from the Brauns', barged in with Sergeant Susan

close behind. He yelled, "Mom's on her way home!" He was full of stories—what Mrs. Braun had said about this and that, how she had called the sheriff, how he got to have cookies, how Mrs. Braun had called Mom at work, how he and the Braun kids had stared out their picture window at everything, how their dog had barked and barked, and how Mr. Braun had come home in the midst of it all and said, "Well, horsesh . . . feathers!"

CHAPTER TWO

MYSTIC CREEK

Georgie shifted to a lower branch in the willow tree. Thinking about Starkton made her squirm but brought everything into sharp focus. It *was* a close call. He'd had a knife! *How had he hid it—curved within his hand and along the inside of his wrist?* She shuddered and shook her head to not think about it. *It's okay. We made it out of there.* The biggest relief: Jackass was out of their lives. The down side: Their family unit was broken apart even further.

Her family used to be a perfect whole. Their five individual parts joined like a puzzle. Though disjointed when Dad left, it still worked. He was still hers, her dad, just a text or call away. His voice would fill her ear and spill down her neck and around into a hug. He was a satellite to the whole, even after Jack showed up. But the calls became less frequent and grew awkward due to less perceived privacy on her part, and probably Dad's too.

Jack's addition to the puzzle initiated a reaction, like a timer on a bomb whose explosion would ultimately shoot the pieces into separate universes.

Mom's bouncier steps and cheerful attitude encouraged Georgie in the beginning. It was a short-lived sentiment. The new guy exposed his true colors early. She wasn't the kind of person to think badly of people, but the gray, gritty unpleasantness around him was hard to miss. While leery, she wasn't prepared for what she saw, metaphorically speaking. The sheen of the oily truth of him seeped through his false, friendly suitor mask. A fleeting disguise, it cracked and slid off the slime beneath to reveal another fake persona, a vermin-ridden costume which should have cast itself away from the stench of his lecherous true self.

She swallowed the bile back and adjusted her perch in the tree. Yeah, maybe her thoughts were a touch dramatic. It was like she had residual dog poop smell on her shoes after she'd wiped them clean on the grass. *I don't want this. I need to figure out a way to let it go.*

When her parents had gone their separate ways, she'd desperately wanted to find ways to keep them all together, like trying to hold water in her hands.

Georgie had never liked the new family picture and harbored a deep longing for what they had been. But, she'd compelled herself to accept the status quo. Its breakup also came with pain and confusion, just a different kind. It was painful to witness Mom navigate through the rugged emotional terrain to step on one land mine after another of betrayal, anger, guilt, and grief.

Confusion came from not knowing how this latest new normal would affect their lives. Perhaps they weren't broken, but changed. Whatever it was, it had to be better. So why did her chest cave thinking about it?

Georgie pulled a willow leaf out of her hair and shifted with the memories of recent days. Held by the tree's branches with her eyes toward Dad's front door, Georgie's mind reached back to the visit to Grandma and Grandpa Ryan's, close-ish to the nearest city, but hours and dimensions from Starkton. The meeting happened a few days after what's-his-face had flipped his lid for good. Dad was there for the meeting, too.

Mom pretended not to tear up on the drive and changed the radio station whenever a love song came on. She apologized at least three times for not having known Jack was a perv, though she didn't use that word. They'd been through it all with the social worker. Georgie, Bill, and Rose weren't to be blamed for not speaking up about the lascivious behavior. *Lascivious*, a word she'd recently added to her vocabulary. Mom wasn't to be blamed for not knowing or missing any signs. The only blame Georgie could see lay with the jackass himself.

Quiet as she could, Georgie had sat on the plank floor landing at the top of the stairs of her grandparents' farmhouse and listened. The voices down in the kitchen discussed, debated, and quieted with pourings of more coffee, during all of which Georgie's butt became numb. *Wait! Am I hearing this right?*

Georgie's dad said, "Let us help, Mary. I can take Georgie to stay with me." *Whoa ... didn't see that coming.* Oddly, the idea felt right. She had an easygoing relationship with Dad and had always been drawn to Mystic Creek.

"No, Will, I can't. . . ." She didn't need to see her mother's face to know the pain there.

"Mary," said Grandpa, "hear us out."

"Yes, dear," said Grandma. "Georgie is the oldest. She's smart and emotionally mature for her age. I shudder to think what would have happened in Starkton without her. It would be easiest for both Georgie and William. Moving will be hard, and you'll be starting a new job. If that wasn't enough, you'll be going through the divorce. It won't be easy for you, and that means it won't be easy for the children."

Ultimately, the adults agreed Bill and Rose would stay with Mom in the city where she would begin her dream job as a commercial artist. They would visit Grandma and Grandpa Ryan in the country on the weekends.

Georgie would live with Dad and visit Grandma and Grandpa

Jones. Meanwhile, they, including Dad, would all go back to Starkton to get ready for the moves.

Aunt Julie, Uncle Walter, and cousin Heather would help Mom once she got to the city.

Georgie stood up, wiped her stinging eyes and padded softly to the guest room she shared with Mom and Rose. Questions swirled like a tornado in her head. Her interest piqued at the idea of going to Dad's, but she'd seriously miss the rest of her family. *This kind of sucks.*

SHE HADN'T BEEN sorry to leave Starkton. The last hectic days spent packing were weirdly surreal with the five of them together again. Hardest was the brave face she wore and her goodbyes to the sibling units. She could not hold back the tears when Mom hugged her. Mom, through her own, had said, "This will be a great new adventure, Georgie." She'd waved goodbye and shouted, "Keep your phone charged. Call me. I love you!"

Georgie moved a branch away from her face and searched for the upside. Not everyone was within arm's reach, but they were each with someone they loved who loved them back. And Jackass was gone.

Now she was in Mystic Creek, a coastal town distant in every way from Starkton. This is where she made her entrance onto this crazy planet and visited, mostly in summers. The name was given by settlers in honor of local Native American medicine people. That's all she knew, except it felt weird to be here. *Normal* was definitely stretching beyond itself. She twisted and slid down the willow's trunk to the ground. Brushing off her jeans, she headed to the house to wash up and see if Dad had finished catching up on emails.

Georgie smiled. Dad, always kind, was super sweet when they arrived at the house. It's not like she hadn't been here before, but he showed her where everything was and which room was hers. Was

Dad nervous? Georgie kind of was. Mystic Creek was still a huge unknown.

She leaned over the bathroom sink and sighed. The mirror reflected a smattering of freckles. Her dark auburn hair sported a wild, windstorm look, just not the kind they gave airbrushed models. Georgie's waves had a mind of their own. Her mouth frog-hopped in an attempted grin—betrayer and telegrapher of thoughts and emotions. She squinted. Her eyes, the kind of blue-green that changed with her surroundings or mood, were bloodshot. Not their normal brightness and intensity, they stared back expressionless. Was it shock, or sadness?

Buck up, old girl. She splashed her face and, in fits and starts, coaxed the wide-toothed comb through her hair and into a pony tail. *That would do.* Despite random compliments—being skeptical of compliments particularly and what passed as truth for most adults in general—she considered herself average looking. Most grownups tried to stuff kids' heads with what they believed to be proper, but was instead unnatural, contradictory, or downright rebel-worthy. Her favorite worst idea was the one about being a lady, a fishy sounding catchall. She nearly grinned. She was like most normal girls, a tomboy—no, that wasn't it—a real girl.

Back during a happier summer, she'd declared to the delight of Bill, Rose, and the neighbor kids, "The best thing about eating cherries is spit-blowing the pits for distance and aim!" This launched the first pit-blowing tournament.

Adult admonishments like "Nice girls do not spit cherry pits across the yard" joined the cadre of earlier others. Loads of these "proper" ideas served only to reinforce how important it is for a person to be herself. She was lucky she'd had people in her life who supported this theory.

"Don't believe everything you hear, Georgie," Dad had told her quietly.

Influenced by reading classics and watching old movies with her parents, she identified with the adventurer, crook outsmarter, and save-the-day'er. *Gumption*, an old-timey word from Dad's black and white movies, had come in handy in Starkton. Imitating the tough-guy line from her favorite, *Thin Man*, she jeered at the bathroom mirror, "Yeah, see!"

CHAPTER THREE

SKIPPER'S

D ad paced the combination kitchen-dining room, his face pulled in a frown. He ran his hands through his thick, black hair. It wasn't like him, and she didn't like seeing him like this. "Hey, Dad." She sat down at the table. "You okay?"

"Look, Georgie, I didn't know what was going on at your mother's. It makes me sick to think about you kids and that . . . guy." His voice was tight, his face not exactly dark, but twisted.

"I couldn't tell you, Dad. I couldn't tell anyone. He told me, told us all, not to tell or Mom would be angry, that he would hurt her. Please, it's over now." She took in a deep, inconspicuous breath and slowly exhaled. He must have agonized since before they were at Grandma and Grandpa Ryan's.

"I know, sweets. I just wish you hadn't gone through it. And I'm glad it didn't escalate further than it did." Anger mixed with anguish washed over his face. He stared off into kitchen airspace until his expression calmed and he forced a half grin. "You always were wise beyond your years."

"Thanks."

"You must've been scared and not sure what to do, like a

hostage, your hands tied, damned if you do, damned if . . . well, you know." He leaned against the counter. "Now you get it, right? What you do and what to say if something weird ever happens again? You understand what's okay and what isn't, right?"

Oh, I'll never take that kind of crap again. Aloud she said, "Yeah, and the counselor went over everything—inappropriate behavior and the importance of telling someone. We knew the whole thing wasn't right. Anyway, it's over now. We're all safe. It could have been worse. He didn't touch any of us, at least physically." How could she help him relax? "Besides, I had planned to call you that last day."

"I don't want us to minimize or gloss over what happened. Do you want to see someone?"

"You mean, like a counselor? No, thanks. I'm good." Maybe she didn't need a counselor, but when she felt around inside of herself with her mind she knew she wasn't done yet.

Dad caught her eye and held it. "This does not define who you are. It's something that happened in your life." He let out a long breath of his own and hugged her. "But it can make you stronger. You done good. I'm glad you're here, Georgie."

She squeezed him back. "I'm glad too. I miss Bill and Rose, but I know they're okay." She didn't say it, but she missed Mom, too.

"I miss them too, sweets." He glanced at his watch." You must be hungry. Skipper's?"

"Okay!" She loved Skipper's Diner, a local spot on the water surrounded by a wooden pier. It was known as much for its food as it was a place to watch seals, otters, and the ever-present pelicans and gulls vying for pier, sky, and fish. The place was also great for people-watching from one of its vinyl booths.

Dusk and the french fry smell hit before they were out of the car. They barely slid into a blue booth when a pelican perched on a pillar outside their window. In the fading light, its brown-grey color blended with the pier's wood.

Inside, the diner was bright light and bustle. Early bird diners shuffled out while the regular dinner shift ramped into full swing. Vince Gill crooned from a jukebox. Wait staff in navy and white-striped sailor shirts and dark blue jeans crisscrossed each other's paths. Mere fractions of time and space prevented crashes. They carried dishes and drinks, ripped orders from pads, and yelled into the kitchen pass-through over the din of sizzling, clinking, and scraping. Here and there, one paused to talk and laugh with customers. A tall, slender, redheaded woman with extra helpings of mascara highlighting her green eyes appeared at their table. She wore a huge smile for Dad, one navy silk scarf around her neck, and another in her hair. The cotton navy apron complimented the sailor's uniform and her figure.

"Hey, William! Good to see you. Is this your oldest?" She didn't wait for an answer. "Hi. I'm Peggy. I've been waiting on your dad here since high school. Handsome Will, we called him. Georgie, right? You've been here with your brother and sister."

Handsome Will? Georgie grinned. She'd remember that. "Yeah, last summer you told us how you and Dad were in the marching band together. You also told us about some ghosts in a place called Crabber's Cove."

"Yes, only it's called Clammer's Cove. Not too far from Andersen Light."

"Yeah, that's it. My brother Bill talked about it for months."

"Maybe your dad can take you sometime."

Their heads swung to him.

"Maybe so," he said. "It's been a long while since I was out there."

Peggy pulled a guestbook pad from an apron pocket. "Coffee for William. . . ." She wrote on the pad. "And you, Georgie? A nice chocolate shake?"

"Yes, but how did you remember?"

"Just practice." Her eye twitched. Fastest wink ever. "You're still looking at your menu. I'll be right back." She whipped around a counter lined with red vinyl-topped chrome stools occupied by widespread diversity and at least one butt crack. A young waiter refilled coffee mugs, retrieved empty plates, and pivoted to place the pot back onto its burner. He whistled as Tony Bennett sang "It Had to Be You" with Carrie Underwood.

Georgie forced her eyes to the menu. "You getting breakfast for dinner, Dad?"

"You bet—fried oysters and eggs over medium with hash browns."

She opted for the veggie burger and sweet potato fries. "Peggy seems nice." She folded the tall plastic-coated menu and stuck it behind the napkin and condiment holder.

"She is, Georgie, and a good person who'd do anything for you. Peggy's worked here since we were in high school. She stayed in the area to help her parents. They were older when they had her and her sister." He shoved his menu behind hers. "Peggy was always one of the smartest kids in school."

"If she's so smart, why is she working here?"

His eye narrowed. "Don't be too quick to jump to conclusions. Appearances can be deceiving. The truth is only Peggy can say, but my guess is she likes it. Not too many people know she is an accomplished author." He looked around the diner and grinned. "I suspect she gets much of her material from the people who come and go from this place."

"Wow. Why don't people know about her?"

"She uses a pseudonym—Maggie Beacher."

"Wow," she said again. "That's so cool."

"Yeah, it is." She followed his gaze out the window. Seagulls flew over the water and through the diner's light. "I hope you like it here, sweets."

She wasn't sure if he expected an answer, but before she could respond Peggy was back with their coffee and chocolate shake. She took their food order and flew off behind the long counter. Her hand darted out to balance a tray of glasses listing like a sinking ship in the hand of the whistling waiter, then clipped their order at the kitchen pass-through. Accident averted, Georgie let out a breath and reached for her shake. It was a work of art in a heavy, frosty, fluted glass. Its rim spilled over like flower petals. A maraschino cherry sat atop whipped cream pierced by a stainless steel straw pointed towards Georgie. "Mmm."

She plucked out the cherry and popped it into her mouth. "Don't worry, Dad."

He peered over his coffee mug. "I guess you know there'll be times when you're by yourself, mainly after school and the nights I play." Dad taught music at the local college, but also played with a band a few nights during the week and most weekends. "I know you're old enough, legally. It's just . . . how much is too much alone time? Your grandparents' place isn't within walking distance." He swirled his coffee. "We'll figure it out."

"I could get around on a bicycle, but I gave mine to Rose ages ago."

His mouth lifted to one side. "I remember your first one." He pointed at her. "You're a smart girl! A bicycle is a terrific idea." Peggy dashed by, suspended in mid-air long enough to refresh his coffee and was gone again. Dad continued without a blink. "Let's go to the city this Saturday and buy you a new bike." He stirred cream into his coffee. "You'll need a helmet."

She tagged onto his enthusiasm. "And a lock. I'll scan the web for sales."

"By Jove, Georgie Jones, you are brilliant!" He slapped the table and she laughed at his horrible faux English accent.

Peggy arrived with plates and a wide smile. They acknowledged both and dug in.

CHAPTER FOUR

DAD TIME

Georgie stared at the image on her phone in horror. Rounds and rounds of duct tape encircled Mom until she resembled a silver-gray mummy. Thick strands of her bright red hair stuck out between the gaps. Terror flashed from her deep blue eyes. *Hang on, Mom! I'll be right there!* Why hadn't she called Dad before now? Then, what could he do from where he was? She strained to see past the wall of water pouring over the doorway which distorted the images on the other side into wavy silhouettes. She zipped the phone in a plastic bag and shoved it in the back pocket of her jeans. There was no choice but to dive through the deep, cascading curtain of water—Bill and Rose were there with Jackass! The water didn't prevent his malintent from emanating from the other side. A tart acidity, stronger than vinegar, and a bitter, burnt taste in her mouth made her want to spit, but her mouth turned in on itself, repelled by the nastiness. She glared through the streaming water. Jack's tall profile loomed over Rose and Bill. *Oh, my God!* "Stop!" she yelled to the other side. No one acknowledged her presence. Armed only with the belief she would succeed, she leapt through the door's waterfall shouting, "Stop!" until her throat was sore, and she woke herself up.

Georgie sat up in bed with a start. Her heart pounded in her chest. She was dry except for the sweat. Hair stuck to her face and neck. Her hand went to her throat. Thirsty but okay, she looked around the room to get her bearings. *It was a dream,* she told her unconvinced self, *residue from Starkton.* The cell phone rested on the nightstand where it charged overnight, its screen dark. *Everybody's okay.* She pulled her knees to her chin and wrapped her arms around her legs. White polka dots vibrated on the lavender sleeves of her new pajamas. A tender, bruised sadness grew in her heart and moved into her throat. The edges of her eyes burned and she rubbed away escaping tears. It was good for Rose and Bill to be with Mom. They would visit Grandma and Grandpa Ryan on weekends. Bill would have fun fishing with their many aunts, uncles, and cousins.

She felt especially bad for Mom. Even though Jack turned out to be a lunatic, it couldn't have been how she pictured her love story with him. Georgie had not seen the appeal from the beginning. Her mother, an otherwise highly intelligent woman, had obviously experienced a gaping lapse in clarity. *Rebound after her divorce with Dad?*

Georgie had not foreseen how her actions from a single day could have such devastating effects on her family. It hadn't been just one day, nor had it been her doing, she reminded herself. Right after the wedding Jack's true colors leaked out like dark, toxic ink into clean water. He hadn't done anything that would explain it, but she hadn't liked the guy since Mom first brought him home. It was just a feeling, so she hadn't said anything. She couldn't blame herself.

Georgie unfolded herself and swung her feet to the floor. Why was she having a hard time wrapping her head around everything? Somewhere, she'd heard or read how things happened for a reason.

Two things were certain: They were way better off without him in their lives, and she wasn't going to dwell on it today.

After a yawn and stretch she took in her surroundings. It was nice not to have to share a room she'd outgrown. There were no bunk beds or toys to step on. This was where Dad stored his music. Musical gear on the floor and bookshelves sat next to stacks of his songbooks and sheet music. Multicolored guitar picks filled a 32-ounce Mason jar. A glass bowl stuffed with packaged guitar strings rested near the lava lamp she'd gone to sleep staring at last night. She opened the mirrored closet doors to a length of empty wooden hangers. *Yeah, I need to unpack.*

Floating shelves mounted over the bed's plain, wooden head-board were bare, except for one framed picture. She, Bill, and Rose were at the beach with Dad, his arms around the three of them. They were all smiles and laughter. She twisted a curl of hair around a finger and bit her lip.

Her eyes moved from instruments suspended on walls to her overflowing ditty bag on the dresser. Yesterday she'd shoved her bags and boxes into the square openings of the tall shelf unit next to the dresser. Unpacking could wait. First, she needed to shower off whatever gunk might still be hanging around from that dream. She wanted to be fresh for breakfast and her first weekend in Mystic Creek. Today she and Dad would visit Grandpa and Grandma Jones on their way to shop for a bicycle. Georgie pictured the bike she wanted. *Yay!*

The bacon's aroma met her before Dad's hummed melody. Officially, he was Professor William Samuel Jones, master musician and, unofficially, excellent cook. Dad turned from the stovetop and smiled. "Good morning, sweets. Are you ready for an exciting day?" His blue plaid shirt peeked out from under a red apron emblazoned with "Musicians Cook It!" written like notes across the lines of a measure. Today wasn't the first time he'd worn that Father's Day gift.

Georgie smiled. "Yeah, and good morning. Whatever you're cooking smells fantastic."

He chuckled. "You're smelling the local apple-smoked turkey bacon." Her eyes slid from the crisp strips to a sizzling, covered cast iron skillet. He tapped the lid with his turner. "Red potatoes, skins on, with chopped sweet onions and peppers, spices, a tiny bit of garlic—paired with the perfect eggs. Want to set the table and handle the toast?"

"I'd love to." Earthy-looking bread and a Mason jar of raspberry jam waited near the chrome toaster. She got to work.

"This is amazing." She guessed he didn't have time to do this often. She slathered the raspberry preserves over the last of her toast.

"All part of the service. The jam's from the farmers market," he said, savoring his coffee. "If you'd like, I'll show you the secret to the perfect egg."

"Cool. I'd seriously love that."

"Okay, but not today. We have bigger plans—dishes, then dashing. Our day awaits!"

THEY DROVE through an open gate and were immediately met by the beagle Sidney and Kelly-girl, an Australian Shepherd mix. The dogs barked and herded the car along the gravel drive to the house. Dad unbuckled his seatbelt. "Ready or not!"

Bouncing and wagging, the dogs escorted them up stone steps to the wide porch and front door. Grandma Grace and Grandpa Sam emerged, him in his good jeans.

"Well hello, honey! You're as tall as your grandma." She gave Georgie a warm hug. Georgie admired Grandma's thick, wavy black hair as she reached up on tip toes and kissed Dad on the cheek. "Let's go inside."

Traces of coffee, a baked treat, and sawdust met them in the entryway. It was pretty much as Georgie remembered it. The wood floor opened into a wide hallway of antiques, art, and photographs. The rough-feeling rug was probably there to cut down on the dirt and dust from her grandparents' continuous remodeling.

"Hi, Dad," her dad said.

Grandpa patted Dad on the shoulder. "Coffee's on, son." His face lit up. "Well hello, Georgie. Aren't you a sight for sore eyes? It's been about a year, hasn't it? Come give your grandpa a hug, then we'll head to the kitchen." She breathed in his smell—sawed wood, shave cream, and . . . apple bread?

Georgie sipped hot chocolate at the familiar round oak table. Grandpa Sam's perpetual jars of something pickled took their place of honor in the center. He sliced zucchini bread while Dad and Grandma talked about wind and solar power.

Georgie munched her slice and drained her mug. A doorway and its unfinished jamb were taped off from the mudroom with clear, thick plastic. Through it, she could see two-by-fours, wires, and insulation peek around open electrical outlets. The conversation turned to today's trip to the city. She excused herself to look around outside.

Nearly out of earshot, Georgie heard, "That child's been through the ringer. . . ." Out the door and down the back, it hit her they were talking about Starkton. That was one place she'd definitely had enough of.

DAD'S PLAYLIST, which weirdly included both Bruno Mars and some guy named Van Morrison, accompanied their ride to the city. He pointed out landmarks and shared tales of his younger days. They sang along to the music.

Rolling hills teased with intermittent views of the sea. She craned her neck for each ocean vista until the terrain flattened out into fewer hills, more traffic, and urban sprawl. They sped by a truck stop, outlet mall, shopping mall, and strip malls. Over time, the same stores repeated themselves. Dad called it homogenization.

"I grok, Dad." It was a reference to *Stranger in a Strange Land,* which they'd both read.

The road spawned more lanes. Signs erupted everywhere posting exit names and numbers. He veered the car over to the far right lane and onto a frontage road. "Lunch before we shop?" His grin hinted that he'd heard her stomach growl. "I know just the place."

"HMM. *RIDICULICIOUS,*" Georgie purred from a taco truck next to the ocean.

Dad wiped his mouth on a napkin. "I don't usually do this, but what do you say we split a churro for dessert?" She liked seeing him like this—smiling, relaxed.

They brushed sugar off their shirts and crossed smooth sand to stand on rough, black rocks closest to the water's edge. Light spray from the crash of waves farther out sprinkled her face. Balanced on rocks and serenaded by the water's rhythm, they gazed in easy silence.

She released a long, deep breath. "I'm ready if you are."

He put an arm around her shoulders and gave her a squeeze. "Let's do this."

BICYCLES POSED like department store mannequins in the wide storefront windows. Her mouth dropped open. "Uh, Dad, my research on bicycle sales and specials only included the main box stores."

"Don't worry about it, sweets. The universe always provides." He winked. "Plus, your grandparents chipped in. We have all the money we need. Let's go find your bike."

Georgie stopped in front of a rack of step-through bikes, dazzled by their shiny newness. Though the pictures she'd seen on the web helped her narrow down the search, they didn't come close to the real deal. Was it just her, or was that aqua blue bike glowing?

Her new bicycle stowed easily into the car's cargo area. Georgie handed Dad the helmet and other accessories and confessed, "I wouldn't have thought of the rain suit."

The last of the day's sun painted brilliant hues through the clouds for the drive home. Her mind waded through the daze of the last couple of weeks. With Dad came a new reality, one she didn't know yet. But she was . . . thankful, and optimistic. She was getting to know him in a different way, maybe because she was older and it was just the two of them. He treated her like a person, not a kid. Gray overtook color as the clouds swelled heavy and dark until rain drenched the landscape into subdued shades. The swish-swish of the windshield wipers lulled her and she sat up straighter. Dad grinned to himself and moved like a bobblehead to the music. This was a good day.

THE SOUNDS and smells of breakfast woke Georgie up Sunday morning. She peeked out from her bed covers. *Yep, still in Mystic Creek.*

She sat up. Tomorrow was Monday. Tomorrow was her first day as a first year at Mystic Creek High School. She was nervous, anxious. Her insides shimmied. There was every kind of unknown out there. *How far behind in studies am I? What are the kids like? Will I make new friends? What will I wear?* Georgie willed herself to calm. *It's going to be okay.* Boxes and bags teased her from around the room. *She'd unpack—after breakfast.*

CHAPTER FIVE

BRIGHT STAR

Evening crept behind twilight as Luther analyzed the life and auric bodies of Georgie Jones. An errant thought seed had taken hold within her. Together, they would impede its meandering growth and prevent it from insinuating itself any further. Stumbling trepidation would not benefit her. Nor would reactions sprung from anger or fear. Conversely, certainty and clarity would serve her well.

His thoughts slid back in time to before his knowledge of Georgia Rae Jones, to when he was a young man, before his acute memory of that fateful conference, and the prophecy. An automatic response to his recollection of the journey, his hand reached out to rub his back side.

"HEY, WATCH IT!" Luther wiped the camel spit from his cheek with his shirt sleeve and adjusted his fedora. He'd had enough of swaying countless miles on this foul-tempered animal. The incessant groaning to its mates in the caravan no longer intrigued him, nor did the indescribable stench issuing from every orifice. He dearly looked forward to the daintier pack animals accompanying them for the journey's last leg. At last he'd be inside the secret sanctuary of caves used for centuries upon centuries, centered high in the mountain vortex.

Had it only been weeks? It felt like an eternity since he and Mother had left behind their beloved lighthouse to attend this year's conference. The modern conveyances of ships, airplanes, and trains were replaced by overland vehicles bent on jarring their teeth loose. The crude horse-drawn carriages and ferry boats were okay, but he was not crazy for these long-legged, humped beasts.

He now gripped a donkey's tether and gazed past switchbacks which yielded no measure of how much more of their journey remained. Luther could almost smell the inside of the cave, though he divided his active focus between distant glances and the immediacy of where his feet might fall behind the donkeys burdened with travelers, luggage, and supplies. The air cooled and his anticipation rose as the convoy climbed.

At last Luther spied the entrance. Voices of bustling conference greeters lightened the drone of the climb. Energetic workers extended smiles and directions to the much-needed necessary rooms, and provided room assignments, conference agendas, and water flasks. Mother was quickly absorbed into the higher ranks of her old friends and peers.

Luther swung open the door of his room and dropped his bag. A modest cave, it easily held the necessities of creature comfort. Water seepage in the walls and crystal formations reflected light from yellow beeswax candles. He ran his hand over an ancient desk's marred surface and sank back into the chair. Age-old lines and divots in the wood kindled his clairsentience. Something about this conference, besides the obvious, had his psychic antennas fanning out.

An urgent call had gone out for all regional mentors to attend this healing conference in person. Normally, a thirty-three percent quorum was enough to provide the energetic anchor required to conduct a session, and in-person attendance was always adequate. Corporeal travel divvied up among the regions freed those who could to teleport. But not this time. For Luther's two cents, this year's in-person requirement underscored the critical need for their combined energies, due to the war.

The world was in peak distress, because of one man in one country. Luther shook his head. (He'd likely be a swivel-head before it was over.) Recent headlines questioned whether key countries would reach beyond their own borders to stop the murdering of millions. At university in Great Britain he'd learned about pacts and alliances forming to combat and defend against the aggression. Lightwork had maintained an iffy balance.

Hence the urgency of this conference. Shielded within their primary tenet, *Anonymity,* the council had joined forces with the unseen realms and their allies around the globe. Together they would focus their powerful, multidimensional healing energy to go beyond merely tipping the balance to achieve another tenet—*Take Light Where There Is Darkness.*

Luther considered the cyclic rhythms of crises as encouraging earth's evolution. Time-spanning spider webs of light raced to spin connectivity in all directions. Healing light stretched across humanity's opening hearts. Humans were evolving, just not at the same pace and not every one.

He ran a hand over his face and stared into the candle flame. Tonight's special event, a prophecy circle, had him jumpy. A persuasive energy, like an electric current, coursed through him. His searches and scans hadn't yielded the source or its characteristics. The elders must be shielding the prophecies. Luther sighed. It would be a short enough wait.

The aroma of melting beeswax pulled him back. He pulled the wrist cuff from his watch. It was nearly time to join the others. Though between university semesters, there'd be no school mates, but perhaps a professor or two. He freshened up, brushed his teeth, and combed at his unruly, black hair. His shoes buffed, he grabbed a pair of gabardines, secured the last button on a fresh shirt, and threw on his jacket. Luther winked back at sparkling blue eyes in the mirror. *Not the cat's meow, but I'll do.* Candles extinguished, he closed the heavy wooden door with a soft hush, and with a bounce in his stroll turned right at the first main artery.

Windows bored through the mountain's exterior opened to vistas cascading into the distance. Ranges graduated in purples and blues until foothills and valleys became desert. *Who wouldn't flip over this?* He couldn't say which impressed him more, that the ancestors had discovered this place or their industrious development of a vast network of caves and catacombs. *Both.* He had to admit the views were spectacular.

Welcome pervaded the mountain's every atom. Glowing light from crystals set in the ceiling and polished floor showcased hanging tapestries and alcoves carved into walls. Niches with cushions and low wooden tables offered hangouts for solitary meditation or meetings. Luther's favorite niches held miniature movie screens. He was no less gobsmacked at their sheer invention this year—there was no evidence of physical or electrical connectivity! Scientists in Europe experimented with transmitting facsimiles of images over wires, so far with limited success. Yet these panels depicted current scenes of events around the world with amazing clarity.

People swerved around him as he gravitated to a panel screen. Animated hands of a storyteller gracefully painted words into pictures for her listeners, their eyes wide and glistening in the firelight. In the next, a man shouted at an outdoor crowd. Permanent creases of anger framed his brush of a mustache and mean, dark eyes. The riled throng shook their fists in the air. Luther hastened to the next screen, a massive aquatic painting come to life. Like the school children in the scene, he stared slack-jawed as colorful fish zipped amidst coral stretching through aquamarine water toward the light. *Oops!* He'd forgot himself in the moment and hustled down the now-empty corridor.

A hum vibrated through his body ahead of the high, arched

entryway to Congregation Hall. The grand cavern reverberated from more than today's quiet conversations. Residual energies from years and thousands of meetings like this one, each with its own agendas and celebrations, amplified his internal buzz. He estimated a hundred congregants sat within the natural bowl formed in the rock floor. Light from candles perched atop stalagmites threw shadows on the walls. They flickered like ghostly spectators. Fragrant incense greeted him as did a few familiar faces. Keen to blend in, he dropped onto a floor cushion.

The old woman sat at one end of the oval, the high wall to her back and some distance from Luther. He was young in chronologic years for a regional mentor—his father's death prompted his early initiation—but considered himself mature for his years and smart enough to know it was easy, but not wise, to make judgments about age. Still, he could see why they called her the *ancient one*. Not only did she look old, she exuded timelessness. Her life's adventures he could scarcely imagine. Her wisdom he only hoped to someday grasp.

Oracle and spiritual elder, Oma, was the kind of person you never forgot. All mentors met with her separately in the sanctuary niche adjacent to her quarters. In her old-timey way of speaking, she provided insights on regional issues, and guidance specific to each mentor's spiritual growth. Last time, she'd identified individuals and situations Luther could expect to support or mediate, and courses of personal study. The rest had to do with building a foundation and preparing the hearth—readying.

With his keister on a cushion, he waited in the circle's emanating glow. Tonight she was scheduled to speak on world affairs. All eyes moved to the end of the oval where David, the cave's resident elder, led the opening prayer. Brilliant violet, blue, and green light pulsed around Oma and David.

Luther focused on her words. "Welcome to our joining in this sacred space. I acknowledge your concern for the global unrest. We will speak of it at length later and during the remainder of the conference. Tonight is our special session, our time to look ahead." She closed her eyes and breathed deeply. Her eyes reopened. "You will see increasing evidence of lightworkers in your regions. Use every available sight, as the effect of this lightwork will manifest in many forms. The result will bring more awareness to aspects of what some may call the world's troubles. Do not be misled by outward panic. The world's attention to these situations is a sign that healing is making its way to these areas. This healing is fortified through your focused intention. I remind you that change comes from awareness, though it may appear circuitous and impeded by human misunderstandings. Do not waiver from your intuitive knowing. Focus, envision, and direct love, clarity, and peace.

"I will not call out specific issues within your regions. Rather, I call upon each of you to follow your hearts and intuition to detect change in the flow of energy. You will discern when the current is dammed and when it moves freely. In this way, you may be ever vigilant and easily know where best to channel the light. Confer with one another, as always. We are pleased with your efforts."

A low, shuffling echoed around the hall as people adjusted their positions and fell silent. "In advance of our healing meditation, I have the honor to announce the coming of a soul of greater potential and expectation than we have yet known. Luther Andersen, please stand."

What? Spontaneous applause resounded in the hall. Dumbfounded, Luther hurried to disentwine his long, lanky frame and get to his feet. Working to normalize his breath and racing heart, he faced Oma. The council quieted.

"Georgia Rae Jones will be born into your region. You, Luther, the youngest mentor in our history, possess many gifts yourself, including those of a multidimensional nature. You will watch over her no matter where she lives, from birth to after, take her under your care and tutelage. The girl has much to offer this world. You will help to make this possible and ensure her unfolding. There are no accidents. She is meant to be an inestimable force of good, and you, her mentor. At times you will find you must will yourself into inaction, while others when expedient engagement is imperative. You are not alone."

Time slowed as the woman made direct eye contact with every person in the circle. Each nodded silent assent. "You may call upon any of the regions at any time." Oma briefly bowed her head to him, grasped the candle burning in front of her, and extended it in salute. Applause and cries of congratulations exploded. Candles were held high around the room. Shadows danced on the walls.

Bowled over and shaking from the announcement, Luther lowered himself onto his cushion. His mother smiled broadly behind her raised candle. He returned a wobbly smile and took in a very deep breath. *So that was it! No wonder I'd had the jitters. Holy smoke!*

HE NEVER FULLY REMEMBERED WHAT else Oma said to the group that day, except she had not talked long afterward. In his memory, her words blended with the soft harmony of voices and ancient instruments into the healing session that followed the prophecy circle he wouldn't forget.

His mother, Sarah Andersen, a loving, insightful woman with a humorous view of life, had lived to see the end of the world war, but not Georgia's birth all these many decades later. Still, her essence remained with him.

Luther snapped out of the memory and chuckled at his younger self. Behind him, Mystic Creek's majestic lighthouse rose high into the night sky, a gleaming giant shooting its beacon of light into the night. The full moon's reflection scattered light across the water's surface and cast Luther's tall shadow across the stone veranda. Late summer wind danced through his thick black and silver hair.

His evening routine usually cleared his mind, but not tonight.

This girl—who would be a meta-normal like no other—had narrowly escaped harm's way.

Luther had willed himself into relative inaction. He'd monitored the girl with his gifts of sight and network of lightworkers. He'd traveled to her dreams, and seeded her thoughts with methods to protect herself and family from the ludicrous behavior of her self-serving stepfather. Georgie, as she liked to be called, coped the best she could. In doing so, she had quickened her gestating abilities.

The divorce of her parents had created the initial internal axis shift. As the oldest child, she had naturally, though misguidedly, assumed responsibility for aspects of those changes. Fortunately, both parents remained in her life. This had enabled her to create and maintain a new normal within her personal landscape.

However, the eventual introduction of the stepfather as an integral part of the new nucleus appeared to have reinforced her need to save the family structure. Behavior of the unevolved, indecent stepfather had had its discernable effects. Unseen fragments within her were also knocked out of alignment. Unseen? Perhaps. Luther could see them as clearly as his teacup.

The girl had stretched her young and developing emotions thin over concern for her siblings. She had striven to understand and predict. She had learned to dance past the edge of normalcy in order to hold their emotional and physical safety together within the re-imagined nuclear family construct. Her subconscious wounds summoned her emotional and psychic energies, and initiated the rerouting of her self-healing. He smiled to himself. It was no accident this healing was perfect and seamless. Her meta-normal abilities extended beyond the seen to the unseen.

Fortunately, many of the traits and skills she'd cultivated—in response to her family dynamics and from living in the fear and silence of emotional abuse—also served to echo and trigger development of her gifts. Georgie had highly developed coping skills, many fostered through her imagination and intuition. She was a bright star of a girl with an effervescent personality and mercurial mind. Her spirit, indeed her future, demanded she surpass early traumas to live her full potential.

Luther would nurture the previously unwavering self-confidence she had brought with her at birth. He took in a long, deep breath—and wove and healed. The effects would ripple through time and space, and eventually through to her conscious mind.

He idly watched lights from a vessel on the horizon.

The rambunctious curiosity of childhood is meant to give lift to dreams, and energy to tackle and sustain creative endeavors. The adults in her life loved and wanted the best for Georgie, as they did for their other children. Only her grandmother, Grace, had an inkling there was something about Georgie that harkened back to her ancestral roots. Perhaps one day Grace would remember the story.

The Jones family affairs would fall into place. Luther crossed his long legs and sipped his Darjeeling tea. Evening's first star winked. *Ah, yes.* It was time to check the light and retire to his room for the evening. Soon Georgie Jones would begin her training at Andersen Light.

CHAPTER SIX

NEW KID

Today was Georgie's first day at Mystic Creek High and she dreaded being the new kid, especially since school had started here two weeks earlier. Maybe she wasn't too far behind, and maybe that would cushion her angst. She was first at the bus stop, a spot under cross-signs labeled Cedar Street and Oak Avenue. It was like she'd been transported to another planet, for sure another life. In one swoop of cosmic cause and effect she was living in a different house in a different state, and starting a new school.

At least Dad is familiar. Georgie allowed herself a teensy grin. Counting her grandparents, their friend Luther Andersen, and now Peggy, the waitress from Skipper's, she knew five people here. *Wow, I've seriously widened my circle.* She didn't like the edge of her own sarcasm, or its tinge of self-pity. *Okay, knowing five people isn't bad for being in town a few days.*

Yesterday's laid back day of riding her new bike, hanging out with Dad, and texting photos to Mom blurred in her mind. She touched the toe of her shoe to the metal pole of the street sign.

Kids arrived and grouped themselves into herds. They stared, not that she blamed them. This was a small town. Next to their bright colors, she second-guessed her decision to go with neutral wear—chambray button-down worn as a light jacket over a plain navy t-shirt, blue jeans, and blue denim Converse, all with minimal logos and no statements. Even her earrings were simple silver hoops. *So much for blending in.* She pulled her oversized canvas bag closer.

The bus arrived and she was the first to board. She jumped too high and surprisingly fast, but landed on her feet. *Yeah, I'm nervous.* And why, since she loved adventures, did her stomach feel like a heavy rock had replaced organ tissue? After a quick scan of the kid terrain, she grabbed the middle of three empty bench seats on the driver's side and plopped down. Pretending a sudden need, she plunged into her bag and searched for nothing in particular as the bus rolled and stopped again. Some kid must be running late. A big boy with spiky red and blonde hair, oversized clothes, and a sneer swaggered down the aisle. He narrowed green eyes at her as he passed, and pursed his mouth as if she was suspicious. *What's his problem?* The driver accelerated and she went back to rummaging through her bag.

The bus stopped and she bounced in her seat as someone plunked down next to her. She edged toward the window as the bus heaved forward, and peeked at who had invaded her space. The intruder, a girl about her own age, smelled of jasmine. Dark black-brown hair wrapped around her head in stylish, complicated braids. The braids outlined a pretty face, which smiled, as did her deep brown eyes. Like Georgie, she wore blue jeans, but sported a red cotton button-down blouse. Bright, multicolored bead neck-laces coordinated her earrings and bracelets.

"Hi," said the girl. "I'm Josefina. You're Georgie. I heard you were coming."

"Hi." *She heard I was coming?*

"If you want, I'll show you around the school."

Before Georgie could answer, the bus braked hard, tossing her bag off her lap. She bent down in an awkward angle to retrieve it.

"Here, let's set our bags between us." Josefina scooted over and dropped her own into the space. "We can always catch them if they fly."

Smart. "Thanks," she said aloud.

A boy launched himself into the empty seat in front of them, landing in a dramatic slide. "Hey, Jo." He swung his arm on the back of the seat and turned to face the two girls.

Jo? Duh. She must spell her name with a J, not an H.

Josefina turned to her. "Shawn's also a first year. We've known each other forever."

"Yeah." Shawn gaped at Georgie through the lenses of his cobalt blue frames.

"Yes, and he *is* always this rude. Shawn, you're staring." Josefina rolled her eyes.

Georgie laughed. The tension in her stomach eased a smidge. Shawn's hair was very curly but not as tight as some of the kids she'd known back in Starkton. The wide, bright white and light blue stripes of his shirt enhanced the blush beneath his tawny brown skin. Wide, rounded, deep amber brown eyes hung at her like she was a candy bar commercial. "What?" she asked. "Do I have something in my teeth?"

He answered; Josefina snickered and his skin tone deepened. He answered, "No. Sorry. It's just . . . I've never seen you before. Your freckles are like the Milky Way. Brilliant. . . ."

Georgie held her breath and mashed her lips together to keep from laughing.

"Okay. . . ." Josefina exaggerated her exhalation. "That's great, Shawn." She turned back to Georgie. "Like I said, if you want, I can show you around."

"Thanks, but I need to turn in some paperwork and pick up my schedule."

"No problem," Josefina said, "I'll take you to administration first."

"We'll probably all be in the same classes," pronounced Shawn. Both girls looked over. He was still staring.

SHAWN WAS RIGHT. Except for P.E., they had all of their classes together, and P.E. was during the same period.

"That wasn't so bad, was it?" Shawn asked.

They ambled toward buses waiting in the afternoon sun like long lines of napping yellow dogs.

"Thanks to you two." Georgie threw them an appreciative smile. The day had passed with no hiccups. There were the expected stares at the new kid, but they didn't last long. Even the herds she recognized from the bus stopped and kept their noses in their phones. "They sure didn't wait to heap on the homework," she added as they boarded their bus.

"You can say that again," Shawn said, and suddenly pulled out his phone. "Incoming comm." He turned away to read and boarded the bus behind them.

Georgie said, "I liked Ms. Valentine's history class. She was kind of scary with the white stubble and crazy mole on her chin, but I liked her stories." She'd been drawn into the fascinating world the teacher described, and temporarily forgotten her new girl status.

"She does have her scary moments," Josefina told her, "mainly related to the pounds of homework she piles on."

"What's with all the dodgeball stuff?" Display cases boasted trophies and dodgeballs, while walls all over the school brandished crimson and gray banners.

"It's the primary competitive sport. Are you interested in going out for the team?"

"Oh, no. It's just usually you see basketball or football, even lacrosse. I've never heard of dodgeball as a school sport, except in P.E., of course."

"Right. Well, it is very big here. It's not just our school, but this whole area. Mystic High competes in the regionals. Go Crimson and Gray, as they say."

"Now I understand why it was the focus in P.E."

"Personally," Josefina said, leaning closer, "I'm not that into it."

Georgie laughed. "So," she began, changing the subject, "this morning you said you heard I was coming. How was that?"

"Oh, right. We didn't finish our conversation." She rolled her eyes across the aisle to where Shawn sat engrossed in his phone, then back to Georgie. "My mom works with Luther Andersen who I guess is a friend of your family."

"Yeah, of my grandparents."

"You've been to Andersen Light?" Josefina asked.

The bus came to another stop. Shawn rose. Still entranced by his phone, he muttered a "I gotta jam" accompanied by a hand wave over his shoulder, and shuffled up the aisle.

"Bye, Shawn," they said together.

"Andersen Light?" Georgie asked, returning to their discussion.

"It's Mr. Luther's place, Mystic Creek's lighthouse. Locals call it Andersen Light."

"I might've been there when I was little. I don't remember. I don't know him well, but he's always been nice to me."

"My grandparents worked there also," Josefina said. "He's like family." Her head craned close to Georgie. "He kind of reminds me of Merlin."

"Merlin?"

"You know, from King Arthur, only without the robes and pointy hat."

Okay . . . She could see Josefina was serious. "I guess I can see that. He's tall and sort of buff for an old guy, but his hair is black with white sprinkles rather than vice versa."

Josefina grabbed her bag. "Hey, this is my stop! See you tomorrow."

Georgie's stop was next. She bounded down the bus steps and to the end of Cedar Street. Dad wouldn't be home for a while. She dropped her bag in a chair with a heavy thud and set off for the kitchen. Armed with a snack, she settled in front of the TV for a re-run of her favorite show, *Star Trek*, the orginal.

Perseverance and quick thinking by the ship's engineer had saved the day with his repeated and frantic attempts to repair the engine just in time to make their hasty getaway from mortal alien danger.

What could she make for supper? The freezer held possibilities —she could handle veggie lasagna. She set the table for two. *No king's fork necessary here, thank God.* The kitchen clock told her there was time for homework. Georgie traipsed to her room.

It was dark by the time she finished her reading assignment. She beat it to the kitchen and had just opened the freezer when Dad arrrived.

"Hello, sweets. How did it go?" He dropped a grocery bag on the counter, gave her a one-armed hug, and kissed the top of her head.

"I met a couple of kids and got a ton of homework. One of them, Josefina, told me her mom works with Luther Andersen, Grandma and Grandpa's friend."

"Wait. I bet I know the mom. Anyway, it's nice you have some-thing in common."

"How was your day?"

He smiled. "Today was a good day. I've got some new gigs lined up. In fact, I have one tonight. But first, let's eat."

"Excellent idea. What would you like?"

"I say we have breakfast for supper." He winked and she saw him. *Handsome Will.* Funny how she never had before. But then, he was the dad.

Dad fried thick turkey-bacon, potatoes, and eggs. He left

Georgie in charge of the biscuits. They laughed when she jumped at the pop from slamming the peeled biscuit container against the counter. The meal was simple and delicious.

Once the kitchen was back to clean, he said, "I expect you have homework."

"Yeah. Where are you playing tonight?"

"It's some fancy restaurant bar up the coast. You going to be okay on your own?"

"No problem." She faked a grimace. "I have plenty of home-work to keep me busy." But first she had a call to make.

"HI, MOM." She tapped the speaker button, sprawled out on the couch, threw one leg over the back and scrunched the pillow under her head. "How's it going?"

"Georgie! Are you okay?"

"Yeah. Things are going great. How are Bill and Rose?"

"They're well. They're in their rooms doing homework. Rose is in counseling now. Bill, too. I start next week."

"I'm glad, for all of you. Tell them hi, and send some pics to my phone?"

"Sure, honey. You want to talk to them?"

"That's okay. I really just wanted to call and ask how the new job's going."

"I love the work and the people are nice. My office has a good view of downtown. I'm finally doing what I've always wanted. How was your weekend?"

"Busy. We went to Grandma and Grandpa's. They're building a new deck."

"They're always doing something. Be careful. I'd hate for you to step on a nail or worse."

"I will. Dad took me to the city and I got a bicycle."

"Good idea. You needed one. How was your first day of school?"

"I met a couple of cool kids. Josefina's mom works with Luther, Grandma and Grandpa Jones's friend. You remember him?"

"Of course. I always liked Luther."

"Well, anyway, except for me being nervous in the beginning, it was a pretty good first day. Josefina and Shawn showed me around campus. Dodgeball is the major sport. Weird, right? And the freshmen, or first years, go to the same school as the sophomores, juniors, and seniors. It's a larger school. I guess that's why."

There was a pause. "How's your Dad?"

Georgie swung her leg down and sat up. "I think he's glad I'm here. He wishes he could have prevented Jack from being Jack." Silence. "I'm sorry, Mom. I didn't mean . . ."

"No, it's okay, Georgie. I understand, believe me."

"It wasn't your fault, Mom."

"Thank you, dear. I wish I had realized what was happening, but I'm glad you kids are safe now. So, you like it there?"

"Yeah, I do. Everything is different, but feels right, if you know what I mean, except I miss you and the siblings."

"We miss you too. If you want to come here just let me know."

"Thanks, Mom. I better get to my homework."

"I love you, Georgie."

"Love you back." She tapped her phone to end the call. *Mom still feels guilty, but she doesn't need to.*

CHAPTER SEVEN

INVITATION

"Would you like to go to Andersen Light?" Josefina asked as they walked toward their bus after school. Turquoise beads danced around the surface of her black cotton blouse. "I go there most days and hang out while my mom is still working."

Shawn trailed behind, hunched over his phone, the hood of his shirt-jacket wrapped around his neck and black curls.

"Yeah, thanks. I'll talk to my dad tonight." Georgie ran a hand along her arm where the afternoon sun warmed it.

"Maybe we could drop you off on our way home."

"That would actually be perfect." Depending on the day, Dad might play that night.

"I'll call you after I talk with my mom." Josefina slung her book bag onto her other shoulder and pushed her sunglasses higher up her nose. She craned her head to one side to pull the braid out from under the bag's strap. "It's really pretty there. Maybe Mr. Luther will give you a tour." She grinned. "And, we can also do homework."

"Good idea, and a great selling point if I need one." Georgie hefted and shifted her book bag. "It's funny you and I have never met." She mentally ran through her Mystic Creek memories. "But, I've only seen Luther at my grandparents' place."

Shawn shuffled their way, still hunched over his phone.

"Who does he communicate with?" Georgie bounced up the bus steps.

Josefina followed. "His aunt, but mainly with his dad and brother. They're at sea most of the time."

"What are they, on a fishing boat?"

"No. They work for the government."

"Oh."

"Exactly," Josefina said in a mock mysterious tone. They took their seat. "I don't know much about it. They work out on a ship for long periods of time. It's all hush-hush."

"Oh. So he stays with his aunt?"

"She lives with them. Mom says the Greens are testing a project, but not to ask about it."

Georgie wondered what they did, but didn't push for more.

Shawn took his seat in front of them and slowly scooted against the window instead of his usual jump-and-slide. He frowned and huddled over to poke into his phone.

"Hey, Shawn, everything okay?" Georgie asked.

He twisted around. "Oh, hey." He waved and reassumed his hunch.

"Shawn," Josefina said in the dogged tone one uses who's known and cared about a person forever. "Is everything okay?"

"Oh, yeah." He turned around. "It looks like Dad and Earl are staying out an extra week. . . and I'll be working on Aunt Darlene's honey-do list." The bus slowed for the next stop and he rose to leave.

Josefina said, "*Hasta mañana*."

His smile was back. "Hasty banana."

They called out, "Goodnight, Shawn!"

Georgie laughed at Josefina's eye roll of fake exasperation.

Josefina retrieved their earlier thread. "From the lighthouse you can see clear across Mystic Creek Bay. And, my mom has a greenhouse on the lighthouse estate."

Georgie imagined the scene. *It sounds really cool.*

Josefina pulled her bag onto her lap and slid to the edge of their seat. "Andersen Light's really cool. Don't forget to talk to your dad about it." She stood. "I'll call you tonight."

"Okay," Georgie said before Josefina was out of earshot. *Okay. .*
.

CHAPTER EIGHT

FAKE BLOG

L uther answered the secure telephone on his desk and punched in his PIN.

"Luther? Derrick Green here. Can you hear me?"

The ship-to-shore connection was clear. "Yes, Derrick. How can I help you?"

"There's been a kind of leak at the lab. I say 'kind of' because the information the receptionist blogged wasn't real. She took the Project Hermes cover story and embellished it, I suppose to gain more followers."

"And now you're concerned even a fake story could draw unwanted interest."

"Exactly. Her blog made it sound like our box is outfitted with communication portals, versus ports."

"Portals?" Luther asked. "For transporting or teleporting?"

"Either or, I guess. It's total fiction. Who knows why anyone would believe it. Just in case we get the wrong sort of attention. . . ."

"Keep an eye on Darlene and Shawn?"

"Exactly, Luther. Thanks a million."

CHAPTER NINE

CURANDERO

Luther settled into his blue chair for his evening meditation. He let go of the thoughts of the day, softened into the chair, initiated breath work through his centers, and abruptly jolted into a dark, enclosed space. He sensed a presence and used his inner vision to scan his surroundings. A lone figure huddled in the gloom. Damp coldness moved through Luther. His clairsentience and clairvoyance sharpened the scene. An old man, a *curandero*, lifted his face and the two merged empathically. Luther saw through the old man's eyes.

The old medicine man sat on a cold floor in the dark and leaned against an even colder wall. He ignored the throbbing and bleeding wounds they had inflicted on his body to force the location of the portal out of him. He would hold them off psychically as long as he could, but it would be but a matter of time before they were back and at it again. Next time they would threaten his loved ones and he would reveal the false location. Until then he would continue to send his telepathic message of warning to Alejandro.

Muffled voices grew louder. A key turned the door's locks. The *curandero* silently prepared himself. He prayed and called forth the *poderosos*, spirits of his *curandero* sisters and brothers. Spirits surrounded the old man, their hands outstretched, denying Luther deeper internal presence, allowing him only to see and envelope the old man in healing comfort.

Many men entered his stony prison. Their intimidation persisted with shouts, beatings, threats, and unrelenting interrogations. His captors could not see how beneath the surface his wounds were already mending. The balm of healing energy quelled his skin's burning pain into numbness. Luther witnessed the face of Alejandro forming through the old man's vision, edging out all else. The *curandero's* message had been received. *"Esta bien,"* he rasped aloud, his voice parched and broken. His torturers fell quiet.

CHAPTER TEN

ALEJANDRO

"I've heard from my brother Alejandro," said Maria Elena Garcia. "It was as you described. The *curandero* was a close friend, someone he had met while on assignment as U.S. Government liaison there in Sonora, Mexico along the Sea of Cortez."

"What were Alejandro's impressions?"

"The *curandero's* captors were looking for a portal. Alejandro didn't have more information, but will let me know when he does."

"Curious." Luther brushed at his mustache.

"You think it's related to the Greens' project?"

"I do. You know what I think about coincidences. I will speak with Alejandro. Meanwhile, we continue our shielding of Darlene Green and the boy."

"Absolutely."

"AFTER I 'HEARD' from my *curandero* friend, I went to my local contacts," Alejandro Martín told Luther. "They tell me the term *portal* is active across many human communication platforms.

Persons yet unidentified are searching for a portal, and not just in western Mexico."

"Are there other keywords associated with *portal?*"

"Only *curandero*. No other words or patterns have been reported, but I will verify."

"Please notify me immediately if there are any associations with the name Green or their government program, Project Hermes."

"Green? As in our our mutual friend Derrick?"

"The same."

"I see."

"Please keep the names within trusted channels, Alejandro."

"Of course. I will contact you very soon."

"Thank you, my friend." Luther replaced the handset and stroked his goatee.

CHAPTER ELEVEN

ANDERSEN LIGHT

Afternoon sunbeams encroached Luther's private sitting room. He placed his notebook on the side table, dropped the pencil into his shirt pocket, and rose to rinse his cup. Birds floating on the water's surface caught his gaze through the tea station's window before he took the spiral staircase up to his gallery level office.

Luther stared into the space above his hibernating laptop.

His father and grandfather were also lightkeepers, and at times, his grandmother and mother. As members of Mystic Creek society, they were admired for their intellect, humor, and musical talents.

That was a very long time ago. Andersen Light had been through numerous renovations since those days, which accounted for his being able to stand in his personal library and office looking through the thick, hurricane-grade windows over the estate.

The towering structure had been in his family since its inception—before the Light House Establishment or its successor, the Lighthouse Service. Lighthouse keepers and engineers, his ancestors dated back to the Northern Lighthouse Board and works of Robert Stevenson in the old country.

Although Luther kept the light burning, the lighthouse was all but retired now. Emergency calls from the Coast Guard or local authorities were rare. He routinely verified the automated alert and warning systems were operational. He and his longtime friends and helpmates, Carl Nelson and Maria Elena Garcia, were required to keep the light, boats, and gear in tip-top condition. They were all trained and ready, with current lifesaving certificates.

Luther closed the laptop and retrieved his cotton navy, Greek-style fisher's cap. He faced the lane that led to the county road, where, shortly, a school bus would deliver Josefina, Maria Elena's daughter, and the Jones girl, Georgie.

He glanced at the main house and outbuildings—carriage, boathouse, old fuel house, and foghorn shed—and allowed his memories as he made another circuit around the gallery windows. Luther donned his cap, descended the spiral staircase, and caught sight of the oceanside guest houses near the property's edge. They were a fairly recent addition and virtually unused. This would change in the coming months.

No expense had been spared to build, rebuild, and expand the original concept of the standard lighthouse, dwellings, and grounds —providing the estate's spacious, comfortable home and work-spaces. Yet even now, he prepared to commit new plans for the second and third floors from drawing program to paper.

His mother and the early Garcia women first built Andersen Light's greenhouse, later redesigned by Maria Elena. Her creative spirit and green thumb deserved credit for today's greenhouse and award-winning grounds.

Carl waved from his grounds cart as he breezed toward the old carriage house, now their garage and workshop.

Luther moved through the foyer into the expansive great hall. Light streamed through its floor-to-ceiling windows onto rugs, tapestries, and paintings hung between windows and built-in shelves. Subtly illuminated artifacts harkened to the everyday lives of lightkeepers.

Beyond their history, beauty, and design, the objects vibrated with the energy of his life's experiences, and those who came before him. He grinned at the hum and glow emanating from each piece. He wasn't the only one eager to greet today's young guest.

The grand sitting room, a generous reception area in soft hues of blues, greens, and lavenders reflected his mother's touch. His father had proclaimed the adjacent fireplace room the great conversation place, now home to a loose half-circle of sofas, comfortable chairs, and ottomans. A massive table Luther fashioned from a rescued tree stump and thick slab of recycled glass sat in the center of the sprawling room. High above the fireplace hung an enormous, round antique clock framed in oak.

Early evenings, he, his grandmother, and mother had howled with laughter at the storytelling of his father, uncles, and brother. Cool winter nights, after Andersen Light and a cheery fire were lit, before Luther was sent off to bed, first one man and then another leaned on the mantle and spun their tales. Tellers and listeners were bolstered by hot cocoa and Mother's shortbread cookies cut into stars and phases of the moon. He could still taste them.

Luther passed by the piano bench where his brother had banged out raucous tunes and sang while Mother danced, cheered on by clapping hands and stamping feet.

Tinkling silverware reached his ears from where Maria Elena prepared this afternoon's refreshments. He walked by the long, wooden dining table, opened the glass door, and stepped outside onto the wide veranda. It was a calm sea day, the breeze light.

Chairs ringed the table, set and ready to receive the Andersen Light family. He looked over the stone wall. Nearby bluffs held sea caves, forests, stories of smugglers, ghosts, and memories of youthful escapades.

It was time. He went inside to lend his hands to Maria Elena.

"WE TAKE a different bus to Andersen Light," Josefina explained.

Georgie stuck close as Josefina wound her way through kids and parked buses, and slowed to keep from running over Josefina's heels. She spotted a man in a black jacket standing across the street. Her stomach lurched. *Weird. That guy's out of place.*

Josefina followed her glance. "That's weird." She climbed the steps of the short yellow bus. "I like riding my bicycle sometimes. On those days, Carl Nelson, who works at the light, throws my bike into the back of his truck and drops Mom and me off on his way home."

"Hey, I have a bike."

"Let's ride out together sometime. We should do it while the days are longer."

"Right." *She must be some kind of season groupie.*

Josefina flashed a one-sided grin. "My mom's kind of a nature freak so we keep up with all kinds of earthy things."

The bus dropped them off where Lighthouse Way intersected with a long lane. Georgie sought its end. The lighthouse rose high above the estate. Shivers ran up her arms. "Whoa."

"Andersen Light," introduced Josefina.

"It's beautiful." The colossal tower gleamed in the afternoon light. Even at this distance Georgie could see sun shining through the lantern and windows on four levels. Lower buildings nestled around the lighthouse, like the humongous house to its right surrounded by seriously big trees. A light breeze carried salty sea air in waves through fields of grass and wild flowers on either side of the meandering lane, which popped up intermittently in low rises. A ripple of something, a kind of low-voltage current, ran over the top of her head. *The wind? No.* The current surged up her spine. *Whoa! Strange.*

The lane terminated into a huge circular drive with branches off to the right and left. A fountain sculpture inside the circle's center depicted a super tall couple—Greek, based on overall buff-ness and classic features. They stood on a natural rock outcropping in a loose embrace with two tridents laid crossed at their feet, as if in offering. Water from the shallow pool splashed up their legs and over the seashells and seaweed adorning the sculpture's base. She and Josefina skirted through rings of wildflowers on stone steps to stand next to the pool's low wall.

Josefina broke the silence. "Mr. Luther calls it *Peaceful Seas.*"

"It's amazing." Live seagulls rested on the tridents.

They tore themselves away from the sculpture, back to the circular drive, and past where the right branch wound through trees toward where the lighthouse towered between brick and stone buildings. Wide, half-moon steps rippled toward them from heavy, ornate wooden doors of the enormous main house. Stone angels leaned from perches on corners of the buildings' roofs. Georgie half expected the angels to wave. Instead, one of the massive doors opened and Luther and a woman stepped out.

"Welcome to Andersen Light," he said, his voice strong and easy. Georgie hadn't seen Luther in a while, and not terribly often. He still wore a navy fisher's cap atop glossy black and silver-speckled hair. His brilliant blue eyes twinkled kindly, and, just as Georgie recollected, the smile was generous. "It is good to see you again, Georgie." His warm hands clasped hers.

"You, too." She returned his smile.

He winked at Josefina. "I don't believe you've met Josefina's mother, Maria Elena."

Pretty in a grown-up way, the woman who hugged Josefina had the same dark brown-black hair as her daughter, but pulled back into a bun. Genuinely welcoming, intelligent brown eyes and a warm smile graced her face. Strands of colored beads of flowers and tiny gemstone animals hung over an apron which partially covered her turquoise blouse and purple slacks. Georgie detected lavender and rose scents as she neared. "It's so very nice to meet you finally." Her hug kind of embarrassed Georgie, but felt good. "Would you like to come in?" Maria Elena asked. "Mr. Luther and I have an afterschool snack ready on the terrace."

"Say yes," Josefina directed in a stage whisper.

Georgie laughed. "Yes."

They entered a ginormous room with the unmistakable aroma of recent baking. The huge space was grouped into distinct areas by furniture and things, like the huge clock over a fireplace surrounded by couches. Georgie openly gaped. *What was the word? Sumptuous. Yeah, that was it.* She picked up her step when she noticed the others had slowed to accommodate her, and closed her mouth.

"Incredible, isn't it?" Josefina asked, a hint of humor in her voice.

"Yeah!" she managed. The group wandered past a piano to the far end where the whole wall was made up of windows. Luther opened one, which turned out to be a door. Georgie embraced the sea air as they stepped out onto the oceanside stone terrace.

A glass-topped table set for five beckoned. Sun sparkled off water in glasses and dishes filled with food as the group seated themselves. Georgie appreciated the protective terrace wall. *Maybe my curls won't blow into my mouth with every bite.* She spied the empty chair just as a man pushed through the glass door, his hair damp from a splash and comb with bits of hair stuck up in the back. He wiped freshly scrubbed hands on his blue jeans.

Luther chuckled. "Welcome, Carl. You are just in time. Georgie, this is Carl Nelson. He and Maria Elena manage most of the operations here."

"Nice to meet you, Georgie." His large, damp hand shook hers as he lowered his brawny frame into the chair. He tipped his head at Luther. "He's being generous. There's not much around here that doesn't have his fingerprints on it."

"Nice to meet you, too."

Maria Elena closed her eyes and held her palms over the table. Georgie glanced at Josefina as if to ask, but it was Luther who answered.

"Maria Elena is thanking the food and water."

The woman said, "I bless the food and drink while I prepare the meal and when we eat."

"Like a silent prayer?" Georgie asked Maria Elena.

"Yes, it is a prayer of gratitude. We thank the Creator, the farmers, workers, harvests, and nature angels. We affirm the food we eat and drink provide us the greatest possible nourishment and enjoyment."

"I get it," Georgie said. *Makes sense.*

Carl threw Maria Elena a wink. "You get used to it."

Maria Elena offered her a plate piled with petite, triangular sandwiches. Georgie selected two and bit into a delicious triangle. Except for the avocado slice, she wasn't sure what was in it. "What makes this so good?"

"Hummus. Mom makes her own," Josefina answered. "The roasted sunflower seeds give the crunch. The arugula comes from her garden. Good, right?"

Mouth full, Georgie nodded her energetic reply.

Luther held up his glass. "To friends and family." Maria Elena and Josefina raised theirs. Georgie and Carl quickly joined them.

"To friends and family!" They clinked their glasses in a toast.

Georgie grinned. *Just like in the movies.*

They polished the so-called snacks and savored the last of their blackberry tarts. Carl excused himself to work on a project. Josefina and Georgie politely declined Maria Elena's offer of hot tea.

"I'll get a cup later." Luther patted her hand. "You have treated us as royalty, Maria Elena. Thank you."

"It's my honor." She returned his smile and tilted her head toward the door. "Time for the tour?"

"If you're ready, girls." He extended his arm in grand gesture. "Shall we begin with the lighthouse?"

Inside the great hall near the foyer, Luther opened a set of heavy, carved, double wooden doors into a wide hallway. Georgie stepped over the threshold to a gentle puff of wind. *What was that?* The air was still. Neither Josefina nor Luther appeared to notice.

She checked behind her but saw nothing out of the ordinary and hurried to catch up.

"We are in the corridor between the main house and the lighthouse tower," Luther explained. "This door on your left opens onto a path to the garage and workshop, also known as the carriage house. You can see it there through the windows. Paths all over the estate are wide enough for the carts we use when not on foot. We created special hybrid carts capable of utilizing either human or motor power—pedaling and the sun charge the motor's battery." They arrived at another set of hefty double doors and stepped over a deep threshold. "This is the ground floor of Andersen Lighthouse. Many modifications have been made since it was first built." His voice faintly reverberated around the room.

Suh-weet. White from floor to ceiling, it was way wider and higher than Georgie expected. Afternoon light poured through tall windows and bounced off the room's white surfaces and circular wall. A staircase ascended from an elaborate pattern in the center of the floor's stone tile and drew her eyes up and up into a picturesque spiral, like a seashell. Stairs and handrailing circled up in varying shades of white. *This could make a girl dizzy.* She gazed up anyway.

Luther drew them over to stand near one of the windows. She grasped the ledge and breathed in a pleasant green scent. "Windows made for extreme storm resistance on each level maximize the use of natural light, heating and cooling," he said. "Each window can be opened manually or remotely, and contains a solar shade. Carl and I have been perfecting our solar and wind power solutions over the years. An energy storage area is immediately below us."

Georgie looked down. "You mean, like batteries? Under the floor?"

"Precisely."

The stone floor of bright whites to the lightest of taupes and grays held in its center a geometric-looking mosaic she didn't recognize. "Nice, there's a perfect view of *Peaceful Seas* from here." She moved around the staircase to find stylish chairs and tables in modern blonde wood, white, and chrome Scandinavian design like those in her mom's art magazines. Plant pockets lining the adjacent house walls came into focus through a windowed door across the room. "Tight idea."

"Right? I call it Mom's living art wall," said Josefina. She waved to several colossal-sized pots around the room. "They're different kinds of citrus trees."

Georgie touched a young, green fruit then glanced around again. A cubic structure with clear sides jutted out from the lighthouse's round interior wall. She refocused. The cube was nearly camouflaged except for the glint of light on its clear surface and a narrow, grooved channel extending up the wall.

"I see you have noticed one of our recent and most challenging engineering feats," Luther said. "Our elevator makes hauling heavier items up to the other levels easier. Shall we?"

He opened the door made of thick, clear composite, like Lucite. *Makes sense,* Georgie thought. *Glass would be heavy.* They stepped inside. The ride was smooth and quiet. "Awesome," she and Josefina cooed as the stone floor fell away. Georgie gauged their rapid speed against the staircase as they arrived at the next level.

"Second floor," announced Luther. He stepped out. "These are my rooms. Beyond that wall is my bedroom and bath."

Georgie stepped onto cork flooring. A breeze moved through the vertical windows. A high wall of variegated bamboo ran through the entire space, and curved around the staircase. Wide, rectangular openings high along the top of the bamboo wall invited light. A carved, wooden door blended into the wall's curve. Near the upper portion of the door was a round, stained-glass window, with the same pattern as in the first floor tile. "I like your door."

Luther beamed. "Thank you. I do too."

"The whole room looks like a yin yang shape with a hole in the middle for the stairs."

Josefina cocked her head for another look.

"You have a keen eye, Miss Jones." He gestured to the right. "On this side of the wall and staircase is my sitting area."

An old wooden table held a lamp and several stacks of books next to a sizeable recliner covered in blue chenille. Georgie strained to read the titles in the bookcases, only making out a few. A shiny, broadleaf rubber plant towered over the cozy sitting room while a glass door opened onto Luther's balcony.

Georgie pointed at curved shelves with canisters, boxes, and cups. "That's where you make your tea?" The tea station with its miniature sink, and a teapot on one burner—in fact, the whole room —exuded a halo of whitish yellow light. *And contemplation?*

Luther smiled. "Precisely, Georgie."

Which question had he answered? *Duh. Don't be ridiculous.*

They returned to the elevator. "Now for the third floor," he said. They arrived in seconds. Georgie speculated whether she could take the stairs faster. *Probably not.* Luther opened the door, but they remained in the elevator. As on the level below, a wall curved across the floor. This time, however, the side within view was empty. "This level is reserved for future use."

Another tingling sensation moved over Georgie's head. *Weird.*

"Last stop—the gallery." His voice mimicked the old-time elevator operators from black and white movies. She laughed. Luther had a sense of humor. They stepped into the gallery.

"Look up," Josefina said.

"What's that?" She followed Josefina's gaze several feet up the staircase to a huge orbital structure of pale green, crystal-clear glass. Afternoon light reflected through faceted concentric circles and waves of curving lines. The color of super clear, recycled soda bottles, the glass dazzled as it refracted the light. She couldn't take her eyes off of it.

"It is our Fresnel lens," Luther answered. "The light shines through that lens many miles into the distance." He grabbed her elbow just as she stumbled forward, her eyes still upward on the lens. "We can get a better look another day."

"Good idea." *Okay, that was graceful.*

Josefina let a soft giggle escape.

Luther waved an arm to encompass the entire area. "This level contains my office, library, and classroom. The kitchenette is an especially handy addition as I spend a great deal of my time here."

Georgie cast a first look. A door butted right up next to the elevator. *A closet?*

"That is the necessary room," Luther volunteered.

"Right." Her grandparents used the term. She craned her head left and right. Waist-high wooden bookshelves wrapped around the entire round wall, leaving room for the ever present, vertical windows.

Georgie's head spun with the feeling time shuffled itself here. Luther's antique desk held a laptop, flat screen, and two telephones, one a bulkier version of the other, amid neatly stacked books and papers. A green shaded lamp vied for space with an ancient-looking brass telescope, modern binoculars, and a printout labeled Tide Chart. Lighthouse-related objects claimed tops of glassed-in bookshelves. She moved closer to inspect the insignia on a billed uniform hat and cup-saucer-teapot set. *Good stuff.* Old fashioned photos and manual-style books crowded other shelves. A worn pocket watch engraved with U.S.L.H.S caught her eye.

Luther held out the watch. "This was my father's." He turned it over in his palm to reveal the initials C.A. She traced the letters with her finger tip. Edwardian was one of her favorite fonts, but this was special. Before she could ask, he said, "His name was Connor."

"You must miss him."

Josefina moved to his other side.

"Yes, I do. He was a good man."

"Tall, like you?" asked Georgie.

He laughed and tapped the tip of her nose. "Yes, tall like me." He replaced the watch. "The initials stand for United States Light House Service."

Adjacent to Luther's desk two chairs faced one another, an ottoman between. Alongside the chairs rare, empty bookshelf space held nautical-themed coasters. Behind the second chair the balcony door marked a half-way point around the room.

"This the counseling area?" Georgie asked. Josefina snickered.

"Wouldn't be a bit surprised," he said.

Two distinctly different areas made up the other half of the room. Closest were three chairs facing ocean-side windows. Next to them stood an impressive telescope on a tripod.

"What do you use the telescope for?" Georgie asked.

"I watch boats and ships out on the water. I also do a bit of stargazing."

The larger space between the telescope and the elevator contained curved tables flanked by chairs arranged in a half circle. *A classroom. The chairs look comfy, and expensive.*

Josefina said, "This is where Mr. Luther teaches—virtually as well as in person. Maybe we can sit in sometime." She looked up to see his reaction.

"I think we can arrange it."

Georgie caught a sparkle in his eyes, or did she imagine it? *Hmm.* They followed Luther out onto the balcony. The railing was high, nearly to her chest, and ran the entire 360 degrees around the gallery. Josefina was right, she could see across Mystic Creek Bay. A fluffy mass hovered further out at sea, fog forming its way inland.

Luther bowed. "That concludes today's tour. If you're to view the grounds and Maria Elena's greenhouse before leaving for the day, you had better get started."

"Thank you!" they said and bounded down the spiral steps.

JOSEFINA AND GEORGIE crammed themselves into the jump seats of Carl's truck. "You two okay back there?" he asked, craning his head around as he drove along.

Maria Elena looked back, the sides of her eyes crinkled. "They're just fine, Carl."

"We're okay!" They grinned to each other.

"Glad you came?" Josefina asked.

"Yeah! It was amazing." Andersen Light was a whole different world, one she hoped to return to sometime. Georgie had a bucket load of questions, which could wait. She was happy to bounce along in the back seat beside her friend while the lighthouse blazed into the night.

GEORGIE HELPED herself to the Thai takeout.

"Everything is medium, except that one." Dad tapped his chopsticks on a cardboard container. "Fair warning: that panang curry is Thai-medium."

"Whatever. I'm sure I can handle it." She generously spooned it onto the brown jasmine rice. "Holy chili curry!" she squeaked and grasped for her water glass.

"Told you." He laughed and helped himself from the variety of containers. "How was your trip to Andersen Light?"

"Oh, it was brilliant, Dad! That place is unbelievable and everyone is so nice."

"It is. They are. I used to go out there with your grandparents." He swallowed a bite of drunken noodle and mused, "It's been quite a while since I was last there."

"You should go again. Seriously, Dad." She squared off at the veggies dripping panang sauce from her chopsticks, and took the bite. "Umm . . . yum."

He chuckled. "Good for you, Georgie."

CHAPTER TWELVE

CONNECTIONS

Georgie maneuvered her bicycle through buffeting wind toward the lighthouse. According to Dad, this part of the country was geographically situated on an edge of utterly unpredictable day-to-day weather. A season didn't guarantee a sunny or cloudy day. Ocean air currents and mountain downdrafts met, and like two rival gangs, puffed themselves up and swelled into storms at their invisible territorial line. The weather had been mostly sunny and not too wet since she'd moved here, and though breezy, today was another beautiful day. A warm sun penetrated the cool breezes. Dad's NPR station had reported partly to mostly sunny with a chance of rain.

Tall grasses in a mix of late, yellow and white wild flowers swayed on either side of the road on her ride to the lighthouse. The more they waved, the closer she was to the shore. There were no high hills on the way to Andersen Light, just rolling rises that allowed her to see further ahead. She used to dislike riding her bike up steep inclines. *One should ride up tall hills,* she'd reasoned, *only if absolutely necessary.* That was then. These days she wouldn't mind. All the recent bike riding was building up her strength and speed. When there was no traffic on the road, which was most of the time—and Josefina was not with her, like today—she would practically fly, catching air off the low hills.

The best part of Andersen Light was hanging out with Luther. He came from a long line of lighthouse keepers. In the past, it was one of the most important jobs in town, right up there with the mayor and fire chief. There was something else about him she couldn't quite put her finger on that made him special to her. She smiled to herself. Maybe Josefina had it right, maybe he was like Merlin. She pulled strands of hair out of her eyes. *Yeah, right. Meanwhile, back in the real world . . .*

Luther said the lighthouse light was hooked up to the Coast Guard's automatic systems. But, in emergencies, like a capsized boat or really bad fog, a call could come in for foghorn activation or shore rescue—which is why they kept boat, rafts, and other equipment ready to roll.

On the way home one night, Carl described the latest rescue. Calls had come in from the sheriff and the Coast Guard about a missing boater. The surf had turned rough and the young man's small boat had crashed on the rocks near Clammer's Cove. "He hit his danged head on something and was knocked out, but there wasn't a scratch on him otherwise." Carl's tone was suspicious and his eyes rolled at them in the rear view mirror. "It was an easy rescue. No doubt he was out there trying to get to one of the smuggler caves. People come around looking for treasure from a yarn spun by some old uncle. It's hogwash. One of them is bound to really get hurt someday, the stupid bean bags." She and Josefina had clamped their hands over their mouths to keep from laughing.

Georgie sped up against the wind to catch some air for an upcoming rise. Time stood still the few exhilarating seconds she was airborne. Since Dad and her grandparents had made a deal with Luther, she rode her bike out to the lighthouse with Josefina after school on most good weather days. Luther was easy to talk with, like he cared what she thought. He helped her and Josefina with their homework, encouraging them to demonstrate things for themselves. They made lists of questions to ask him during hikes along the beach trail or discussing homework. Afternoons breezed by and Maria Elena's call for time to pack up always came as a surprise.

She landed squarely on the downhill and followed her thoughts to a recent weekend at her grandparents. Her job was to fetch tools and materials, and fill coffee or water orders. Georgie pondered Grandma Grace's peculiar expression as she laid down an armful of lumber and handed her a fresh pack of nails, until the conversation turned to Luther.

Luther was a longtime fixture and honorary member of the Jones family. He regularly dropped by for a cup of tea, and they'd get his opinion on their latest renovations.

Grandpa liked his gentle way. "He's humble. Rarely talks about himself, being more interested in the folks he's with. His brother and uncles died in the war, but their buddy Thomas Nelson came back and married your grandma's Aunt Betty. They eventually had Carl."

Georgie quickly calculated. "So, that makes Carl Nelson my third cousin."

Grandma smiled. "Good catch, dear." She brushed debris off a stained and marred wooden saw horse, took off her gloves, and sat on one end.

Grandpa stepped around Kelly-girl and Sidney to sit next to Grandma. "And it was Thomas who taught your dad to play the guitar."

"Thanks to Thomas Nelson, I have a job tonight." Dad stood and brushed off his jeans.

On the drive home, Georgie had played movies in her mind of Jones-Andersen dinner parties from the old days.

The wind gained force. Grass and flowers flailed wildly on either side as she flew down the lane to the lighthouse. She circled around *Peaceful Seas* and glided into an open door of the old carriage house garage just as big, fat drops of rain pelted her back.

CHAPTER THIRTEEN

DODGEBALL DAY

Georgie and Josefina changed into their P.E. clothes and wandered outside. Kids kicked dodgeballs and milled around in their usual herds. P.E. dodgeball was considered coed, but more boys had made it to class so far, and no teachers. She could see Shawn across the school yard next to the wall, holding and twirling the dodgeball like a basketball.

A kid shouted at him, "You just going to stand there twirling, or what?"

"Who's that guy?" she asked Josefina. She'd seen him at the bus stop, on the bus, and around school. Larger and taller than most of the kids, he wore a constant sneer. It ranged from the full face scowl to the evil-looking sideways mouth twist, as if he had something real nasty in his mouth. Bits of blonde hair fought their way out of shocking red, unruly cowlicks spiked all over his head. *There's no way someone would do that to their hair on purpose.*

"Oh, that's Harvey Smith. He's on varsity. He can be obnoxious." Her eyes narrowed into a frown. They strolled toward Shawn. He was as tall, but slender compared to the big, red-headed kid he appeared to be ignoring.

"What are you, hard of hearing? I asked you a question," Harvey demanded.

Shawn didn't answer. Other students began to cluster nearby. A girl named Ruby—thin, like a model from teen magazines Georgie knew only from the checkout line—hid behind a tree, face ashen and rigid, one hand over her mouth.

Harvey's scowl reddened. His body was tense, hands clenched. He stalked over, grabbed the ball out of Shawn's hand, and bounced it on the ground—thawt, thawt, thawt. "Let's play, twirler." The cheerful tone mismatched his stance. He bounced the ball some more then tossed it hard from one hand to the other. "Ready to play?"

Shawn moved to leave, but didn't get far before Harvey threw the ball at him. "Hey!" Shawn yelled.

"What's he doing?" Georgie asked. This couldn't be normal. And it was escalating. She met Josefina's glance. They picked up their pace.

Harvey caught the rebounding ball and threw it at Shawn again. "Ready to play?"

"Stop it!" Shawn shouted.

"Ready to play now?" asked Harvey. He threw it again. He kept at it, a game now. He threw the ball over and over at Shawn, every throw harder than the one before. Harvey grabbed the ball from each bounce off Shawn's frame, now folded into itself and lowered to the ground.

"Stop it, Harvey!" Josefina and Georgie shouted. They rushed to the scene.

Why wasn't anyone stopping him? "Stop it!" Georgie yelled again. A burning sensation grew low in her stomach. She visualized a protective force field around Shawn.

Harvey ignored them and continued to pound Shawn. Other kids hollered for him to stop.

Harvey ignored them all.

The burn in Georgie's stomach erupted like wildfire through her arms and legs and intensified in her hands and feet. She was in motion before the blaze hit her face. "He's not ready to play, jack-ass!" She wrenched the ball from Harvey's hands and threw it away. It hit the nearby wall, leaving a two-foot spider crack, and bounced back directly at Harvey. He issued a visceral grunt as the ball rocketed into his stomach. His arms curled around it as the force knocked him backwards. To Georgie's surprise, the impact of the ball did not knock him down, but caused him to fly yards through the air before he landed on his butt. *How was that possible?* She stared after him, stupefied.

Clapping and shouting grew through her muffled shock. She stared at the bully sprawled on the ground. He clutched at his stomach as the ball rolled away. Shawn and Josefina edged closer to her.

"Hey, thanks," Shawn said.

She pulled her eyes away from Harvey and replied numbly, "Yeah, sure."

"Are you okay?" Josefina asked her.

"Yeah, sure," she repeated. Georgie couldn't decipher the odd expressions on her friends' faces. *Surprise?* She focused on Shawn. "Are *you* okay?"

"Yeah. But how did you do that?"

"I don't know—fight or flight response, I guess."

Josefina suddenly grabbed their arms. "The coaches are here. Let's head over."

The three hustled toward the center of the court. Josefina put her fingers to her mouth in a zipper gesture to the kids who followed them. The whistle of one of the coaches pierced the air and they all broke into a jog.

Other than a few odd glances from Harvey, the rest of P.E. moved quickly. He went through the motions of play, but hung back. There were no retaliatory throws from anyone and the enthusiasm from the rest of the class was, according to Josefina, at an all-time high. Even the remainder of the school day went as usual, if she didn't count the low buzz of students repeating and texting the story.

But she wasn't okay. She was quiet on the bus ride. Next to her, Josefina gave her space and didn't press her with any questions. Instead of having his nose in his phone, Shawn twisted around in his seat silently staring at her. But she didn't care. *What the hell happened?*

HER STOMACH SCREWED into itself clockwise. Distracted, she lifted her bike off the porch, threw on her helmet and headed off toward Andersen Light. *What had happened?* She'd been angry with that big kid Harvey for continuously pummeling Shawn with the ball. *What was his problem anyway?* Everyone told him to stop, including herself and Josefina. Ruby Lee, a girl she only knew from a couple of classes, ended up cowered in a ball against a tree. Shawn had teared up from the pain by the time she and Josefina arrived on scene. That's when Georgie had lost it.

She reviewed how she'd grabbed the ball and thrown it away. *Fiercely.* It hit the nearby wall and bounced back squarely into Harvey's stomach. Instead of the ball deflecting, the force sent Harvey flying backward, but not to the ground. He actually flew backward, bent over like a less-than sign, for at least fifteen feet. *Okay, maybe it was more.* The throw had been hard, but not *that* hard. *What happened?* She wasn't a violent person.

How was she going to explain something she herself didn't understand? Prickles of sweat pestered her. *Weird.* It wasn't hot. Luckily Harvey had not been hurt, except for his pride and possibly his intimidation cred. The wind and swagger was knocked out of him, and he hadn't said anything to any of the coaches or teachers. Not that she'd heard. Maybe he couldn't admit a girl had knocked him down—well, knocked him through the air and then down. Still, she had a feeling it wasn't over with Harvey. It'd be a miracle if someone didn't post a photo or video.

Everything had happened so fast. No one had been more surprised at the effect of her dodgeball throw than Georgie. It was unbelievable. She hunkered into the handlebars and wind.

Shawn had said thanks and wiped his face with the back of his hands. Kids told and retold of how Georgie had thrown the ball so hard she had sent the big bully flying backwards onto his butt. Maybe she could claim exaggeration. But she had not meant to hit him. Or had she? She was angry when she threw the ball. Had she been thinking of hitting Harvey when she threw it—or had she just thrown the ball away so it could no longer hurt Shawn?

She peddled furiously to put as much distance between herself and the most horrible day of school she'd ever had. *What a way to make an impression at a new school! What would Dad say? Would he hear about it?* She sped down the road on her way to the lighthouse. Her face burned. The wind glanced off. She probably looked like the blur she felt inside. The bicycle whined. All she wanted was to be inside the protective walls of the lighthouse. *Was that selfish?*

Josefina and her mom were doing stuff at their house and wouldn't be at Luther's. Good. Talking to him would be tough enough alone. The landscape streaked in her peripheral vision and her hair whipped at her neck, shoulders, and back. Her eyes stung.

Luther watched her skid into the carriage house and leave her bike standing without its kickstand. The girl didn't hear it fall. He followed her in his mind's eye as she crashed through the doorway. She leapt up the spiral staircase, wild-eyed, wild-haired, red-faced, and ready to explode—which she did as she fell into a heap of heaving sputters into her usual chair.

He listened intently from the gallery kitchen as she recounted her day, colorful descriptors included. Georgie decried her ruined new life. Her questions were imbued with anxiety and uncertainty.

She demanded to know which was worse—what she had done or the impossibility of what had happened?

"How the hell could it happen?" she asked. "It can't be normal."

This was the day he had been waiting for. "You are experiencing a perfectly normal reaction." He handed her cold lemon water. "Who would not be shocked?"

"Exactly." She uncurled an arm out of the tight ball she had wound herself into and accepted the glass.

He pretended not to see her dab at the corner of one eye with the back of her wrist as he patted her shoulder and took the facing chair. "But you're not normal, Georgie."

"Excuse me?" She sat up.

"Georgie Rae Jones, you are not a normal girl. Clearly, you have meta-normal strength."

"No kidding." When he didn't respond to her sarcasm she said, "Wait. What?"

"You are meta-normal, meaning you were born with the potential to develop senses and abilities beyond normal human ranges."

She stood straight up. Her feet wouldn't move.

He motioned for her to sit. "You may have noticed odd or exceptional occurrences since your thirteenth birthday."

"Wait!" She sat on the edge of the seat. He had to be kidding. She searched his face. "Is this a joke?"

"I assure you, Georgie, this is no joke." His answer was gentle. "Look back. Take a breath and scan the last couple years of your life."

His expression was serious but kind, definitely not smiling or humorous. She sat back, put one ankle up on her knee, her arms on either arm of the chair, and took a deep breath. Plenty had happened in recent years, so much to scan.

"Does anything you've done stand out, other than your powerful dodgeball throw?"

Can this be real? She reviewed. Things were weird back there in Starkton with Jackass. Memory flashed on her surrounding Bill, Rose, and herself with the invisible force field, and later, toward the end, also Mom. *Is that what Luther's talking about?* She'd only prayed it would work. Maybe it did.

"What is it?" he asked.

"It's something I do." She described it to him.

"I see." One of his eyebrows lifted. "We call that shielding. What else?"

"I used to run to clear my mind. I got pretty fast." She didn't go into how she ran to shake off Jackass slime. "Lately I've gotten faster on my bicycle, but I figured it was from all the riding." *And today . . . yeah, there had been lots and lots of air.*

"I believe we can agree something else is going on. Today's incident may seem isolated, but it was an accelerated response." He paused, his expression grave. "From today forward, I must ask you to use caution when you engage in physical activity away from Andersen Light. And, you must not speak to anyone about this."

"Wait!" cried Georgie. "You think something like what happened today will happen again?" *Holy crap! I am a freak!* She covered her face.

"Look, Georgie." She lowered her hands. "Yes, I do expect your strength will increase. No, you are not a freak."

Did he say freak? "That's easy for you to say."

"Yes, I suppose it is."

It wasn't his fault. "Hey, I'm sorry."

"You will refrain from using your super strength outside of Andersen Light?"

"Yeah, okay." She wasn't even sure about her strength. Maybe this was a fluke. Either way, if it did happen again she wanted it private, not public.

"This is not a fluke, Georgie. Tomorrow we will talk about it more and have our first lesson." He stood. "How about a snack before you do your homework? Carl will be ready to take you home soon."

He did it again! How did he know she'd been thinking those words—*freak, fluke?* Was this the end of the conversation? But she was going to explode with questions! She followed him down the spiral staircase.

"You're not going to explode, Georgie."

I know I didn't say that out loud. This keeps getting weirder and weirder. But she wasn't at all sure of herself. They were almost to the ground floor on the last curve of their descent when she spotted a very wide smile on Luther's face.

WHAT AM I BECOMING? The questioning cry screamed into her every hidden corner. No answers soothed. The silent question shouted and reverberated from her chest, up her throat, across her face, and down into her fingers and toes. It vibrated her gut, tingled the top of her head, and left her legs shaky, her arms weak. On the edge of her bed, head in hands, she held back tears. She fell backward and waited for the sensations to pass. The wall clock ticked off the seconds. Tears escaped from her eyes into the hair at her temples. Their release left her still. Was this the quiet before the storm in her mind, or the empty place waiting for the answer to her question?

Drying trails from her tears tickled. She swiped at them. The question of who she was stood on top of the pile of questions she had not allowed herself to consider. Whatever was happening in her body, maybe her whole being, had nothing to do with family affairs. Unless they triggered her?

Family stuff, specifically her parents' divorce and the unhappy stint with Jackass, had become the place her thoughts drifted to understand her feelings. She had acknowledged to herself the emotion behind her parents' actions, but had logically rationalized them away—one event had resulted in another, and so on.

The ceiling's blank canvas hovered in the quiet until understanding dawned. She had not been a participant in the decisions that lead to the divorces or moves. Those issues or problems weren't hers. They belonged to other people. There was no denying she had been affected, but those whys weren't hers to carry around or answer.

The pile of questions tumbled down to one level, rolled away and dissipated, except for one. *What am I becoming?*

CHAPTER FOURTEEN

ASSESSMENTS

An uncharacteristic twinge of alarm caused Luther to expand his sensors for any connection between the dodgeball incident at school with Shawn Green and Project Hermes. Seeing none, he scanned the Smith boy but discovered only that young Harvey's less than ideal home life had nurtured his bullying.

Luther sipped his tea from the familiar comfort of the old blue recliner and turned his attention to Georgie. The time had come for him to pass on wisdom from the oral tradition. After years of watching over her from a distance, his cursory assessments and her visits to the lighthouse filled in a few blanks. Outwardly she was in a good state of mind and emotion despite her recent family experiences. She was also acclimating well to her new circumstances. All that changed today. Rage ignited her newly kindled meta-normal strength, and her dodgeball throw left a telekinetic energy trail. Later he would conduct a thorough scan of Georgie's auric bodies to gauge her true progress.

His preliminary scan of Josefina indicated self-shielding, an understandable reaction to protect herself from her sudden clairempathy catalyzed by the schoolyard event. Luther also observed telepathic receiving in Ms. Garcia, perhaps not altogether new. Georgie had been shielding since Starkton. Directing both girls to shield Shawn would be a good first practice as lightworkers.

Luther rubbed a frown from his face. Georgie had been alone much of the time at her father's home at the end of Cedar Street before she began coming to Andersen Light after school. William's evening music jobs left her alone many nights, for now.

The girl's awareness had not yet caught up with her destiny. It was time to begin the next phase of her training, as well as young Josefina's. He rose, rinsed his cup at the tea station, and retired to his room for evening meditation.

CHAPTER FIFTEEN

BALANCE

The day struggled toward autumn and the weather was pronounced unpredictable by the local NPR station. Georgie rode her bicycle to Luther's anyway, glad for the afternoon warmth. She wound her way past one neatly-arranged neighborhood after another. Sun flickered through the trees and bounced off branches and leaves. Josefina was off with her mom again today. Georgie was glad in a way since she was too distracted to keep up a conversation. Good or bad, the ride gave her time to think about what had happened with the dodgeball yesterday. She had the feeling Luther wasn't finished talking about it either.

Waves boomed and crashed on the rocks outside the lighthouse gallery windows. What was it about the ocean that plucked her heart strings into aching chords of longing? Georgie poured herself a glass of water from the kitchenette, walked into Luther's library, sat in the same chair as yesterday, and stared blindly.

She hadn't slept well. Her focus at school had been crap. Thoughts bounced around inside her head all day. They ricocheted wildly as if her mind was a pinball machine—and she'd shot the game ball into play with her so-called meta-normal strength. Logical thoughts acted like flippers. Questions flew, deflected off bumper guards, and raced off at panic-stricken speed just to glance off another guard. The ding, ding, ding in her head's arcade served as endless alarms triggered over and over. *Not normal? It can't be true! Things were working out here. What if people find out? This can't be happening! Real life is not a comic book story. Is Luther crazy? Did Harvey really fly through the air? I'm probably making all this up. Maybe the stress of Jackass and the move has caught up with me. What if it is true? I did have a hard time regulating my speed on my way out today. Maybe something is wrong with my bicycle! Right . . . the bicycle didn't throw that dodgeball.*

The rowdy pinball tournament waged on. How could she make it stop? She absently rotated her water glass on its coaster. Josefina had asked her a few times if she was okay, and Shawn had said "hey" more than usual. Georgie told them both she was just thinking about stuff — a freakin' understatement. Footsteps moved up the spiral staircase and silenced her mind momentarily.

Luther took the chair's twin across from her, crossed his legs, and steadied a mug of tea on his knee. "Let's talk about balance."

"Balance." She tossed the word around in her mouth to test the flavor. It tasted like it didn't have anything to do with her.

"Balance forms a foundation in our lives. Think of a beautiful, well-formed tree."

Like it had a mind of its own, hers raced to Dad's giant weeping willow.

"Good. Its roots are deep. Branches reach out from its trunk in all directions with stability and strength. Because it is balanced and flexible the tree regains its posture once the wind has dissipated."

"Okay, but what's this got to do with what's happening?"

"Patience, my friend," he said gently. "Picture a peacefully flowing spring. See how it is neither dammed nor stagnant? Balance strives to exist in harmony within natural laws, such as rhythm, balance, and counter-balance." Luther sipped his tea.

"Okay. So you're saying," she jumped in, "balance tries to exist in nature." She gulped her lemon water.

"Yes, and more. I am saying balance is a part of everything even though it may not be apparent. The tide isn't always out, nor in. Eat too little and you may feel hungry, too much and you're uncomfortable, overstuffed.

"A gyroscope or centrifuge must be perfectly balanced in order to function correctly. An emotionally balanced person may merely be challenged in the face of failure, even if at first she is discouraged. Like a top that runs into something, she wobbles slightly but regains her balance and continues on her path." He paused. "You follow?"

"Yeah, I think so." There was more to it than what he was saying, she just didn't know what, yet. Like, why bring this up now? Was she the top?

"Good. Let's focus for a moment on the balance in your life."

"Okay." She hoped this answered her thousand questions.

He grinned briefly, and continued. "As you can surely imagine, balance is inextricably tied to the natural law of cause and effect."

"Natural law?"

"Think of a natural law as something that just is, like gravity. If you stay up late reading it is harder to get up the next morning. Everything vibrates, nothing is static. When you throw a rock into the water, you will see ripples. The natural laws of polarity and duality demonstrate hot and cold, soft and hard, warrior and protector. Swing a pendulum one way, it will swing the other way. You know this, although you may be hearing it differently. Learning is often remembering."

She couldn't wait any longer. "Why are we talking about this now?"

Luther calmly replied, "Because now it is critical to employ more balance in your life. Again, think of balance as your foundation. What do we do before nearly every physical act? We center ourselves." He stood to demonstrate. "Our feet are firmly placed in alignment with our shoulders. Knees are slightly bent for added stability. From this position we swing a bat, lunge forward and back, and catch or ward off a ball." He returned to his seat. "We also center ourselves to create mental and emotional balance."

Her mind whirred to make a connection to his esoteric discussion. "Okay," she said, "this is about the dodgeball thing." *Duh.* "I was not centered, so to speak, when I reacted."

"Yes." He smiled. "Today we discuss the unseen and the unsaid. Let us examine yesterday's dodgeball incident. You became angry at the boy who picked on your friend Shawn."

"Harvey." She tapped the tops of her sneakers together.

"You asked Harvey to stop. Did you say anything else?"

She hit her mental replay. "He's not ready to play, jackass."

"You said this while angry, before you seized the ball and threw it at Harvey?"

"Yeah. I threw the ball away and it hit the wall. The ball bounced back at him."

"Recall your feelings and thoughts at the moment you threw the ball."

"I wanted the ball out of the way so it couldn't hurt Shawn. I was angry at Harvey for hurting Shawn."

Luther waited.

"There was anger toward Harvey when I threw the ball. I guess it was rage. Maybe I wanted to throw it at him, even though I threw it at the wall. I don't know, but I wanted the ball out of there, gone. It was about him but it was also about Shawn and the ball, that it was being used as a weapon."

"You reacted to the cause, in this case, Harvey's actions. I suspect a combination of meta-normal strength and emerging telekinetic abilities was in your throw."

"Tele-what?"

"Telekinetic energy is the ability to move things with your non-physical being."

"Okay. I might have seen a movie. . . ."

He grinned. "We will discuss telekinesis later."

"Wait, you're not mad about Harvey?"

"This was your first undeniable manifestation. You literally did not know your own strength when you reacted to a highly-charged emotional situation."

Luther paused to read her auric fields. "We may not always agree with others on what is proper. But, we do need to know what is appropriate and what is inappropriate for *us*—so we may better blend in with others. Otherwise, it would be difficult for us to help them."

She let out a heavy sigh, and went back to turning her glass around.

"You have beat yourself up enough about it, have you not?" Tiny crinkles appeared around his eyes, then were gone. "Mind, it is important not to display your strength or other talents in public. Don't worry, you will learn how to control your abilities and emotional reactions. There was another jackass, wasn't there?"

"Yeah. . . ." Her stomach dropped. *Where's he going with this?*

"We agree a balanced stance is our ideal?" She nodded. "The anger you carry from Starkton was present in your dealings with Harvey yesterday. You brought it with you unconsciously." Luther quoted, his voice gentle, "He's not ready to play, jackass." He waited.

She narrowed her eyes at him and sifted through his words. "I see the connection, but I don't see the problem."

"To be most effective in any circumstance, especially highly emotional ones like yesterday's, we must operate with the clarity of a balanced stance, one uncompromised by the anger of another day. Clearly weigh each situation on its own merit. Yesterday's baggage need not shadow our today. History and its lessons need not rule every thought, word, and action of our present or future."

She thought back to what Dad told her when she first got to Mystic Creek, "This does not define who you are. It's something that happened in your life."

She refocused on Luther. "Okay, how do I keep the old anger from taking over?"

"You let it go. Letting go is not forgetting or saying it was okay. You move from anger to willingness to accept the facts—not to condone, but to let things go. If there are pearls of learning, pick them up. Leave the rest."

She was incredulous. "What pearls?"

"For starters," he spread one hand and tapped each finger, "you learned it wasn't about you—you didn't think it up or cause it. You rescued your family from prolonged trauma, or worse. You began your shield work. And, I am pleased to acknowledge, you moved to Mystic Creek, which has led you to Andersen Light."

"I see." She returned his smile. "Good things *have* come from it." Doubt clouded her emotions. "What if the anger comes back?"

"It may, Georgie. You didn't build up the emotions overnight, but you can intend their rapid release. Replace the old feelings with how you want to feel now."

"You mean it is up to me how fast or slow I let things go, and how I want to feel?"

"Precisely. Of course, you may experience heightened teenage emotions. It remains unclear how or if these will manifest meta-normally. You are not alone, my young friend. I am here to help."

"I feel better knowing you have my back."

"Always." His pause was nearly imperceptible, but she caught it. "About the bicycle, Georgie, you've been testing yourself to see how fast you can go. You've been lucky. No one witnessed your speeding blur. The bicycle maintained its integrity—you did not experience a flat tire or the flying off of a chain—but it was not built for flight."

She raised her head as she relived the moment.

"Notice how different you felt between the anger in the school yard and the joy which literally propelled you through the air on your bicycle?"

"That was fun."

"You were happy."

"Yes," she laughed.

Luther slapped the arm of his chair. "Happiness is powerful. Happy is good!" He selected two apples from a bowl on the kitchen bar.

"Oh," she said around a bite, "this is tasty."

"These are Maria Elena's babies. She has a special relationship with the trees. Back to our discussion on balance . . . we will strive for balance as we explore your gifts."

She looked up abruptly. *Gifts, plural?*

"Yes, gifts. You have power within, Georgie. Most people are completely unaware of the power inside them. They deny, ignore, or unintentionally give it away. Those who do acknowledge their inner power often lack the discipline to focus or channel it. They squander their power through distraction and confusion. You have more than most. Yours will only grow, and require great focus and equilibrium. There is a delicate balance with using your gifts and the need to protect them."

"What's the big deal about keeping this part of me secret?"

"First, it is for your own safety and well-being. We don't want you waking up locked in a laboratory being tested every which way for the rest of your life." His tone was matter of fact. He finished his apple and held the core between his thumb and index finger.

She sputtered. "No. Yeah, I don't want that!"

Luther leaned forward, patted her arm.

Georgie pictured horrors of needles and biopsy forceps. "Thanks," she whispered as he took her apple core.

"Secondly," he said on his way to the compost bin, "you are not alone. There are others of us we also protect with our silence." He returned to his chair.

"Us? There are others? Who are they? You? What do you do?" Eyes huge, she grasped the arms of the chair.

"Careful," he chuckled. "I like that chair."

She released her grip and looked down. "Oh, wow." There

were deep indentations where her fingers had been. "This isn't going to be so easy."

"We'll do the best we can."

"Who . . . ?"

"One thing at a time for now." He held his hand up as if to slow her down.

"But . . . !"

"I do understand. Your mind bursts with questions. We will answer them in time. Remember *balance*." It wasn't a question. "We will live each happy moment as you learn and remember your way into being you."

She stared. Sometimes he spoke in circles.

"Breathe," he told her.

She took a deep breath. Then she took a deeper breath, let out a long exhalation, and settled into her chair.

"It is rare," Luther began, "for a child to be born into this family, a tribe of extraordinarily gifted souls. Yet there are many of us, each doing our part. We work and play in anonymity. Most of us are known to each other. Others live in deep secret in order to work behind the scenes. Your birth was foretold as a future legend. As your mentor, I will not now reveal all of my own abilities to you so as not to plant thought seeds, or ideas, which could distract you. Instead I encourage the natural unfolding of your gifts."

She struggled to take it all in. He could have been talking about his shopping list for the hardware store. But he wasn't, he was talking about her life and she didn't recognize it. Sure, it had changed a lot lately, but this was different. Other people apparently knew more about her than she did, people she didn't even know. Or . . . ? "Do my parents know about this?"

"No. Your grandmother Grace was in position to hear things as a child, but doesn't appear to remember. We agree not to approach her, do we not?"

"Yeah, okay." It was all so strange.

"This must be strange to you," Luther said.

There he goes again. I wonder if he does hear my thoughts. Freaky.

He stood. "Let us do something normal . . . "

Oh, yes. That would be a relief. She jumped up.

" . . . and see what Maria Elena has left us for dinner downstairs. She and Carl have already left for the day. I'll take you home myself tonight."

"Maria Elena?"

"Yes."

"No, I mean is Maria Elena . . . ?"

"Yes."

"You mean she knows?"

"Yes, and she has gifts of her own."

Georgie trailed behind him down the circular stairs, through the main corridor and into the great hall. Arms of the giant clock above the fireplace pointed five. The dining room windows framed a horizon of orange sherbet melting into the ocean. They passed through the double doors into the kitchen. *Yum . . . something this way smells savory!* Her mouth watered. Maria Elena had left food warming in one of the ovens. Two simple place settings waited on a wooden table. Ice floated in the two glasses of water. A single beach flower stood in a glass jar. "It was nice of her to leave us a flower. What can I do?"

Luther opened the refrigerator. "You may take your salad." He extended a wide-rimmed, shallow bowl of lettuce mix, sliced strawberries, and pumpkin seeds, and a cruet filled with dark fluid and tiny floating bits.

They were nearly done with their salads when she asked, "What about Josefina?"

"It remains to be seen."

"Does that mean Josefina will have extra abilities?"

"I believe so. She is highly intuitive, yet many people are. Meanwhile, we wait in silence." He gave her a meaningful look.

"Okay. Got it. Silence. Don't ask her about it." She saw the look again. "Right, I don't talk to her about it either."

Luther smiled. "Exactly. Her gifts must unfold naturally as well."

"But . . . ," she started to protest.

"You have your own to process," he said kindly.

She nodded in agreement and sipped her water, but had every intention to watch Josefina more closely.

"If you carry the bowls to the sink, I will see what other deliciousness waits for us." He was at the oven door before she'd even reached for the salad bowls.

How did he . . . ? She shook her head but didn't ask, distracted as she was by their pizzas.

Later, tummy and head both full, Georgie grabbed her school bag and shadowed Luther out to the garage. Bright moonlight poured over them. Sounds of the surf lapped around her like snuggly blankets.

The main garage door opened at their approach. Luther announced, "We will let Woody take you home tonight." His eyes twinkled as he gestured to the wood-paneled station wagon.

"What? Really?" She'd admired the gleaming old red and wood-paneled car whenever she parked her bicycle. She'd assumed it was never used. Except for the body style, it sparkled and shined like brand new. She peeked through the windows. "Oh my God! This is so cool!"

Luther laughed. "Woody is a Packard Deluxe station wagon. Bring your bike over." He opened the double-windowed back door, lowered the wooden tailgate, and swung her bicycle into place in one fluid motion. "Fits like a champ." He closed the doors and reached down to remove a heavy duty electric plug.

Georgie climbed into the passenger's seat and glanced around in the dim light. She sat high in the seat, its leather like new. Luther and Carl must polish everything.

Luther interrupted her wonderings. "This buggy has been through several modifications since my mother purchased it. The first to acquaint you with are the modern seat belts." He fastened his own and pushed a button, possibly the original key insert. 3D displays lit up every surface on the dash with system, sound, and environmental icons. She ran her eyes over them before they faded. The engine was almost silent, though wood creaked faintly as the station wagon went into reverse. They backed out in a long, wide turn. Solar spot lights, Woody's headlights, and the nearly full moon illumined *Peaceful Seas*.

"How old is this car?"

"This is the 1941 model. We bought it to get supplies in town. We also took it on drives, as we called them back then."

"Drives?"

"Short jaunts up and down the coast to the beach or mountains, and picnics."

"What other changes have you made, besides the seatbelts and space age dash?"

Luther pressed a knob. Music came from everywhere, clear and crisp, as if the musicians were in the car.

"Wow!"

He pressed another knob until the music faded to the background. "The engine alternates between solar, electric, and clean hydrogen power. Technology is embedded in such a manner as to blend in with the manufacturer's original design and detail. Perhaps we can take it on a picnic one day with Maria Elena and Josefina."

"Like taking a drive," Georgie ventured.

The girl stifled a yawn as they pulled up to the house on Cedar Street. The porch light was on, but William had left to play with the band somewhere. Luther waited until she was safely inside the house before he drove away. He made a mental note to speak with her parents about Georgie's next move.

CHAPTER SIXTEEN

GEORGIE AND JOSEFINA

"You've spoken with Georgie?" Maria Elena smoothed a lock of hair behind her ear.

Luther grinned inwardly. "As you already know, I have introduced the topic." He poured a round of morning tea and served Maria's freshly baked, lemon-raspberry scones.

She sipped her tea. "Josefina was also triggered by the dodge-ball incident at school—intuition, along with empathy, and reactive shielding."

"I detect telepathic talents within her also."

"She and I had recently talked about her intuitive abilities. Her gifts were growing so fast I became concerned she would scare herself or say something in mixed company. You know how much they want to fit in at that age."

"I think it likely our two young women may avoid that folly."

"They'll have to, won't they?"

"It's time they had each other," Luther observed.

"Tonight then?"

"Tonight."

They lifted their mugs. "Cheers."

. . .

GEORGIE HADN'T BEEN much company since that day before P.E. class, dodgeball day. Other kids, even older ones she didn't know, gave her wide berth. Josefina spent more time with the fashionable Ruby, which gave Georgie less occasion to observe her for unexplained abilities. Shawn hovered around them in a silent orbit, and unabashedly stared at Georgie. He had plenty of opportunity to gape since they had all their classes together, though it was more like he studied her.

She and Josefina threaded their way out the school's front entrance through throngs of kids. Tethered and locked, their bicycles waited in the white-washed metal bike racks. The racks were screwed into the concrete not so coincidentally situated in front of the school administration's picture windows. No doubt it was a handy way to spy kids leaving early. A pang of appreciation ran through Georgie as she unfettered the turquoise frame and pulled it into position beside Josefina's cherry red bike. Bags on shoulders and helmets adjusted, they waved at Shawn. He waved back from under the expansive tree.

Georgie pedaled slowly. "So . . . , Ruby is extra excited about homecoming."

"It's definitely her thing. She said her older sister Rachel had been on all the event committees. Looks like Ruby caught the obsession. Rachel attends cosmetology school in the city and practices on Ruby when she's home."

"That explains the makeup, hair, and clothes."

"Exactly. Ruby loves fashion. She tailors her clothes to get her own look."

Georgie glanced down at the blue Converses she labored to keep from peddling too fast. Not sure what to say, she settled for, "Stylish."

"It's creative, anyway."

They veered onto their lane. Georgie changed the subject.

"Hey, thanks for giving me space lately. I guess you could say I was processing what happened with Shawn and Harvey that day in P.E. with the dodgeball."

"I think we all were." Josefina smiled, but her glance assessed. "No worries. Do you still want to go to the farmers market this Saturday?"

"Yeah, it sounds fun." She grinned. Fun would be a welcome distraction.

Bikes parked in the carriage house, they blew through the front door of the main house, scurried through the great hall, and headed for the bathroom. An ornately carved wooden panel depicted female goddesses and divided the two commodes. Georgie washed up one side of the smooth, stone vanity lit by the overhead skylight. She waited on the chaise and traced a Goddess arrow with her index finger. "I hope Dad says yes to the farmers market."

"He goes there himself sometimes, doesn't he?"

"Yeah, I think it's where he gets his raspberry preserves."

Josefina rummaged through her bag. "I've got to fix my hair." Several wisps had escaped the weave of her ordinarily perfect braids.

Georgie peered into the mirror. She hadn't paid attention while washing. *Yep, this hair's even wilder than usual.* After a fast few minutes with her wide-toothed comb her hair looked about the same, but with fewer tangles.

Josefina asked, "Shall we?"

Hmm . . . this is different. Luther and Maria Elena were seated in the great hall on one of the fireplace sofas. Georgie and Josefina took up their positions on the facing sofa, the red one closest to the front door they used for hanging out and doing homework. Halos surrounding Luther and Maria Elena distracted Georgie. *Or was it the afternoon light from the dining room windows?* The silver specks in his hair shone brilliantly.

"Hello, girls," greeted Luther.

They seem happy, so it must not be bad news. Her eyes

wandered to the trays of snacks and drinks on the tree trunk table.

Maria Elena handed out cold glasses of red liquid she identified as raspberry hibiscus tea. "Luther and I have something we'd like to tell you girls." Maybe it was the halo, but Maria Elena was crazy beautiful. Her black hair, pulled back and up as always, elongated her regal neck. The apricot dress warmed her natural cheek color.

"Yes," Luther began. He interrupted Georgie's observations, though he couldn't agree more with her assessment. Maria Elena was beautiful. "We'd like to introduce you each to another meta-normal."

Both girls sat up straight, rigid, looking only at their respective confidant.

What? Georgie opened her mouth but slammed it closed. Josefina turned to her. Her eyes changed from surprise to comprehension. Georgie quickly refocused on Luther.

"However," he continued, "you already know each other."

"I knew it," Josefina said.

"You mean . . . ?" Georgie regarded Josefina.

"Yes," Maria Elena answered, "it's time you know about each other. We don't want you to feel isolated. As close as you've become, you'll soon notice your gifts unfolding."

"You may help one another and ensure your secrets are maintained from the so-called outside world," Luther added.

"What a relief." Georgie sighed, as did Josefina. "No more secrets."

"No more secrets between each other," Luther corrected.

"Got it," Georgie said.

"That morning before P.E. with Shawn and Harvey?" Josefina asked.

"Yeah."

"Right."

Maria Elena explained, "The incident at school with Shawn and the other boy triggered Josefina's developing abilities to the next level."

"The same as it did for you, Georgie," Luther said. "I would like to begin your joint training right away—this Friday after school if it is agreeable. We can make an evening of it."

"Pizza?" asked Maria Elena.

"Yes!" came the simultaneous reply.

"I think Dad's playing Friday night."

"Excellent," Luther said. He leaned over to the untouched food tray, selected a wedge of sandwich, and lifted his drink in salute. Hungry, Georgie grabbed two.

Well into the celebratory snacks, he spied the girls' bags on the floor. "Maria Elena and I will leave you to your homework."

"Okay, spill it," Georgie demanded once she and Josefina were alone.

"What I do, you mean? Intuition and empathy. And shielding, like putting protective barriers around someone. I guess you could also put them around things." She cocked her head to consider this new twist. "Anyway, it happened by accident. I reacted automatically that day in P.E. when I saw Harvey hit Shawn with the ball. I thought it was an emotional response."

"I did the same thing!" Georgie stared at her friend. "You think it worked?"

"I think so. I mean, who's to say how Shawn would have looked otherwise?"

"Good point. I used to put a force field around my brother and sister whenever I thought they needed protection. The idea came from watching reruns of a television show."

"I know the one." She reached for an orange slice. "Tell me about you."

"Besides what happened with the dodgeball, I'm getting stronger, and really fast on my bicycle." She grinned, then fell quiet. "This is all so crazy, right? I was just getting used to my new life here in Mystic Creek . . . "

" . . . then you find out you are meta-normal. Your head must be spinning."

"Yours too. I'm glad we're in this strangeness together."

LUTHER AND MARIA ELENA sang along to 1940's music from the Packard's front seat.

Josefina leaned in. "What are you going to say to your dad?"

"I'll tell him we plan to hang out longer Friday night, and have dinner, too, if it's okay with him."

"And Saturday's farmers market?"

"Right. I almost forgot with everything else going on."

Swaying branches of the weeping willow tree welcomed her home. Outside lights spilled over Dad's parked car. Luther extricated her bicycle from Josefina's and swung it onto the ground next to her. Georgie consciously paced herself as she walked her bike to the porch. She pushed the kickstand with her toe and waved goodnight. Luther waited for her to open the door before he pulled away.

The house smelled terrific, of garlic and cooked onions. Georgie registered the clanks and clatters as Dad at work in the kitchen. She dropped her bag in a chair and, almost instantly, stood in the kitchen doorway. *Okay, that's new.* "Hi, Dad! What are you cooking? It smells wonderful."

"Hi, sweets. Black beans—they've simmered all day in the slow cooker." She moved in for a closer look. "Want a taste?" he asked and kissed the top of her head.

"Heck, yeah." She took the wooden spoon he offered. "Phenomenal."

"Oh?" He laughed. "Phenomenal beans shall be paired tonight with our transcendent market-procured vegetarian tamales and house salad created in our very own house." Georgie laughed with him.

"I'm ready to create." She pushed up her sleeves to wash her hands. "Hey, are you playing Friday night?"

"Yes, thanks for reminding me. We have a job down the coast a little ways. There's another on Saturday at the Coast Valley Farmers Market, then later that night at the Solar Gardens in the city." He handed her a cutting board, knife, and green onions.

"You okay with me hanging out with Josefina Friday night out at Luther's? Her mom is going to be there too."

"Of course. It's perfect."

"And Josefina asked if I would go to the farmers market." She finished the green onions and reached for cilantro. "Maybe we could do a sleepover Friday."

"That would work." His knife hovered over an avocado. "I was thinking of your grandparents, but I'd bet you'd have more fun with Josefina." He winked. "That leaves Sunday for us—for something besides laundry."

"Thanks, Dad." Georgie diced the tomatoes. He hadn't mentioned Saturday night, but she'd remind him later. There was plenty of homework, and, yes, laundry. She might even get some extra homework from Luther Friday night.

SHE TURNED on her left side and hugged the spare pillow. Pieces of past conversations swirled in her mind one after the other. She counted breaths to still her mind. The comforting sway of the weeping willow branches swept around its base like a carousel. Strangely, outlines of forms took shape as the branches swung around the tree. Crouching figures became visible as the passing branches trailed over them. Why were they hiding in the tree? The scene shifted to Shawn Green on Old Mystic Creek Bridge. He leaned over the side rail and watched the creek rush toward the sea. Shawn flinched as the shadow of a huge bird, a hawk, passed over at the same time a fish jumped out of the water at him. His cell phone buzzed. "Hi, Dad," he said and crossed back over the bridge. Shawn didn't see it, but Georgie witnessed the hawk double back and fly high above him. Was it trailing him? Concern creased the space between her eyebrows as she slipped deeper into sleep.

CHAPTER SEVENTEEN

ANONYMITY

S hawn escorted Josefina and Georgie to their bicycles before heading to the bus. Georgie caught sight of that same man wearing a black jacket standing across the street. "Don't let him see you looking, but have you seen that guy before?" She tipped her head in his direction.

Josefina said, "Looks like he's staring at you, Shawn."

Shawn peeked over and back. "How can you tell? He's way across the street. He's probably checking you two out."

"Should we report it to the admin office?" Georgie asked.

"And say what?" Shawn retrieved his slipping backpack. "There's a guy in a black leather jacket. He's standing on a sidewalk."

"No need to be a smart aleck, Shawn," Josefina chided. "Still, you have a point."

Shawn licked his index finger and held it up. "Point given by Ms. Garcia."

Josefina rolled her eyes. "Let's just see if the man turns up again."

Georgie couldn't shake the feeling that Black Jacket Man was a creeper. By the time she and Josefina arrived at Andersen Light, she'd decided to tell Luther.

Josefina beat her to it. "Unless he's a parent or something, why is he even there? Georgie thinks he was staring at Shawn."

After further questioning, Luther said, "Thank you, girls. I'll make a few phone calls." He'd also reach out clairvoyantly. "I had intended to discuss anonymity this afternoon. However, the situation you've reported provides us opportunity to practice the art of shielding. What do you say we practice on your friend Shawn. Georgie, you go first."

"I like to use a force field, like from *Star Trek*, only with light," Georgie said.

"Light?" asked Josefina.

"Yeah, like a halo force field."

Once the girls had Shawn well shielded, Luther changed the subject. "Josefina, please indulge us. You will soon see the relevance. Georgie, your bicycle is a perfect place to begin our subject of anonymity."

"Oh." An image of riding her bicycle at top speed popped into her mind. She brushed a curl out of her face. "So you've noticed some things." Doubt colored her effort to be cool. Luther took another sip of tea like there was no hurry. Maybe he was thinking about what to say. A gull flew by the window.

"I have noticed some things," he said at last, "and I am hoping no one else has."

No more being cool. "Like what?"

"Let's stretch," Luther suggested.

Outside next to the gallery railing they stretched arms, shoulders, and back muscles. Georgie reached back, pulled one ankle back in leg stretch, then the other. Waves bathed the rocks below as seagulls flew in and out of the spray. The sun held its own in the sky. Even in Georgie's distracted state, the beauty of the ocean charmed her.

"Over time you will notice each other developing certain

talents," Luther said. "It is important we mentor and nurture these abilities in privacy. This is one reason we are in each other's lives. I am here to help you develop fully and maintain balance in your life. I realize you have both been educated on the need for anonymity. Still, I remind you, tell no one."

"Not even Dad?"

"For the time being." They returned to their seats in the gallery. "In light of the stranger lurking around the school, I ask that you refrain from drawing unnecessary attention to yourselves. Georgie, you must be very careful not to display your meta-normal strength and power outside the safety of Andersen Light. Okay, girls?"

"Okay!" came their tandem response.

CHAPTER EIGHTEEN

HARVEY

Georgie couldn't believe she was riding her bike to Harvey Smith's house. Josefina was off with her mom again. It was just as well. This was something Georgie had to do, though it wasn't like she'd come up with it on her own. It was an assignment from Luther, one she was neither sure nor keen about. He had offered to drive her, and as tempting as it was, she'd refused. An adult hanging around would be weird, and probably spook Harvey. She dismounted, removed her helmet, and walked her bike along the sidewalk, helmet strapped to a handle bar. She replayed the conversation with Luther in her mind as she searched for house number 155.

"WHY DO you think Harvey acts the way he does?" Luther had asked during their last dodgeball discussion.

"I don't know, because he's a bullying butthead?"

He spoke slowly. "Yes, it does appear to be all that is happening —on the surface."

"What are you getting at?"

"I ask you to again consider the natural law of cause and effect. He bullied your friend Shawn, you responded by throwing the dodgeball, which in turn embarrassed and humiliated Harvey. What now, do you think, will be his reaction?"

"I don't know. So far there hasn't been any. I've kept my eyes and ears open."

Luther had ensured evidence of her activity from that day weren't on the human internet. He said, "As a meta-normal, you look beneath the surface to learn and understand the root of things, and to discover if there is an opportunity for healing."

"Okay." Georgie worked to make the connection, and wasn't sure she liked the direction this was heading.

"I suggest you get to know Harvey," said Luther.

"What? You're kidding me! Why would I want to do that? He's a bully!"

"I'm not suggesting you become friends. I am asking you to *know* him."

"Seriously?" She couldn't believe what she was hearing. The idea was repellant. Her stomach clenched. She swallowed metallic tang. "How am I supposed to do that?"

"You begin by listening."

"Okay . . . ," she drawled out.

"Between now and then, I'd like you to keep in mind something about anger."

"Like what?"

"Anger is a useful energy from which to fuel action, but it obscures clarity. When we act from compassion, another powerful energy, our vision and understanding of the situation are not clouded. Clarity is important when speedy and decisive actions are demanded."

"Okay . . . ," she repeated doubtfully.

"Compassion enables us to back away from our myopic view,

one which may cloud our minds with emotions and keep us from fully understanding what we are seeing. When we back up to a larger view, we see more."

She sort of understood, but said nothing. Her opinion of Harvey could be limiting a broader view.

"Imagine, for example, you are floating in a stream and you have suddenly come across a massive boulder. It appears to span the breadth of the stream and block further travel. You become frustrated, then become even more upset as the current pushes you into the boulder and you feel stuck. The longer you are smashed into and forced to look at the boulder's face, the angrier you become."

"Ugh."

"So it would seem." His mouth widened into a grin. "Imagine you are instead inspired to wrench yourself away and swim or wade to the side of the stream. You climb up the bank, scale up a small distance, and sit down to catch your breath. When you look down you are surprised to see the boulder isn't as large as you first believed." He had her attention.

"The boulder only sits to one side of the stream. You relax when you comprehend the situation is not as dire as when you were crushed up against the cold, hard rock. From your new position you shrewdly examine the geography and begin to map out the steps you'll take to complete your journey down the stream."

"Shrewdly?" she asked with a light laugh.

"Yes." He leaned toward her and raised his abundant left brow. "You shrewdly, calculatedly, and most astutely—from your higher ground, perspective, and understanding—may now decide in the clear light of day, free from confusion and anger, what you will or will not do next."

"Heck, yeah! I will take my tube and enter the stream past that pesky boulder and enjoy the rest of my float. I'll leisurely take in nature's sights and sounds with gladness in my heart!"

"Good, girl!" He clapped her shoulder.

She was caught up in the moment and hesitated to bring up the piece of the picture that wasn't filling in for her, but it might be important. "How does compassion relate to the boulder?"

"You may not feel compassion for the boulder in our illustration. But, the perspective you gained allowed for your anger to melt away and your understanding of the situation to grow. Reaching for compassion is like climbing up the bank. The circumstances and how they relate become clear when you see the lay of the land. Compassion lifts you to a place where you can take in the bigger picture, its pieces and parts, how they go together, and how they all work."

"You put a lot on Ol' Compassion's plate."

"Compassion is very powerful. You will become more familiar with its power over time, and utilize various tools in which to access it. We will discuss it more after your exercise with Harvey. Keep in mind—to listen is an act of compassion."

"Oh, okay. I see the logic trail. I'm not feeling the compassion, but I can do listening."

GEORGIE KNEW INSTINCTIVELY that somewhere in her there was an unbreakable bond with Luther. In the short time she'd known him, she had grown to trust him and accept him as her mentor. He was the one to show her the way into the meta-normal life, and to live it normally. However, just now as she scrutinized the front of 155 Scrub Oak Street, she doubted his wisdom, and sanity. Had the jackass experience tempered her spunk?

The beat-up aluminum mailbox was loosely nailed to a bleached out two-by-four. Once embedded firmly in the ground, it now listed to one side. A hand-painted *Smith* with street numbers were scrawled across the aluminum. White paint aged to a light gray peeled away from the house. Windows framed with a flaking and oxidized red-brick color flanked either side of the splintery front door hung to accommodate left-handers. The framed screen door, its top hinge rusted free, drooped and creaked.

A wide, plank-board porch spanned the front in chipped, industrial gray. A boy's bicycle lay in a heap in front of three old chairs. In a past life they were cheerful primary colors of red, blue, and yellow. Now they sat dusty and washed out, witnesses to the comings and goings here, whatever those were.

Georgie toed the kickstand and parked her bike next to the mailbox, just off the cracked and gouged concrete sidewalk. The gleaming turquoise and chrome of her bicycle contrasted starkly. She stared at the front door and rehearsed in her head what she would say. She hoped for the best, but she said a quick prayer to the vast, impersonal universe, *please let there be no guns or knives.* She mentally amended it to make an exception for the flaming sword she pictured at her side.

A shoving and pushing sound preceded the unsticking of the front door. Harvey shot out like a bull launching from its pen into a rodeo arena. The screen door wobbled behind him. He stood on his front porch, green eyes narrowed into his trademark glare of suspicion. Nostrils flared and hair flamed in every direction, the blonde at war with bright red spikes. His t-shirt slouched around his substantial body and saggy, dirty, oversized jeans. "What the hell do *you* want?"

"Hey, Harvey." She kept her tone and expression intentionally neutral, and added to her earlier appeal. *Please help me keep my perspective.*

"What the hell are you doing here? You here to throw me through the air again, or what?"

"I just came to see you."

"What the hell are you talking about? I don't know *you*," he spat.

"That's why I came to see you."

"You're a freak and you need to leave."

She stood in place, probably like an idiot, and worked to figure out what to say. *Correction: I'm not an idiot, though I may look like one now.*

"Are you still here?" He stood near the porch steps, arms crossed.

"Hey, I think we got off on the wrong foot, Harvey."

"There is no right foot, Jones." He moved down a cracked step.

She didn't respond, stayed where she was, and watched him watching her. He wore his usual sneer, buttressed now with increased suspicion, sizing her up. Finally, she said, "Okay, well, I just came to talk."

"What do you want, a freakin' medal? What would *we* possibly have to talk about?"

"I was hoping we might get to know each other."

"Is there something wrong with you? Is that it?" His feet moved down another step. "Why would you . . . would I want to know you, Jones?" He ran his fingers through his hair. Apparently the spikes were natural.

She stood in place and ignored the slip. "That's a fair question. I just moved here. I don't really know too many people, even though I was born here."

"Yeah, I heard."

"You heard?"

"What's it to you? It's a small town, in case you hadn't noticed. You look pretty chummy with Garcia and that wimp, Green."

Georgie winced but clenched her teeth so she wouldn't react further, and snuck a deep but quiet breath through her nose. "Yeah, what about you?"

"What about me?" He narrowed his eyes into a scowl.

He didn't tell her to leave. Luther had said to ask questions and listen, so . . . , "Are you from here?"

"Yes." Behind his answer was, "Of course, where else would I be from? Everyone who's worth a damn is from here." She waited.

"My family came over on the *Lion of Glasgow*, a Scottish Viking ship."

I'm pretty sure the Vikings were Norse, but I can roll with this. But, isn't Smith *an English name? Oh, well, there must have been loads of intermarriages back then.* Aloud she said, "Then you're practically originals, right after the natives. Old blood, it's called?"

"Hell, yes, we're old blood." He appeared to savor the way it rolled off his tongue, but it gave Georgie the creeps.

"Do you have brothers and sisters?" She'd only seen one bike and no other kid stuff on the porch or in the yard.

His face darkened. "No, it's just me and my dad, not that it's any of your business."

She disregarded the snide ending. "That's me. I live with my dad. My parents were divorced. It's a long story. My little brother and sister live with my mom."

"So you're the reject." He stated it as a matter of fact and sat down. His long legs stretched out across the cracked steps.

It wasn't true, but maybe it's how he felt about his situation. "Yeah, maybe," she said finally. She remained where she was, but shifted her weight.

He'd caught the pause. "Cheer up, Jones, it's not the end of the world. At least your mom's not dead—it just feels like it." He relished the twist at the end, his natural sneer. Her head snapped back like she'd taken a blow to the face. "You get way more alone time this way, more independence," he was saying. "Am I right, or what?"

"Yeah, it's true." Recovered, sort of, she added, "Still, it must be hard."

"Not really. I'm used to it."

"Has it been a long time?"

"Yeah." He cocked his head to one side and calculated. "It's been six years." She'd bet he could say exactly how long, to the month and day. She would.

"Do you have other family here, like grandparents?" she asked, thinking of her own.

"Of course," he snapped. "Old blood, remember?"

"Of course." She prayed her tone didn't reflect the snark in his. This wasn't the easiest of Luther's assignments.

"One side is a bunch of stuffed-shirt blowhards. They barely acknowledge our existence." Resentment dripped like syrupy acid from his words. "My dad didn't follow the family's plan for his life. We're the black sheep."

"That bites," she said, like she was casually commiserating. "What was the plan?"

"He was supposed to go into the shrink business, be another doctor of psychology. What a freakin' joke. That bunch is as dysfunctional as they come. Seriously, they could be their own embarrassing reality show."

Georgie laughed. She couldn't help it. He regarded her with the first real smile she'd ever seen on him.

"Talk about skeletons in the closet . . . ," his laugh was dry, "I could tell you some stories."

"That must be normal for an old-blood family, what with more time to create history."

"Normal!" he guffawed, riled. "There's not a damned thing normal about them!"

"What about your mom's side?" she quickly asked to avoid a tirade.

He went quiet, his face passive. "They're pretty cool. They're laid back. Don't see them much. I guess I remind them of my mom. We go over there for holidays." His expression changed to amusement. "My aunt is always trying to set my dad up with one of her friends, but he's too smart for her."

"Too smart?"

"He sees them coming from a mile off and is ready for evasive action. Women love to glom onto him."

The last sentence rang like it had been said many times before, likely by his father. Not wanting to touch that one, she conceded with, "Yeah, my dad's not dating either."

"Why complicate life?" This one sang like an oldie too.

"So, I hear you're really good at dodgeball, on the varsity team, or something. I was wondering if you would explain the game to me, like the rules and stuff."

He inspected her face, possibly for teasing or ridicule. Georgie braced herself but was confident he wouldn't see either. She really didn't know much about this hallowed Mystic Creek sport. Or was he thinking about the day she threw the dodgeball? She held her breath. He visibly relaxed and she breathed. "Okay, Jones. Let's start from the basics."

She walked over and sat on the far end and down one from the step he was on. First he corrected her—he was on the junior varsity team, regular varsity was next year. His tutorial began with positions, both team field and individual. Next were the rules for the field, the balls, and the players. He was surprisingly patient with her questions, picking up where he left off between clarifications.

"Wow! There's more to it than it looks from gym class. I can see why you like it."

Harvey smiled, but suddenly frowned and checked the sports watch on his right wrist. "Hey, you really have to go." He stood. "My dad will be home any minute now."

Was there a trace of fear in his eyes? "Sure," she said, and hustled over to her bike. "Thanks, Harvey. See you around."

She donned her helmet, was down the block, and turned the corner before she let herself think. *That was painful, and surreal, especially at first.* He was an angry kid, but now she could see he was probably lonely, and afraid of his dad. Maybe that's how he learned to be a bully, and why. *It's sad and sucky.* Harvey could be smart and articulate, when he wanted to be. She was unexpectedly glad he had dodgeball. Not that she could forget what he'd done to Shawn, but she had to admit she had some compassion for Harvey.

Her bike took the corner onto Cedar and she remembered her

prayer. *Hey! There'd been no guns or knives. Maybe the vast universe wasn't so impersonal after all.* Georgie smiled and whispered a thank you. She caught sight of her dad pulling into their driveway and pedaled faster toward the porch, though not enough to raise the brows of any watchful eyes.

CHAPTER NINETEEN

PLANTS HAVE HALOS TOO

Georgie mulled over her meeting with Harvey, and could report tentative success to Luther this afternoon. She, Josefina, and Shawn made their way toward the school buses and congregated under the canopy of their usual tree. All three glanced across the street. They'd acquired the habit of checking for Black Jacket Man. He wasn't there today.

"Ruby's hyped up today," Georgie commented to Josefina. Their classmate styled in chunk-heeled boots and a short dress. She stood out like a tall, thin tree in a group of girls, talking and waving her hands.

"Yes, she can't stop talking about the homecoming dance."

"Homecoming?" Georgie kicked at a rock and grinned at Shawn's eye roll.

He leaned against the tree. "You know," he punctuated with another eye roll, "it's the night the dodgeball jock and queen are surrounded by their doting entourages, and school alumni relive their glory days."

"Oh, Shawn," Josefina said good-naturedly. "First, there's the big game with our school rival, followed by a dance. Ruby is on the dance committee."

Georgie had a funny feeling in her gut, a flutter. *What was it? Apprehension?* "Is that something we're expected to go to? Because I'm not feeling it."

"You're a rebel then, Ms. Jones?" Shawn asked with mock authority.

She screwed her face up, pretending to search for the answer. "Yeah, maybe I am."

"Anyway," continued Josefina, "it's all Ruby will talk about for the next month."

At least she won't be talking about me.

Josefina leaned in and whispered, "At least she won't be talking about dodgeball day."

"Right," Georgie whispered back. *Right . . . ?*

"Attention spans are short," Josefina said, her voice still muted. "There'll be some new drama any minute now for everyone to yack about."

Shawn bent down toward Georgie, his face uncharacteristically close. "I heard you're going out for the dodgeball team."

"What?" She was aghast.

"Shut up, Shawn. Seriously." Josefina rolled her eyes. "Don't worry about it, Georgie."

Georgie glanced up at a deadpan Shawn.

"She's right." He grinned, "You shouldn't worry about it. Seriously."

Unsure how to reply, she went with, "Thanks, Shawn."

His grin slid wider. "No problem." His attention swung to his phone.

Josefina and Georgie boarded the bus for Andersen Light. Josefina asked, "Ever been to the Coastal Valley Farmers Market?"

"I've never been to any farmers market, only roadside stands and pick-and-pay farms with my family." A lump suddenly formed in her throat. She looked away and pulled the collar on her jean jacket up around her neck. Though it wasn't, it seemed like a long time ago when they were all together, before the divorce, before Jack-wad. Her mind wandered to Bill and Rose, but she stopped herself so she wouldn't make herself sad.

"You must miss them," Josefina said.

"Yeah, I do." *How did she know? Is it her gift?* Georgie perked up. "There are some things, though, I don't miss, like my little brother's pranks. He likes to bring nature indoors and hide things where they'll be discovered later, like the frog in my underwear drawer."

"Gross." Josefina made a face. "I miss my brother Adolfo, too. He's been away forever going to school for environmental engineering. Plus, he interns at some company full-time during summers. I'm not sure what they do, exactly. Adolfo comes home for the holidays and a couple of weeks every summer. Dad died when I was a baby. Maybe I should miss him more, but I don't remember him." She was quiet and gazed out the window. "What were we talking about? Oh, right, the Coastal Valley Farmers Market. Would you like to go this Saturday? It's fun—not all about the produce."

"Yeah, I'm definitely in."

The bus slowed to a stop. "Andersen Light!" A placard to the right of the angled mirror above the driver's seat read: Nancy Blackeagle. "Good evening, ladies," she said as they exited.

"Good night, Nancy," they said.

They'd barely passed through the kitchen's double doors when Maria Elena extended two glasses of cold, thickish green liquid. "Luther and Carl are in their workshop studying wave energy." She ushered Josefina and Georgie through the mudroom and into the greenhouse. Georgie tentatively sipped her smoothie. Weirdly, given it looked like pond algae, it tasted good. They stood in front of long rows of shelves on a wall shared by the greenhouse and the main house. Lights fastened underneath each shelf glowed onto the plants below.

Maria Elena, asked, "Did you know plants have their own energetic vibrations? We'll experiment seeing those vibrations and the differences between them. After today you'll perceive the plant kingdom in a different way."

Georgie hadn't thought about plants like this. She'd seen plant energy mentioned in movies and books, but those were all fiction. *Right?* Optimistic, she replied, "Sounds fun."

"You've learned in science class that everything vibrates differently. For example, rocks are notoriously slow." *Did Maria Elena just wink?* "You can actually see the energy the plants exude. Look at the zucchini and cherry tomato plants on the top shelf vining down in front of you. It doesn't matter where on the plants you focus. Try using the periphery of your vision."

"Like with those 3D posters Adolfo used to have?" Josefina asked.

"That's right. Okay, girls, stand with your feet planted somewhat apart and your knees slightly bent. Take in a deep breath. The idea is to be centered in your own bodies, and grounded with your head and heart connected. When you're centered, you see with the part inside of you that isn't being filtered by the intellect."

Say what? Georgie flashed on Luther's description of centering stances. She moved her feet shoulder width apart and relaxed her knees.

"What are we looking for?" Josefina asked.

"Look for the aura, an energy field emanating from the edge of the plant. It may look like the heat coming off asphalt in the summer, or you may see a faint light or glow."

Georgie saw it right away. She'd seen halos her whole life, though not on plants, and learned early to never mention it. She'd told her kindergarten teacher that one of the kids, Jeremy Thompson, was sick. When the teacher asked Georgie how she knew this, she'd said his halo was dim and slipping to one side, like a lopsided frowny face. Other kids laughed until the teacher told them to be quiet. At first she thought the teacher understood, but the woman looked at her strangely and said nothing. Jeremy was out the rest of the week and the next with chicken pox. Until then she thought everyone saw halos. The teacher never treated her the same, but Georgie knew what she'd seen. It was as real as the wind blowing the leaves around. You couldn't see the wind either.

"I see something!" exclaimed Josefina. "It's a narrow, extremely pale, translucent light around the leaves and the zucchini there." She pointed to the five-inch vegetable growing at eye-level. "If the light hadn't waivered I'm not sure I would have seen it."

"Now look at the tomato plant. What do you see?"

Georgie said, "Light radiates around the plants from clear to yellow. It's concentrated around the tomatoes and zucchinis themselves. The light moves, like fingers stretching."

Maria Elena directed, "Can you detect a difference in the energy of the two plants?"

Georgie said, "The energy patterns are slightly different, but those around the blossoms are especially pretty." The flowers' energy stretched toward her, and her own reached out in response. The halos radiated in a rhythm like a heartbeat. It flowed through and from her. Was this the stuff of the force field she'd visualized around Rose, Bill, and Shawn?

Josefina had been studying her, then refocused on the plants. "I see what you mean."

The girls followed Maria Elena through the greenhouse while she quizzed them on the energy patterns of vegetables, herbs, and flowers. Enthusiastic, she volleyed questions until they'd worked their way back around to the mudroom door. "Very good! Next time we'll focus on what you can hear and feel, as well as see. You might even see a plant spirit or nature angel, girls! Ready for your snack and homework?"

Luther wasn't kidding. Maria Elena definitely had a special relationship with plants.

CHAPTER TWENTY

FIRST CLASS

Friday after school Georgie led the way past Nancy Blackeagle to the back of the bus for maximum privacy. She trusted the moving bus to muffle their conversation and whispered to Josefina, "How did you grow up not knowing about all this meta stuff?"

"I know, right? Mom taught me to meditate super young, like four. I've always tied meditation and intuition together."

"You never suspected something else was happening?"

"I knew Mom was intuitive, and Uncle Alejandro, her brother. There again, they're both big on meditating. To me, Mom's beliefs and work with plants are normal."

"What about your brother?"

"Adolfo? Good question. He's the best big brother, my best friend before he left for college. His big-brother teasing is what I'd call love-spirited. We used to talk about everything and go shopping together. Mom taught him to braid my hair—he'd search the internet for new braids to try. For such a guy's guy, Adolfo's very in touch with himself and others. So maybe he's empathic. I don't know about his meta-ness."

"Your whole family might be meta."

"It wasn't until I was in school that I thought anything about it. Even then, it was our normal. What about you?"

"The Jones grandparents are eccentric remodelers, but that isn't too weird. Both of my parents are artists, but so are a lot of people."

They were quiet until Josefina asked, "Do you want to talk about what happened before you moved here?" Her pretty face shaped into sympathy, her brown eyes deep and soft.

Josefina genuinely cared. Instinctively Georgie knew she could tell her anything, but today wasn't the day. She grasped her hand briefly. "Another time, okay?" *Saved by the bus stop.*

After a tandem "good weekend, Nancy" and hustle from the bus stop, they took a quick bathroom break and scrambled up the spiral staircase. They silenced their phones and stowed their bags. Luther and Maria Elena swiveled toward them on the gallery's kitchen barstools. The girls gravitated to the water pitcher with floating lemon and lime slices and a bowl of hummus surrounded by petite triangles of sprouted grain pita bread, celery sticks, and jicama spears. Georgie's triangle hovered to scoop hummus once Josefina's hand cleared the approach zone.

Luther gauged their satiation levels. "Are you ready for a different kind of class?" The chomps continued, but the girls bobbed their heads. Luther moved around the bar toward the classroom, a semi-circle anchored by curved, conference-type tables. The girls familiarized themselves with the ergonomic chairs.

"Our first class will be easy. We'll start with an assessment," began Luther.

What, a test already? Georgie couldn't believe it.

Josefina whispered, "No, not a test."

That is definitely one thing she does, Georgie thought before she could stop herself.

Luther said, "Let us slow down the energy of rushing about and allow the feeling of being where we are catch up with us. Get

119

comfortable, take in a deep breath and relax into your chairs." Less than a minute later, he said, "Very nice. Thank you."

Resituated next to Maria Elena, he continued, "Meta-normals generally exhibit one primary skill, although many do have a secondary talent, and occasionally a third. Normally, we would assess the two of you separately in order to preclude comparisons and to encourage your individual talents to manifest naturally. However, as you spend most of your time together it is inevitable you will witness each other's gifts.

"Josefina, please describe your experiences which occurred both before and after the dodgeball incident. Any of us may ask a question to better understand. If what you are describing has a particular name we may call it out."

"I wasn't aware of anything different going on."

"You are speaking of . . . ?" Luther asked.

"Intuition. Mom saw it first. I didn't realize it happened more for me than other people. It's just how I think to myself in the privacy of my own head, how I get a feeling, in my gut, or here." Her hand went to her heart.

"Those who give attention to their intuition experience its improved development," Luther pointed out. "Instead, it is often ignored or made to fit logical explanation. People tend to second guess themselves into denial. Please describe how yours is manifesting."

"I know the answer, especially in simple either/or situations—like, should I turn left or right? And I usually know who's texting or calling before I check. Sometimes I know what to say when I have no prior knowledge. At school, I can feel my way into a scene or theory as my teachers lecture. It's kind of like I connect the dots and shades of color in the blank spots with pictures and feelings." She glanced at her mother. "And I feel other people's feelings."

"Empathy," Georgie called out.

"It happens most when I am near a person experiencing strong emotions. But, if I am close to someone personally, like Mom, I can feel them even when they are miles away."

"How do you know the feelings aren't your own?" asked Georgie.

Josefina turned to Georgie, then her mom and Luther. "There's a change in emotion. It's abrupt, like I'm being interrupted. For instance, I can be on the bus with my own thoughts and feelings when the bus stops and a kid gets on. I haven't looked up or changed what I'm thinking about, yet suddenly I feel frustration and anger. Neither emotion fits my own. Like I said, the stronger the emotion, the easier it is for me to feel it. It can get pretty crazy at school. Not to be obvious, but I look around to see who's feeling something really intense, like cheerful excitement, rage, or sickness. But then I feel kind of guilty, like I'm invading their privacy." She studied her hands. "Some days I wish I didn't feel them at all. It can be so extreme, from happiness for getting a date to the dance, to miserable despair. I shield myself to shut it out, but then I feel like my head's in a bucket."

Georgie stared at her. *Wow. That's rough. It's a wonder she's so upbeat most of the time.*

"You are quite empathic, Josefina, and it grows stronger," Luther said gently. He glanced at Georgie without moving his head. If they hadn't made eye contact she might have believed she imagined it. *He must hear my thoughts.* He said to Josefina, "You will learn how to access your internal tuning and volume knobs, so to speak. By managing our own emotional reactions, we may minimize the impact the emotions of others have on us. In fact, we can use the underlying energies in emotions to focus our powers. Permeable shielding will help with the bucket effect."

"Can the underlying energy help zero in on the source of the emotions?"

"Yes, Josefina, among other things."

"Talk about the shielding, *mija*," suggested her mother.

"I have no idea where I first got the idea," Josefina responded.

"I imagine throwing something over the person to protect them, like a blanket, but stronger. Georgie does it, too."

Surprised to have everyone look at her, Georgie nodded in silent agreement. *It would've probably come out anyway.*

"Please allow me to interject here." Luther leaned forward. "Two primary elements of shielding are belief and intent. Energy we use to shield comes not only from within us but everywhere. We merely channel and focus. This power is universal, divine. It is the energy which animates life, and inherently desires our highest and best." He straightened his posture. "The act of shielding does not assume all the world is unsafe. Shielding focuses your intention to step away from the cliff's edge, use a potholder to pick up the hot kettle, and protect yourself or others from malintent. Self-shielding for empaths is a delicate dance. Please continue, Josefina."

"Except for attempting to shield myself, the first time was the day at school, right before P.E., when Harvey repeatedly hit Shawn with the dodgeball."

Dodgeball day, the day Georgie would never forget. Maybe Josefina would talk about her mind reading. Josefina's face was blank. *Hmm. Maybe it doesn't work all the time yet. Or, maybe she's not ready to give that one up. Either way, I'm pretty sure Luther's doing it.* Her theory hadn't yet been corroborated, but her suspicions were strong. She shifted in her seat and sipped her water. Everyone looked her way. *Great. It must be my turn.*

"I can see halos," she blurted. "Auras," she amended at their expressions, "or whatever you call them." She quickly added to head off any discussion, "I also have strangely vivid and active dreams." She weighed whether to speak further, then forged ahead. "Last night I dreamed people were hiding in my Dad's tree and a huge hawk followed Shawn across a bridge."

Luther stroked his goatee. "Most interesting."

Georgie hesitated. This one felt like a confession. "Sometimes, I feel a puff of air or tingling on the top of my head. It only just started, but it kind of feels like, 'Pay attention'."

There was more goatee stroking by Luther. When no one commented, Georgie continued, "And I am getting stronger physically."

Josefina laughed. "There's an understatement!" Georgie swung around to see whether the laugh teased, but her friend's smile was impressed.

"True," Luther agreed. "We don't yet know how fast you are, or strong. We will measure you at given intervals—both of you and all your gifts. Please continue, Georgie."

"About the speed. I have to be extremely conscious of my movements, to focus on moving slow or not breaking something, like a door handle. It's distracting." She grinned at Josefina. "It helps to have someone to pace myself with."

"We appreciate your efforts to normalize in public," said Luther. "Please tell us more about the halos, or auras."

"I can see them around everyone. The auras look like the glow around a lamp, like when we practiced seeing plant energies the other day, but bigger, and with colors too. They're really strong when the person is speaking in front of a group. I'm pretty sure I saw your auras last night before you told Josefina and me about each other."

Luther tipped his head toward Maria Elena. "We will teach you how to interpret them."

"Yes, *mija*. Now tell us about the shielding."

"Oh," Georgie responded, "the idea came from a television show. But then I sort of fashioned it for my own use. I imagined a force field around members of my family, for protection. It seemed to work the first time, so I kept doing it. Until that day with Harvey and Shawn, I hadn't shielded here in Mystic Creek." The image of her sword came to her, but the moment had passed and she didn't mention it. *Why hadn't I remembered the sword when Shawn got pummeled with the dodgeball?* With the thought of the sword and the stranger who helped her build it, also came a question. *Was Luther the stranger?*

A lull held the conversation.

Maria Elena broke the silence. "Here you will learn to shield in many ways." She rose. "Thank you for sharing your experiences, girls." *Her smile was what? Prideful?* She clapped her hands. "I'll see you later in the kitchen for pizza building." She disappeared down the stairs with an empty food tray.

Georgie swished her drink around in her glass. Josefina stared at the end of her braids.

"We have made a great first foray," Luther said. There was considerably more to explore, but he wanted to encourage a natural flow. "Maria Elena and I will share techniques to fine-tune and increase the sensitivity, accuracy, and power of your gifts. Next time we will measure baselines. Josefina, do you know how to use a stop watch?"

"I sure do. This should be fun."

Georgie slipped a half-grin. Josefina was enjoying this too much. She had to admit it sounded fun to her, too.

"Excellent!" Luther grabbed a tray. "Let us see if you can navigate a spiral staircase, carry your school bags, and the remaining dishes."

MARIA ELENA STOOD at the long wooden kitchen worktable, blender pitchers filled with a green mixture in one hand and red sauce in the other. Piles of chopped vegetables lined one side of the table opposite four pizza crusts engrained with so many seeds they kind of reminded Georgie of the bird blocks at her grandparents' house.

Maria Elena lifted the pitchers of sauce. "Everyone ready?"

Pizza building involved a focused parade around the worktable. Georgie fell behind Josefina, who followed her mother's lead. Luther shadowed Georgie, which shouldn't have made her nervous. She poured both pesto and red sauce on her pizza crust before choosing her toppings. Two petite bowls contained what looked like grated cheese.

Maria Elena gathered from mounds of vegetables, and paused before the piles of herbs and greens. "For something different," she suggested, "wait until your pizza comes out of the oven, then add the cilantro, basil, or arugula-kale mix."

Josefina asked Georgie, "Did you try the hemp seeds?"

"What? No. Are they legal? Which pile were those?"

"The first bowl with the small whitish seed-looking things in it . . . , and yes, they're legal. I sprinkle mine on top before I eat it."

"Okay, I'll give it a whirl." *Life is full of firsts lately, why not another?* Georgie asked of no one in particular, "I was wondering, how else might one fine-tune their shielding process?"

"An excellent question," Luther replied. "Consider dimensions. Let's say we want to place a shield around our vehicle. Size the shield so that it and the vehicle are contained within one lane. Drivers of other cars are apt to be unconsciously aware of something in the space. If too large, they might swerve, give too wide a berth, and potentially cause an accident."

"Wow! I never thought of it like that."

Josefina said, "The same must go for how far you shield in the front and back of the car."

"Precisely. You can make other adjustments, such as density, strength, and conditions. For general shielding, I like to allow for positive thoughts, words, and actions to penetrate the shield as appropriate. The primary purpose of a shield is for protection. You can and may need to customize it according to the situation, and infuse it with specific qualities, such as camouflage or varying density and permeability." He picked up one of the glasses and drank.

"Josefina, *mija*, you could experiment with your self-shield when you are at school."

"Definitely," Josefina agreed absently.

Georgie could almost see her constructing possible

applications. A companionable silence followed. The pizza's aroma wafted. She peeked through the oven's window.

"Almost ready," Maria Elena said, joining her.

They settled around one end of the long dining room table just outside the double doors of the kitchen with their customized pies. Munching sounds, satisfied yums, and murmurs of "this is really good" traveled around the table.

After cleanup they relaxed on sofas around the fireplace, their feet up on ottomans or the tree table, and raspberry hibiscus iced tea in hand. A low moan sounded. Georgie threw a quizzical glance at Josefina as Luther rose and walked briskly to the front door.

"The doorbell sounds like a fog horn, doesn't it?" Josefina smiled. "It's your dad."

"Georgie, your father is here," Luther called from the foyer.

Georgie twisted around. Dad stood next to Luther with her overnight bag.

"Oh!" She ran to the end of the great hall to join them. Josefina, who struggled to keep up, whispered, "Not so fast!" Maria Elena followed somewhere behind them. Dad's pink shirt accented his navy suit and electric blue tie. Musical notes played up and down the tie's length.

"Hi, sweets. You might need this." The bag was stuffed to over-flowing.

"Thanks, Dad! I forgot all about it. Wow, you look great."

"Tonight's a fancy jazz affair. I thought I might spruce up a bit. Did I do okay?"

"Yes," the girls answered in unison.

"You remember Maria Elena, Dad? And this is Josefina."

"Yes, of course. And it's very nice to meet you, Josefina."

"You look very nice, Professor Jones," said Maria Elena.

"Thank you, William," said Luther. "It was very thoughtful of you to bring this all the way out here."

"No problem. Andersen Light's kind of on my way. Speaking of, I should hit the road. I'll see you all tomorrow at the Coastal

Valley Farmers Market, right? Our band will set up on the stage in the center of the market."

"We'll be there," Luther assured him.

"Terrific. And thanks. It's a relief to know Georgie is safe and having a good time."

"It is our pleasure, William." He glanced at Maria Elena.

"We do have a good time." Maria Elena smiled, an arm around each girl.

"Have fun tonight, Dad."

"Goodnight, all." He whispered in her ear, "Love you, sweets," stepped through the door and was gone.

CHAPTER TWENTY-ONE

COASTAL VALLEY FARMERS MARKET WEEKEND

L uther hung up the secure phone. It was quiet in his
office, except for sounds of the light's rotating beacon
and waves breaking on rocks. There had been a break-
in at the Greens' home workshop. Nothing was missing. Everything was in order. Derrick said he wouldn't have noticed, except
the door was ajar and the locks were broken. How fortuitous
Project Hermes had been moved to the secure lab many
months ago.

WORN OUT AFTER DINNER, old movies, and more Q&A,
Georgie and Josefina crashed into a queen bed centered in the
sparse but comfortable spare room on the third floor of the lighthouse. Georgie had thanked Josefina for opting to stay with her
rather than with her mom in the guest house. Josefina had said,
"Duh."

Awake early, they took turns in the en suite bathroom. With a
last glance in the wardrobe mirrors they wound their way down the
spiral stairs, each with an overnight bag over one shoulder and their

school bag over the other. Morning light poured through the towering windows and bathed the ground floor citrus trees.

Their stomachs growled in response to cinnamon, vanilla, maple, and hot griddle smells wafting across the great hall. Morning greetings hailed them from the bright kitchen. Maria Elena had transformed the spacious worktable into a breakfast bar. Luther placed bowls of berries and nuts next to a familiar glass vase holding a single beach flower. He winked. Georgie smiled at their shared memory. "Anything we can do to help?" she asked.

"Drinks need poured and seats need taken," replied Maria Elena. She passed the syrup to Luther and continued flipping slices of sizzling french toast on the large griddle.

"Smells *delicias*, Mom." Josefina kissed her cheek on the way to the orange juice and almond milk.

Georgie pulled her stool closer. "These berries are huge! How . . . ?"

"I talk to their spirits."

"Oh, okay." She threw a verification glance at Luther and Josefina. Both nodded. *I must be getting used to things here.* Maria Elena's hands hovered in her silent food blessing.

"As a young girl, my mother and grandmother taught me to speak to them. The practice is found in nearly every culture," Maria Elena said. "One of my favorites is Findhorn Garden in Scotland. There are books and stories on the internet. I'll teach you what I can, if you want."

"ART IS my favorite part of the market." Josefina said from the back seat of Woody. "There's jewelry too. You can find nearly everything there. It's crazy."

Georgie reflected on finding the money Dad had put in her overnight bag. A warm sensation traveled from her heart to her throat. Josefina's lips curved in a soft smile.

Sunny with the occasional drifting cloud and an expected high to hover above seventy, the weather was ideal. She had imagined it would take a long time to get to the Coastal Valley Farmers Market since they started at the coast and would presumably end in a valley. Yet only twenty minutes had passed once they drove down Main Street, through town, and crossed Old Mystic Creek Bridge. The road wound through rolling hills and tumbled into flat country reaching across the valley toward distant mountain foothills.

A generous sprinkling of vehicles sat alongside the road and within graveled parking lots snatched from surrounding fields. Acres upon acres hosted colorful conglomerations of buildings, tents, tarps, and trucks or vans in various utility and size. Evergreens established themselves among deciduous trees in their first whispers of autumn foliage.

Quiet grew inside the Packard as Luther navigated through a busy parking lot into an empty space close to the entrance, like it was reserved for him.

"That was lucky," Georgie said.

"Oh, but luck had nothing to do with it," Luther said to her in the rearview mirror. Before she could ask, he twisted around to face her and Josefina. "Everyone has their phone switched to audible ring, correct? Good." Surprised, Georgie and Josefina heaped thank-yous upon him as he handed them each a fold of money. "If you need more come and find me."

Maria Elena doled out canvas shopping bags. They would meet at high noon in the market's center at Dad's bandstand. The four set off toward the smell of fried food and sweets. Enormous stacks of pumpkins, gourds, and squash funneled them through the entrance. Georgie took a picture to text to Mom of the life-like farmer scarecrow greeters.

"Are you looking for anything special?" Georgie asked Josefina.

"Maybe some holiday gifts."

They came to a beautiful black woman selling hand-knitted scarves in every color of the rainbow, and some in between. She wore a long flowing, gauzy dress with matching vest in lavenders, blues, and greens. Long necklaces strung together with various gemstones and yarns matched her earrings. Her hair fell in long, obsidian box braids interspersed with delicate curls minimally streaked in copper, and lavender.

Georgie peeked at Josefina. They followed the lure of color.

"Your work is beautiful," Georgie gushed to the woman.

"I love all the colors," cooed Josefina.

"Thank you. I'm Melanie. The yarn is spun with contributions from my happy alpacas." She showed them pictures of her animals, and gave their names. "I dye the yarns with organic plant materials, but the colors are set and won't run or stain your skin."

Georgie ran her fingers over the scarves. "They're soft." She selected one in violets, lavenders, and blues, and continued browsing.

"I'll get one for myself and Mom." Josefina picked one in similar colors but with a line of maroon, and another in various shades of purples and greens.

"Let's go in together and get one for Luther." Georgie asked Melanie, "Do you have more earthy colors?" The woman showed them to a rack of scarves in blues, reds, greens, grays, and black. "Perfect!" Together they chose scarves for Luther, Georgie's dad, Josefina's brother, Georgie's brother, and Carl. Afterwards, Georgie selected a scarf for her mom and one for Rose.

"Who gets the one in chocolate brown, juicy orange, and turquoise?" asked Josefina.

"My mom. It'll go with her red hair. Rose gets the pinks mixed with ivory."

As they paid for the scarves, Melanie asked, "Excuse me, you mentioned Luther earlier. Would that be Luther Andersen?"

"Yes," they answered together. Josefina added, "My mom works with him."

"You must be Josefina. I know your mother well. And, you have to be Georgia."

"Yes," Josefina said, and smirked at Georgie.

"Actually, it's Georgie." Georgie corrected. The woman studied her, like she searched for something. *Weird.*

"Of course. I'm glad to meet you both. Please say hello to Luther and Maria Elena." She pointed. "I see him over there."

Luther stood under a tree on the other side of the main walkway in deep conversation with two men, their heads close together.

"That's Shawn's dad," Josefina said, "and his big brother, Earl. I wonder what they're talking about."

Except for the short, cropped hair, their resemblance to Shawn was clear. They were as tall as Luther, well over six feet. Given their expressions, whatever they were saying was serious.

The girls thanked Melanie, who gave them a healthy discount, and said their goodbyes. Once they were a safe distance away, Georgie asked Josefina in a low voice, "Do you feel or hear anything?"

"No, but she did seem interested in you."

"Yeah, that was weird. But I mean, do you feel or hear anything from over there with Luther and the Greens?"

"Not really. It feels vaguely intense. Maybe he's using some kind of privacy shield. Wait." Josefina's face was guarded. "What do you mean, do I *hear* anything?"

"They seem urgent about something. I just wondered." Georgie plowed past Josefina's raised eyebrow. "Oh, I know you can read minds, or hear thoughts, or whatever you call it."

"What are you talking about?"

"It's a bit of a giveaway when you answer my thoughts before I say them out loud."

"Hmm . . . ."

"Exactly."

"I'm not sure I knew that." Josefina brushed at a stray hair.

"You do it with me all the time." Georgie offered, "Maybe it's all mixed up with your empath stuff."

"Maybe. You can help me with it?"

"I'm in. We can do our own field testing." Georgie bumped shoulders with her.

The numbers of people had grown into crowds.

Josefina said, "Let's head over to your dad's bandstand. It's nearly noon. We can say hi while they set up."

"I'm down!"

They arrived at the market's center. "There's your dad." Josefina pointed under a wide red sail stretched over a stage. Georgie dodged her way through the gathering crowd with Josefina on her tail. They stepped to the edge of the stage where musicians in crisp, turquoise shirts and black jeans bent over cables and equipment.

"Dad!" shouted Georgie. He smiled and waved them over to the steps at stage left.

"Hi, girls. Having a good time?"

"Yes," they answered in unison.

"Do you need anything? Water or something?" Georgie asked.

"No, we're all set. Want to meet the band?"

"Yes!" they exclaimed.

"Okay, watch the cables, girls."

One by one, he introduced them to the band members. "I'd like you to meet my daughter, Georgie, and her best friend, Josefina."

Marion, the drummer, Larry, who played bass guitar, and C.J., the rhythm guitarist, shook their hands. Josefina explained she knew C.J. since he was Carl Junior.

"As in Carl Nelson's son? We're like third cousins." Georgie shook his hand.

"That's right. It's nice to meet you." His hands were like his father's, enormous.

"And this is Earl Green," Dad said.

The tall man swung a saxophone strap over his head. He dipped his head at them as he finished adjusting the strap. "Nice to meet you." His eyes narrowed at Josefina. "Wait—you're Shawn's friend. And you must be the Georgie Shawn mentioned. I didn't make the connection with the Professor—I mean your dad."

Josefina asked, "Is Shawn at the market today?"

Georgie considered Earl while they talked. *What are the Greens and Luther up to?*

"No, he's helping Aunt Darlene with a project at the Mystic Creek Botanical Gardens."

They left Earl to follow Dad. Georgie thought hard at Josefina. *You think Luther told Earl and his dad about Black Jacket Man staring at Shawn?* Josefina shrugged. Georgie added, *Hey, this mind reading thing could be handy.*

Before Josefina could respond, Dad presented Stephanie, the keyboard player and one of his graduate students. She flipped her long, brown hair out of her face. "Any requests, girls?"

Josefina named a song, then suddenly looked away. Georgie followed her gaze. Luther and Maria Elena stood at the foot of the steps. The girls thanked Stephanie and darted to the end of the stage.

"Hello, Luther, Maria Elena!" called William. "I've just finished showing these teenagers around. If you'd like, take the table reserved for the band. You can eat your lunch there and listen as long as you want."

Luther surveyed an empty wooden picnic table beneath a wide, red umbrella. Neon green tape with black lettering reserved the bench seats. "Thank you, we will."

Maria Elena said, "We're delighted to catch one of your performances."

"I hope you still are once we start playing." William laughed and tipped his head toward the din of tuning instruments and sound checks.

"I'm sure we will." Luther exchanged glances with Maria Elena. "Do you play somewhere tonight also?"

"Oh, yes. Thank you for reminding me." William looked toward Georgie to speak, but Maria Elena broke in.

"We're happy to have Georgie with us until the morning." Maria Elena peeked at Luther. "Breakfast at Andersen Light?"

"Magnificent idea," agreed Luther. *Excellent, my dear.* "You will love Maria Elena's breakfast."

"On the condition I may assist the chef."

"I would welcome it."

William laughed at Georgie and Josefina's bouncing. "You two don't mind, I take it."

"Thanks, Dad!" Georgie hugged him. "See you later."

The women followed Luther through the crowd to the musicians' table.

Georgie remarked, "I'm amazed no one else sat here."

Luther winked as Maria Elena threw a red checkered cloth over the table. They dispensed generous samples from various vendors. The music began. He raised a cup to William's nod.

LUTHER DROVE them by their respective houses on the way back from the farmers market to grab fresh clothes. Georgie and Josefina finished their biology homework and said goodnight.

Georgie sprawled out on the lighthouse guest room bed in turquoise pajamas sprinkled with lavender stars. "So . . . ," she drew out playfully, "you're a mind reader."

Josefina draped a blouse over a hanger. "I think the term is *telepath*. I am a receiver and you are definitely a transmitter." She closed the wardrobe door and leaned against it.

"Aren't we supposed to do both?"

"It makes sense. Let's ask Mr. Luther."

"Did you shield the gifts you bought from the market?"

"From their intended recipients? Yes, before we got to the stage."

"Me too." Georgie rolled over on her stomach and crossed her ankles. "How do you know if it worked?"

"Good question. I just do it and believe it will work. Is that how you do it?"

"Honestly, I've used equal parts of hope and belief. Belief and faith would probably put more oomph into it."

Josefina let out her braid. "You see the shield too, right?

"Yeah."

"On another subject, do you plan to go to the homecoming dance?"

"Not seriously. You don't sound too excited either."

"I'm just tired. It's been a long day." Josefina yawned and got into her side of the bed. "But you're right. I'm not excited about it."

"Did Shawn ask you yet, or did you ask him?" Georgie sympathy-yawned and slipped under the covers.

"No, he's not into it either. Besides, we're just friends. I thought you knew."

She let that one drop. "Let's all do something else that night?"

"Okay, but let's not tell Ruby." Another yawn. "She breathes homecoming."

"Yeah, okay." Yawn. "Sweet dreams."

WILLIAM CIRCLED the drive and parked.

"Good morning!" Luther shouted out as the professor closed his car door. "How did the job go last night?"

"Good morning, Luther." They shook hands. "Very well. It was low-key but high energy, if that makes sense. Several of my past and present students were there which gave me the chance to ask some to sit in. The music was lively with new twists and takes."

"You're a musician, but always the teacher, eh, William?"

"Yes, life has evolved that way, but I am also always the student. There is a world of music, and I've only begun to tap into it."

"How exhilarating, William. We are both fortunate our work and passions align." Luther gestured him inside the foyer.

"I haven't spent time here since before college."

"Do you recall exploring the tidal pools as a boy?"

"I do." William took in the great hall and gravitated towards the piano. "I remember this beautiful instrument."

Luther tapped the piano's top. "There's always room for more music."

William sat before the keys, ran fingers through his hair, and played "On the Sunny Side of the Street." His voice and music filled the huge room.

Maria Elena appeared in the kitchen's open doorway. She wiped her hands on her apron and joined them. Soon, the three of them sang. Luther took Maria Elena's hand. She looked up as he placed his other hand on her waist and they danced.

At the song's end, William went right into "Someone's in the Kitchen with Dinah." He substituted Maria Elena's name with an exaggerated sustain at the end. Applause and laughter came from the front of the hall where Georgie and Josefina held their cell phones high, flashlight apps shining. William, Luther, and Maria Elena took a bow.

Good mornings shared, Maria Elena and William left for the kitchen.

"Are you young meta-normals up for a hike?" Luther asked. At their unanimous nods, he said, "Good, let us gear up in the mudroom!" He donned his fisher's cap. The three grabbed lined windbreakers and thanked the cooks for travel mugs of hot tea and chocolate. They stepped into a bracing ocean breeze, and after a few fortifying sips descended the stone steps to the path that led down to the shore.

He paused at the viewing bench and sipped his tea. Yellow light concentrated around the girls' heads and extended beyond their physical auras. "I see you have questions."

They both spoke until Georgie gave a nod to Josefina. "We have questions about telepathy," Josefina explained.

"Shall we walk and talk?" Luther suggested. "What is your first question?" The path descended into a sharp curve to the right.

"Are telepaths supposed to be able to send as well as receive?"

"Customarily, but not all telepaths do both. Why do you ask?" He faced them at the bend.

"She says I'm a transmitter, and I know she's a receiver," said Georgie.

"She's not *just* a transmitter," Josefina explained, "she's super strong, and clear."

Georgie's eyes grew wide. Luther bit back a grin at her silent *What?*

"Georgie's the strongest I hear, even more than Mom."

"Your mother is strong. She also focuses, modulates, and adjusts the intensity of her transmissions." He set off down the trail. "First, to fine tune receiving telepathically, focus on one person at a time and shield yourself from all other thoughts." He kicked a sizable rock off the path. "This might sound counterintuitive—you shield but your focus is tighter." *You understand what I am talking about, right?*

His grin escaped at Josefina's aloud, "Yes, I do."

"Do what?" Georgie asked.

Josefina said to her, "Luther wanted to know if I understood."

"Georgie, my young friend, you can also receive. Practice the same two things." His rearward glance confirmed she was analyzing the process. "Concentrate on the person sending. Meanwhile, shield your mind from your own thoughts and outside distractions. Incorporate openness and receptivity into your focus."

Her eyes narrowed. "Okay."

He slowed his pace as Georgie stopped to pick up a piece of trash. "Second, practice fine tuning transmissions by varying the process I just described. Envision the shield the same way you have in the past, but this time protect your own thoughts from radiating. Once you feel comfortable, practice on one of us. Focus on the person and simultaneously shield the thought in your mind. Imagine your thought travels in a protective conduit and its message is destined only for its recipient, or recipients."

Georgie's eyes narrowed into a squint. "Okay."

Luther resumed his pace. She was already working on it, as was Josefina. The footpath opened onto a flat beach with a circle of squat, stone benches and a fire pit in its center. Oversized rocks protruded from the water. He rested on the bench closest to the shoreline and faced the waves. Cool, gentle wind flowed over him. Luther loved the sea's breeze and welcomed the water's energy with deep breaths. The girls stood on rocks at the shore's edge conducting a telepathic exchange. *Ah, that's working together.* He took another long breath, dropped into a familiar meditation, and merged with the vast ocean of the universe.

His time in silence was brief. The girls shouted over the surf, "It's time to go up!" They hiked over the rocks and sand to him.

"Mr. Luther, Mom says breakfast is ready."

"We decided to experiment," Georgie explained. "I sent the question and Josefina got the answer." Smiles lit up their faces.

"Which were?"

"I asked Maria Elena if breakfast is ready. I isolated the thought the way you said," answered Georgie.

"And I waited to hear the answer," Josefina said, "which I got loud and clear from her, accompanied by images."

He studied her. "Images?"

"I saw the dining room table set for five and Georgie's dad carry the teapot and orange juice pitcher from the kitchen." She grinned at Georgie. "He has on one of Mom's aprons."

"Well done, both of you." He stood and brushed off his pants. "In fact, you've done so well, let's ramp up your practice. I want you to send and receive when you are together or apart."

"You want us to switch what we do?" asked Josefina.

"I would like you both to do both, with each other, and devise ways of verifying. If you verify by text, be sure to give sufficient lead time." He clapped them each on the shoulder. "Let's go eat!"

"Not so fast, Georgie!" cried Josefina.

Luther shook his head. Georgie, already at the viewing bench, posed dramatically.

Reclined with her legs crossed and elbow bent, Georgie's head rested on one hand. The other hand lifted her mug in the air. "What?"

"Your father might look out a window, or a boat could pass by," Josefina replied. "I don't want to have to rescue you from some scary laboratory." She feigned a scowl.

"You're right. I didn't think of that." Georgie glanced up at the house, as did Luther. There were no windows from the kitchen in sight.

"Okay, so no windows," said Josefina. "But, still."

"No, I get it," Georgie assured her.

Luther wrapped an arm around each of them and gave a squeeze. "Lessons well learned. Anybody hungry?" He scaled up the footpath like a mountain goat. They gaped from the viewing bench.

"There they are," William called to Maria Elena.

"Nice apron, Dad." Georgie grinned.

"It came in handy." He pointed to culinary evidence splashed across its front.

Maria Elena asked, "Ready for breakfast?"

"Yes we are," declared Luther. "Their stomachs rumbled all the way back."

"William?" Maria Elena extended her arm in invitation.

Luther followed Josefina mentally as she compared the table before her with the images she'd seen earlier. Fresh flowers in a glazed pottery vase anchored the far end while bowls of colorful vegetables, condiments, and spices held the table's center. Vibrant shades of greens dominated from cilantro, green onions, green chile, avocado, along with shredded cabbage and lettuces. Reds popped with chopped tomatoes, radishes, and salsas.

"Breakfast tacos, I love breakfast tacos!" Georgie grinned like a clown and rubbed her abdomen.

"Beautiful presentation." Luther caught the eye of both

Georgie and Josefina and, with hand to head, said, "Hats off to the cooks!"

The girls saluted, "Hats off to the cooks!"

Maria Elena leaned over Luther's shoulder to pour his tea. *Good morning,* she whispered telepathically.

Good morning, Maria Elena.

BACK AT DAD'S, Georgie hauled her bags to her room and unpacked. She hadn't talked to Mom all weekend. Did texting photos count? She fished for her cell phone. Mom answered on the first ring. Georgie told her about pizza night and sleeping over, the farmers market, and breakfast at Andersen Light with Dad. She shoved at the pile of clothes and sat down on the bed.

"I'm glad you had a good time. Did you get any homework done?"

"I have about an hour and a half's worth left, but it's early. Did you go to Grandma and Grandpa Ryan's?" She tapped the speaker button and sorted clothes into clean and dirty piles.

"Yes," Mom laughed. "They got another goat. Bill caught a fish as big as he is. Your Uncle Kenny had to help reel it in—they both nearly fell into the water. Rose helped your grandma make biscuits. She was covered in more flour than the biscuits. Your grandma thinks she's sneaky, but I know she's been adding almond flour to her recipes. Good for her, I say."

Mom's in better spirits this week. No need to make a big deal of it. She said, "Me, too. When I was there she baked her fried chicken. Go, Grandma!"

"Washer's available!" Dad called.

"Better go, Mom. Talk soon?"

Georgie joined Dad. "Great breakfast, right?"

"Luther and the Garcia women are super people. I'm happy you can spend time there, sweets. I don't worry when you're with them." He closed the dryer door and pushed a button. "Enough mushy dad talk. Grab your first load then we'll plan the rest of our day." She moved to leave, but hugged him first. "Whoa, take it easy with the neck. Are you working out, or what?"

"Whoops! Sorry, Dad. Guess I don't know my own strength." *That's an understatement.* She patted his neck, then measured her pace back to her room.

ALONE WITH HIS EVENING TEA, Luther pondered the break-in at the Greens' carriage house workshop, the fictional blog written by the Project Hermes receptionist, the stranger lurking at the high school, Alejandro, and the *curandero's* portal. He checked the time. By now, Derrick and Earl Green would be back at work on the ship.

CHAPTER TWENTY-TWO

HOMECOMING

Homecoming buzz flew through the air like an orchestra tuning up in a wind storm. Flyers and voices swooshed from every which way. Georgie nearly physically ducked. Information on the homecoming game, homecoming king and queen, or homecoming dance was plastered everywhere. Ruby Lee walked on air when she didn't jiggle up and down with excitement. Luckily, they only shared a couple of classes.

Georgie kept an extra eye on Josefina to monitor her shielding. Every open mouth yacked about homecoming, even the teachers. Josefina must be bombarded with their thoughts. Hopefully the frenzy would peak soon, but Georgie doubted it. It was only third period on Monday. She peered over at Shawn and rolled her eyes. He shook his head and lowered it to stifle a laugh.

Josefina's face looked intentionally blank. Georgie wished she knew what was going on behind it, but only got occasional, fleeting inklings. They were so nebulous she let them float away. She focused a question to Josefina. *You okay?* The blank face crossed her eyes. *Need any extra protection?* Josefina shook her head. Georgie mouthed an okay and faced the teacher.

By Thursday morning Georgie, Josefina, and Shawn settled on their plans for Friday night. Dad would be playing music somewhere while Shawn's Aunt Darlene hosted a party at their house for Botanical Gardens volunteers. Luther and Maria Elena had suggested a moonlit, seaside picnic. Georgie was stoked. According to Josefina it was supposed to be an extra bright night with some kind of special, super full moon.

"The weather will be clear, but cool," Josefina warned, "so bring coats." Georgie and Shawn had obtained parental permission and the three arranged to meet at Josefina's house. "Luther will pick us up at five Friday night. So get there a couple of minutes early."

They endured the last two days of homecoming bombardment. Josefina finally accepted extra shielding. By then Georgie herself heard, or felt, the muted edge of people thinking about their plans, parties, and dates. There was no shortage of sappy teen inner lives. Did she imagine the hyped up, devastated, and elated emotions? Almost constant, it was crazy distracting. Georgie bolstered her efforts to shield Josefina. She pictured and believed. It had some effect. Josefina's face changed from unexpressive to semi-relaxed, though mainly around her hair line.

She boarded the bus with Shawn and Josefina Friday after school. Josefina reminded them, "At least for tonight, curb your text crave and need to read the feeds every sixty seconds."

"I don't do that anyway," said Georgie.

Shawn flashed his ultra-white teeth. "No problem."

The ride, always longest for Georgie, seemed to take forever. Shawn and Josefina had already gotten off the bus when she heard an unmistakable voice from the seat behind her.

"Going to the freak show tonight, Jones?"

She twisted around. "No, Harv. I'm staying out of the fray."

"Probably a wise move." He rose to exit as the bus slowed. "I can't resist it myself."

Not thinking, she jumped off without taking the steps. *Shoot.*

She pretend-stumbled. "I'm okay!" she yelled to the driver and stuck a thumb up. He shook his head, but waved, pulled the door closed, and drove off. *Close one.*

"Smooth move, Jones." Harvey's remark was less snarky than amused.

"Right? Well, have fun tonight." She made a self-regulated run for home. Dad's car was in the drive. She blew through the front door, but forced herself to slow down once inside. 4:05 p.m.—she had less than an hour to get to Josefina's house. "Dad!" she called and dropped her bag in a chair by the door.

"In here, sweets," he yelled from the kitchen. She skidded to a stop at the sight of the pizza cutter in his hand. Sprouted grain tortillas folded into green chile quesadillas filled two plates. Glasses of raspberry iced tea and napkins sat on the nearby table. "I figured we could use a snack."

She hugged him, gently. "You're the best dad ever."

He kissed her cheek. "Thanks, sweets." They conversed between bites and slurps. He'd meet the band early for set up and still needed to shower. She'd put on some warmer clothes before she jumped on her bike to ride over to Josefina's. Dad would be home late and suggested she stay overnight with Josefina, if she wanted, which she did. "Text me and let me know for sure, okay?" he asked.

She packed an overnight bag, just in case, fumbled around in the bottom of her closet for her boots, and changed into warmer clothes. She searched in vain for a hat to keep her hair from flying around. Resigned, she shoved a ponytail band onto her wrist. There was always the hood on her coat.

Dad met her at the front door. "Why don't I drop you off at the Garcias' on my way?"

Shawn and Josefina sat on porch steps of Josefina's house in sweatshirt hoodies, jeans, and hiking boots, with heavy jackets and bags piled behind them. Georgie dropped down beside Josefina. "Where's your mom?"

"She's at Andersen Light preparing for the picnic."

"How are you?"

Josefina glanced at Shawn, then back at her. "I'm just relieved we made it through the homecoming madness. And, I'm excited about tonight. It'll be fun."

"Right?" Shawn nodded and rocked back and forth.

Georgie grinned at his bobble-headedness.

Luther drove up in Woody. Shawn jumped to his feet. "Suh-weet! For us?"

Luther parked the Packard at the curb and tipped his navy fisher's cap with a wave. "Is anyone here looking for a ride to Andersen Light?"

"That would be us, Mr. Luther!" Josefina said.

They gathered their piles and bounced down the stairs. Luther opened the double-windowed back door and stowed their coats and bags. Georgie slid into the backseat beside Josefina and leaned forward to better see metaphoric drool drip from Shawn's lips when he got in. She covered her mouth to keep from laughing out loud. Josefina shot her a lifted brow, and Georgie could swear she heard her say, "Really?"

I can't help it. He cracks me up. With both hands clamped tight over her mouth to keep from laughing, she caught Luther's wink in the rearview mirror. That was it. She doubled over with the giggles. It had been a long week.

Luther's voice mimicked an old-style train conductor. "Buckle up, ladies and gent—next stop, Andersen Lighthouse and the great full moon seaside picnic!"

The rest of the car laughed with her.

Shawn shot Luther with questions about Woody the rest of the way while she and Josefina practiced telepathy.

Georgie sent first. *Do you think it would be okay if I stayed over with you tonight?* A full minute passed before she sensed more than heard Josefina's whisper in her mind, a *yes* so light it was barely discernible. Georgie sent back for confirmation and mentally strained to hear her reply.

Josefina said aloud, "Yes, and Mom called Shawn's aunt to clear it for him to stay too. I guess his dad and brother are gone. Anyway, I think Mom and Luther plan for this to be a late night."

"Cool," Georgie said, "I'll text my dad and let him know."

The late afternoon sun cast its rays wide through the Fresnel lens and lighthouse windows as Woody turned down Luther's Lane, as she'd taken to calling it. She couldn't believe her eyes the day a new street sign had appeared with *Luther's Lane* in official lettering.

Luther pulled into the carriage house, and distributed coats and bags before the teenagers headed inside. He closed the garage door and walked through the workshop to the back path. A feeling niggled at him. After a cursory scan of the nearby ethers he detected nothing more and resolved to step up his vigilance.

Maria Elena directed Georgie and Josefina to the lighthouse guest room and Shawn to the guest house. Bags deposited, Georgie raced down the spiral staircase to the ground floor. She leaned against the door jamb and waited for Josefina to come into view, her legs crossed and coat in the crook of her elbow. She feigned interest in her nails, peeked out of the corner of her eye and, for the cherry on top, transmitted. *Are you coming?*

"Very funny, Ms. Jones. I trust I didn't keep you waiting too long," Josefina quipped. "Don't forget Shawn will be with us tonight."

"No problem. I have you around to remind me." She fake-punched her friend's arm. They entered the kitchen as Shawn returned. Josefina delivered her surreptitious eyebrow lift, to which Georgie responded with her best faux-serious face.

Maria Elena and Luther glanced up from the kitchen work-table. "*Mijos*," greeted Maria Elena. "Shawn, you found your room?"

"Yeah, thanks, Ms. G. I forgot toothpaste and stuff, but you had everything there." His eyes bounced around the kitchen. "This place is dope!"

"You haven't seen the half of it," Josefina said.

Maria Elena and Luther went back to packing a soft-sided cooler and wooden box. Two tall and ancient looking thermoses plus one short and wide thermos flanked a tower of waxed paper packages, a box of wholegrain graham crackers, and a bunch of bananas.

"What can we do?" asked Georgie.

"There's another wooden crate on the floor there," Maria Elena gestured. Shawn retrieved it. "You can load the water jug," she directed with her elbow, "plus these thermoses, that lantern, and the blanket over there." She pointed to a roll of thick, plaid cotton lying on the smaller table.

"Shawn, do you have room in your pocket for matches?" asked Luther.

"Yes, sir." He caught them midair. Georgie and Josefina cushioned the water jug with the blanket roll.

"Choose one." Luther indicated a row of brightly colored flashlights. "Bring your coats!"

Shawn grabbed a wooden crate. Josefina and her mom carried the coats out. Georgie made for the other wooden box, but Luther offered her the soft-sided cooler instead. She replied telepathically. *I get it. It's better not to flex my muscles.*

A heavy duty utility wagon with fat, knobby tires waited outside the mudroom in the covered pass-through to the greenhouse. They loaded everything into it but the coats and flashlights. Luther grasped the sturdy handle and slowly pulled the wagon forward.

OOHS AND AHS of delight escaped Georgie and the other teenagers as they entered the greenhouse. Countless strings of varied lights guided them through rows of raised plant beds. Early twilight accentuated strands draped high above from sides to center ceiling.

"This is so cool," Shawn breathed, his eyes bright.

Luther chuckled to Maria Elena, "We may have to leave these up all year."

"I vote yes for that," said Georgie. Shawn and Josefina concurred.

"I am inclined to agree, but I must first ask the plants." Maria Elena swung open the exterior door of the greenhouse to expose the footpath.

Shawn's head swiveled in a double take. Georgie caught his barely audible, "Say what?"

Josefina and her mom were first to reach the trailhead. "Oh, Mom, this is . . . "

Georgie was right at their heels. "Magical." Solar lights stretched along both sides of the sharp, descending path. They snaked around curves, encircled the fire pit area, and led off toward the water.

Shawn reached the trailhead. "No way."

"I'm glad you approve. Light is our specialty here." Luther chuckled at his own humor. "Please file behind me as I navigate this wagon downhill." They stepped to the side as he pulled the cart forward. "Fire building will be easier while we still have light."

They approached the nearly 180 degree turn. The tires slid and sprayed rocks. Luther crouched slightly to redistribute his weight.

Impressive. He's very quick for an old guy. Luther laughed. *Oops.* Georgie forgot to shield her thoughts. *Not that you're old.* Josefina snickered and poked her shoulder. Georgie's face burned. She tried emptying her mind but failed, and focused instead on the path.

The breeze grew colder as they reached the circle of benches around the fire pit. A utility wagon identical to Luther's rested next to a picnic table outside the circle. Sets of long metal handles with wood grips and a bundle of wrought-iron rods protruded from the wagon's cover.

The teenagers slipped on jackets and circled the fire pit.

"Shawn," asked Luther, "can you build a fire?"

He looked over the three stacks of different sized wood. "Yes, sir!"

"Excellent. You and Josefina get started while Georgie and I help Maria Elena unpack."

Maria Elena stopped unloading when Georgie approached. She said in a low voice, "*Mija*, you will master your thoughts more with each passing day," and hugged her.

Luther gave her a one-armed side hug. "Don't worry. I enjoy the comic relief, Georgie. You are unconditionally loved and accepted here."

Georgie had sensed her welcome, but didn't know they felt that way. Her throat grew thick, and a warm sensation moved throughout her chest. "Thank you," she choked out. The adults smiled and Luther gave her another quick hug before he extracted the wrought-iron rods and headed back to the fire pit.

Maria Elena spread the plaid table cloth over the sturdy, full-length table. Georgie followed her lead, pulled the lengths under, and tied the corners into tight knots at either end to hold the cloth in place against the breeze. She placed the lantern on the table. "What you both said—that was really nice."

"It's true, *mija*." Maria Elena removed a set of long handles with square, flattish baskets from the cart.

Georgie placed the thermoses and water jug on the table and peeked over to the fire pit. Shawn and Josefina arranged split logs into a teepee with twigs and wads of paper stuffed inside. Luther erected a wrought-iron kettle frame.

The three stood back from the pit and against the chilly breeze. Luther called over to Georgie and Maria Elena, "We're ready to light the fire!"

Shawn held the box of matches and Josefina moved close to

shelter him from the wind. Georgie shifted to his other side and the three of them crouched down around the pit. Shawn cupped his hands around the tiny flame until it grew, more paper caught and fire reached nearby twigs, cheered on by clapping.

Georgie left the fire to help with dinner prep. A tinge of darkness edged into the sky. She held the lantern closer.

After a few clumsy attempts, toasting baskets, crammed full, hovered over flames. Luther toasted Maria Elena's sandwich while she poured hot chocolate and tea. A corner of Shawn's sandwich caught fire. Giggles erupted when he frantically blew at the burning bread.

Stadium cushions insulated them from the cold stone benches as they ate. Georgie took it all in—her friends, the robust fire. Life was good.

"My sandwich," Shawn proclaimed, "its edge sealed with slightly charred cheese, is by far the tastiest."

"It's definitely crunchier, right Shawn?" poked Georgie. Josefina snort-laughed.

"Look!" Georgie pointed to the sky and a cresting moon. "The full moon is humongous."

"It's called the Blood Moon," Josefina said.

"Say what?" asked Shawn.

"Blood?" asked Georgie.

Maria Elena expounded, "It is one of many names for October's moon. Every month's full moon has a name, or sometimes a few names." She slipped away to the table.

Georgie said, "It's so bright it's hard to find the stars. Oh, I see some." She pointed away from the moon, "Way over there, low in the sky." She, Josefina, and Shawn made a game of naming the planets and stars, and fell under the spell of the advancing moon until roused by Maria Elena's hefty, steaming hot mugs of chili.

"Delicious," Luther said between spoonfuls.

Maria Elena extended a wide-mouthed thermos to Shawn's, "Is there more?"

Luther sipped his tea, grateful the fog had not obscured the evening. The moon rose to a brighter height. His eyes followed the teenagers as they took off to the water's edge. Moonlight reflected off the rocks to create dazzling whites and a continuum of lavenders and indigos where there were once tans, grays, and blacks. He joined Maria Elena at the table and packed used dishes while she prepared her special cocoa sauce. Later, they would dip fruit and graham crackers in chocolate bubbling in its kettle over the fire.

"Oh!" Maria Elena's shoulders slumped and her hand went to her solar plexus.

"What is it?" Instantly at her side, Luther placed a hand on her shoulder and examined her face.

"A vision. . . . Something's happening. Look." She grasped his hand.

A strong clairvoyant and telepath, he didn't need to hold Maria Elena's hand to share what she saw in her mind's eye. Yet, it appeared to ease her and he used the moment to reinforce her psychic shield. She stared off into the night and he opened himself to join her sight.

Her vision took him to the high school gymnasium. Celebration of Mystic Creek High's winning game pervaded the dance. A confusion of reflective balls, colored lights, and crowds of people forced him to pan out and refocus. Three men dressed in black, from leather jackets to cowboy boots, thrust their way through masses of dancers and people laughing and conversing. A girl screamed. Kids fell to the floor. The interlopers searched for someone.

"Who?" Luther asked her. The men scowled as they combed the dance floor. They swung a black kid around, then pushed him down, hard. It wasn't who they wanted. The intruders worked the room until they found another black boy, but shoved him away. The process repeated several more times. Her gaze moved to Luther when he quietly asked again, "Who?"

She closed her eyes and Luther waited. Maria Elena winced,

her face twisted in anger and frustration as she scanned the room through the eyes of one of the men. The man glanced down at a photo in his palm. It was Shawn! The vision dropped, and her eyes opened wide. She let go of his hand. "Oh, no!" she said to Luther.

He squeezed her hand and gently directed, "Stay with it. We need to see where they go."

Maria Elena closed her eyes again. The men grew more agitated as they elbowed their way through the crowd. They shoved people, grabbed phones from kids taking pictures and videos, tossing the cells over their shoulders. Occasional clusters of bigger boys, possibly varsity players, protested with shouts, but quickly backed up, hands raised in the air. Some stumbled over others to get out of the way and fell to the floor.

Luther felt Maria Elena's apprehension. "Those men must be carrying weapons," she whispered, but closed her eyes again. More people screamed, the fire alarm sounded, and the men left the gym. They stalked down halls, busted into boys' rooms and slammed open stall doors, injuring boys in the process. Red faced and frowning, they left the last restroom, cursed in Spanish, and stormed out the nearest exit. The men scrambled into a black sedan waiting in the emergency lane. It sped away, the license plate number in full view.

"Can you see ahead?" he asked, and took her other hand in his. She tightened her hold in silent acknowledgement. The car sped along the edge of town to the old side of the Port of Mystic Creek. Maria Elena opened her eyes and looked directly into Josefina's, visible from the distance in the Blood Moon's light, then back to Luther's.

"Let me," he said, and transmitted to Josefina. *Please stay there with the others for a few more moments. Distract them.* Josefina nodded her head slightly. Georgie turned, as if she had also received him.

He returned to Maria Elena's focus. The men boarded a small running boat. She flashed forward to observe them climb a side ladder onto a motor cruiser yacht anchored well out of the way of sea lanes, its running lights off. Its name was clear in the bright moonlight as the boat pulled away—*Halcón con Sombra. Shadow Hawk.*

"Maria Elena, are you all right?" Luther asked.

"A little shaky, and concerned."

"Please, take a moment to center yourself. We will discuss this later."

She sat with him near the fire. "Josefina knows something is . . ."

"I'll communicate with Josefina to let her know we will talk tonight. The boy is safe here. I will call his father when we go back up." He glanced over at the teenagers running their flashlights over the rocks and shallow water. "Do you wish to finish the evening?"

She squeezed his hands. "Yes, I do."

SEVERAL FEET AWAY, Shawn crouched at the shore's edge, his flashlight beamed into the water. Georgie sensed Josefina was on high empath alert. She leaned closer. "You okay?"

"Yes."

"Something going on?"

"Whatever it is, they'll talk to us about it later." Josefina threw a meaningful look Shawn's way.

"Let's head back to the fire." Georgie shouted over the surf, "Hey, Shawn!" and waved her arm in a swim stroke.

The evening's seaside picnic carried on. They speared fruit with long skewers to roast in the fire and dip into the kettle of hot chocolate sauce. Graham crackers caught the dripping mess. Luther told stories of life-saving adventures from the early days of Andersen Light. Shawn asked if he knew any ghost stories. As if on cue, Luther launched into the first of many. Georgie suspected the stories were real, especially those about conquistadores who came to shore. His hilarious telling of greedy but stupid smugglers who cheated each other, only to end up with nothing and nearly drown, made her laugh until her jaws hurt.

The Blood Moon's brilliance illuminated as they packed picnic remnants into the utility carts and tended the fire pit. Crunching boots, rolling tires, and crashing waves serenaded their uphill trek. Georgie admired the light reflected in the dew of plants near the trail's edge.

Luther and Shawn pulled the empty carts away. At the kitchen worktable, Georgie and Josefina paused to gulp water. Maria Elena turned from unpacking the last of the wooden crates. "Luther and I would like to talk with you once we get Shawn settled in the guest house for the night. Do you mind putting off going up to bed?"

"Not at all. I'm still wired from the hot chocolate. . . ."

" . . . and the yummy chocolate sauce," added Georgie.

"Very well. Bring your extra energy over here, *mijas*."

Georgie spun off her stool, hung leftover bananas on their hook, gathered up and arranged things to be washed next to the sink, slowed, and shoulder-bumped Josefina.

"Hey!" yelped Josefina. "You're going to make me break a chili mug."

"Oops." *Just checking in.*

Translation: you're trying to lighten the mood.

Yeah.

Josefina returned the bump. *Thank you.*

Luther entered from the mudroom with Shawn speaking overly fast. "Aunt Darlene, she's my dad's sister, takes care of things when Dad and Earl are gone. I try to help, but except for opening a jar, reaching the top shelf, or lifting something heavy, she points me to school work and stuff. But I do organize her photo files—she takes tons of pictures of birds and plants. Plus, I manage both the house and workshop networks. I've been doing it for years. Dad and Earl taught me stuff early, when I was a kid. Like, when I was in elementary. Thanks, Ms. G." He accepted a glass of water from Maria Elena and took a seat. "So I manage the security, firewalls, software updates, malware protection, and backups." Luther joined him at the worktable with a cup of tea. "Lately, Dad lets me handle his comms, special government gear that sometimes need attention, when him and Earl are out."

"*He* and Earl, *mijo*," corrected Maria Elena.

"Oh, right, Ms. G." His head sunk forward with a sheepish air. "I forget sometimes." Josefina and Georgie sidled up either side of him.

"It has become an afterschool job," observed Luther.

"Yes, sir, it has."

"It keeps you out of trouble, right Shawn?" teased Josefina.

"Most of them time," he said, suddenly deflated.

Georgie saw an image of Harvey's face warped by meanness. "Yeah, like when you hang out with us," she said, seeking to return his good mood.

He rallied. "Yeah, tonight was dope. You really know how to throw a picnic."

"I'm glad you came." Maria Elena patted his arm. "It's getting late ...."

Luther interrupted her with a telepathic bow. *Allow me.* "I'll walk you to the guest house, Shawn. You've got your flashlight?"

Georgie observed their exchange, and Josefina's raised eyebrow.

"Thank you, Luther," Maria Elena said. "We'll see you for breakfast, Shawn. Josefina can give you a wakeup call, so don't worry about setting an alarm."

"Thanks, Ms. G." He fist bumped the girls. "Goodnight, Jo, Georgie."

Luther and Shawn slipped out onto the veranda and into the moonlight. Luther peered over to the guest houses, their stone and brick architecture corresponding with the main house. Everything appeared to be in order. The two descended stone steps to the walkway which ran parallel to the bluff overlooking the sea then turned right toward the guest houses. He scanned the structures as they approached, and would double check the oceanside balconies and parking garage before heading back to the main house. Automatic spotlights illuminated as he and Shawn approached the guest houses.

"Solar . . . nice," said Shawn.

"We use as much solar and wind power here as technology will allow." A dim light glowed in the first guest house, Maria Elena's. They continued to the second. "Here we are. Did Maria Elena give you a key code?"

"No."

"Use this number." He punched in a six-digit code. The locking mechanisms disengaged with two clicks. "Got it?"

"Yes, sir."

Luther followed him into the suite and surveyed all the rooms. "You won't need the balcony tonight?"

"No, sir. I'm gonna catch some z's."

Luther opened the French door and inspected the balcony and its low wall. Satisfied, he secured the door.

"Be sure to lock up behind me." Luther paused at the front door, but the boy didn't question the security checks. "I will see you at breakfast. Sweet dreams, Shawn."

"Yeah, you too."

Luther physically checked the perimeters, then, with his mind's eye, the roofs. Satisfied, he strode to the parking garage and repeated the process. The side door was good. He peeked inside the window. There was no sign of trouble or unwelcome visitors. Halfway to the terrace steps, he turned and faced the guest houses. He raised his hands high in the air, palms out, took a long, deep breath, then opened himself as a clear conduit. Energy filled him as if a dam had opened. He allowed it to rush through him. He deftly wove the protective light in and around the grounds with no space untouched. With another deep breath he intentionally slowed the flow. Hands clasped together momentarily, he swiped them against each other, then shook them out. *That should do it.* Luther didn't expect trouble, but it didn't hurt to play it safe.

He reentered the kitchen and assessed the atmosphere. Maria Elena had told the girls what she'd seen in her visions. He took a seat, hung his cap on his knee, and gratefully accepted a cup of tea. The teenagers were quiet, expectant.

"As you have surmised from Maria Elena, we are not certain why the men searched for Shawn at the homecoming dance. I suspect it has to do with the Greens' government work. I will call Derrick tonight. For now, we shield Shawn, his family, and his home. We are but instruments for this powerful, loving, and protective energy. Release any fear, as it may inadvertently serve as an obstruction or filter. We shield not out of fear, but in confidence of divine protection. You are the channels. Keep yourselves clear." He asked Maria Elena, "Did you look in on Darlene?"

"Yes, she is sleeping peacefully. In my vision I saw the men stop their vehicle and look through her house windows. Darlene had a good amount of guests, all adults. The men drove off without intruding. The girls and I have directed shielding around her and the home."

"I've done my best," Georgie said after a moment. "I've never met her or been to their house, so it was all imagination. I admit I am afraid for him, but shielding together helps with the fear."

"Awareness opens the door." Luther's eyes crinkled over the rim of his tea. "Won't it be interesting to learn the accuracy of your imagination when you see Darlene Green and her home in person? I would not be too surprised if I were you."

"It's good Shawn was here with us tonight." Relief rang through Josefina's voice.

"And those men didn't know to come here looking for him," Georgie added.

"Meanwhile," Luther interjected before their thoughts and words marched off into unpleasant possibilities, "here in the present moment we are all safe. Let's all get a good night's sleep. Tomorrow we meet another day." They said their goodnights to Maria Elena and the girls followed him to the lighthouse. They took the elevator to the third floor. "Goodnight, girls," he said and took the remaining stairs to his office on the gallery level.

"THERE'S no way we don't listen in," Georgie whispered once he was out of earshot.

"He'll know we're there," Josefina warned.

"Don't worry, we'll sit a step or two down. We'll still be able to hear him on the phone."

"Okay, but this is your idea."

"Fine, but you have to 'hear' Shawn's dad's side of the conversation."

"Oh, all right. If I can."

"You're as curious as I am."

"I know. Let's just do this."

They took off their boots and padded up the stairs in sock feet. Georgie selected a step where their heads wouldn't be visible from the gallery floor. They sat and waited. They heard a flush, faucets turn on and off, and the opening and closing of a door. They craned their necks up and around in time to get a clear view of Luther leaving the bathroom. He stared directly at them. Busted.

"Do you girls have somewhere you'd like to be?"

"Yes, Mr. Luther. Goodnight," said a red-faced Josefina.

"Yeah, goodnight," Georgie echoed.

"I'll fill you in in the morning, if there's anything to tell."

"Thank you," they said and raced down the stairs.

"That went well," Georgie said, subdued. She'd brushed her teeth and now lay in the queen-sized bed next to Josefina. She shined her phone's flashlight at the ceiling. "I apologize for getting you into this one."

"It's okay. I wanted to hear, too. But now I don't even want to listen telepathically."

"I don't blame you. He's probably shielded the conversation anyway."

"Probably. The best thing to do now is go to sleep knowing Shawn is safe."

"You're a wise soul, Josefina."

"Just a sleepy one." She moved onto her right side toward the wardrobe and bathroom door. "Goodnight."

"Goodnight." Georgie put down her phone, turned over on her left side, and fell asleep staring at the curved wall.

HE TAPPED in his PIN and made the call. "Luther Andersen for Derrick Green, please," he told the person who answered the secure line. The connection was mediocre. Luther sat down and checked his watch. It was well after midnight.

After a few minutes, a tired voice said, "Hello? Luther, are you there?"

"Yes, Derrick. I apologize for the late call. First, everyone is okay. Can you hear me?"

"I hear you five by five, Luther. What's happened?"

THEY COULD'VE SLEPT IN, but she and Josefina anticipated news about last night. Light strains of classical music and wonderful breakfast smells drifted across the great hall. Luther and Maria Elena met them at the dining room table. Georgie's face fell at the shake of Luther's head.

"We have nothing new. However, Mr. Green concedes a connection may perhaps exist between the armed intruders at the dance and what he and Earl are working on for the government. This is merely speculation. Derrick will speak with Shawn when he and Earl return to shore. As far as we know, Shawn's name has not been linked with the incident at the homecoming dance. For now, we must neither hypothesize nor comment on this to anyone except for the four of us. Do we all concur?"

"Okay, but what about the black jacketed man we saw hanging around?" Georgie asked.

"I'd like the answer to that myself," Luther said. "Did either of you clearly see his face?"

Georgie glanced at Josefina.

"*Mijas*, hold the image of this man with the black jacket in your minds. I will compare his face with the men I saw in my vision last night." Maria Elena's eyes briefly belied her inner focus. "The face is distant, Hispanic. I cannot be certain he is one of the gunmen." She stood with Luther. "Thank you, girls. Breakfast is calling."

Shawn entered the dining room through the glass terrace door and dropped his bag and coat on the floor. "Good morning. I slept like a rock. Those ocean waves z'd me out."

"Good morning, Shawn," greeted Georgie.

"You're cheerful," Josefina said.

"Yeah, last night was fun. I'd definitely do that again."

Luther and Maria Elena returned through the double doors with the breakfast trays.

Luther said, "The gang's all here—just in time for pancakes!" He placed a heaping plate of steaming pancakes on the table.

"Hey! Are those chocolate chip pancakes?" Shawn's eyes popped.

"Buckwheat with dark chocolate chips— Josefina's favorites," answered Maria Elena.

"You're awesome, Mom! Shawn, you are going to love these."

Georgie noticed an extra place setting. "Are we expecting someone else?"

Luther said, "Your father has undoubtedly just driven up to the house."

Georgie scrambled out of her chair, but slowed down at Josefina's expression. She moved to the front door at a brisk, though measured stride as the doorbell's foghorn sounded. "Hi, Dad! This is a nice surprise."

"I can't pass up Maria Elena's cooking." Georgie stayed in step with him. He asked, "Would you like to take a drive down the coast later, after we take the Garcias home?"

"You know I would!"

She officially introduced Dad to Shawn. The party around the table dug in. Not a single morsel remained. Dad and Maria Elena left to discuss recipes.

A loud belch bellowed from Shawn. "Oh! My bad . . . please excuse me."

Once the teen guffaws died away Luther said, "Shawn, your aunt asks you remain here until she comes to pick you up. That gives us time to show you around the solar and wind power systems, if you'd like."

"Yes, sir! That'd be righteous!"

CHAPTER TWENTY-THREE

FALLOUT MONDAY

"Freaky, right?" Shawn careened into the bus seat. Monday morning was here and *freaky* was the word of the day. The ruckus at the high school got a smallish write-up in Saturday's edition of the *Mystic Creek Clarion*, but splashed across Sunday's front page. Georgie had read it with Dad at breakfast. He'd already heard most of the story Saturday on local NPR, and had asked her what she knew. She'd truthfully told him she and Josefina had been texting about it. One text relayed a telepathic message from Luther to keep their eyes out, though he and Maria Elena suspected the black jacketed man may have left by sea Friday night. Georgie hadn't mentioned to Dad they were shielding Shawn, his family, and home. "Lucky you were at the lighthouse," he'd said.

Prominently displayed under the *Clarion's* headline banner of "Gunmen crash homecoming!" was a candid shot of dodgeball varsity team members falling over each other to get out of the way of the intruders. Pictures of the three gunmen, taken with phone cameras, were positioned alongside the article, stacked one over the other, with the caption, "Do You Know These Men?" The write-up had little substance and was aerated with student and faculty quotes. It ended with an appeal for anyone with information to call, text, or email the authorities. According to newscasts and school bus chatter, Mystic Creek thumbs and fingers flew with texts at an all-time high over the weekend and videos ran viral on social media.

The bus queued up to the school entrance. Georgie rubbernecked with the rest of the kids at the media vans parked as close to the school and newly erected vehicle barricades as possible. She and Josefina followed Shawn through the maze. Police attempted to keep out reporters, their crew, or any evil-doers, and asked to see school IDs.

Flyers plastered everywhere announced an assembly called by Principal Storey. Georgie crammed into the gymnasium with Josefina and Shawn and the rest of the school. "Ironic choice of venue," she whispered. This was her first gathering of all the classes and faculty, first year through senior. She gawked freely. The principal and several other adults, possibly teachers or staff, milled around in front of the crowd on the platform, and periodically checked their watches. At exactly eight-thirty, Principal Storey took center stage and spoke into the microphone. Who knew what she said since everybody in the gym was yacking. The varsity coach sprinted over to center stage and blew a shrieking high pitch with his whistle. People covered their ears and a collective groan replaced the vocal chaos. The principal leaned closer to the microphone.

"Good morning, Mystic Creek High" echoed and reverberated around the gym's high walls and ceilings. "The administration would like to express our relief that everyone made it through homecoming with their lives. A few boys were injured but are recovering from home, except for one student with a concussion who is being monitored at the hospital. Several others, both students and alumni, experienced bumps, bruises, and scrapes. It could have been worse, as iterated in the media, and we are grateful it wasn't. We take this very seriously. Police are here to investigate and conduct interviews. You are all asked to cooperate fully. Chief of Police Ganzhorn is with us this morning to speak to you." She extended her arm. "Chief . . ."

The man who stepped forward could have passed as a teacher, except that both his tweed blazer and hair were way nicer, and his shoes had what Georgie imagined was a military shine. Wide yellow and blue auras extended several feet around him. His deep voice, not quite gravely, soothed. "Thank you, Principal Storey. Good morning. As she said, my officers will interview you all. Their teams are set up here in the gym. Anyone knowing anything is asked to come forward now. Cell phones taken and tossed by the gunmen Friday night have been confiscated as evidence and will be returned. Contact us if you believe your cell was among them. You'll find posters with our contact information displayed throughout the school. If you think of anything now or after your interview, please call, text, email, or otherwise come forward with your information. We appreciate your support. Ms. Storey . . ." He stepped back.

"Thank you, Chief." She said to the assembly, "Counselors are available in the gym. Please take advantage of their presence. Students with pertinent information *and* those whose last names begin with A, B, or C please remain. We will call the rest of you over the P.A. system. All other students and faculty are asked to report to their first period classes. Thank you."

Decibels rose. People funneled through the gym doors like molasses being poured across a cold plate. The remainder of the day resembled the morning. Josefina was on overdrive to glean any helpful information out of the noise, and looked like she had a headache by the end of second period. Georgie was not immune, but the bazillion thoughts were garbled and faint, like conversations behind glass. She picked up the emotions easier. That wasn't the problem. Their onslaught hit her like a sneak attack and left her first dazed, then frenzied, in her efforts to sort them out from her own. Nearly every emotion was some form of fear—paranoia, worry, anger, revenge. A few were giddy, as if some of the kids were

165

high, riding waves of communal excitement. She tried pinpointing their sources, but it was too much like eavesdropping. Besides, she didn't want to invite in more outside feelings. Instead she visualized protective light around herself like an invisible force field emanating several inches from her body. Within seconds the gamut of intense emotions muted and dissipated, leaving her to her own, which were surprisingly calm. She felt—no, sorry wasn't right—compassion for the fear-infused kids.

She and Josefina strolled to third period. "You doing okay? Need extra shielding?"

Josefina drooped for effect. "Yes, thank you!"

"You've got it. Must suck to be you today. I picked up emotion, but not every random thought. It's crazy how much fear is flying around, and that doesn't count the energy stirred up by the drama mongers. You've sifted through it?"

"Nothing useful so far. I'd hoped to learn why those men were looking for Shawn specifically."

"Maybe we should go directly to the source—tap into the men."

Josefina hedged. One side of her face pinched into a pained squint. "You may be right, but it feels dangerous. Let's talk to Mom and Mr. Luther about it after school."

"Dangerous?"

"Like I'm not ready to cope with that much rage, or whatever else is going on."

"Oh! Right!" She knew first hand about being around someone in a toxic mental state. There were some real sickos out there. "We should wait." Who could say how their stuff could affect Josefina's emotions, or her own? *Better safe than sorry.*

Exactly.

Shawn nodded his greeting as they entered the classroom. Georgie detected the outer shimmering of a protective shield being reinforced around him.

. . .

LUTHER DISCOVERED Maria Elena in her verdant herb garden nestled between the walls of the lighthouse, kitchen, and main house. Her shiny, black hair fell under a sun visor in loose waves around her light blue flannel shirt as she talked to plants still thriving late into the season. The worn tool belt and canvas pouch hung low over her jeans, heavy with trowels and clippers. She made her way around pots and patches of ground to the garden pockets adhered to the house wall. Their heartiness was a testimony to her ability to commune with plants on levels most folks didn't know existed. He sat down on the meditation bench without interrupting.

She turned to him. "It's time I take a few plants into the greenhouse."

"Tell me," he asked kindly. She was in the curious state she sometimes held—here, but preoccupied, the center of her inner being present and her mind's eye wandering.

"I've not seen more into what happened Friday night. You said the attempt was meant to gain leverage over Derrick and Earl Green—I understand that. What I mean is, I have been unable to see what those other men are doing now, or are planning for the future."

"Have you been able to locate them?"

"Not specifically, but they are in the western regions of Mexico."

He said, "I will check in with Alejandro and speak with those regional leaders."

Handles of the longer trowels clunked as she sat down on the bench beside him.

"Maria Elena, when either of us speaks with him, we must do so with caution. Say nothing over the phone beyond establishing contact. He is a government employee; his phone traffic may be routinely intercepted. But, telepathic communications are very strong with him."

"Yes. And we need to call for a local meeting."

Luther's mind followed hers to the local area meta-normals, then to Josefina and Georgie. "Would an afternoon tea work for you?" He kept his tone conversational.

She grinned. "Perfectly."

"I will speak with the local allies separately. Meanwhile, we shall accelerate our work with the teenagers."

"I love how we work together."

They sat in silence until he asked, "Spot of tea?"

They passed through the greenhouse into the mudroom. Luther threw his hat on its hook, put the kettle on, and turned from the stove. She had three mugs. He raised an eyebrow, but dropped it. It wasn't yet lunchtime, but . . . *Carl is coming.*

"Yes," she answered aloud, patting his back as he prepared the teapot. She sliced the pumpkin-zucchini bread she'd made with almond flour, a new recipe. They set the tea out on the kitchen worktable as Carl entered and seated themselves on the tall stools.

"Can't sit," the man declared and breezed through to wash his hands. Carl stirred an ample spoon of honey into a tea mug with one hand and reached for a slice of bread with the other. "Uh . . . mm . . . this is real good." He sat down and poured a glug of coconut cream into his tea. "Here are the measurements for the new safe," he told Luther, and handed him a folded paper from his shirt pocket. "I checked on those batteries while I was in town."

His pumpkin-zucchini bread finished, Carl took a gulp of tea and grabbed another slice. "We're looking good for the winter. Of course, there may be more wind than sun, but the batteries will work fine. Plus the reserves are there." He grabbed a napkin and wiped his mouth. "This is real good, Maria Elena. Pumpkin?" He slurped his tea.

"Pumpkin and zucchini. Would you like another slice?"

"Don't mind if I do. I know it's healthy if it comes from you."

Luther accepted another piece and refolded Carl's note. "Thank you for these dimensions. I'll get the safe ordered right away. Will you have time to check the wall today?"

"I did that first thing." Carl poured himself more tea and held the pot up in offering. At their shake of heads, he set the pot down and went for the honey. "It looks good. There are no breaches or cracks in the stone or concrete. At over six feet, it's pretty high. Do you think we need to reinforce it?"

"No, we can take care of it." Luther threw him a wink. Carl nodded his understanding. Luther added, "Will you check the front gate? I know we usually leave it open, but let's keep it closed for now."

"Good idea," agreed Maria Elena.

"Will do."

"We'll give the code to the girls and William." Looking to Carl, Luther continued, "Please look into upgrading the key device. The cover can be pretty rough to handle in winter." He drained his tea. "Has the contractor finished the specs for the gatehouse?"

"I'm on my way there now to pick them up. I'll check the back gate and close the front on my way out. I'd better test the intercom. Maria Elena, be ready for the check?"

"Ready and waiting," she said over the rim of her cup.

"See you tomorrow, Carl." Luther waited as the realization hit Carl.

"Thanks, boss! See you tomorrow. Maria Elena, thanks for the tea and pumpkin bread." He put his mug and plate in the sink, threw his napkin in the used towel basket, and left through the mudroom door.

THE STUBBY yellow school bus ambled along to Andersen Light. Georgie rode in silence. Fields of grass bent in the breeze like blonde hair from a wimpy blow dryer. Her mind wandered. Josefina's phone buzzed.

"It's Mom." Josefina read the text aloud, "Contact me once you're at the gate.'"

"Gate?"

"You didn't notice it because it's always open."

"But not today." Georgie changed the subject. "Have you recovered from today's crazy energy?"

"I guess. I confess I'm worried about Shawn, and trying not to be, which makes me more worried." Josefina bit the corner of her lip.

"Worried? You're not a worrier." She gently shoulder bumped her friend. "Luther and your mom will tell us more this afternoon and we can relax."

They rolled to a stop. Nancy announced, "Luther's Lane!" The gate, painted to blend into the rock wall, stood in plain sight, closed.

"I may already know the code, unless they've changed it." Josefina faced the gate's metal keypad entry box. "It's been awhile since I used it." Georgie lingered quietly for Josefina to receive her Mom's message. "It's a new number," Josefina said suddenly. "Come watch." She swung open the weather protection cover, punched in numbers, and pressed her index finger on a sensor pad. A small light at the base of the keypad flickered, followed by a clunk. The gate drew itself behind the wall.

TODAY'S TRAINING would begin outside. Georgie and Josefina rushed up the spiral staircase and dumped their bags in the third floor guest room. Josefina had suggested last week they leave exercise clothes in the wardrobe, just in case. Georgie grabbed a t-shirt and running pants, then made a mental note to leave an extra pair of training shoes here too.

Luther and Maria Elena waited near the foyer, he with his navy blue fisher's cap and she in her herb and fairy patterned apron. Maria Elena handed them each a stainless steel water bottle and retreated to the kitchen. "Have fun!" she volleyed over her shoulder.

The girls rushed around Luther and out to the front steps.

Josefina spoke into her phone in an official tone, "Stopwatch."

"Georgie, are you ready?" Luther asked.

"Yeah!" She shook her legs out and pawed at the walkway with her sneakered feet. Her hands tingled. She could finally let go.

Luther stepped down to the sidewalk. "We will measure your speed and time you from where this walkway meets the circular drive." He bent down and drew a white chalk line. "You'll run to the front gate and back to this line, slightly over a mile. First, I will measure you for baselines, then you may stretch and take a couple of warmup laps around *Peaceful Seas.*" He tapped the toe of his boot on the chalk line. "Return here."

"Okay."

He briefly held her wrist, then made notes in his notebook. "You are within good meta-normal range." Her forehead creased at her third eye. "The pulse rate is normal, for an extremely excited human."

"Oh, okay." *Was that a joke?* She handed her water bottle to Josefina whose expression snickered, "This is going to be good."

Georgie stretched in a modified lunge on the fountain's low wall. Next, she pulled each arm back and away in wide stretches. She twisted her torso, clasped her hands behind her head, then bent forward, extended, and held her ankles with her hands.

Luther jotted in his notebook and Josefina practiced with her stopwatch app as Georgie ran circles around the fountain. After six rounds she loped over.

"I was in track and field in my old school." Unexpectedly, Georgie understood she wouldn't be on the Mystic Creek teams. She swallowed hard and tightened her ponytail.

"Oh?" He raised his eyebrows. "Did you discover marked increase in your times?"

"I did run a lot faster this last summer." *Probably because I was mad at Jackass.*

"Who's Jackass?" asked Josefina.

Crap. I keep forgetting they can hear what I'm thinking. "He was my stepfather. It's a long story."

"A story for another day," Luther said. "But, you were right. Your anger and frustration at the situation initially prompted your abilities. Meta-normals often exhibit around a significant event sometime after we are thirteen. It occurred for me when my brother, his best friend, and my uncles enlisted for the war." He laid his hand on Josefina's shoulder. "Although the development of Josefina's intuition had begun, her other gifts were triggered by the infamous dodgeball incident. More of yours were too, such as your strength." He studied Georgie's heart and respiratory rates. Both remained normal. "Everyone ready?" Luther steered Josefina a few steps back off the walkway with him, clasped his hands together and pointed. "Georgie, from that chalk line." She assumed the crouched start position. "Ready, set, go!"

Georgie launched in a blur. He gave silent thanks for the high wall surrounding the grounds. He would speak with Carl tomorrow on ways to increase the gate's decorative iron work to provide better privacy. She made it to the gate and was heading back. Josefina faced the chalk line and hovered her index finger over her phone. In less time than it took to blink, Georgie passed the fountain, crossed the line and was up the steps. Her foot kicked a stainless steel water bottle which missed a window, but crashed into one of Maria Elena's autumn flower beds taking out a few chrysan-themum blooms.

"Oops!"

"Two forty eight—that's impossible!" Josefina exclaimed. "It's faster than the world record, held by a full-grown man!"

"I can do better." She peered around Josefina's arm to see the time for herself. Luther took her wrist and held it. "I was off. I had Jackass in my head, but once I got him out, I . . . "

" . . . flew!" finished Josefina.

Luther released her wrist, completed his notes, and clapped her on the shoulder. "It was a good first run." He stowed his notebook in his pocket. "Let's go up, team."

Georgie retrieved her errant bottle from the flower bed, took a quick slug of remaining water, and was beside Josefina in a flash. The two trooped behind Luther to the lighthouse's side entrance. The soft whoosh at the threshold hit her again. She had sort of grown accustomed to the greeting, likely an aspect of the powerful shielding surrounding Andersen Light. They spiraled up the staircase to the fourth level classroom.

Three plum-colored smoothies rested on a thick tea towel on the kitchenette's bar counter. Luther gestured, "Maria Elena's wild blueberry green smoothies are the best. Shall we?"

Luther flipped the chair in front of their desk around and sat down with his glass. Georgie slurped her drink and studied him over the rim of her glass. His eyebrows were works of art, like a squadron of dragonfly wings ready for take off. They had a kind of beauty, like rolling waves breaking on the beach, or synchronized swimmers, a team of black, silver, and charcoal hairs poised over his eyes.

"Georgie," Josefina whispered, "you're spacing out."

"Right, sorry . . ." She cleared her throat. "I'm back now."

"Please, no sorries," said Luther. "You are not in a sorry state, and it is not necessary to affirm yourself into one. Daydreaming is healthy. No need to apologize."

"Thanks." *This is what sheepish feels like.* She snuck another peek at his brows then at Josefina's straight—no, her holding-back-the-laughter—face.

Luther moved to the bar, placed his hand under the counter, and pressed a button. An invisible seam in the adjacent wide, gray metal pole cracked open and swung into two halves. Clear umbrella-like spines unfurled from the pole's interior like a slow-motion video of flower petals opening. It expanded into one wide, flat, and transparent sheet. He pushed another button. The panel became opaque and stretched into its final, rigid position, the folds of its previous accordion shape gone.

"Wow!"

He leaned toward them. "Would you like to deviate a

moment to see my favorite kind of whiteboard?" Their heads bobbed. "Envision a matrix or a web, a living, breathing, pulsing, sentient light energy which connects us all. It is infinite in every way we measure things, like time and space, or success and happiness.

"As you might imagine, there are smaller parts to the whole of the universe, like a family unit is part of a larger family tree. You and your best friend have your own connection which connects to other friends, your own families, me, and so it goes.

"Some connections are stronger because of the energy we give them. For instance, you've never met your great great-grandmothers, so little focus is given and the link is not strong. You strengthen it when you give it your attention. It is your choice where and how much energy you intentionally direct. And, as in the Native American proverb, whatever one person does to the web, she does to herself, himself, or themself."

As he spoke, his hands threw images into the air. The girls gasped. A giant web of light appeared near the ceiling. It looked crystalline, yet organic, like branches and roots of a tree pulsing with light. Another web in a new color appeared with each illustration. As webs multiplied, each connected to overlay and underlay horizontally and vertically. The ceiling pulsated with multidimensional light matrices.

Georgie gazed at Luther's glowing illustrations. The points where connections came together looked like stars. Some blinked, or did they wink? "Magical," she breathed.

"It is like magic, only better," Luther said.

"Better?" Georgie asked.

"Yes, because it is real." He beamed. His teeth gleamed white beneath his mustache. He waved a hand and the colorful connectivity dissipated from the ceiling to astonished ohs.

"But . . . ," Georgie objected.

"What was . . . ?" Josefina began.

"Ah, there'll be more at another time." Luther assured them, then redirected their attention. "Now, *this* whiteboard works with today's technology."

He held up a pen resembling a combination marker and stylus. "It works wirelessly." He drew the number one and the black number was instantly outlined, as if backlit in a muted blue. Beside it, he wrote, "Shawn" in letters which contrasted sharply against the milky, opaque screen.

2. Protection and Telepathy

3. Thought Shielding and Direction

4. Meditation

5. Summary of Initial Development Plans

He slipped the stylus into his shirt pocket. "I doubt we will get through much of this before dinner, but we will give it a go." He rejoined the girls at their table and finished his smoothie. "By the way, dinner is here tonight. Professor Jones will be joining us and taking you all home." Josefina gathered up the empty smoothie glasses and returned with lemon water.

Number three caught Georgie's eye. *Thought direction?*

"Thank you," Luther said, accepting the water. "Now, let's begin with young Mr. Green." Georgie and Josefina scooted closer. "Shawn's father and brother have developed new classified technology for the government. An employee at their research and development lab leaked information about their project, but the leak was not true to the facts."

"What do you mean?" asked Josefina.

"The employee embellished, overexaggerated the cover story. She changed the facts."

"Cover story?" asked Josefina.

"A cover story is used to describe a project in terms suitable for public consumption. They have been used throughout history to intentionally mislead would-be enemies—think of the famous Trojan horse—or, in this case, to describe the Hermes project in benign, unclassified terms. The cover story was provided to those not working directly on the project."

"So it is the story a person gets if they're not briefed in?" suggested Georgie.

"Exactly." He tilted his head to one side and narrowed his eyes.

She shrugged. "What? I read books."

"Then you can imagine how projects in research and development are at a delicate phase, and not just from an engineering or technical perspective. Fierce competition for money puts projects with the slightest hint of a hiccup at risk for cancellation."

"What does that mean for the Greens?" Georgie asked.

"On the plus side, the employee blogged a modified version of the cover story, technically not real project information. Yet even a perceived security breach is not viewed favorably. Their security team will have to shore up any problems while the program management convinces their bosses the project remains viable and stable."

"Do you think they can?" Josefina asked.

"Time will tell. The unfortunate result remains that someone has believed the fake story. He, she, or they are willing to kidnap in order to gain access to its technology."

"Do you know the *un*-cover story?" asked Georgie.

"No, but I do know this project began as an idea Derrick and Earl Green conceived in their garage workshop. Once they convinced the government of proof of concept they were funded and provided a secure lab environment in which to work."

"What is it, Mr. Luther?" asked Josefina.

"I apologize, but I have signed a security agreement for what little I know about it."

"Why?" Georgie asked. "Are you helping them with it or something?"

"Not technically. Before Derrick and Earl Green had their secure lab, the government authorized them to store sensitive and classified aspects of the project here."

"Here?" asked Georgie, dumbfounded. "Do you have some kind of secret vault?"

"As matter of fact, I do." Luther chuckled at their saucered eyes. He used his professorial voice, "This lighthouse has a long history. At a time when our country was at war, U.S. Naval and Coast Guard ships began patrolling the coasts. Lighthouses and their keepers were enlisted to aid in a complex network of secure communication, passing along information and reporting suspicious activity, among other things."

"No way," breathed Georgie.

"Yes, way. You may have noticed we have a wonderful view of the water here, making it quite easy to observe seafaring vessels."

Georgie nearly snorted her lemon water, which would not have been good.

"Good one, Mr. Luther," chuckled Josefina. "So, you can't tell us anything about the project?"

"Perhaps Mr. Green will tell you more."

Their postures sagged. He bent forward and asked in a dramatic voice, "Now, aren't you glad I can keep a secret?" They nodded slightly. "That's good," he said, now solemn, "because I must ask you to keep what I have told you to yourselves."

"You bet," agreed Georgie.

"Even from Mom?"

"Maria Elena knows this."

"Okay."

"Excellent, girls." He wriggled his eyebrows and retrieved a utility knife from his pants pocket. "Shall we seal it with a blood oath?" They answered with incredulous stares, and he paused a few seconds for effect before he stashed the knife away. "I am joking. But," his tone serious, "I never jest about the security of people, especially you two."

Georgie was first to recover. "We get the point." She laughed at her own joke. "Our lips are sealed."

Josefina rolled her eyes. "Do you think Shawn is still in danger?"

"I don't know he isn't. There is no physical proof what

happened Friday night had anything to do with Shawn. Although Mr. Green trusts the knowledge I 'receive,' he knows he can't use it to ask the government for additional security. He can, however, pass along his suspicions, point out the coincidental timing of the security leak, and attempt to correlate it with the gunmen's appearance at the high school." Their eyes narrowed. In a lighter tone, Luther said, "No matter what, we remain vigilant in our shield work for their family, right?" The girls nodded. "Very good. Do you have more questions?" He took a long drink of water.

Georgie grasped her glass. "What does Shawn know?"

"His father has asked him to minimize activities outside of school and home. I believe Shawn is unaware of the real situation. It is best we support his father until he is ready to talk with Shawn. We will reevaluate if the need arises. Derrick Green has told his sister, Darlene. Meanwhile, I ask you to continue your telepathy practices and be prepared to assist with additional shield work if necessary."

Georgie and Josefina were outwardly quiet, yet their minds whirred. Luther waited for their faces to register understanding. He witnessed their thoughts make connections, mend snags, bridge gaps, and broaden views until a new determination settled in their faces.

"We're good?" They smiled and nodded. Luther pointed over to the list on the high-tech chalkboard. "We'll pick this up next time. I believe Maria Elena and William have dinner ready." He placed two fingers on his forehead. "I see Anjou pear and arugula salad, tomato-basil soup, potato-pepper hash, and pumpkin empanadas for dessert."

"I love that hash!" Josefina pushed her chair back. "I hope she made enough empanadas for breakfast, too."

DAD UNLOCKED the front door just as Georgie's phone vibrated.

"Georgie, are you okay?" Her mother's voice soared in a frantic pitch. "Your high school was in the news—the national news!" This last was more like an accusation.

She gave Dad's cheek a goodnight peck and headed to her room. "I'm okay, Mom. I wasn't even at the school that night, remember? I texted you about the moonlight picnic. You texted back how it sounded cool, and asked who all was going. I told you Josefina, Shawn, and I had decided to go alternative and skip homecoming. Remember?"

"Oh, yes, honey. I remember now. I guess I didn't connect the dots," her voice almost normal. "Thank God you weren't there. I thought that town was safe. Nothing ever happens in Mystic Creek. It's a freakish thing no one talks about. It's like it's in its own protective bubble where people don't get mugged, the fire department always arrives in time, and nobody gets the flu. It's why I thought you'd be out of harm's way there."

"I'm sure it was a fluke. This place is very laid back." She paced around her room. "The authorities believe the men weren't from around here. Things do happen here, if you count the farmers market and weird regional dodgeball."

"That I can handle. It's when gunmen in Mystic Creek make the national news that I start freaking out!"

"I get it, Mom, people fret. This may be the most excitement Mystic Creek's ever had. But I'm fine. No need to worry. Really."

"I just want to know you're safe."

"I am. There's a whole team of adults making sure I'm okay and where I am at any given moment. Seriously, I more feel protected and at home since before you and Dad split up. I have friends here. I like my life. I even like school again." There was too much silence. "Mom, are you still there?"

"Yes, Georgie, I'm here. I am glad, dear. It's a relief to know you're happy, and safe."

"Thanks."

"Well, dear, I have a million things left to do tonight. Promise me you'll be careful."

"I will. I love you, Mom."

"I love you, too, honey. We'll talk soon."

The short conversation left Georgie uneasy. She tried to run her fingers through her hair but they tangled up in the curls. What was going on in her mother's head? What was the pause about? It came after she told her she was happy and liked it here. Did Mom feel bad because she wasn't with her, and she was happy here? Maybe Mom felt guilty about Jackass and it had nothing to do with her. That could be partly right, but it didn't feel like the whole story. One thing was for sure, she didn't want to leave Mystic Creek, especially since she just found out about being meta-normal and began training with Luther. She needed to find a way to make this okay.

She tossed her phone on the bed and dropped into the chair, too hard. The wood protested with a crack. She jumped up to check the chair for breakage. Another close call—a creak, not a crack. But it was a sign. How was she going to learn how to live with herself if she had to move? There was no way. What could she do? She obviously couldn't talk to Dad. Oh, she could imagine that conversation! "Uh, Dad, I'm a meta-normal and I need to stay here in Mystic Creek so I can learn what to do with all these abilities growing inside of me. Will you talk with Mom and get her to understand?" *Right.* Should she call Josefina, or ask Luther for his opinion, or both? *Maybe later.* Was she overreacting? She didn't like feeling this way, afraid of being uprooted again. This might be a good time to try out the meditation Luther recently taught her and Josefina, although Josefina already knew how.

Georgie kicked off her shoes, piled the bed pillows against the headboard, and leaned back. Her eyes closed, she took in a deep breath and held it for a count of three. This was the breath she was supposed to use to get in touch with her body, sense where any tension was, and release it. But worry was everywhere. Georgie settled deeper into the pillows and counted her breaths—inhale-one, exhale-two, inhale-three, exhale-four—and willed any stress to leave with the exhalations. *Ah . . . better.* Mom's voice intruded, "Georgie, are you okay?" Where was she, on inhale-seven? She started over . . . inhale-one, exhale-two.

She made it to exhale-ten before seeing an image of Harvey flying through the air, his hands and arms and abdomen wrapped around a dodgeball, his eyes all but popping out of his head. She forced herself back to her breath counts. "Acknowledge your thoughts and let them go," Luther had said. *I'd like to let go of all images of dodgeball day, but I have a feeling it will be with me forever.* Maybe she could just let go of it right now . . . six-exhale. Her nose itched . . . eight, nine in, ten out, one, two . . .

CHAPTER TWENTY-FOUR

ICE CREAM

Tuesday afternoon Georgie bolted up the spiral staircase, tossed her school bag on a chair, hopped up on a bar chair, and poured herself a lemon water. "Oh, hey, Luther." He stood in the gallery's balcony doorway with his amused, eye-crinkling grin. She gulped her water. "Josefina's doing stuff at her house today."

"Very well." He gestured to the two facing chairs in the library with his tea mug. "Today we talk about Jack."

She dropped into her usual chair. "Jackass?"

"Yes."

"Okay, though I'm not sure why."

He bestowed his encouraging smile. "Yes, well, that is part of it, isn't it? You said you had him in your head during yesterday's run."

"Yeah." Her fingers tapped the chair's arm.

"Our goal today is to begin to change your reactions so stray thoughts of him will no longer affect you. We neutralize the charge to similar situations or people, and weaken the triggers and responses to emotional memories. You have immense power within you. You need not dilute or give this power away—to him, or people and circumstances which remind you of him. Shall we continue?"

The finger tapping stopped. Her bottom lip stilled between her teeth.

"This involves complete self-honesty. Where in your body do you first feel a response when you hear Jack's name?"

Taken off guard, she managed, "Uh . . . my stomach."

"Anywhere else?"

"My throat, like it's tight."

"Okay."

"And my hand twitches like it wants to smack someone."

"Really?" One eyebrow's synchronized swim team raised their arms.

"No," she laughed, "but I can imagine hurtling him into deep space."

His lips curled to one side. "I see that, but let us circle our focus back to the other two reactions, beginning with the feeling in your solar plexus. What feelings or ideas could you name to this quite literal gut reaction?"

She considered as he sipped his tea. "Rejection, like I reject him—everything about him."

"Go on."

"Disgust and fear." She grimaced and pushed deeper into her chair.

"Whatever you felt is okay. You know what you like and what you do not."

"Exactly." She straightened her posture. "I don't like what he said, what he did, or whatever he probably thought."

"You sensed the tone of his thoughts."

"Right, and sometimes I knew what he was going to say."

"So you know what you didn't like. What did you like?"

"I liked how it was when he wasn't there—we could breathe and play and joke around. I liked how Mom would smile more and laugh with us."

"Okay, let's turn it all into ice cream."

She gaped. "What?"

"You know what you like and don't like, so let's look at the menu. Right alongside the usual selections of vanilla, chocolate, butter pecan, rocky road, and black cherry are the feeling good, joking around, smile-like-you-mean-it, and Jack flavors. Which do you choose to have in your life, to feel in your stomach today?"

"Oh, I must have chocolate, some feeling good, joking around, smile-like-you-mean-it, a dab of black cherry, and whip cream." Georgie smiled.

"You know what you like."

"I know what I like."

"There may be Jack on the menu, or someone might bring Jack to a potluck. You decide what you want. Put another way, you focus on what you want. How is your stomach now?"

"It still feels a little funny."

"And your throat?"

"It feels better, clearer."

"Let's take a walk."

They descended the beach trail and headed north with a light sea breeze. She admired the silvery white parts of Luther's hair sparkling in the afternoon sun. "Why the sudden walk?"

"Walking helps sort and balance. Thoughts fall into place, understandings dawn, and ideas bubble up."

"All that from walking?" Skepticism crept into her tone.

"And more. Walking engages us in multiple ways. It calls on both sides of the brain which affects, among other things, thought, emotion, and creativity. On an energetic level, we are literally in motion. Walking raises our vibration which positively influences our physical world. One affects the other, and so on. Everything is connected."

She pictured yesterday's webs of pulsing light on Luther's favorite "whiteboard" and kicked a rock off the path. "So what are we doing now?"

"We are giving you the opportunity to know, on many levels, how Jack is a person outside of you."

"I guess I know that much."

"Yet there is still the stomach response."

"You're not wrong."

"We walk in order to jiggle loose those feelings, to let them fly away in this breeze." He grinned. "See, your brain is on fire now."

Georgie raised her brow. "Is that what is happening?"

"Yes, indeed." Their trail took a wide curve into Clammer's Cove. "Let us review. We've identified your body's physical responses to your emotional reactions to Jack. Follow?"

"Yeah." The playful breeze danced around them. She pulled a strand of hair from her mouth.

"Next we relate those reactions to thoughts."

"Okay. . . ."

"Of those thoughts, you were clear about the ones you liked and didn't like."

"Right." She was catching on now. "And you used ice cream to show me I can choose what I think."

"Exactly," he replied, "yet there were lingering physical and emotional responses in your body to the memories."

She nodded in agreement.

"You can choose how you remember."

"Oh, really?" Her eyebrows scrunched together.

"History did occur, and what you thought during the events created certain responses in you. But your reactions to those events can be changed, now. You can rethink them. Essentially, you can remember them how you choose."

"Hmm."

"Jack, let's call him an unenlightened entity."

"You're generous."

"The thoughts, words, and actions of the unenlightened entity were separate from you. They were not caused or created by you, your mother, Bill, or Rose. You agree?"

"Yeah, I see."

"The fear response in your stomach was normal. There was real danger to you and your family. The subtle choking or holding back sensation in your throat was a natural reaction to being told not to tell your mother what was going on." She raised her hand to her throat and slowed her pace until she stopped. He took her hands and looked into her eyes. "The danger has passed now and you have spoken. You are safe. You are here, now. Any remaining sensations are residual memory."

"And I can choose new sensations, how I relate my feelings with memories."

"Precisely. Memories, like accounts of events throughout time, can also help you recognize similar situations or people." She kept pace as he turned back toward the lighthouse. "You may view historical memories as tools in your tool chest. They aid your intuition."

"For example?"

"If you feel a similar sensation in your throat, you will know, from your own past, someone is trying to muzzle you—even if that someone is you." They hiked for a time in silence.

"I think I understand."

"You may sense fear in your stomach when your intuition is telling you there is danger."

More silence, then, "I get it."

"Excellent! Another successful excursion into the ways of thoughts and intuition. We'll revisit this, add new methodology to your meditations, and employ different techniques as needed, like tapping."

Georgie gave him a sideways glance.

"How about a bowl of Maria Elena's ice cream?"

"I'm with you!"

CHAPTER TWENTY-FIVE

A FEW ADJUSTMENTS

Georgie strode alongside Josefina up Luther's Lane into a brisk afterschool breeze. She shoved her hands into jacket pockets against the autumn chill and cinched her scarf closer—to fend off both the cool air and interloping memory of Mom's panicked phone call. Yesterday's work with Luther had been an intense distraction, but she went to sleep with the call on her mind. She felt kind of bad about fretting over Mom with Black Jacket Man slinking around the school. Georgie didn't even know if her mom was thinking about moving her. She peeked at Josefina. Dark pink edged her ears and nose.

"What?"

"Your ears and nose are pink."

"So are yours."

"And, well, my mom kind of freaked out about the homecoming raid. She saw it in the news. I'm worried she might move me back with her."

"But it was a freak incident. At least that's what the town thinks."

"Yeah, I told her."

"Well, stop worrying. You don't want to attract what you're worrying about, do you?"

"Duh."

"Let's talk to my mom and Luther." She added, "If you'd like."

Bright new stools graced the kitchen worktable. Georgie swiveled into one between Luther and Josefina. Maria Elena's hot chocolate and warm almond flour raspberry scones hit the spot, and she hesitated to bring up the topic of her mom. Maybe she was paranoid about the whole moving thing, but part of her didn't think so. She sipped the cocoa and searched Josefina's profile for the words and will to speak.

"Georgie's worried," Josefina announced as if briefing the day's news.

She started to "thank" her for spilling the beans, but stopped at Josefina's I'm-trying-to-help expression.

"What is it, *mija*?" Maria Elena asked.

Everyone studied Georgie as she related the phone call with Mom and her fears of having to leave. "I love it here. Dad and I are closer." She looked around the table. "I have a best friend. I love coming here to Andersen Light and spending time with you. How else would I learn about being a meta? I can't imagine living somewhere else."

"It's normal for your mother to think of your safety, *mija*. Did she say something to make you believe she might take some sort of action?"

"It's what she didn't say. I told her what I just said to you, except for the meta part."

"Keep in mind your mother also contends with changes in her new life," Luther said.

"It couldn't have been easy to see the news about Mystic Creek High, made scarier in national media," Josefina offered.

"Yeah, I should have called her right away."

"It's done. No amount of 'shoulding yourself' will make you feel better," said Maria Elena.

Shoulding—Georgie liked the word. "You're right."

"Your mother might feel better if she could see for herself where you spend your time," Maria Elena suggested.

"She's been in Mystic Creek before. I was born here. Has she been to the lighthouse?"

"No," Luther explained, "your family moved away after you were born. Subsequent visits to your grandparents did not present the opportunity, although we were well acquainted."

"Should we invite her?" *If Mom had the chance to look around and meet everybody maybe she'd be glad I am here.*

"Your mother is welcome to stay in a guest house." Luther and Maria Elena locked eyes. His tone changed. "We have been planning to speak with your family."

What? "Why? Is something wrong?"

"No, everything is fine." Including Josefina, he said, "You are both eager to learn. Training is progressing well. But we must proceed with care as Georgie's skills develop, and as Josefina's gifts become outwardly apparent. This environment is better suited to developing your abilities, especially for those manifesting physically. . . ."

"This environment?" Josefina interjected, her face taut.

"We have been discussing a few adjustments," Luther said, "one of which is inviting you all to move to Andersen Light."

"What?" Georgie asked, echoed by Josefina.

A restless quiet settled around the table, the shuffling of thoughts palpable. Georgie's own were frenetic. *What about my family? What would Dad say? I would miss him. Would Mom agree? It'd be good not to have to literally watch everything I do all the time. Where would I sleep? Would everyone agree to it? How would it work? What about Dad?*

"What?" Josefina repeated, and leaned away from the table, her eyes seriously wide. *Was she in shock?* "What about our house? What about Adolfo? Where would he live? Where would we live?"

Maria Elena placed her teacup into its saucer with a soft tinkle.

A delicate sensation of warmth came over Georgie, followed by a vague sense of peace. Judging from her visibly relaxing shoulders, Josefina felt it too. "This won't happen for a while, perhaps after the holidays, or in the New Year," Maria Elena explained. "Adolfo's employment will likely take him away from Mystic Creek when he graduates, but we'll keep our house for now. You and Georgie will each have rooms on the third floor of the lighthouse."

"What about you? Where will you be?"

"Where I always am when we stay overnight, in the first guest house."

Josefina's stare bordered on a scowl. "I see," she replied stiffly.

"The news is sudden, but I can assure you there has been considerable deliberation," Luther stated. "Georgie's concern regarding her mother moving her away from Mystic Creek only accelerates this conversation."

Georgie squirmed on the new kitchen stool and sneaked another look at Josefina. She didn't like being the reason for her friend's discomfort.

Luther's voice softened. "We are aware this will be an uprooting change, right on the heels of learning who you are." He caught their eyes. "We must all adjust our lives at times in order to thrive."

"What do other new metas do?" Georgie was curious.

"Exactly!" cried Josefina. "They can't all move to lighthouses."

"Some live rigidly secretive lives. A number of regions have training schools. Your regional training is right here at Andersen Light." He winked. "I am confident you will easily assimilate before you finish high school."

"Funny," Georgie said, then her mind blew back. "Other regions? How many? Where?"

Luther enjoyed her inquisitiveness. "We are not the only meta-normals here in Mystic Creek. You will soon learn of the others."

Maria Elena asked, her voice tender, "Beyond surprise, *mijas*, how do you feel?"

"I'm not sure how I feel, exactly. I guess I'm okay." Josefina conceded, "We're here most of the time, anyway. It makes sense. Everything has been crazy different since school started. There's the thing with Shawn. Now this. It's so . . . tumultuous."

"True," Georgie agreed. "But, I'm not sure how my family will take to the idea."

"Your mother's visit will provide the perfect occasion to confer with your parents," assured Luther.

Maria Elena placed a basket covered with a blue plaid tea towel next to Josefina, and an arm around her shoulders. "Please carry these sandwiches up to the gallery with you, *mija*."

GEORGIE AND JOSEFINA settled onto their sofa in front of the fireplace. Luther's firehose session on telepathy had cracked Georgie's block to tele-receiving. Neither girl had much focus for the homework now sprawled around them on the sofa and glass top of the tree table.

LUTHER RESTED with Maria Elena in the gallery. "Did you mention Thursday's meeting?"

He reached for her hand before he answered. "Yes, I explained it is a protection strategy meeting. The girls are keen to meet the others."

CHAPTER TWENTY-SIX

LUTHER AND MARIA ELENA

Womenfolk gone for the day, Luther leaned on the balcony outside his sitting room. He faced the sea's horizon but scanned the terrain of the last several days. Andersen Light patrolled the buffalo-shaped cloud masses roaming across the sliver of waning Blood Moon before scattering across the stars. Overall, he was satisfied with today's progress and could move forward to logistics and family concurrence. There had been many nights like this when he had gazed at the stars and contemplated Georgie coming to live and train here.

Ah, but more than one change is afoot. The decades-old plan metamorphosed to include Maria Elena and Josefina, a natural progression given they had long been like family. He had known Maria Elena all her life. Her parents, Marco and Elena Magdalena, had worked at Andersen Light, and before them, her grandmother, and great-grandmother. Luther was a boy when Maria Elena's grandfather Alejandro worked the lantern and grounds before going off to war with his brother and uncles.

Luther had come home from school occasionally, but his ultimate return occurred after attaining advanced degrees followed by his many internships with the world's meta-normal regional mentors, assignments which had been arranged by Oma herself. As result, Luther returned long after Maria Elena left for his alma mater, the esteemed United Kingdom meta-normal university that fanned the fire of her interest in the natural world. He recalled with sharp clarity the day his mother revealed Maria Elena had met a young man, Josef Adolfo Garcia. They married after her graduation. Her husband's sudden death of heart failure within months of the birth of their second child, Josefina, was a devastating shock, unexpected even to a family of seers.

Luther worked at Andersen Light while he developed meta-normal teaching programs when Maria Elena moved back. She brought her young son and baby daughter to live with her parents. The woman she had been, a student alive with curiosity and bride filled with hope, returned a wilted young widow. Yet, she rapidly grew stronger as she fashioned gardens in the earth and worked alongside her mother at the lighthouse. Thinking back to those earlier times, he chuckled to himself.

"Digging in the dirt suits you," he'd told her.

She stood, trowel in hand, eyes ablaze. "Yes, I prefer it to the mundane." She looked him over. "Or to the grease of the garage."

He glanced down at his oil-stained coveralls. "If only you knew of the magic we make in our often spotless workshop." He produced a thermos. "Please accept this iced tea, from your mother."

"Well, if it's from my mother." She took the thermos eagerly, her good nature returning. "Thank you, sincerely." She chugged at the tea. "I have heard of your so-called magic, though I have yet to witness the results."

"I heartily extend my personal invitation to tour our workshop."

She smiled and offered a drink which he accepted, though he wasn't thirsty.

They became fast friends once again. His willing ear and words of encouragement provided solace in the years following Josef's death and those of their parents. The two became intellectual, as well as spiritual colleagues, deliberating ideas and concepts with the ardor of young students. While both the business of running Andersen Light as well as meta-normal matters brought them together, they made room for outings with Adolfo and Josefina. Long coastal and mountain drives, picnics, Sunday dinners, and family birthdays were regular affairs.

Luther mentored Adolfo and involved him in after-school activities around Andersen Light with Carl Nelson and himself. He encouraged the boy's fascination for engineering and the environment, and provided a college scholarship. Luther and Maria Elena jointly included Josefina as she grew curious of lighthouse and garden activities. They were mindful not to venture into meta-normal conversation so that tendencies of the children would surface naturally.

Neither had noticed, for a very long time, something more made them especially attentive to one another. He couldn't pinpoint the exact moment when he became aware his love for Maria Elena had grown beyond friend and coworker to the boundaryless domain of his soul's heart. They accepted their camaraderie without question or comment. It did not seem unusual for Maria Elena and the children to go home at the end of each day. Likewise, over the years he had accepted their expanding love without question, regarding it as normal given their years of familiarity, and a likely effect of their spiritual growth.

These days he was acutely conscious of it being more. Though he had not yet given voice to his feelings, he held the notion that the two of them had always been evolving, ever slowly, toward a more personal love. Daily interactions were an easy, seamless, unchoreographed dance—intuitive and companionable, with a timeless familiarity which more recently brought them closer, as if an angelic realm urged them forward. Their smiles wore longer, their arms brushed more often, and the touch of a hand lingered, suspended in place and time.

He lifted his mug to his lips and held Maria Elena in his mind. She captivated him. Meta-normal aging radically decelerated around the twenty-fifth year, yet years could affect neither her inner nor outer beauty. Maria Elena's loveliness was itself meta-normal.

The two had spoken often of Oma's prophecy of Georgie, "a soul of greater potential and expectation than we have yet known." Only with time would he and Maria Elena learn what faculties would evolve. They respected the importance of protecting both Georgie and Josefina.

The dodgeball incident, which truly ignited her meta-normal gifts, created an urgency for Georgie's relocation to Andersen Light. Previously, the view into what talents she would develop remained shrouded. She had the potential for any and all meta-normal traits, and possibly some yet to be categorized. However, her physical gifts, the most difficult to camouflage and deflect unwanted attention, were the first to manifest.

Georgie's escalating strength and speed would launch her off the meta-normal chart, but also demanded further training. He and Maria Elena would work with her as long as they could before reinforcing their team. No meta-normal had developed to the extent Georgie was expected to grow. Besides Luther, few around the globe were capable of giving their assistance. *Ah, those concerns are for the ifs and whens of it.*

Josefina's growing capabilities complemented Georgie's. Training the two of them proved especially effective, as evidenced by their recent telepathic practice. Maria Elena's skills were keenly suited to aid him in guiding the girls through many of the more esoteric lessons.

He and Maria Elena would prepare for the move, talk over the wheres and hows, and present them to Georgie's parents without the use of meta-normal influence. Georgie and Josefina would have another weekend sleepover in the lighthouse, while Georgie's mother stayed in the guest house next to Maria Elena's. The way was paved for the parents' approval. He would proffer invitations right away.

CHAPTER TWENTY-SEVEN

MEET THE METAS

There was no evidence of trouble save the gravelly-edged feeling in Luther's solar plexus. He stayed with the awareness, but got on with scheduling the emergency meeting of the local meta-normals to discuss protection for Derrick Green and his family. It would be an afternoon of acquainting, serious discussion, and light refreshments.

Georgie and Josefina would officially meet the area meta-normals, most of whom they knew or had met in passing, just not as meta-normals. As regional mentor, he could call for any of them at any time, but rarely did so outside of meta-normal lightworking missions. These were good people and a joy to be with. A pang of wistfulness stirred and he resolved to gather together more often.

Mystic Creek Chief of Police Phil Ganzhorn accepted right away, glad to attend, as he put it, Luther's "meta-normal hootenanny." Luther laughed and thanked him. Chief Ganzhorn was a powerful intuitive and clairvoyant, abilities he used quietly and regularly in his work.

Next, Luther called Peggy Hanna, a local waitress and famous author who wrote under a pseudonym. An intuitive, she also had the gifts of strength, endurance, flexibility, and extreme coordination, the last of which she regularly exhibited to unsuspecting patrons of Skipper's Diner. Peggy confirmed she was off Thursday, "Count me in."

He moved down the list, tapped in the number for Nancy Blackeagle, a cross-sport assistant coach at Mystic High, school bus driver and protector, then Melanie Ball, local artist and empath-healer, both of whom happily accepted his invitation.

CARL WAITED at the front gate. Luther had asked him to set up new identification and authentication codes, including thumbprints, for each guest as they entered the estate. He encouraged Carl to take the rest of the afternoon off once everyone was inside.

Freshened up, Luther gave himself a friendly wink in the mirror and left his room to find Maria Elena. He smiled to himself. Maria Elena's idea of light refreshments meant no one left hungry. She stood over the oversized wooden worktable cutting sandwiches into triangular quarters. The fresh ingredients came from the year-round herb and kitchen gardens she had developed using both ancient and breakthrough organic methodologies.

"Everything looks scrumptious, Maria Elena." Dips and sauces complimented an arrangement of sliced pitas, home baked, ripple-cut sweet potato chips, and vases arranged with vegetable spears. Cake plates delicately stacked with slices of her delicious pumpkin-zucchini bread anchored one end.

She handed him a sandwich triangle. "We better give these the taste test."

"Mmm," he murmured. The bread was hearty but not heavy. Its filling held a hint of sweet basil. *Delicioso.*

She gave him the once over. "You look ready, too."

"I pass muster?"

Her mouth broke into a dimpled smile. "As always."

"And you, Maria Elena, are a beautiful, magnificent cook and charming host. Shall we?" They readied the table. He followed the image she shared telepathically to arrange dishes.

Georgie and Josefina bounced through the front door, disappeared, then reemerged with combed hair and fresh faces to volunteer to carry the drink pitchers.

Maria Elena set a teapot on the table and stepped back.

"I love it, Mom," said Josefina. A large sunflower stood in a tall pottery vase surrounded by autumn leaves. "Sunflowers are still alive?"

"Your mom still has a few surprises, *mija*."

"Yes, she does," Luther agreed. "I'd like to remind the teenagers in the party that all our guests are meta-normals. This afternoon provides an excellent opportunity to practice your shielding techniques—for thoughts *and* feelings."

"He means you," Josefina stage whispered to Georgie, garnering a shoulder bump.

"If not," he continued, "that is okay, too. You are safe and among friends. Now, I believe the first of our guests has arrived."

Everyone hastened to the entrance. Luther swung open the heavy wooden door as the doorbell's signature foghorn sounded.

"Chief Ganzhorn, welcome. It is good to see you." Maria Elena hugged the chief and Luther took his trench coat and wide brimmed fedora. The chief assumed a formal posture when introduced to Georgie and Josefina. He shook their hands and gave no sign he noticed the girls stammered their nice-to-meet-yous.

Though Georgie struggled to prevent projecting her mental correlation of the man in front of her with the one in her memory, Luther clearly witnessed her image of the chief standing in front of the student body. He patted her shoulder, suggested she and Josefina walk their guest to the fireplace, then turned to open the door for Peggy Hanna and Melanie Ball.

Georgie returned to the foyer to escort Peggy and Melanie. It was weird, out of context, to see them here. "Peggy, I saw you at Skipper's, right?"

"That's right."

"Oh! My dad doesn't know about the meta . . . ?"

"Your secret is safe with me." Her wink was so fast Georgie almost missed it. The woman's makeup and clothes were softer today. A perplexing wrap in soft, natural fiber draped in subtle movement around her curves.

"I met you at the farmers market," said Melanie who wore a version of the long flowing dress she'd had on at the market, also in lavenders, blues, and greens.

"Exactly! I remember. Josefina and I bought . . . ," started Georgie. "Wait, please don't think anything. Those are gifts," she whispered. "I tend to forget about the thought-listening mind readers lurking about."

Peggy and Melanie acquainted or reacquainted themselves with Josefina and hugged Chief Ganzhorn after which laughter immediately filled the air. Georgie didn't hear the joke but did catch Maria Elena and Luther next to the piano. She held his face in place and gently dabbed at lipstick marks on his cheek with a handkerchief. *Okay, then.*

Georgie glanced at the chief and her mind again flooded with images of Principal Storey introducing him to the student body. Self-conscious, she sought to bring up her shielding, but that horse had escaped through the gaping barn door. Worse, he was coming her way.

"It's okay, kid," he said. "You'll get it with practice." Grinning changed his face. It was kindly, crinkly, and somewhat sparkly. He held her hands. His were big, dry, and warm. Her earlier mortification dissipated and she liked him instantly. She returned his smile. "How do you like it here in Mystic Creek?" he asked.

"I love it here, Chief Ganzhorn."

"Kid, you can call me Chief Phil, or," he added in a conspiratorial tone, "just Chief." His gruff voice juxtaposed a kindly grin.

"Uh, thanks, Chief."

The others drew near.

Luther said, "Nancy Blackeagle has checked her bus in and is on her way."

"Nancy?" asked a stunned Georgie.

"Yes," Luther replied. "She drives your bus and is an assistant P.E. coach at your school." He winked. "It is good to have someone on the inside."

"This day is loaded with surprises," Georgie said to Josefina.

"You can say that again."

"Something to drink, anyone?" offered Maria Elena. Peggy and Melanie joined her at the dining table.

The foghorn moaned and Georgie and Josefina hightailed it to receive Nancy. Rustlings of mock formal introductions accompanied their distinctive giggles as they crossed the great hall. Nancy's work uniform—khaki pants and polo shirt in the Mystic Creek High crimson and gray—contrasted with her Native jewelry, bracelet cuff, and matching earrings intricately fashioned in silver. Her thick, shiny black hair grew back from a shorter cut, accentuating a roundish face, and wide smile. The others welcomed her with hugs and affectionate exclamations of long-time-no-see. Nancy was the youngest meta, not counting Georgie and Josefina, and her easy laugh and bouncing gait expressed her happiness to be with them.

Luther shared his *curandero* meditation with the encircled group and fielded initial questions before Maria Elena and Peggy steered everyone to the dining room. As always, there was no chair at the table's head. Luther took his usual place at the end closest to the kitchen, his back to the veranda door and windows.

Georgie faced the seaside, next to Josefina, and across from Chief Phil. She worked to shield her random thoughts, difficult through her awe of all the meta-normals sitting at the same table.

Josefina leaned over and whispered, "You're doing great."

Georgie thanked her but didn't miss the irony of whispering at a table full of people who could hear you thinking. She almost laughed out loud, but held her breath for a couple of seconds. Relieved she'd stifled her laugh, she let out her breath louder than planned and the entire table cracked up. While embarrassed, she had to laugh with them. *Who needs an ice breaker?*

A second round of laughter dissipated. Luther thanked the Great Creator for providing, Maria Elena for preparing, and everyone for coming and being who they are. They passed food around family style and caught up with each other's latest goings on. The conversation turned to the subject of the Greens and their connection to the homecoming raid. Georgie's every sense activated. The table fell quiet as Maria Elena described her visions from the night the men showed up at the high school looking for Shawn. She spoke clearly and deliberately, giving every detail. It was the first time Georgie had heard the full telling. A different cadence to Maria Elena's speech accompanied the distant look on her face, as if she relived it right then and there. She identified the boat that sped away into the night as *Halcón con Sombra*. Georgie mentally translated—*Shadow Hawk*, like her dream about Shawn!

Chief Phil slid his plate of angular sandwiches aside and took out an official-looking, black leather notebook. Georgie fixed on the flipped up cover, the embossed Mystic Creek Police Department emblem, on him jotting notes—and rocketed back to Starkton.

On the couch with Rose, Georgie held her breath as Deputy Susan Jensen took notes in her black leather notebook. She was in shock at what had happened with Jackass, upset she had been surprised, worried about Rose, and scared at what could have been. Her scalp prickled. Everything felt taut, as if she clenched every muscle, especially those in her abdomen, and her hands were sweaty, but cold.

The vision, or whatever it was, lasted only seconds, then she was back. Two hands held hers under the table, one Josefina's and the other Melanie's. Her chest was tight and it was hard to breathe. A sensation of comfort moved up her arm and throughout her body until the tension eased. Melanie's hand relaxed but remained firm and Josefina's held tight. Afraid to look away, Georgie stared at the black notebook. Everyone must be looking at her. Tears threatened. The bathing comfort from Melanie was stronger than the urge to run.

Georgie, the memory has resurfaced for you to let it go. You are safe and loved here.

It was Luther. She forced her eyes to move to his. He wore a soft smile. Slowly, she glanced around the table. Every face held encouragement. She transmitted, no shield. *I hear you, Luther.* Verbally, she said, "Loud and clear."

"Your visions will be as powerful as that memory, kid, but stronger," said Chief Phil, "and with multidimensional clarity." He focused on her as if she were the only one in the room.

Her eyes tightened. She stared back and moved her head in acknowledgement.

"He's right, *mija*." Maria Elena embraced Georgie around her chair's back. "Your experiences are catalysts and serve to make you a deeper, more capable person. They sculpt you within and increase your capacity for empathy and spiritual understanding."

"And clairvoyance," added Chief Phil.

"Clair-everything, girl," said Peggy. Her eyes twinkled.

"I never thought of it like that." Under the table, Georgie squeezed Josefina's hand and released it to take a drink of her cider. She released Melanie's hand and thanked her. "I'm not sure what you did there, but it really helped."

"Melanie is an empath and healer, with the convenient twist of being able to transmit just the right remedy to help counteract emotional . . . distraction," Luther said. "Just now, she sent you comfort to aid your distress and allow you to relax and regain clarity." He glanced at Josefina. "Josefina, also an empath, felt your suffering. Her grip anchored you to your here and now, and brought your attention back to your body, to your hands in particular." He inclined his head. "Good team work."

"Thanks, everyone," she met the chief's eyes and returned his smile. A chorus of voices and laughter erupted as she asked, "Can I eat now?"

Tinkling glasses and delighted murmurs over Maria Elena's so-called light fare intermingled as conversation meandered back to the Greens.

"Luther," Peggy asked conversationally, "what made Shawn Green the gunmen's target?"

Luther leaned forward. "Chief?"

"Please, Luther," he returned, "you've been in contact with Derrick Green."

"Very well. I suspect the intruders anticipated Shawn would lead them to the black box Derrick and Earl Green built for the government."

"Black box?" asked Nancy.

Luther explained, "It is a generic term for a classified item or project—Project Hermes, in this case. An employee from their research and development lab leaked an embellished version of the project cover story. Someone is pursuing something that doesn't exist, or at least not in the form they think it does. Whatever the details, it is of keen interest to whoever the intruders work for. Derrick and Earl were deployed at sea for testing the night the men searched for the black box. The Greens' carriage house/home research lab had been broken into once before, but this time it was tossed. The intruders may have settled on taking Shawn when they didn't find the box, or it was their intent all along. It is still a mystery as to why they didn't enter the family home."

Josefina cleared her throat and took a drink of her cider. Georgie adjusted her posture.

Luther asked, "Is there something you girls would like to tell us?"

"Well, Georgie and I chose Shawn's house to practice our shield work on."

"Yeah, exactly," said Georgie. The hall rang with laughter.

Metas sure laugh a lot. And, come to think of it, they wink a lot, too. Chagrined, Georgie realized she hadn't shielded, again.

"You see, Luther," Chief Phil said, and wiped a tear from his eye, "there's a perfectly meta-normal explanation." Guffaws followed.

"Way to go, girls!" Nancy beamed and raised her fist in solidarity.

"I am proud of you," Maria Elena said. "You likely saved Darlene Green's life that night, and those of her guests as well."

"What's that?" asked the chief.

"Darlene was hosting a party for the Botanical Gardens volunteers. In my vision, the men peered into the windows at her guests, and left. At first I thought they took off because there were so many people. They proceeded from there to the high school." The girls dove at the bowl of hummus with pita triangles. *Use your plates, mijas.* They spooned hummus onto plates and grabbed sweet potato chips. Maria Elena continued, "We initiated shielding later that night. Looks like the girls were already doing it." A grin dimpled her cheek.

Luther stretched a long arm and high-fived them. "Keep up the good work, girls."

Once the laughs died down, his face grew serious as he looked around the table. "The Greens' safety is the primary reason I asked you all here today. Members of the Green family have been allies of meta-normals for generations."

"Allies?" asked Georgie.

"There have always been individuals throughout history whose keen minds and huge hearts can contain the knowledge of people like us. We call them allies—believers who are not meta-normal, but on whom we rely for their discretion and cooperation. Many demonstrate remarkable human capacity and have purposefully or naturally developed skills such as intuition and telepathy. Derrick Green and his sister inherited their knowledge from their mother, Nordeen. It is an oral tradition."

"What kind of tradition?" Georgie asked.

"An oral tradition is knowledge passed by word of mouth. Explanatory drawings or notes are destroyed immediately, typically burned."

"Who knows? Does Shawn know?" Josefina asked.

"Darlene and Derrick Green have known since long before Nordeen made her transition from this earth plane. They passed the knowledge to Earl when he was a college student. I am not aware that Shawn has been told, yet." Luther shot a meaningful glance to Josefina and Georgie. "That is up to his father."

"Is Carl an ally?" asked Georgie.

"Yes, as was his father and mother, Thomas and Betty Nelson," Luther replied.

"Right." Memories from a day she helped out with her grand-parents' deck resurfaced.

"Betty and her sister Jane, your great-grandmother, were both allies. Jane shared their history with your grandmother Grace when she was a child, but Grace has since forgotten."

"How did the men get the photo of Shawn?" asked Peggy.

Chief Phil responded. "The high school's administrative data-base was illegally accessed." He slipped something out of the back of his notebook and passed it to Maria Elena. "Is this the image from your vision?"

"Yes, that's it," Maria Elena replied.

"That confirms it. This is his school I.D photo. I'll put a call into the school board about beefing up their network security." He turned to Luther. "We think these perpetrators got the Green name from the project's cover story?"

Luther nodded. "Their names would have been listed as project managers or lead engineers. Knowing what we do now, that listing proved to be an operations security weakness."

"Yes, it did," the chief agreed. "What do we know about this person who leaked the fake cover story?"

"Nothing at this time. Check with the project's security

manager. You can get the name from Derrick." Luther accepted a slice of pumpkin-zucchini bread from Maria Elena and passed the platter to Peggy. She took a piece and handed it to the chief.

"Thanks, I'll call him." Chief Ganzhorn pulled a slice and gave the bread to Nancy. "I would like to know if the leaker has a connection to Mexico." He took a fork-full of dessert and his eyes rolled up. "Maria Elena, this is your personal best."

Melanie licked a large crumb off her fork. "Moist and light, as if baked by the fairies."

"I'll work the local angle first, using conventional means. . . ." The chief winked an eye at Georgie and Josefina, " . . . as well as my own personal methods." He waved his hand in a circular motion. "And we'll utilize our combined meta-normal means to pursue the Mexico connection."

"I agree. It will be safer for everyone," said Luther. "Maria Elena believes the men hail from somewhere in western Mexico."

Maria Elena said, "Luther is in communication with my brother Alejandro. Most of you know he works as a government liaison at Mexico's CEDO, Intercultural Center for the Study of Deserts and Oceans, or *Centro de Intercultural para el Estudios de Desiertos y Océanos.*"

Luther added, "Outside the scope of CEDO, Alejandro networks with lightworkers of all backgrounds, including meta-normals within various government entities in that region."

"A short time ago, he began receiving telepathic messages from an old friend, a well-known and respected medicine man, a *curandero,*" said Maria Elena, "the same *curandero* from the meditation vision Luther described earlier. The medicine man was rumored to have knowledge of a gateway, a portal enabling a person to transport through time and space."

Luther continued, "Alejandro has contacted meta-normals in our Western North American region for help." He redirected the focus to those in the room. "I recommend empaths, intuitives, clairvoyants, and telepaths direct their attentions to this region, but not exclusively. Use caution, everyone. Although we don't know anyone will detect our searches, be cognizant of shield triggers. Activate enhanced shields to preclude being tracked back to Mystic Creek."

Luther leaned toward Georgie and Josefina. "We will all work together to protect and shield the Green family and their home. And, because you young women spend so much time with Shawn, we will include you and your homes. Still, you are to shield yourselves, and all vehicles." He looked to Nancy. "That includes the school bus."

"You've got it!" She saluted.

"Excellent." He abruptly glanced at Maria Elena, then back to the teenagers before continuing, "Georgie and Josefina, you are to conduct only protective shielding for now. If you happen to receive any impressions in dreams or visions, please tell Maria Elena or me as soon as possible." He turned to the adults. "If there are no questions, let's meet back here again in a few days. Shall we say Monday or Tuesday?"

Tuesday took the vote. They lingered awhile in each other's company while the last of the dessert made its way around the table. Georgie liked how everybody cleared the table before Maria Elena could protest. Each received a wax-papered package of pumpkin-zucchini bread Maria Elena had reserved. The metanormals instructed Georgie and Josefina to call them if they ever needed anything and gave the girls their business cards—except Nancy, who shared her contact information directly to their phones.

The door closed on echoes of goodbyes and see-you-next-weeks. Luther and Maria Elena returned to the kitchen. Georgie and Josefina kicked off their shoes and collapsed like jellyfish onto their sofa. Their heads were propped on pillows at either end and their legs intermingled to keep from falling off the sofa's edge. They lay there for a long while and silently processed the last few hours.

Georgie broke the silence. "Shield triggers?"

"Really? That's all you've got?"

Georgie's laughter shook the sofa and Josefina with it. They caught the giggles, fell onto the old silk rug and bumped their heads into the tree-trunk table, which made them laugh harder.

Giggles calmed, they descended like floating feathers into sprawls on either end of the sofa then bolstered themselves into reading postures worthy of their homework assignment. Low voices drifted out from the kitchen. Georgie glanced at her friend. The conversation grew difficult to ignore. Dips of chins and eyes repeatedly cast toward the double doors confirmed they had the same idea. They tiptoed towards the kitchen in sock feet, stopped outside the doors, and leaned against the wall. Georgie threw a mental shield around herself and Josefina to prevent their discovery.

Luther said, "I'm certain more will be revealed." There was a short pause. The girls held their position. "We must ready the girls to defend themselves, and each other—in the unlikely event the situation necessitates."

Georgie looked sharply at Josefina.

"If you believe it is related to the Greens' issue, then I understand, Luther. But . . . I just don't know." Maria Elena's voice wavered. "Less than two months ago they believed they were normal teenagers."

"They have mastered every lesson thus far. We don't have the full picture at this point, but they can, at the very least, provide shielding. And, if it comes to it, they can also assist in communications."

"Dark communications, if they're anything like what you saw with the *curandero*."

His voice was gentle. "We merely discuss the enlistment of their help—for a mission our collective endeavors to prevent."

"We don't know what the girls are capable of at this point." A teacup tinkled on a saucer.

"Nor what abilities are yet to be developed."

"Perhaps I am overprotective."

"I love them too, Maria Elena." His thirty-second moment of silence lasted forever. "They may be new, even to themselves, but the girls have championed every challenge. This is what they were born to do."

"Yes, I know." She was quiet. "If needed, they can shield and communicate with *us*, without being in the middle of it, wherever and whatever *it* turns out to be."

"Indeed, *if* it turns out to be, they can be safely hidden. Meanwhile, we proceed with their training as planned."

After a long break in the conversation, Georgie caught Josefina's eye and jerked her head towards the fireplace. Josefina nodded. They turned simultaneously and tiptoe-ran to the sofa.

"Oh my God!" Georgie exclaimed in a hushed voice. "What are they talking about? What mission?"

Josefina leaned toward her. "I don't know. Mom's been sort of tense lately but won't say what's bothering her."

"What could possibly bring them to consent to using us?"

"Right? I don't know."

They leaned back and stared at each other. Georgie's mind searched for explanations.

"Maybe it has something to do with Uncle Alejandro. He contacted Mom a few days ago, but she only relayed his hello. She's been distracted ever since, not her usual self."

"Have you tried to pick up on it empathically?"

"Yes, but she must be filtering or blocking it somehow. She might feel it if I probe."

"Why didn't you say something?" *We tell each other everything.*

"I didn't think to mention it. It was between Mom and Uncle Alejandro, not anything to do with us. Of course, now . . . "

Again silent, they gazed into the fire. And jumped when Luther and Maria Elena appeared out of nowhere.

"Hello, girls," said Luther. "We didn't mean to startle you." He and Maria Elena seated themselves on the facing sofa.

Several minutes later Georgie recounted, "So, let me see if I've got this right. Luther had a vision about an old medicine man who, while being tortured, gets a telepathic message to Josefina's Uncle Alejandro. And, visions come for a reason, so it's important."

Luther nodded but said nothing. He needed to ascertain how much she had gleaned.

"And," continued Georgie, "Ale . . . , er, Uncle Alejandro got meta intel while these bad guys interrogated the medicine man. . . ."

"*Curandero*," Josefina interjected.

"Yeah, interrogated him about a portal. And you," she swept her hand toward Luther and Maria Elena, "think the portal and these bad guys have something to do with Shawn."

"It could be associated with the misinformation given about the Green's government project, and the resulting raid at the homecoming dance," Luther said.

Josefina said, "So you want to us to boost our shield work."

"Yes, and we, as you say, will boost your training."

"You want us to put out some meta feelers to check on the bad guys?" asked Georgie.

Luther held both palms up. "No."

Georgie became quiet. *I'm going to miss all of this if I have move to Mom's.*

CHAPTER TWENTY-EIGHT

SAD TO CURIOUS IN SIXTY SECONDS

Friday after school and back at Andersen Light, Georgie stared down the length of the sofa at Josefina's nose pointed into her textbook like the needle on a compass. *Thank God for Josefina, especially on days like today.* To say it was hard to concentrate at school after yesterday's meeting with the local metas, and last night's chat about Alejandro and the medicine man, was a crazy, freaking understatement.

It hit Georgie harder today that she wasn't normal—as she sat in class, walked the hallways with other kids, and tried to act natural. She and Josefina and the other metas all lived regular lives. They looked ordinary, did everyday stuff, yet their secret lived behind each and every normal thing they did.

Now that she "heard" telepathically, she picked up all the personal dramas emanating from people's heads. *Isn't that lovely? Hmm. Sarcasm—not helpful.* On one level it was cool she'd improved on receiving, but the storm of thoughts sometimes hit her like a tornado.

She'd begun to accept her new self, whoever or whatever that was, out of necessity. Out of fear she'd move too fast or break something, Georgie constantly monitored her actions. Perhaps keeping an eye on her physical movement would one day be second nature and fear wouldn't play a role.

It was one thing to know you're different. It was another to see the effects, like the reflections of mirror images within mirror images. Meta-ness affected everything and very likely things she hadn't yet thought about. It was like she'd crossed over a threshold or gateway into a new world. She adjusted the sofa pillow behind her. She was probably just being weird.

Did seeing the other metas yesterday punch through a layer of denial she didn't know she had? She'd never strived for normalcy, so why did she feel this way? Who thinks about being normal? Didn't most people want to be different? She was off her center, with the homecoming raid, the talk of the move, and yesterday's meta meeting. Then there was her flashback from the chief's black leather notebook to Sergeant Jensen's in Starkton.

Plus, Mom was coming tonight for the weekend. Georgie was excited to see her, but worried, too. She glanced down at her feet. The trainers were still on from self-defense maneuvers with Luther and Josefina.

She stood and touched Josefina's shoulder. "Hey, I'll be right back."

Josefina looked up from her book. "You okay?"

"Yeah, I just need to run off some nervous energy."

"Okay." She went back to her reading.

Georgie blurred through the dining room door, onto the veranda, then left toward the back path. She skipped the steps, caught sight of the old fog horn and fuel houses, jumped off the veranda and flew. *That was different.* She'd looked at the old buildings and was practically there in an instant!

Not stopping, Georgie took the cart path left past the carriage house garage and zipped around the circular drive. *Let's try that move again.* The front gate wasn't visible from *Peaceful Seas*, so she pictured the gate in her mind, and launched. There was no sense of her feet hitting the ground, of inhaling or exhaling, or time. It was like she skimmed across gently, rippled water. Buffeted wind streamed over her, whipped her hair back, and burned her cheeks. She let go. Freedom burst inside her chest and tingled up and through her entire body.

At the front gate, Georgie made a long, wide arc to her left and ran along the perimeter. Years of Andersen, Nelson, and Magdalena/Garcia boots must have created this trail Carl now drove his cart along. She flew by the guest houses toward the back wall parallel to the sea, and slowed her blur once she hit the path to the veranda to complete the circuit. A single jump over the steps landed her slightly off balance. Georgie skidded on her feet before coming to a stop on the stone deck. She straightened to find Luther seated at the table with a cup of tea, a warm smile, and his navy blue fisher's cap tilted up over black and silver-speckled hair.

"That was impressive. Do you feel better?" He patted the seat of the adjacent chair and pushed a glass of water across the table.

Her face split into a wide grin. "Yeah, I do." She gulped the water, sat down, rested her elbow on the table's glass surface, chin in hand, and looked up at him.

"Did you understand what Chief Ganzhorn and Maria Elena told you yesterday after you flashed to Starkton and back?"

She squinted. "Refresh me?"

"The intensity of your experiences, those you have probably wished a hundred times you'd never had, creates in you a deep capacity for greatness. Where some might speak of the wounds of childhood, I see potential in the fertile soil of your strong spirit. To the depth which you have felt the pain of fear and sadness, you may also experience courage, soaring joy, and more. Life makes spaces inside of us from events in our lives, things we go through, decisions we make, and our encounters with others. While some are larger than others, they all provide us room to grow. Even so, we have the free will to choose to grow or not."

"You mean a person could feel sorry for themselves over something that happened in the past *or* they could use it to try and understand things better?"

"That's right, Georgie. People often find it difficult to let go of the pain from their past. It can cause problems for them in the present. Some find ways to numb their feelings. . . ."

" . . . like using drugs?" She thought of Harvey. "Or bullying?"

"Yes, escapes of various forms."

"So they won't feel the full brunt of their feelings?"

"Yes, exactly, and they get stuck. They may be in pain, but to move forward would involve change, usually of the mind, and change is scary to most people, at least at first. Yet, everyone has a choice to shift out of the repetitious loop trapping them in a mindset of powerlessness. One small change in thinking and perception can be, for example, as simple as the desire to feel better. A few seconds of feeling good can open a person's mind enough to receive new ideas, view a situation differently, or see it clearly. The decision to feel better can be enough to see a solution, and begin to let go."

"I get the whole change-is-scary part. My life's been like a fast-moving bumper car ride, and drastically different since I moved to Mystic Creek. Then the whole meta thing . . . but I guess that had been happening. Anyway, you know. . ."

She took a deep breath and glanced up from the imaginary circles she drew with her finger on the table's glass surface. "Maybe instead of feeling overwhelmed, I could just see how cool it is where I am now."

He smiled. "Yes, if it feels good. If it feels forced, sneak up on it. Listen to your heart and gut. You may be surprised by the reliability of your own intuition."

"Will we have more intuition exercises in class?"

"You bet." He patted her shoulder. "Just now I have a question for you."

"Okay. . ."

"Have you allowed yourself to process the changes in your

life?" When her eyes narrowed, puzzled, he asked, "Do you let the tears fall for the loss of how your family used to be, for the physical proximity you once enjoyed?"

"Yeah." Her face colored. Why was she embarrassed? This was Luther after all. "I was both relieved and sad when I first came here. Some nights after I got to bed—I guess I relaxed or something —I basically cried myself to sleep. After a while, I stopped. Maybe I stopped because I had stuff to look forward to, like new friends, new things. I miss Mom, and the sibling-units. That hasn't changed. You could say my focus got bigger."

"Things happen in life. Your parents' divorce and your later experiences with your stepfather brought suffering. Suffering is one type of mud, or clay from which we form and grow new dimensions of us. How long we suffer is our choice."

"Kind of like the phoenix who hangs out in the ashes to heal the burnt spots, biding her time until she flies out?"

"You bet, and you are your own phoenix. It is okay to feel. Name the feeling and allow it to change before your eyes."

"You mean I could go from sad to curious in sixty seconds?" She flashed her half-grin.

"Absolutely!" He laughed. "You can also transition from anger to compassion, or fear to a calm inner knowing in even less time. You create your world, Georgie. See it, feel it, and make it. You have come a long way in these many weeks since coming to Mystic Creek." He finished his tea and slid his chair back with a wink. "Now we must travel the distance—to the kitchen."

CHAPTER TWENTY-NINE

PIZZA NIGHT, FAMILY NIGHT

"**F**riday night, pizza night!" Luther exclaimed as he and Georgie headed to the sink to wash up. Josefina and Maria Elena looked up from piles of vegetables, chopping boards, and blenders.

"Just in time." Josefina shoved an empty cutting board and knife toward Georgie.

Georgie aimed the knife at a red bell pepper.

"You must be excited to see your mom, *mija*," said Maria Elena.

"Yeah, it's been awhile."

"You're a little worried, too?" asked Josefina.

"Maybe. Hey, a girl can't get anything past you empaths, can she?" Georgie chuckled but chopped the pepper vigorously, which elicited snickers from Josefina and laugh lines from the adults. She was surrounded.

"You could practice self-shielding your thoughts and emotions," suggested Luther. "Or, relax and accept that you are among friends."

"Oh, pick 'relax and accept'," urged Josefina. "You can be very entertaining."

Maria Elena shook her head. "Pay no attention, *mija*. You are the sister Josefina has wanted her entire life."

Georgie smirked and pink blossomed up Josefina's neck and face.

Luther raised a hand. "I believe Georgie's parents have arrived."

Maria Elena removed her apron and the four of them soon stood on the broad circular steps of the main house.

Georgie scoped her mom's red hair through the car window as her dad darted around to open the passenger door. She was taken by how pretty and fresh Mom looked, even after the flight and long ride from the airport. A dark green denim jacket set off her hair which, longer than Georgie remembered, flowed in waves below her shoulders. She wore dark blue jeans in a stylish cut with chestnut brown canvas clogs, none of which Georgie recognized, but liked enough to borrow had they worn the same size. Then she got it. Mom was happy.

"Hi, Mom. You look fantastic!" Georgie bounded down the steps and nearly hugged her off her feet. Dad lent Mom a steadying arm.

"Georgie! I've missed you too."

Dad escorted Mom up the steps for introductions. Georgie linked hers with his other arm. He kissed her cheek and whispered, "Hi, sweets."

"Hello again, Professor," greeted Luther. "Mary, it's been a long time. Welcome to Andersen Light." He took her hands in his. "I am delighted to see you again. Please allow me to introduce you to my long-time friend and coworker, Maria Elena, and her daughter, Josefina."

"Thank you, Luther. It has been too long." She turned to the women. "Georgie's had nothing but good things to say. I am glad to meet you both."

"The pleasure is ours, Ms. . . . ," said Maria Elena.

"Oh, it's Jones." She glanced at William. "I changed it back. It's easier for the kids and me to have the same name. But please, call me Mary."

"That's easy." Maria Elena smiled and turned to Georgie's dad. "William, are you ready to reprise your role as sous-chef?"

"Ready and willing." His eyes brightened. "It's pizza night, right?"

"Yes. But first, will you please take Mary's luggage around to the guest house closest to guest parking while we show her around?"

"With pleasure." He memorized the security code. "Be right back."

Mary oohed and aahed at her first look inside the great hall. She peppered Luther with questions and admired the art, historic lightkeeping tools, and books. They meandered through the first sitting room and into the second, before pausing in front of the coffee table with its tree trunk base and thick glass top. "Your design?" Luther nodded confirmation from where he leaned near the fireplace. She lauded, "It's magnificent."

Content to observe the comingling energies, Luther witnessed wild, multihued light splash as Georgie and Josefina jumped onto their sofa like cannonball into water.

"We do most of our homework here," Georgie said. The two girls lounged on either end.

"This is quite a cozy spot." Mary ran her hand appreciatively over the sofa's sumptuous material.

"It's perfect," William said, returning to the group.

The girls rose and trailed the adults into the dining room. Georgie's mother stopped at the table. "How beautiful!"

"An artisan friend, Val, burns and paints the gourds I've filled with floral arrangements," explained Maria Elena. "She has a gallery downtown, but sells them all around the world. Farmers market potter friends create these bright stoneware plates and dishes in primary colors." The sun's descent spread broad fingers of pinks, peaches, and oranges into the paling turquoise skyline. "May I show you your guest house while there's still light?"

"Take your time," Luther said. "The girls and I will be in the kitchen with William rolling pizza night into high gear." Facing the dining room double doors, he asked, "Shall we roll up our sleeves?"

WILLIAM AND MARY were quickly indoctrinated into the round-the-table pizza building method, beginning with sauce selection. William and Maria Elena created a slicing station while the pies baked, and Luther produced enough of the new kitchen stools to accommodate everyone a perch around the worktable..

Maria Elena cast a glance at Luther. Georgie was pretty sure you didn't have to be an empath to catch the look that passed between them. She volleyed a left-eyed wink at Josefina who raised an eyebrow.

Maria Elena turned from the oven. "Girls, please carry the cold teas and water to the table? The pizzas will be done shortly."

"You saw that, right?" Georgie whispered as they passed through the double doors loaded with pitchers.

"Do you think they're getting closer?"

Georgie glanced to measure how Josefina embraced the whole Luther and her mom getting-closer thing. "Looks that way."

"This should be interesting."

"Interesting to watch, you mean?"

"Exactly. Let's keep an eye on them," Josefina said, her whisper conspiratorial.

The pizza slices, laughter, and talk traded around the dining table.

Mom beamed as she described her new job. Her boss allowed her to work at home part of the time, and outfitted her with a modular desk designed for a manual drawing table and oversized electronic drawing pad. Her computer had all the latest graphics software, multiple displays, and included a scanner. The company paid for everything—internet connectivity, wireless router, phone, tablet, and supplies. She stopped suddenly and eyed Georgie with a pained expression.

"What is it, Mom?" She lowered her pizza slice.

"Oh, honey, I'm afraid my home office was meant to be your bedroom."

"What do you mean? I don't live there." She held her breath.

"I know, but it's where you would stay for visits. That's why I chose the apartment with an extra room."

The energy fell a few inches. Luther stepped in. "It's good you did, Mary. A part of you must have known you would need that space. I think it is a wonderful arrangement. Surely a daybed would fit alongside a wall, should the need arise." His wink disarmed her.

Georgie watched as a soft light relaxed Mom's shoulders.

Mom's face brightened. "Of course. Thank you, Luther. I can easily accommodate a daybed." She smiled at Georgie, pleased.

Everyone pitched in to clean up until Maria Elena cast everyone from the kitchen, except William, who stayed to help prepare dessert. Luther seated them in the half-moon shaped area near the fireplace. He prodded at the burning composite logs. "Everything in them is recycled and organic. A local couple makes a variety of these on their farm. I prefer those embedded with white sage."

William poked his head and a shoulder through the kitchen double doors. "Hot cocoa, cider, or tea?" he asked, then disappeared with their answers.

"Mary, would you like a tour of the lighthouse and grounds tomorrow?" Luther threw another log on the fire and stood against the side of the hearth.

"Oh, Mom, make sure you try out the elevator!"

"It's really cool," Georgie and Josefina said simultaneously.

"Okay, I'm sold." Laughing, she asked Luther, "Do they . . . ?"

He answered her unfinished question. "Yes, all the time."

Maria Elena and William gently placed trays on the tree table's glass top. Josefina and Georgie jumped up to serve, demanded everyone sit, dispensed hot mugs and desserts. Each stoneware dish contained a bulbous, half-moon pastry with a generous scoop of ice cream.

"What is this yummy ice cream?" Mary asked, "And delicious pastry?"

"Maria Elena's famous pumpkin empanada and her very own homemade pumpkin-vanilla coconut milk ice cream," answered Dad, as proud as if he'd made it all himself.

Maria Elena laughed and said, "It's a team effort. William's sprinkled cinnamon is the finishing touch." She reached for her tea. "Will you join us for breakfast tomorrow, William? No cooking required."

"My entire weekend is free." He stole a glimpse at Mary, and replied to Maria Elena, "However, I'd be honored if you allowed me to join you in the kitchen."

With empty dessert dishes spirited off to the kitchen and drinks replenished, the six relaxed in front of the fire. Conversation lulled. Luther leaned forward. "William, Mary, we would like to talk to you about Georgie."

Her parents' faces spun to Georgie's.

"Why? What's wrong?" Mom's eyes narrowed and her eyebrows flew into check marks. Her aura pointed off sharply in every direction, like fur of a cartoon character jolted with live electricity.

"What's happened?" Dad asked. "You okay, sweets?"

Georgie gripped her hot chocolate mug. Josefina scooted closer to her on the couch. "Yeah, never better." *Did her smile look too forced?* She knew this was coming, and had imagined possible scenarios. But she hadn't anticipated the blast of energy from their attention. Josefina shifted and suddenly it wasn't as strong. *Thanks. Anytime.*

"It is quite the contrary," Luther said. "Your daughter is an extraordinary young woman."

Ease returned to William's face. "Thank you." Mary said nothing but turned toward Luther, her eyes searching.

"I am saying Georgie truly is extraordinary, meaning she can do things most people can't. In time, we expect she will be capable of doing things no one has been able to accomplish."

Her parents' eyes bounced between Georgie and Luther.

"What do you mean?" Georgie recognized her mom's suspicious tone.

Dad leaned closer to Mom. *Was it unconscious?*

"Your daughter is special," Luther said kindly. "She is extremely fast, and strong."

Show them. It was Josefina.

Georgie looked to Luther.

Go ahead, Georgie.

She rose and strolled over, her back to the tall, glass door leading from the dining room to the veranda. All eyes were on her as she gauged the over two hundred foot long walkway to the front door. Georgie crouched and leapt into her running blur. She slid, but landed on both feet, pivoted, and glanced back down the stretch. Focused on a spot a safe distance before the glass door, she again crouched. She wasn't aware of her leap or landing, only the focal point and suddenly being there. Her dad's "holy crimini!" and community gasps filled the great hall. Any other time Georgie would have laughed at Dad's pseudo-expletive. Everyone stood. Were they freaked out? Mom's hands covered her mouth. Uncharacteristically timid, Georgie moved in a slow, normal pace back to the group.

Well done, mija.

She exchanged a grateful look with Maria Elena.

Josefina, shoulder bumped her. *When did you pick up that move?*

Before she could reply, Luther spoke into the silent room. "Georgie," he said and crooked his head to the sofa. Josefina moved to a nearby chair.

She cranked one eyebrow up for Josefina's benefit and bent down into another crouch. She slipped one arm under the center of the sofa's frame, and stood, lifting it over her head.

"Georgie!" cried her mother. "Put that couch down before you break it!" She sputtered, "Or yourself!"

Startled, Georgie lost focus for a split second and the sofa teetered. She quickly stabilized, then lowered it, but too fast. It nearly crashed before Georgie, in a blur, stepped forward and caught the couch, lowering it to a gentle landing.

"Holy mackerel!" Dad ran both hands through this hair.

"Please, everyone be seated." Luther continued once the girls had resituated onto the sofa. "My intention is not to shock you. As I said before, Georgie is extraordinary. To be more precise, she is a meta-normal."

"A meta-what?" asked William.

"Meta dash normal," Georgie enunciated, but zipped it at Josefina's expression.

"Meta-normals and their allies have quietly existed throughout history," said Luther. "The knowledge is passed down by word of mouth. William, you have a long line of allies in your ancestry. Your mother was told as a young child, but has since forgotten. Georgie is the first meta-normal in your family. Mary, as far as I have been able to learn, there have been neither meta-normals nor allies in your family until now. You are the first."

"You mean Georgie is so strong she's different, not normal?" Mary's voice squeaked.

"She is indeed different. Think of her as being *beyond* normal. Speed and strength are but two of her developing abilities."

"When you say *ally*, I'm guessing you mean 'friends of'?" William asked.

"Yes. Allies are friends and supporters of meta-normals, keepers of the secret of our existence. Without *Anonymity*, the first tenet of meta-normals, our efficacy would be exceedingly diminished, or worse."

"Wait! I used to know this old guy . . . ," William recalled, "when I was a boy. He is the man who shared his love of music with me. His name was . . . "

" . . . Thomas Nelson, the grandfather of your rhythm guitar player."

"Yes, Thomas Nelson. I vaguely recall his stories about people who talked to each other with their minds, protected people from harm, and had the power to heal. He spun them like fairy tales, and that's how I took them. I haven't thought about it in years. They were fascinating tales, ones that ended with a prophecy of some kind, if I remember right. He really stressed the word *ally* in every story. I don't know. It may have nothing to do with what you're talking about. I was just a kid. We mostly played guitar."

"Like the Jones family, many Nelsons have been allies. I have no doubt Thomas planted seeds in your young mind." Luther raised his hands as the corner of his mouth lifted. "And, here you are."

"What does this mean? When did all this business start?" Mary asked, her voice tense.

Maria Elena offered Mary a fresh cup of tea, "Lavender chamomile."

"After I turned thirteen," blurted Georgie, "but I didn't notice it until after I moved to Mystic Creek."

"Abilities begin to surface around the age of thirteen, often in barely discernible ways," Luther confirmed. "As for what this means . . ." He paused to sip his tea.

Maria Elena stepped in. "Meta-normals easily blend in with the rest of society, which is how we have coexisted throughout time. Most meta-normal abilities are not the kind you see, but at least two of Georgie's are. She needs to develop her gifts in safety."

"Safety?" asked Mary and William at the same time.

"Her physical strength cannot be explained away, and she is expected to grow even stronger and faster," Luther said. "She monitors herself and does not exhibit her speed or strength while at school or in public so as not to draw unwanted attention. However, she needs to train in a protected environment. She is able to do that here."

"Whose unwanted attention are you concerned about?" questioned Mary.

"They don't want me to end up as some kind of government lab rat, Mom."

"Oh!" Mom's face stretched like an animation.

"That makes sense." William scowled and scratched his head.

"Well, none of this makes sense to me." Mary shook her head. "If I hadn't seen it with my own eyes . . ." She was quiet for a moment. "Maria Elena, you used the word 'we' earlier when you talked about coexisting with others. Were you talking about yourself?"

Luther held Maria Elena's hand as she answered, "Yes, my daughter and I are both empaths with telepathic abilities, and protectors. As are my brother and the women in my family—my mother, grandmother, and her mother, God rest their souls."

Georgie elbowed Josefina. *Looks like your secret is out.*

Misery loves company?

Exactly.

"Telepathy?" inquired William.

Maria Elena grinned. "Our daughters have been communicating silently all evening."

William took in their full-faced smiles, and laughed. "Who needs texting? Right, girls?"

"I do, Dad. I still have to be pretty close to Josefina to receive."

Mary flapped her hands in the air. "Okay! All of this is overwhelming." She took in a deep breath. "What does it mean?"

"Let me guess." William swiped at his hair. "One, it sounds like Georgie needs to be out here a whole lot more in order to train in private. Two, Mary and I are being enlisted as allies, plus three and four, we need to keep your meta-normal identities secret and lend a hand when necessary. Is that about it?"

"An excellent summary, William," Luther replied. "Georgie living here in Mystic Creek, her instruction at Andersen Light, and future in-residence training is critical to her development and safety. I have also asked Maria Elena and Josefina to move here sometime after the first of the year. I am training both girls, with Maria Elena's assistance, and anticipate other students here in the future. "

Silence.

"You should know," Maria Elena said, "your daughter is not just meta-normal. Her coming was prophesied, as was her tutelage by Luther. It is said she will be . . ."

William gasped. "Prophesied? Thomas Nelson was talking about my own future daughter?"

"I apologize. I have said too much." Maria Elena's eyes went to Luther.

Luther placed his hand briefly over hers. "It is all right."

"What?" Georgie demanded, her eyes wide. "I'll be what?" Already on the edge of the sofa cushion, she twisted toward Josefina.

Josefina shrugged. *I don't know. Honest.*

"It is better you unfold without the burden of expectation," said Luther.

"What are you all saying?" insisted Mary. Her frustration was beginning to show. William put a hand on her shoulder.

Luther quietly let out his breath. His plan had always been to foster their natural progression without these added expectations. Still, both girls would inevitably hear more about the prophecy as they learned meta-normal history and became involved in the meta-normal world. *Ah, but the story yearned its telling.* "She could very possibly be the greatest meta-normal ever known. This greatness is her potential, yet it is her choice. Meta-normals are poised around the globe to watch and support her unfolding."

"Shut up!" Georgie jumped to her feet.

"You said that out loud, you know," Josefina said, sotto voce. *Sit down?*

"Young lady!" cried her mother.

"But . . ."

"No buts." She wagged her index finger.

"Right, Mom. It's just . . ."

"I don't care what you are, you will speak with respect."

"I apologize. It's just an expression," Georgie replied, contrite.

Her mother pretended to clear her throat.

Georgie said, "I apologize. No excuses."

"Apology accepted," said Luther. *We will speak more of the prophecy later.*

Josefina's shoulder bump was gentler. Georgie felt the room's taut energy shift.

"Thank you, dear," Mom said with the first hint of a smile since the conversation's start. "Maria Elena," she asked, "have you agreed to move here?"

"Yes, Mary. Luther and I are already discussing plans, including a remodel of the lighthouse."

Mom said to Dad, "Would you be spending more time here too?"

Georgie held her breath.

Luther interjected, "William, you are welcome here at any time. You may join us for meals and sit in on any of the classes. I would go so far as to invite you to move into the other guest house if you find it convenient."

Mom's eyebrows elevated.

"Thank you, Luther. I'd be fascinated to hear what you're teaching the girls and see more of Georgie's capabilities. I would also welcome any opportunity to learn from the venerable teaching chef Maria Elena. But honestly, I'd have to mull over the guest house offer."

"Fair enough. The offer is always open."

"Georgie, what do you think of moving here to the lighthouse?" her mother asked.

"It's a terrific idea. If you think about it, I am at school all day then I come out here for training. After that Josefina and I work on our school homework, then Carl Nelson or Dad drives us home. So I am here tons already. At home I basically eat with Dad, then sleep. On weekends, we do laundry, go see Grandma and Grandpa Jones, or I come here. Dad comes here sometimes, too." She studied her parents. Mom sat back, her spiky, scaredy-cat aura smoother.

"William, you often pick us up after work, or meet Georgie at home. Why not have dinner here?" suggested Maria Elena.

"What do you think, sweets?" He acknowledged her nod and opened his hands to the room. "Time spent with all of you is the highlight of any day." He inclined his head toward Georgie and Josefina. "You two would make splendid roommates." His eyes met Georgie's. "If I could see you every day, sweets, and your mom could visit sometimes, the arrangement could work. We can still go out and visit Grandma and Grandpa Jones, at least until next month when they drive their RV to Yuma for the season."

"As a reminder," Luther said, "moves will not occur for awhile, until after our remodel."

Everyone's attention swung to Mom. Georgie held her breath.

"Okay, I'll go along with it. But, I want to know more about meta-normals, and what Will and I are to tell family and friends about why our oldest daughter lives here."

"Then we are in agreement," William pronounced.

Georgie caught Luther's eye. *Thank you, Luther.*

He winked. *It is my privilege, Georgie.*

How many other parents sat around a cozy fireplace tonight to hear a fantastical tale about their teenager, and how many believed it? Georgie leaned into Josefina's shoulder and they sank into the sofa pillows. The adults discussed legal stuff and logistics until, without feigning boredom, the girls said good night and spiraled up the staircase to the lighthouse guest room.

"What do you know about the prophecy?" asked Georgie.

"So, years before we were born and Luther was very young, there was a worldwide council of metas where the oldest, a woman called Oma, told everyone your name and that Luther would be your personal mentor. I was just as surprised as you were to hear about your destiny of greatness." She elbowed her. "The destiny where I'm your BFF." They entered the third floor. "Maybe I wasn't *as* surprised as you, since it was about you."

"You've got that right, bestie. They were vague, but I didn't want to ask more questions." Josefina cocked a brow at her. "Okay, yes, but I didn't want to raise more issues for my parents."

Josefina threw her a toothy smile. "By issue, you mean the move?" Her hand went up in a high-five and she sing-songed, "We're going to be roommates!" She grabbed Georgie's hands and they twirled around the wide, open space until they fell on the floor, dizzy and laughing.

Josefina was asleep as soon as they fell into the queen bed, but Georgie lay awake. She reflected on the prophecy and wondered at what she was expected to become until sleep came.

CHAPTER THIRTY

WEEKEND WITH THE JONESES

G eorgie yawned and wound down the stairs with her sleepy eyes on Josefina's messy braid bouncing against her back with each step. They waded into a chorus of good mornings from adults deep into breakfast preparations. Maria Elena nudged Josefina towards the mudroom door to repair her braid. Mom kissed her groggy forehead before Georgie moved out of everyone's way and idly observed her parents' interactions. Their ease felt organic to her, free from meta influence. *Harmony is good.* A full hand clamp over her mouth failed to squelch another yawn. She hadn't slept well. Dreams of unfamiliar faces and strange places woke her throughout the night.

Josefina leaned her head against Georgie's shoulder. *Didn't sleep?*

Not much. Did I wake you?

I don't think so.

I hope not. Maybe we're worn out from all the expectation we'd built up for last night. You know, like the air's been let out of a balloon, or a stormy high tide has come and gone.

Right? Well, get ready for another jam-packed day.

They transferred to the dining room and after a few bites of yummy country french toast with berries, nuts, syrup, and two kinds of sauces, she and Josefina perked up to their elders' discussion. Her meta-normality still shocked her parents, but less so after a night's rest. After they'd adjusted to the news in the morning's bright light and engaged in Q&A with Luther and Maria Elena, talk turned to the mundane: syrups, toppings, and sides.

The six of them sketched the day's agenda alongside slow, casual conversation between bites and second helpings. The tour of Andersen Light after breakfast included the lighthouse, greenhouse, workshop, and *Peaceful Seas*. Georgie agreed to a speed demonstration. Josefina would clock her run while Luther took notes.

Luther handed the blueberry bowl to Mary and added to the schedule, "Later, during dinner preparations, the teenagers and I will proceed to the classroom." *We shall practice active shielding with Shawn, answer any questions, and conduct other exercises as time allows.* He swirled his tea, and said aloud, "After we're spruced for dinner, we three will help with any last minute touches." He topped off teacups with green Darjeeling.

The girls trailed Maria Elena into the kitchen with stacks of sticky dishes. Georgie asked Maria Elena, "Did you and Luther decide what we'll tell people about why we've moved here? What's our cover story?"

She turned from the sink. "*When* the time arrives we'll be prepared for the question. We won't conjure a public story line. Every situation will be different, *mija*. For example, you already spend much of your time here, and people in your life know it. Your mother's family is not here to see where you sleep at night. If it should come up, Mary will likely tell them you and Josefina attend in-residence preparatory classes here, which is true. However, I don't expect she will need to explain. William wishes to be the one to tell his parents, though he says he may not need to until they return from Yuma in the spring. As for school, Nancy

Blackeagle will pick you up for school and bring you back. The stop is on her route."

Josefina slipped silverware into the sink. "Shawn will want to know why we aren't on his bus anymore."

"It's not until after the first of the year, *mija*. Shawn's father will tell him everything long before then."

Josefina said, "We could invite Mr. Green here to talk to him."

"Good idea. I'll suggest it to Luther, but today we focus on the Jones family."

Luther gazed at the sea's horizon through the dining room's glass door. Not precisely surprised, he was relieved and gratified at William's and Mary's general acceptance of the meta-normal Georgie. Their energy presented as natural and relaxed this morning, although understandably curious. They were highly intelligent, talented artists who loved their daughter. Creativity in their workaday worlds may have enhanced their intuitions and enabled them to clearly sense the sincerity and importance in last night's meeting. Not incidentally, these two people, of all the couples on this earth, had come together to conceive Georgia Rae Jones. He recognized the light touch on his shoulder. *Ah, good morning, Mother.* Animated voices in the kitchen brought him out of his reverie.

"Everyone wearing your walking shoes?" Luther asked the reassembled party. He waved over his shoulder for them to follow, grabbed his fisher's cap, and joined Maria Elena in the greenhouse.

While everyone held steady interest in Maria Elena's easy explanations of light, beds, vegetables, herbs, and flowers, Mary was enamored. She inquired about soil and organic fertilizer, seed harvesting and sprouting, and growing seasons. The women continued their discussions as the party proceeded to the old carriage house workshop.

Autumn's late morning light poured through the windows and a constellation of skylight tubes positioned throughout the ceiling. Everyone lobbed questions at Luther about his many projects with

Carl. He described the solar and wind power used at Andersen Light, and their recent work in harnessing wave energy. "And, last but not least, we've also had some success with residential desalinization. We employ it in a few applications around the estate." When their eyes searched the workshop, Luther added, "Its infrastructure is located seaside, below the kitchen and terrace."

"Holy mother of pearl! Is this for real?" When William's delight over the shining Packard unleashed a battery of queries, Luther allowed himself a measure of pride. The others circled Woody. A hand occasionally ran over its smooth surface.

Luther coaxed them away from the garage, onto the footpath and in front of the lighthouse. He heard Georgie work out mentally whether jumping to the third floor balcony would be a good demonstration of her recent development, and quickly made eye contact with her. *May I suggest, instead, a nice run from* Peaceful Seas *to the gate and back? There is no need for your parents to question your safety here at Andersen Light. You agree?*

She pulled her mouth over to the right. *Yeah, okay.*

Josefina won her struggle over snickering with Luther's amused warning glance.

He gathered the tour around the low wall of the pond and conveyed the history of the Poseidon and Amphitrite sculpture. "Here they have placed their tridents at one another's feet in an act of peace. *Peaceful Seas* was an early gift from the community to my family."

Luther turned and announced in a dramatic sports announcer voice, "Georgie Jones shall now display her speed and agility." He outlined her path as Georgie and Josefina positioned themselves. Josefina pulled up her stopwatch app.

Georgie crouched and rocked forward into place. At Josefina's "Go!" she propelled herself to the gate and back in a whoosh. She arrived to clapping cheers.

"The time?" Luther asked, pencil ready over his pocket notebook.

"It reads one minute forty eight seconds," exclaimed Josefina. "One minute shaved!"

"Holy speed racer! Way to go, sweets!" William wrapped his arms around her.

"But that's impo . . ." Mary stammered into an open-mouthed smile, her freckles stark across her flushed face. She sat down on the low wall and gazed up at her daughter.

"Very nice, *mija!*" congratulated Maria Elena.

Luther reached for Georgie's wrist. Satisfied, he released her. *No Jack this time?*

Nope. Georgie beamed. "I don't know what the meta record is, but I plan to beat it."

Luther grinned. "I have no doubt you will." He again recognized pride in himself, but deferred the thought to his evening meditation.

His attention turned to Mary who scoured her mental terrain for answers like a hen frantically pecking at pebbles for prized insects. "Mary," he said quietly, "the answers you seek will come. Relinquish the need of your intellect to understand. Rather, allow your heart to hear."

She took in a deep breath and exhaled. "Thank you, Luther."

Luther ushered the company around *Peaceful Seas* and through the side entrance of the lighthouse walkway.

Josefina held Georgie back with a raised left eyebrow and silently ribbed her. *Really? You actually considered jumping the balcony?*

Yeah, but I wasn't sure if I would make it. Maybe another time.

Please give me a head's up. I want to be there in case I need to call an ambulance.

Georgie sensed her underlying concern, but kept it light. *You'll be the second to know.*

The tour reached the third floor of the lighthouse. The girls' attention popped up like prairie dogs when Maria Elena and Luther described the remodeling plans. The curved wall would extend to make way for two bedrooms, one for each teenager, connected by a shared bathroom flanked on either side with two independent wardrobes. The outer room would shrink in size but provide ample lounge and study space for those times when home-work operations moved up from the sofa in the great hall.

Luther volleyed a colluding glance at the girls. "Naturally, we will confer with the future residents on design details."

Georgie turned to Josefina. *It's going to be amazing! I may not miss my old room after all!*

They smiled up at Luther. *Cool!*

AT TOUR'S END, light snacks served alongside answers to more questions satisfied the peckish appetites of both mind and body. Half remained in the kitchen while the rest trooped off toward the lighthouse gallery classroom.

Georgie hesitated. *I'll be right up. I need to ask Mom about the sibling-units.*

True to her word, she rocketed in, reported her sibs coped surprisingly well without her, and settled in at her the desk.

Josefina's brows narrowed inward. "What?" Georgie asked.

"Did you fly up the stairs or jump the gallery railings?"

"I flew of course."

Luther directed their attention to Shawn and his family. "Just to reiterate, when we visualize a protective shield, whether it be a force field, a cloud of light, or what have you, be mindful to intend the flow of positive energy through the shield.

"Until now, you have worked with broad, encompassing shields. Today you'll learn a different technique." He drew a stick figure on the whiteboard and encircled it. "Imagine a band of protective light around Shawn's waist, *his* clockwise."

"Kind of like a wide hula hoop?" Georgie asked.

"Precisely. Envision the hula hoop made of light." His lips curled to one side under his mustache and he observed their mental work with the light energy. "Good. Do it again, but vertically, so that this time the circular band goes from his toes to his head and back to his feet in a complete circle." When their eyes registered completion, he said, "For this next pass, start under his left foot and take it out past his right hip, over his right shoulder, and down his back toward his left foot. Then, repeat this step, but start with the right foot." He completed the sketch.

"It kind of reminds me of that famous drawing of Leonard da Vinci," said Josefina.

"Right," said Georgie, "the one where he's in a circle. Only in my mind, Shawn has his clothes on."

"Well, yeah!" Josefina sputtered, turned red, and glared.

"I'm just saying . . . Leonardo is buck naked in that picture."

Josefina rallied her composure and retorted, "You're very funny, Ms. Jones."

Luther squelched his chuckle. "Let us all maintain a suitably clothed image of Shawn for both his dignity and this shielding exercise. Now, who can recap for me?"

They wrapped every member of the Green family and their property in protection. Afterward, they discussed asking Derrick Green to bring Shawn to Andersen Light for "the talk." There were implications. Luther would need to tell Derrick about the two of them, but briefing his friend on the girls' meta-normal growth was already on his list. A visit by the Greens could link them to Andersen Light, and alert any wrongdoers. Shawn had not visited since the homecoming seaside picnic, Derrick or Earl even longer.

Luther was not inclined to allow fear to rule his decisions. "We strive to balance our day-to-day lives, and proceed with prudent caution. We do not sacrifice the very relationships we work to preserve."

"So it's okay if Shawn comes here?" asked Josefina.

"Let us plan for tomorrow afternoon. I will call Mr. Green."

"Thank you, Mr. Luther!" Josefina clasped her hands then high-fived Georgie.

"Today's was a good session. There will be more on shield work later. I am pleased with your progress thus far. Monday we will introduce visions."

The downstairs team had dispersed for personal preparations ahead of dinner. Luther dispatched Georgie and Josefina to do the same. He stood at his desk and picked up the handset of the secure phone for the third time this month. The meeting with the four members of the Green family arranged, Luther spiraled down the staircase to the main house.

Maria Elena flitted about the dining room table. Her understated attire and intricately swept up hairstyle flattered an already beautiful woman. She was stunning. Even her apron enhanced her grace. Impossibly, his gratitude for her magnified. He placed his hand on his chest at the quiver of soft warmth and fluttering anticipation. "You look lovely, my dear. May I help?"

"Thank you, Luther." Her aura sparkled. "The table is set, the appetizers and drinks are ready to go, and the main dishes require only last minute touches. I'll finish here while you ready yourself before the others arrive."

"Right-oh!" He retraced his steps to the spiral staircase.

GEORGIE VIEWED Josefina's reflection in the bathroom mirror. It was Josefina's third attempt to braid her hair into some design she kept to herself. Someone knocked on the door. They exchanged quizzical glances. Josefina smiled. *It's your mom.*

Georgie bounced off the bed and opened the door. "Wow, Mom. You look nice." The sky blue blouse made her red hair flame and deepened the pink in her cheeks.

"I won't stay." She adjusted the green jacket draped over her arm. "I just ran up to see if you had a minute. Hi, Josefina."

"Hi, Ms. Jones." She waved from the bathroom doorway. "That blue is good on you." Josefina closed the door with, "Just giving you some privacy."

"Sit?" Georgie grabbed her phone and jeans off the arm of the chair and sat on the bed. "Everything okay?"

"Other than our brief chat about Bill and Rose we haven't had time alone. I just came to tell you I love you and I've missed you, and I know things haven't been easy for you. Now I know it was even harder than I imagined. I don't care if you're a meta-whatever, Georgie. You'll always be my girl. You're doing well here and I'm proud of you." She leaned forward. "I'm grateful you have a strong support system—people who care for you *and* know what you need."

"Thanks, Mom. I'm still just me. You're not too freaked out?"

"At first." She patted Georgie's leg. "I don't pretend to comprehend what it will mean for you, but I do know you will succeed wherever this takes you." She rose to leave.

Georgie stood and dabbed an eye with a knuckle. "I'm proud of you, too." They'd both healed in their new lives.

"Hey." Her mom put her arms around her. "These are exciting times. Enjoy the journey, as they say." She kissed Georgie's cheek and shrugged into her green jacket. "See you at dinner."

"I love you, too, Mom."

Georgie closed the door, sat down and stared into the space Mom had vacated. *Okay, that was way cool.* She rubbed the tight knot of emotion in her chest until it released a soft sensation. Flopped back across the bed, she let herself feel—until the bathroom door opened. Josefina's hair hung soft and wavy, free to her waist. Strands of her own braided hair held it out of her face. Reverie over, Georgie sat up. "Sweet. I like it."

"I wish I could say the same about yours." Josefina jerked her head toward the bathroom. "Give me two minutes with it."

Josefina positioned her in front of the bathroom mirror. Georgie could see her point. Black and auburn curls roiled out from her head in every direction. Josefina deftly twisted, twirled, and pulled lengths of curl up and away from each side of her face into a sweep-up. She secured the two twists together near the top of Georgie's head with a hair claw and stood back for a look. The pull of her lower lip said she wasn't done. Josefina moved back in, fluffing and mussing with the remaining hair until the rest of the waves and curls hung in harmony. She smiled and handed Georgie the over-sized hand mirror.

"Nice," she said to Josefina's reflection. "I may even attempt this myself. Thanks."

"No biggie."

"You know that was more like six minutes, right?"

Josefina didn't take her bait. "You're worth it."

THE WARM GLOW of tens of dozens of candles welcomed Luther into the great hall. Maria Elena adjusted the tall pillar candles and stood back to scrutinize the dining room table. Vibrant, multicolored stoneware warmed the crystal goblets and created a festive, artful composition. The rotund soup tureen at the table's head balanced the symmetry of the eight colorful place settings with the centerpiece and ancillary dinnerware at its far end.

"Delightful, Maria Elena."

"Thank you, but it has been a team effort." She broke their gaze and pulled at his sweater vest, presumably to straighten it. "Mary arranged the flowers." Seasonal flowers reached up and out from a pear-shaped gourd, lovingly etched and painted by Val, one of Maria Elena's artist friends.

Luther carried an appetizer tray toward the sitting area, passing Josefina and Georgie as they lit the last of the piano's tea lights. "Hello, girls. May your candlelight illuminate our evening's conversation."

Luther placed the tray next to Maria Elena's platters on the glass-topped tree table, and lit the sage composite log in the hearth. Back in the kitchen, he poured himself a strong blend of the black Darjeeling he favored for a brief respite. The deep and haunting moan of the doorbell would soon chime. He locked eyes with Maria Elena. *It's time.*

He traversed the length of the hall ahead of the silent bantering of his escorts.

Think we can get there before they push the doorbell? asked Josefina.

Oh, yeah.

Luther interjected. *How nice it is for the three of us to receive our guests together.*

Flanked on either side, he opened the door.

"Hi, Grandma, Grandpa." Georgie greeted them with hugs. "This is my friend, Josefina."

"You've grown two more inches, haven't you?" said Grace Jones, relinquishing an arm from around Georgie to shake Josefina's hand. "Josefina, it's been a while. And, Luther, good to see you, as always." She appraised the great hall, her eyes sparkling. "It's as lovely as ever."

"Thank you, Grace. It reflects a group endeavor." He kissed her cheek and turned to shake Sam's hand. "Welcome, Sam. How have you been?" Luther recognized the going-to-town hat Sam hooked onto the foyer coat rack.

"Busy at it, Luther. Keeping my thumbs away from hammers." He chuckled to himself. "Sure is good to see you again."

Grace laughed, "You know what it's like, Luther. The place changes every day. It's been a few weeks since you were last out."

Luther grinned as he pictured their continuous home renovation projects. In contrast to Grace's usual rugged jeans, an attractive dress draped her figure. The subtle blues and greens played off her eyes. Like her husband, her body and energy portrayed an active lifestyle. He guided the couple to the oval sitting area formed by sofas and wing-backed chairs in front of the fireplace. The girls plopped down on their usual sofa just as Maria Elena returned from the kitchen. He lightly touched her back.

"Maria Elena," said Grace, "your advice on shrubs and berry

plants when we last met at the farmers market was excellent. They've all done quite well."

"I'm so glad. Please call should you ever need more ideas."

Luther sensed William and Mary whipping around the circular drive and excused himself. The two were all smiles when he opened the door. Given their windblown appearance, they had had a good time in the covered cart. Mary smoothed strays of her bright red hair toward its ponytail while the professor's hand moved to tame a black curl at his forehead.

William leaned in. "Thanks for pulling this together, Luther."

"It is my honor." He, William, Mary, and the teenagers entered the great hall. Maria Elena and Sam were in conversation near the fireplace. Luther veered the group toward Grace and her study of the wall tapestries in the first sitting room.

"Hello, dear." Grace greeted William, then her ex-daughter-in-law. "Hello to you, Mary. I am so very pleased to see you again."

William waved at Sam as everyone migrated to the fireplace.

"Hi, Dad."

"You girls look nice," said Mary. She nodded at Maria Elena.

"It was her doing." Georgie tapped shoulders with Josefina, who rolled her eyes and shrugged.

Luther sat beside Maria Elena and asked across the tree table. "Can I get you a drink, Sam?"

"Maria Elena poured me some coffee, but I'd try one of those appetizers. What are they?"

"These are miniature vegetable bundles, and these," she pointed, "are pumpkin bites baked in coconut phyllo dough."

"They both get my vote," Sam said around his first one and sipped some coffee.

Luther asked, "How goes the remodeling work, Sam?"

"We are looking to shut down for the season. Grace and I are heading to Yuma right after Thanksgiving. We like the RV subculture, as you know." He popped another appetizer in his mouth as Grace and the others joined them. They talked at some length about Yuma, friends they expected to see, activities organized, and how long they planned to stay.

Luther winked privately to Maria Elena. The energy was lively. Sam described their deck remodel. Josefina and Georgie chatted telepathically, primarily about the friendliness of Luther and Maria Elena, and William and Mary. Mary updated Grace on her other two grandchildren, and her own new job. William listened to Sam and sporadically checked if Georgie and Josefina were in telepathy mode. Luther and Maria Elena rescued themselves from laughing out loud at the nonverbal communications by moving to the dining room.

Luther raised his sparkling apple cranberry to the seven other goblets held high as Maria Elena extended her palms over the table. "A toast," he said," to family and friends. May our bonds be ever strong!" Hear-hears and clinks of crystal echoed around the table. Sam and Grace entertained them through the remainder of dinner with tales of RV adventures and the colorful people they'd met.

Maria Elena wiped away tears of laughter and began to clear the table. William was quick to join her, but she said, "Warm up the ivories? I can find other helpers."

Luther and the Jones elders gathered around the fireplace. He and Sam swung a sofa around to open the oval sitting area to the piano, then reinforced the fire with another log. William played a tune Luther recognized as "Take Five." He left Sam to the sofa and ambled over to the dining room table, whistling and snapping his fingers to the Brubeck song. He picked up the soup tureen and carried it through the double doors.

He stopped. Georgie faced the doors, trance-like. Josefina hovered next to her. Luther handed the empty tureen to Josefina. He placed his hands on Georgie's shoulders and searched her unfocused eyes. *Georgie, can you hear me?* No reply. *Georgie, what do you see?* The girl slowly turned her gaze to him, but her focus remained elsewhere. It was enough. He caught the edge of her thoughts and sailed along with her. They rode wave after wave of color and sound, crests then spirals, swirls of blues, splashes of orange and sprays of violet, only to descend, and nearly crash. The two of them marched through shallow turquoise blue waters. She kicked the water into sparkles high in the air. They caught another wave and rode it to its end onto the sand into quiet and stillness.

William reprised "Take Five" and Georgie's waves returned. Luther felt her nuances of color and light. They played on the water and danced with the melody and harmonies. He retreated to her mental edge, whistled to the song, and took her hands until she resumed her march, kicking the shallow water until toes met sand. *Georgie, feel your hands.* She squeezed his with light pressure. He slowed his whistle and, without taking his eyes from hers, transmitted to Josefina. *Please ask William to stop playing.* Luther stood with Georgie on the sand. The music stopped. The water pulled back into the ocean and away from their feet. He asked, *Shall we go back? Are you ready?* Her eyes focused.

His voice low, he said, "That was quite a side trip. How do you feel?"

"Okay. Thanks. Yeah."

"Are you disoriented?"

"Yeah."

The others crowded around them at the kitchen entrance. Their auras emanated concern. Luther spoke. "She is fine. Bring cold water, hot tea, and hot chocolate and let us all relax near the fire. William, we'll need an intermission." He lowered his glance to Georgie. *Shall we?*

A respectful silence pervaded the room. William and Sam returned the sofa to its cozy oval. Georgie settled on the homework sofa with Luther on one side and Josefina on the other. Their feet sought the glass-topped tree table, but though there were no exchanges from the women, verbal, mental or otherwise, a simultaneous descent of all six feet occurred as Maria Elena, Mary, and Grace arrived with the drinks. William snickered.

Georgie checked with Luther telepathically, stole time to ground herself, then described her experience in the kitchen.

"It was weird. I mean, I love music, but this was so intense. One second I was on my way from the kitchen to the dining room and the next I was riding waves of music. It was like I transported into a scene of a movie, only I was *in* the song. The music was vivid and existed on different layers or levels. The tones were colors and movement, flowing like water, with texture and motion. It doesn't make any sense, but that's what it was like."

"This vision is another demonstration of how powerful your clairvoyance will be," said Maria Elena. Everyone but Grace turned to her.

Grace stared at her granddaughter. "I've heard about people like you," she blurted. All attention in the room swung to Grace.

"Grandma?"

"Yes, Grace?" Luther asked. Had this episode unearthed her memory? The woman's look was inward and distant.

"It was a fairy tale," Grace said. "My grandmother told me about people who could do special things. I was a very young girl. She told me lots of fairy tales. As I got older I recognized they were just stories. Maybe there was something to them."

"Truth is often woven into fairy tales," Maria Elena offered. After a brief silence she asked, "What else did your grandmother say?"

"She said we were allies, our family had always been allies. I didn't understand what she meant then, and I still don't. Grandmother said it like it was something special. She never spoke of it again. My mother never mentioned it. I believed it was another fairy . . . ," she peeked at Maria Elena, " . . . another story."

"You've never said anything," said Sam.

"No, I forgot about it. Until Georgie described her trance or vision, or whatever you call it, into the music," Grace said. She reached for his hand.

"What's all this about, then?" Sam looked around the room.

Luther chose his words carefully. "Grace, I could not say anything until you remembered on your own, even if it meant you could not pass on the tradition to William." He told her and Sam of allies, about Georgie, and why it was necessary to reveal this information to her parents.

Sam ran one hand over his face. He took a deep breath, scooted forward to the edge of the wingback chair and leaned toward Georgie. "I can't say I care what you are, girl, as long as you're healthy and happy. You'll always be special to us."

"Thanks, Grandpa." The prickly tingle of a blush edged up her neck and over her face.

Luther cleared his throat. Georgie had asked he continue and, after a telepathic check for consent with Maria Elena and Josefina, he elaborated to include mother, daughter, and himself in the company of their granddaughter. He concluded, "You may understand why it is imperative to protect meta-normal identities."

Grace had been staring at her granddaughter and her parents. She expanded her silent appraisals to the rest of them. "Life is full of surprises. Never a dull moment, right, Sam?"

"You've got that right!" His smile widened as Maria Elena reappeared with dessert.

No one else had registered Maria Elena's speedy exit and entrance. Luther allowed himself a hearty chuckle as she parsed out wedges of moist pumpkin-zucchini bread with dollops of her whipped vanilla coconut cream.

"Is that why you're such a good cook?" Sam's eyes danced his plate.

Maria Elena burst out in laughter. "You are kind, Sam. I do pay attention to details, but listen to my intuition more."

"I think it's both, Mom." Josefina smiled.

"Me, too," said Georgie.

"Whatever it is, you've got my vote!" Sam declared.

"Mine, too," Mary and William said together.

"Me, too," said Grace, "and I want this recipe."

Luther breathed an internal sigh of relief. Resurfacing memories could create firestorms. Instead, Grace held hers like a young girl fascinated with her first firefly. Nor was he too weathered or seasoned to appreciate life's miracles.

GEORGIE LEANED against Dad outside on the top of the concentric steps. He sighed, "That went pretty well. . . " They and the others waved goodnight to her grandparents. Their cherry red taillights dipped out of view. He put his arm around her shoulders. " . . . even with your unexpected trip to music land. Luther, I see what you mean about her needing to be here for her development. Let's hope she doesn't drop into a trance while she's at school."

"Agreed, William," said Luther. "No one expected it tonight, though she experienced something similar last Tuesday. I expect Josefina will soon have visions as well. They will learn to manage this ability, like all their others. We are fortunate they have each other." The girls linked arms.

"Yes, we are," agreed Mary. She dropped her head between Georgie and Josefina and gave them a tandem hug.

William held his arms out as if to encircle everyone. "Thank you all for everything. Today was a good day. Life with you is interesting, to say the least." To Mary he said, "I'll be here tomorrow to take you to the airport. May I drop you off at your guest house?"

"Good idea. We can call Bill and Rose and tuck them in."

"William," interjected Maria Elena, "join us for breakfast? You'll still have plenty of time to get Mary to her plane."

"I'd love to." Turning, he offered his elbow. "Mary?"

"Thank you, Will." Mom looked tired, though her eyes were clear and bright and her face was relaxed. "Goodnight, everyone."

Luther closed the door behind them. "William said it. Life *is* always interesting."

Georgie and Josefina stretched out on their sofa, kicked off their shoes, and rested their sock feet on the tree table. Luther sat down on the adjacent sofa with Maria Elena and relaxed his arms over the back. The four of them gazed at the last of the burning embers of the sage log.

Luther broke the companionable silence. "I need to ask you all to stay a little longer tomorrow. The Green family will be here after their church service lets out."

Josefina sat up. "Yay! Thanks, Mr. Luther."

"They'll be here in time for lunch?" inquired Maria Elena.

"Yes, a late lunch. But we will all pitch in, right girls?" asked Luther.

"Of course!" said Josefina.

"I'm in," agreed Georgie.

Luther cautioned, "Remember, we do not yet know what, if anything, Derrick Green has told Shawn about the intruders at the homecoming dance, or anything else."

"Exactly, we won't say anything yet," replied Georgie.

"Outstanding. Shall we clear what remains and call it a night?"

THE MORNING FLEW from breakfast and goodbyes with Mom, to Dad's promise to pick Georgie and the Garcias up later. Georgie tempered stinging tears with feelings of relief at how everything had worked out. She reminded herself she'd see Mom and the sibs next month for Thanksgiving. Had it sunk in she'd be staying in Mystic Creek?

She and Josefina washed a joint load of laundry. They threw everything in at once and judged the load safe from bleeding since they used cold water and vinegar. Lucky or smart, the clothes were okay. They folded and organized them on the queen bed in their third floor guest room.

"How about those vibes this weekend?" Josefina divided socks and underwear into ownership stacks.

"Like?" Georgie folded the jeans and sat on one corner of the bed to work on t-shirts.

"Like how well your parents get along, or is it normal for them?"

"They've been okay, especially since Dad helped with the last move." She replayed a few scenes in her head. "Mom was quiet at the time. I think he was extra sensitive to her emotions. You're right, though. They seemed friendlier this weekend. What about your mom and Luther?"

"What? Oh, they've always been close, best friends close."

She looked up. "Seriously, there's no way you, of all people, with your empathic abilities, have not picked up how intimate they are with each other."

"Perhaps you, with your budding imagination, see things that don't exist."

"Or, perhaps," Georgie retorted, "you don't see things where they do exist." She sensed her friend's confused emotions. "I'm just saying . . . it wouldn't be horrible, would it? They deserve to be happy."

"Whatever. I guess. Of course." Josefina scanned the piles of sorted clothes and homework and slouched into the bedside chair. She studied the end of the braid, as if looking for split ends. "I've never thought about it. I haven't needed to. I might have spotted a couple of things. They don't hide or shield much . . . that I know of."

Georgie let it go. Josefina didn't often talk about her own feelings. She would share when ready. "So, the Greens will be here soon."

Josefina perked up at the change in subject and retreated into the bathroom. Georgie slipped her hair into a ponytail, and leaned against the door jamb. Josefina wound her braid into a ball, then pinned it to the right of the base of her head. It would bug Georgie, but it looked good on Josefina, who added a pair of silver hoop earrings. Fashion adjustments complete, they spiraled down to the kitchen to assist with lunch prep.

CHAPTER THIRTY-ONE

TELL IT LIKE IT IS

Georgie took her seat next to Josefina while Luther sat in his usual place, his back to the tall veranda door and across from Maria Elena. His dark blue, long-sleeved cotton shirt accented the silver in his black hair and the blue of his eyes. To his left was Derrick Green, still in his shirt and tie from church. His deeply rich, amber brown eyes, bright and intelligent, were tense. Random tight, white curls grew around his temples. How many had sprouted since Luther's call to him homecoming night? Derrick loosened his tie.

Darlene sat across from her brother. "It has been a long while since I was out here to your place, Mr. Luther. I believe our mother was still alive. Oh, the stories she would tell . . ." She smiled and shook her head.

"We had our share of adventures," Luther agreed. "She was a wonderful woman, with uncanny intelligence and abundant humor, as have you, Ms. Green."

"Our mothers were good friends, Darlene," said Maria Elena. "They swapped recipes and gardening secrets. I have their notes and recipes for healing tinctures and salves—among other things."

Maria Elena passed her the basket of cornbread muffins. Her grin was covert, but Georgie caught it and Darlene Green did too.

"This meal could have been made by our grandmother, Ms. Garcia." Earl said from his place across from Georgie. She'd learned he also played his sax in the church band and the dark lavender of his shirt was the band's signature color. "This is one of my favorite meals. Right, Aunt Darlene?" Anyone could see it. Georgie swallowed her giggle. The bowl of pinto beans on his plate was so full the broth rippled in waves toward the mountain of fried potatoes. His fork dove in for another generous bite.

Josefina either caught her thought or witnessed the same thing, because she choked down a chortle and grabbed her apple cider for cover. She tapped Georgie with her right elbow and grinned across at Shawn who, sandwiched between his dad and brother, struggled to remain straight-faced.

Shawn pointed to the bowl next to Georgie's glass and asked, with no small measure of control, "Would you mind passing the coleslaw?"

Maria Elena responded to Earl, "The recipes for this meal came from your grandmother, with the exception of dessert, which is a cross between her apple pie recipe and my empanadas. She was a true pioneer in cooking—for taste as well as health."

"It's perfectly delectable, Maria Elena." Darlene sprinkled green onion pieces into her beans and reached for a bowl of diced radishes. "Where on earth do you find these this time of year, girl?"

Maria Elena passed a dish of sautéed summer squash with sweet onions to Luther. She replied, "I grow them year round," and offered to show Darlene around the greenhouse.

"Hey! What about dessert?" Shawn asked when the party rose from the table.

Earl shot his brother a wide-eyed look and mouthed, "What?"

"Mind your manners, Shawn," Derrick said through the chorus of teen snickers. He dabbed his mouth with his napkin to cover a grin.

"Don't worry, *mijo*, we'll have dessert," Maria Elena told a blushing Shawn.

Georgie sensed Shawn's squirmy feelings. His tawny brown color tinged with red and contrasted handsomely against the white collar of his wide-striped, button-down shirt.

"In the meantime," Maria Elena implored, "everyone please relax in front of the fireplace."

They all ignored her and cleared the table. Georgie spied Luther catch Derrick's attention before the two headed to the fireplace with Earl. Maria Elena insisted they leave the dishes stacked in the sink, and led them into the sitting room where Luther, Derrick, and Earl spoke in low voices.

Georgie positioned herself at one end of the homework sofa while Josefina took the other, which left Shawn to sit between them. Darlene sat in an armchair nearest the fireplace and smoothed out the dark brown velvet piping in the hem of her forest green twill dress. The others settled in. Georgie flashed Shawn an encouraging smile and fluffed her cushion against the sofa's arm.

Shawn's dad, his tie now draped over itself, sat forward. "Shawn, I need to tell you something about our family."

"Okay . . ." Shawn's drawl held uncertainty.

"From as far back as we know, the Greens and the Bells, from Grandma Nordeen's side, have been what are called *allies*."

Georgie glanced at the serious faces around the room. Earl, one arm up across the back of the sofa next to his father, shifted his position and crossed his leg, his wingtip shoe motionless. He scrutinized his father and brother as his dad spoke.

Derrick described allies and how the fact of meta-normals—people with abilities beyond the range of the extremely gifted human—had been communicated to him as a boy. "The information is only revealed to an ally as it becomes necessary to do so, and, for many reasons, your time has come."

Shawn said nothing while his dad spoke. He adjusted his sitting position once, crossed his legs twice, scratched his head, and pushed his glasses up higher on his nose. "Can I ask what makes this my time?"

Georgie felt a rush of empathy, but aborted her mission to ease the atmosphere at seeing Josefina's raised eyebrow. She offered Shawn a half-hearted smile.

His dad said, "Your two best friends recently discovered they are meta-normals."

"And that's just for starters," Earl added.

"Get out! What? Is this a joke?" Shawn bolted off the couch and gaped first at Josefina then Georgie. He looked around the room as if he expected a punch line, then back to Josefina.

Luther rose and put an arm around Shawn's shoulders. "It is no joke, Shawn. You may as well get comfortable. We have more to tell you."

Shawn stared at Josefina. "You have super powers?"

"Sort of." She hugged a throw pillow.

Shawn's brows and eyes widened at Josefina. "What? Why didn't you tell me?"

Luther answered, "Neither Josefina nor Georgie could say anything until your father first told you of your own family legacy."

Shawn sat down and leaned forward with his hands clasped together between shaking legs, an expectant expression on his face. His eyes were on Josefina and didn't see the nod his father gave to Luther.

Luther stood in front of the fireplace. "Meta-normals have coexisted with the rest of humanity since the beginning. We live around the world, on every continent, and then some. You are welcome to attend my class on meta-normal history and geospatiality. Your father explained the need for privacy and protection for meta-normals. These also extend to allies."

"Are you ready to take the blood oath?" Georgie asked Shawn.

"What . . . ?"

Earl laughed out loud with Georgie, but Josefina glared at her like a protective mother bear. *Hilarious, Georgie—he's already in shock.*

Just lightening it up, girlfriend.

Go easy. . . .

Okay. He's my friend, too, you know. "Nah, I'm kidding, Shawn."

"We will not be administering a blood oath," Luther assured him, "although it is practiced in some regions. Georgie's remark does shine the light on the importance of our meta-normal/ally relationships. Generations of our families have shared the secret of who we are. They have acted to preserve it, worked together in local crises, and provided routine and vital world support." He held a hand up at the looks of surprise from Georgie and Josefina—they weren't yet familiar with the full scope of meta-normal work life—and continued speaking to Shawn. "Today, I will tell you about your friends Josefina and Georgie. I'm certain they will later elaborate. After, your father will discuss a project he and your brother are working on."

Maria Elena and Darlene appeared with sizeable trays of desserts and drinks. Luther moved quickly—too quickly—to relieve Darlene of the listing drink tray slipping from her grip. He preferred not to display his abilities, choosing instead to employ camouflage or shield them. Ignoring the gasps from around the room, he smiled at Darlene and eased the tray onto the table's glass surface. "No need to worry, Ms. Darlene. These things happen."

"Whoa," breathed Shawn.

Georgie and Josefina exchanged impressed glances.

"Apple empanada a la mode, anyone?" Maria Elena asked into the silence, as if nothing unusual had happened.

Over the clinks and scrapes of spoons at work, Luther recounted how Maria Elena and her family were associated with Andersen Light and his family, beginning with her great-grandmother Florencia. He detailed the prophecy foretelling the birth of Georgie, and how the fateful dodgeball incident triggered different meta-normal abilities in both girls. Settled into the armchair next to Josefina's end of the homework sofa, he paused for a bite of empanada and raised his dessert plate in salute to Maria Elena. "Josefina and Georgie had previously begun to exhibit abilities in what you might call the subtle or self-denial stages."

"You mean," Shawn asked," they didn't believe what was happening and chalked it up to something else to explain it away?"

"Precisely," Luther said. "For example, Georgie told herself her growing strength was due to increased exercise, primarily bicycle riding. But it could not explain how the boy flew through the air with her dodgeball throw that day at school."

Shawn's face slackened. "Yes, I remember that day." Josefina and Georgie gave him simultaneous shoulder bumps. He rubbed his left shoulder from Georgie's bump. His curious glance juxtaposed a half grin.

Luther continued, "Maria Elena and I had been monitoring them, and the catalytic event of the dodgeball incident necessitated we tell them who they are."

Maria Elena put in, "They needed to know in order to protect themselves."

"I get the whole lab rat avoidance angle. Otherwise, what's the big deal?" Shawn asked.

Luther said, "We are meta-normal, but from another perspective we could be viewed as abnormal, or threatening. Recall legends of people, different in whatever way, and how the societies of the time treated them."

His brother interjected, "Think about your science fiction books, movies, and games, Shawn. Aliens get experimented on and are usually depicted as a dangerous menace, bent on the destruction of the planet rather than an intelligent species who want to be friends." He colored deeply, "Not that I think meta-normals are aliens or anything."

"Thank you, Earl." Luther's lips gave way to a grin. He placed his empty dessert plate on a side table. "You are correct. The unfortunate end in those stories portrays annihilation and extinction of the perceived enemy. Earth history as well as current events show the repetition of this dynamic in—I hesitate to call it this—real life."

Thought images raced across Shawn's face. "I totally get that." Georgie sensed some of the prejudice he'd experienced.

Luther said, "There is a subtler reason we remain anonymous. Human beings are evolving. This is being measured in scientific circles today. In fact, we are all evolving. The inherent need in humans to strive for improvement, to be and do better within themselves and in their world, is paramount. A prime tenet of every meta-normal is to support and protect this in every way. It has long been held that if the knowledge of our existence upset this primordial drive it could lead to disastrous effect for humanity."

"You mean if we knew you all existed some people might think, 'Why bother?' So, to protect the human race, basically from itself, you have this prime directive to remain anonymous," Shawn observed. Georgie hadn't heard this explanation. It made perfect sense. She respected his reference to *Star Trek's* Prime Directive.

"Precisely," Luther said.

"And human allies are the ones who help you protect this anonymity so you can do whatever you do, whatever that is?"

"Our allies not only protect the sanctity of our existence, we work together to lessen or eliminate pain, suffering, and disaster on an infinite continuum—individual to global. We bring understanding, healing, and compassion. Many, both meta-normals and allies, as well as those in other realms, call themselves lightworkers, in reference to another tenet, *Take Light Where There Is Darkness.*"

Darlene poured more tea and hot chocolate. She winked an eye at Shawn and sat down with her cup.

Luther continued, "Our work is based on cooperation. We operate as a community with common visions shared by each person, team, and region. We are empowered by the desire to restore, nurture, and protect nature's balance in its many manifestations, by cooperation rather than competition."

"I'd say there's plenty of work to go around." Shawn eyes narrowed. "It must feel like an impossible job."

"You refer to the world disharmonies. It may appear as if there is no progress, but oftentimes our work results in what you don't see."

"I get it. We don't see it because it didn't happen, thwarted by meta-normals and allies, and, wait a sec! Other realms?"

"We predominantly work locally," inserted Maria Elena, "with ourselves, our communities, and so on. We are autonomous, but also connected around the world. Luther is our Western North American Regional Mentor. Yet, his calls for direction for specific help are responded to locally, globally, and anywhere in between."

"Let us save the topic of other realms for another day." Luther winked at the teenagers.

"It could be easy to get lost in the glamour of this new information," explained Maria Elena, "but it is important to remember that meta-normals, like their allies, are people who live normal lives. We brush our teeth, go to school, hold jobs, fall in love, learn life's lessons, cook meals, do our laundry, make friends, . . . "

" . . . take out the trash, and make our beds," joined Darlene.

"We all share the charms of this worldly experience." Luther asked, "Derrick, would you like to begin after a short break?"

"SO WHAT DO YOU DO?" Shawn tapped the right elbow of his crossed arms with his left hand. The girls first looked at him, then each other.

"Josefina's an empath. She can read your thoughts." Georgie wiggled her eyebrows. Shawn stilled, but Georgie observed his pupils dilate.

"Georgie," Josefina added, "can run inhumanly fast and leap short buildings." His eyebrows rose and his mouth dropped open.

Georgie swung open the heavy wooden door she'd been leaning

on. "Be right back." She grinned, closed the door on his sigh, and ducked into the necessary room behind Josefina.

The girls returned a fast few minutes later. Shawn still leaned against the wall. "So what am I thinking, Jo? *What's this about other realms?*"

"Oh that. Mom must have meant spirits of plants and things of that sort."

"No vampires." Georgie added with a dose of intrigue, "But I'm just guessing since we haven't covered that topic, yet."

Shawn abruptly straightened from the wall, his expression incredulous. "You heard me, too?"

"Yeah," she answered, apologetic. He teetered somewhere between freaked out and amazed excitement, and she didn't want to add to the former.

Shawn didn't respond. He followed them to the sofa with an unfocused stare of deep, internal analysis,.

"Are you okay, Shawn?" asked Josefina.

"Let's just say the sponge that is my mind is close to saturation."

"I feel you. It hasn't been that long since this all started for me. I'm not going to lie. I've freaked out about this. I still don't know what I'm becoming," said Georgie.

"It must be weird, but cool." He tilted his head to each of them. "Of course, I haven't witnessed your new skill sets."

"Later," whispered Josefina.

Georgie warned, "Get ready for more overload because your dad has more to tell." When he wilted, she added, "This will grab your inner geek." His face brightened.

Pitchers and glasses of lemon water on silver trays rested on the thick, greenish glass of the tree table. Adult conversation stopped as the teenagers approached, took their seats, and pretended not to notice.

"Shawn," Derrick Green said to his son, "I know this is a lot to take in. . . ."

"No, Dad, I'm totally cool. But you're right. It's, well, a lot. But how cool is it that I'm part of a long family legacy I didn't know existed, and my best friend—friends," he corrected, "are super girls? I'm seriously good with it."

Looks like he just swung from freaked out to amazed excitement.

Josefina tipped her head to peer around Shawn at Georgie. *I think you're right.*

As do I. Luther's eyes twinkled.

Earl's brows lowered into a squint, equally suspicious and curious, at their exchange.

"We've had an unfortunate mix up at work," Derrick told Shawn.

"Mix up?"

"You know the latest device Earl and I worked on in the carriage house workshop?"

"You called it the black box."

"The government named it Project Hermes once they accepted the proof-of-concept and contracted it. We then moved the black box to our secure lab down by the old port and married it with the classified portion we'd already engineered. We worked on it there until it was ready for field testing."

"You mean out on the ship?"

Earl nodded. "We'll return it to the lab for tweaks and modifications."

Derrick said, "Because of the device's sensitivity, a cover story was created."

Shawn shifted on the sofa. Georgie craned for a peek. Questions raced across his face.

Derrick saw it also. "A cover story is an abbreviated, for-release version used when dealing with outside entities, such as parts suppliers and others who don't need to know all the program particulars." He rubbed his face. "It is a watered-down description of the project. Ours was written in the blandest of government language. Some cover stories are classified. Ours was labeled as sensitive and for official use only."

"So what's the cover story?" Shawn asked.

"It describes in simple, unclassified terms a communication device engineered with advanced encryption for communicating extremely dense video, voice, and data packets . . . "

" . . . with limitless capacity," Earl added.

"It was designed for initial use by the U.S. Navy and Coast Guard," Derrick said.

"What makes your device better than what's already out there?" asked Georgie.

"Holographic? 3D? 4D?" Shawn asked.

"I can tell you Project Hermes is multispectrum, which is not new. It is the way in which we deliver through the spectrums that makes it special. It's faster than light and utilizes quantum cryptography."

"Wow! But why would your black box cause a problem?" asked Shawn.

"Our box is not the problem," said Earl, "It's that someone, an uncleared individual, blogged an exaggerated version of the official cover story." His mouth twisted like he might spit.

"Oh."

Derrick picked it up. "The blogger was not briefed. As a receptionist, she worked the program's periphery. The nondisclosure agreement she signed when she was first employed cautioned against the release of information, including for official use only and sensitive data. She's been disciplined, but, for the time being, remains in her position as the lab's entry receptionist so security can keep an eye on her."

"What did she blog?" asked Josefina.

Derrick shook his head as if he couldn't believe it himself. "She wrote that the box was engineered with *portals*, rather than communications ports, and changed the description to say it would support communication of packets *and things*. It took the tone of science fiction when she embellished how it would be used by the 'U.S. Navy and Coast Guard, and other countries to transport sea life out of harm's way.' According to her, Project Hermes would 'transmit dolphins and sea turtles from tangled fishing net, or whales out of reach of a whaling boat or fleet'."

"Cool," Georgie said.

"Right?" Shawn agreed. "That is a way cool idea, but you'd have to change the name to Project Poiseiden."

"Meanwhile, back in reality . . . ," said Earl.

"Reality. Like the one I had before today?"

"Touché, little brother."

"What did she mean by transport and transmit? Like teleport?" Josefina asked.

"I'd say teleportation was implied," Derrick Green answered.

"So what's the big deal, Dad? You seem contrite."

"Contrite," Earl repeated with a half-faced grin. "There's a five buck word, bro."

Shawn took it in stride. "Thanks, Earl. I'm glad you caught the meaning."

"Let your father finish, boys," said Darlene. Her tone belied an often used request.

"Thank you, Dar," Derrick said. "I'm getting there. During her, uh, interview, the woman said her friends pressured her to write about her job on her new blog, despite her having told them she couldn't talk about where she worked. These friends, according to her statement, continued to egg her on, until she got the idea to use the project cover story. By the time the entry was removed, the damage was done."

"Makes you wonder why anyone would believe her," Georgie said, mainly to herself.

"Wait," said Shawn, "what damage?"

His dad responded, "Though it was a far-fetched work of science fiction or wishful thinking, the blogger appears to have drawn the interest of a person or persons wanting to use the fictitious technology for their own gain, beyond the eyes of global law enforcement—movements of drugs perhaps. Of course, *that* black box doesn't exist."

"Then what's the problem?" asked Shawn.

Earl replied, "We don't want the real project endangered because someone wants the imaginary one, and now we're on their radar."

Derrick caught Shawn's eye. "At the homecoming dance . . ."

"What? Those dudes . . . ?" Shawn interrupted.

Georgie listened to his mind run through possible causes and effects.

His father replied, "The intruders at the homecoming dance have since matched law enforcement facial recognition searches. One of the men was related to a friend of the receptionist, a first cousin."

"But why would they look for the black box at the high school?"

"We don't think they were," Earl said.

He shot up and paced in front of the fireplace. "Then . . ."

"They were looking for you, Shawn," Luther said gently. "Maria Elena had a vision of the men. She saw them search the crowds at the high school, the boys' restrooms, then leave the Port of Mystic Creek."

Shawn stopped walking back and forth and stared at Maria Elena.

Luther continued, "It was the night of our seaside picnic, while you and the girls investigated the water's edge with your flashlights —before the chocolate fondue."

"Oh." He turned to Luther. "How do you know they were looking for me?"

Maria Elena answered, "Each man carried a picture of you."

"It was your school ID photo, Shawn. The school network was hacked," Josefina said.

"But none of this makes sense. Why me?" He plopped down and gulped his water.

Earl expounded, "Dad's name is listed in the contract paperwork as the lead scientist and development engineer. My name is there as his senior assistant. The info's open source. You could find it on the internet with the right search."

"They could figure out you were the right kid by checking for family on your online profiles," Georgie offered.

Luther waited for Shawn to set his glass down. "We suspect they learned your dad and Earl were aboard ship, then intended to kidnap you as leverage. Fortunately, you were here with us that night. They drove by your house where Ms. Darlene's party for her Botanical Garden volunteers was underway but drove off without intruding on the festivities."

"You knew then? But why . . . ?"

"We couldn't say anything then, Shawn. You didn't know about us," reminded Josefina. "What would you have said if we told you about Mom's vision? We had to wait for your dad to have the talk."

He rose and threw his hands in the air. "You let me walk around, not knowing bad guys were trying to kidnap me? To get their hands on something that doesn't even exist?" He turned to Georgie. "Was one of them the black jacket guy we saw across the street from the school?"

"I don't know." Georgie didn't have to be an empath to read him. His pacing accelerated. He was guarded, in shock, and angry, all of which made sense. *Is he tipping over to freaking out mode?*

Let's wait. Josefina's audible exhale drew no attention. Georgie squeezed her hand.

"Now, Shawn Robert Green, you just calm right down." His aunt's voice was stern. "These people—these meta-normals, our friends—have been working to protect you since that night." He stared at her, mute. "Your father and brother have been working day and night with the authorities and government representatives to keep you safe so you can live a normal life."

Shawn stood motionless. "Wow." He rubbed his face with the same gesture his father used. "Okay, Aunt Darlene." Taken aback, he searched the faces in the room and took his spot between Josefina and Georgie. He winced and held his shoulder when they shoulder bumped him. "Of course you'd be doing something. Thanks. I didn't . . . , but that's cool."

No one spoke. Georgie observed a lessening veil of shock. She caught Luther's eye. He saw it too.

Shawn relaxed and processed the situation. Another minute passed. "Thanks, everyone." He clapped his palms on his thighs. "What's next?"

Georgie rested her head back on the sofa. *He's teetered to amazed excitement.*

I know. Josefina didn't hide her smile.

Luther answered, "The official investigation continues. Composite sketches, surveillance camera imagery, and cell phone photos taken at the dance were run against criminal databases. The three men were identified as Mexican nationals. Although officials believe they will not return, facial scans are programmed at all applicable travel points."

"Our government program managers gave our receptionist a new cover story to blog in exchange for keeping her job," said Derrick. "Among other changes, references to transmitting matter and sea life have been removed."

"We must maintain an active stance," Luther warned. "These people may construe the changes as mere obfuscation. Maria Elena and I have alerted our contacts in Mexico to monitor without raising attention. I am collaborating with other regional mentors."

Luther shifted toward the teenagers. "You may like to know there are meta-normals who do something similar to what the blogger had first described." All eyes but Maria Elena's opened wider, incredulous.

Georgie recovered first. "You mean, like mer people? Or Green Peace?"

"Mer people?" asked Shawn

"You know, mermaids."

Luther resumed, "The Oceanic Global Initiative, an international and inter-realm network of meta-normals, allies, and environmentally-minded humans who work behind and under the scenes, in anonymity. These lightworkers operate within society, yet beyond its gaze."

Georgie questioned how anyone could do anything in anonymity without every move being posted. Her thoughts raced. "Wait!" She jumped ahead. "Maybe the bad guys heard stories about the Initiative and that's why they believed the blogger."

Shawn caught the thread. "They read the blog, and saw a new avenue for their business."

"Whoever *they* are." Derrick rubbed his face.

"I suppose," considered Maria Elena, "stories could have been passed along as folklore."

"It does conjure many more questions than answers," said Luther. He exchanged a glance with her. "We will sleuth amongst our sources to learn what we can."

"Thank you, all." Derrick Green's gaze took in the group.

Luther said, "Local meta-normals are briefed on the general situation, including Chief Ganzhorn with whom I work closely. We will continue to shield your family and home."

Comprehension spread across Shawn's face with a wide grin. "Chief Ganzhorn is . . . ?"

Luther continued, "Beyond our behind-the-scenes efforts, my young friend, we wait."

"We need to extend our protection digitally." Georgie was urgent.

"Oh . . . ," Josefina said.

"Whoever hacked the school network has the skills to cyber stalk us," Shawn agreed.

"Lay low for a while, Shawn," Josefina suggested.

"It's not like I'm posting my life's every move."

"No, but you're an active gamer."

"You're right. I've never thought about those footprints."

"I suggest you minimize your exposure and increase your system security," Luther said.

Derrick agreed. "You don't have to go cold turkey, which could raise suspicion, but be cognizant of what you post. Let's all increase network firewall and system security, including mobile devices."

Shawn said, "It's drastic, but we could disassociate our phones, or phone numbers, from online social media accounts and disable location tracking."

"And boost password strength on everything," said Earl.

"With numbers, caps, and characters, like *3arlzNut$*." Shawn spelled out the password.

"Very funny, Shawn."

Georgie kept her use to a couple of mainstream social media apps. Not that she wasn't curious, but who had time to live online? Besides, there was so much teen meanness and toxic stuff. An anonymous site called *Shh* targeted insecure kids in cruel ways. "Do you like me?" "No, you suck." Some kids even sent themselves hateful messages on the down low. She'd "heard" some students who were addicted and depressed. A kid near Starkton had tried to kill himself after he was cyber-bullied. The family moved to Alaska or Iceland—someplace cold.

She'd read somewhere how the part of the brain that deals with actions and consequences hadn't finished developing in the teenage brain. *Talk about your frontal lobe karma.* Georgie shook her head to clear it. *Glad I'm not a total social media junkie.*

Josefina spoke to Shawn. "You still need to be careful. After the dodgeball incident, Harvey's minions posted a photo."

Shawn's face fell. Georgie imagined a web photo of Harvey, Shawn, and the dodgeball. She refocused.

Luther's eyes were on her. "I know someone who can help us with web protection."

Shawn bounced to the edge of his sofa cushion. Eagerness wafted from his pores. "A meta-geek? That's fly! I've gotta meet this person!"

CHAPTER THIRTY-TWO

INTERLOPER

Georgie snuggled up against the pillows in her bed on Cedar Street. Her homework was done and she'd laid out everything for school tomorrow. Mom had texted she'd made it back home. The Greens had left Andersen Light by the time Dad returned from taking Mom to the airport. They dropped Josefina and her mom off at their house, then headed to Skipper's for dinner. The waiter, a student who recognized Dad as Professor Jones, told them Peggy had Sunday nights off. His tiny brown pony tail did not rein in the mop of hair that flopped over his face when he spoke. "Peggy's cool people."

Dad had looked worn-out at Skipper's, but something rode the track below the fatigue. Happiness? Expectation? When asked how the drive to the airport went, he'd replied with a breezy, "Splendidly."

Scenes of the weekend played in her mind. Images of Shawn's reactions were replaced by the renovation of the lighthouse's third floor. She imagined shades of lavender and sounds of waves through open windows, until sleep took over.

Was she still dreaming? She knew she had gone to bed in her

room on Cedar Street, but she got out of bed and walked out to the seaside balcony. It was barely dawn. Grainy darkness strained her focus on the grays and shadows of the waves and rocks below. A few birds, already awake, dove and skimmed for an early breakfast.

"I love this time of day."

What the . . . ! She nearly jumped out of her pajamas. Her slippered feet backed away from the interloper. She brandished her flaming sword. "Who are you!?"

"Whoa, there!" The boy, his back against the balcony's railing, held his palms out. "No need for weaponry. I'm not looking for trouble."

Conscious of the ocean's cool breeze, she wrapped her arms around her chest, the sword upright in her hand. He was a couple of years older than Georgie, tall with chestnut brown hair and natural red-gold highlights evident even in the shadowy light. "Where did you come from?" His kind face was handsome, which could be how people like him burst their way onto other people's balconies to scare them half stupid. "Answer me," she commanded, as if she had the upper hand. She wiggled her sword at him.

"Truthfully, I'm not certain. I . . ."

"That's it? You're telling me you don't know? Speak up before I call the authorities!" She pictured waking Luther.

"No. I mean to say, you must have summoned me."

He didn't appear to be dangerous, but that could be faked. People don't just appear out of nowhere. Maybe he was a nut job. "Why would I summon you? Are you nuts? Spill it."

"Please, don't be afraid. You're dreaming, right? *I* am in *your* dream. You called me in."

She glanced around her. He remained on one side of the balcony. His posture was non-threatening, though not exactly what she'd call submissive. The navy sweat pants and dark green t-shirt with "Meditate" in white letters did not disguise his athletic build. His feet were bare. It did feel like a dream.

"See?" He'd observed her inspection. "I was asleep too, taking a nap. Or rather, I am asleep, but in your dream."

"Why would I call for you? I don't know you, or know how."

"That's a good question."

Her eyes narrowed. "You've done this before, then?"

"No, I never have. You're my first." His grin came and went so fast she might have imagined it. "I have heard of this, though it's believed the parties involved need to be acquainted. Since we've never met, at least in this life, I'd say this is an anomaly."

"Anomaly." She considered it.

"It's when . . ."

"I know what an anomaly is." She leaned against the cold railing and looked out where the horizon would be if she could see the difference between ocean and sky. She must have relaxed enough to let her arms and guard down because her sword was gone and he'd moved a little closer. "How do you know you didn't call me into *your* dream?"

"I'm only guessing, but you live here, right? I've never been to or seen this place before."

"Does it matter? Besides, I don't live here, yet."

"I don't know the answer, but I will study up on dream logic. What's your name? Mine's Arthur." He had an accent. She was no expert, but it had to be from somewhere in the UK.

"Georgie."

"It's nice to meet you, Georgie." He extended his hand with a smile.

What the heck? She shook his hand. His grasp was firm, his hand warm, almost hot. "Sure," she said, "you, too." Her smile was automatic, a traitor. He chuckled softly. Was he laughing at her? She peered right into his very blue-green, hazel eyes, but saw no malintent amidst the brown and gold sparkles. They were clear and easy, like he was centered and happy where he was with himself. She saw something else. What was it? Curiosity? She glanced away before she embarrassed herself.

"We may never see each other again, Georgie. We may as well get to know each other."

She scooted away from him, crossed her arms, and glared at him.

"No, I didn't mean . . ." He shook his head. "I'm not doing this well. Please, this is new for me, too." His manner was uncertain. The lopsided smile looked genuine.

She blurted, "Are you meta-normal?"

"Let's get right to it then. There's a brilliant question, Georgie."

"That's how I roll. And the answer is?"

"Yes. The answer is yes. I take it you are as well?"

"I found out recently."

"Then you must be . . . ," he calculated, "fourteen?"

"Almost fifteen, and you?"

"Sixteen, almost seventeen. How did you find out?"

Why not? Georgie told him about dodgeball day and confessing to Luther. She scrutinized his reactions. Arthur was a good listener which encouraged her to share, even the embarrassing parts where she thought she'd lost it and worried she was a freak.

"So you're *that* Georgie." Comprehension spread over his face.

"What's that supposed to mean?"

"I expect all meta-normals are told about you during the coming-of-age talk." He asked in an amused tone, "Weren't you?"

"Well, I'm me, aren't I?" she said shortly. Did he poke fun, or just have a good sense of humor, which normally she appreciated? "Anyway, sort of."

"And Luther, he's your teacher, right?"

How could she describe him? "Luther is an old friend of the family, and . . . "

"He's your teacher, your mentor, if you will?" Arthur smiled to himself. "But of course he is. Did you know he was only eighteen at the time of the prophecy? "

Uh, no. "Really?"

"Did Luther help you trace your first exhibited abilities?"

"Early on it was mainly about speed and," she paused, opting to leave out any reference to Jackass, "something he calls shielding." Her mouth slipped into a side grin.

"What is funny?"

"I wasn't sure it if it would work at first. I got the idea from a space show on TV." She peeked to gauge his reaction and claimed one of the chairs.

"Pretty clever, that. I know the one—*Star Trek*." He took the other chair and put his feet up on the side table and crossed his ankles.

The sky lightened to gray-blue. She could see clearer. Self-conscious, she reached up to check for eye boogies and attempted to run her fingers through her curly bed hair, but they got stuck. "What about you?"

"Oh, I'm still in training, too. I suspect it never ends."

"What?" She gaped at him. "We never get out of school?" He laughed, a friendly kind of laugh which softened the blow of going to school forever.

"There's always more to learn, different ways to hone your skills, and more depths and heights and dimensions to things. Life itself is a classroom. Take this dream, for example." He gazed into her eyes. "Do you think we could learn to do this again sometime?"

She forgot to be cool. "I hope so."

Georgie stirred in her in bed, the one on Cedar Street, but lay still for fear the memory of the dream would float away. *How am I going to remember it?*

"I'll help you. Write it down." It was Arthur's voice, accent and all. She untangled herself from the bed covers, flipped on the desk light, fumbled for her journal, and wrote as fast as she could.

CHAPTER THIRTY-THREE

JAVATEA NOVELTY MONDAY

She stared blindly at her handwriting in the journal, flipped off the light, and shook her head at the intensity of the dream. Morning was still dark outside her bedroom window. Her chest and guts quaked but the rest of her was sleepy. The dream had left her off kilter, or was it the boy? His dream charm had disarmed her, enough to interact. How did she hear his voice afterward if he was a dream?

Georgie sunk deep into her pillow, moved her focus to the lava lamp and pondered Arthur—interloper or dream walker, real or imagined—until her heavy eyelids won out. She drifted into sleep like a feather floating through multiple layers of air. Each layer moved in different directions until the feather neared the ground at last, then blew back up in another light wind. Far from rested when the soft strokes of a harp sounded from her phone alarm, she sat up groggy. *Hmm.* The things in her room were out of place. *Whatever. I'll investigate later.* Breakfast with Dad and a school bus demanded she hustle to get ready.

"You okay?" he asked over his coffee mug. "You seem distracted."

"Yeah, I just didn't sleep well."

Thanks to last night's pre-planning she made it to the bus stop appropriately dressed with everything she needed for the day. She inclined her face at Harvey. He and his boys stood on the grassy area between the sidewalk and the low wall that butted up to the yard of whoever's house had the luck to be a school bus stop. Harvey returned the gesture with his usual imperceptible nod. Georgie opened her phone's e-reader and dove into her current book until the bus came.

"You look different." Josefina bounced onto the bus seat, sunny, rested, and inquisitive.

"I didn't sleep well." She didn't bother to shield her unprocessed emotions. "You ever hear of people visiting other people in dreams?"

"No."

"Me neither."

"Really? That's all you're giving me?"

"Yeah, it was just a weird dream." At Josefina's skepticism, she hastily added, "You must have them too." *I guess I need to thought shield.*

"Yes, I guess so." Josefina didn't push for more. Georgie sensed her curiosity and said a silent thank you when Shawn landed in a smooth, twisting slide and turn. She admired his recovery from the weekend's information overload.

Dressed in one of his signature polos with alternating wide stripes of forest green, white, and orange-yellow, he hung over the seat back. "What are you two talking about?"

"Dreams," Josefina replied, too upbeat. "Ever have lucid dreams, Shawn?"

Georgie self-shielded and groaned internally. *So much for a break on the subject.*

"Actually, I have." He colored a reddish dark honey and inadvertently shared mental images of Josefina—clothed and decent, thank God.

"Maybe they're not uncommon," put in Georgie. *Poor Shawn. He's so transparent. It's not fair. There must be a way to shield his thoughts when he's around Josefina. Starting now.* She imagined a force field very close around his head, imbuing the intention into the shield, as Luther instructed, to filter only Shawn's thoughts of Josefina. His aura pulsated. *What if our bodies also radiate our thoughts? They must.* She extended the field to include the rest of him. The metas continued to place their protective shield around him—this was just a little added something. She ignored Josefina's raised eyebrow. "What? Lucid dreams do show up in books and movies."

Josefina contributed to the verbal conversation. "You're right, but how many people direct their own dreams?" Her eyes moved up and left in thought. "I have dreams where I remember something, like déjà vu, or where parts of the dream happen later."

"So cool," said Shawn. He cocked his head to one side. "Is it part of your, you know . . . ," he looked around to see if anyone could hear, " . . . special talents?"

"Gee, I've never thought about it," Josefina answered. "We haven't covered dreams yet. What do you think, Georgie?"

"I think I'll read up on lucid dreams. It may prove useful one day."

Josefina caught her eye. *Yeah, okay. Whatever you say. Or don't say.*

"What?" Georgie asked in a staged whisper. "It might."

"Wait up. Did I miss something?" Shawn, whispered, "No fair with the telepathy."

"He's right," Georgie concurred.

Maybe this time. Her smile uncharacteristically feeble, she responded, "Okay."

Georgie leaned in for a shoulder bump.

Josefina returned the bump, but narrowed her eyes at Shawn.

Georgie let out a slow, quiet breath, and thought of her own dream. She would replay its delicate memory later in the privacy of her bedroom with a shielded mind before it dissolved into the ether. Some things were personal. Besides, she didn't know how she felt about it. Her attention flew back at Shawn's voice.

"Thanks," he said. "It'll be difficult enough keeping up with you two."

They exited the bus into the slow flow of students. Ruby called Josefina over. It was the perfect moment. Georgie leaned nearer to Shawn, her voice conspiratorial, "Hey."

He hunched down so their faces were level. "Yeah?"

"I've shielded you so Josefina can't read your mind—specifically, any thoughts about her. I've never tried this before, but it should work okay."

He stared at her for a fraction of a second. "Thanks." He straightened. "Sweet," he said, as Josefina rejoined them.

School got out early after an assembly to update the students on the homecoming investigation and provide cautionary guidelines for Friday's Halloween costumes. Georgie and Josefina solidified their afternoon plans at their lockers—they'd take the bus to their respective homes, grab their bikes, and meet up at Javatea Novelty Shop.

Once outside, Georgie checked across the street. That's when she saw him.

The man stood in a different spot, but wore the same black jacket. Georgie glanced over to see if Shawn stood beneath the canopy of their tree. He did. She looked back to Black Jacket Man, his face pointed toward Shawn. The man started to cross the street! Now what? What could she do? She slowed down and threw an arm out to stop Josefina.

"Is something wrong?" Josefina asked. *You're acting weird.*

It's the Black Jacket Man. Wait here.

"But . . . ," Josefina objected.

Just wait! Georgie turned toward Shawn. Her promise to Luther to keep a low profile screamed inside her head. If she couldn't run or knock the bad guy out, what could she do? She focused on Shawn and pushed extra shielding his way.

"Oh! What just happened to Shawn?" Josefina took a step forward.

"Wait, Josefina, please." Georgie whispered. *I put some extra shielding around him. The force must've knocked him down.*

Black Jacket Man dodged afterschool traffic in the street. Georgie's heart pounded. She assumed her stance, aimed at the man's knees, down to the soles of his cowboy boots, and shot. The force shield, like a barrier, stopped him in his tracks.

She peeked over to the tree. No Shawn. *Oh, no!* Georgie scanned the students and spotted him ambling toward the bus. Her eyes locked onto Black Jacket Man who had tripped in the street and struggled to get back on his feet. Shawn boarded the bus.

Now! Let's go! She and Josefina hurried to the bus before it left. Georgie glanced over to the street. Traffic had stopped. People got out of their cars to help Black Jacket Man.

Georgie slid into the seat behind Shawn. The bus pulled away.

"What the . . . !" Josefina glared at Georgie and dropped into the seat beside her. *Why did you stop me from going to Shawn?*

Because I don't think either one of us wants Black Jacket Man to know we exist.

Where was he? What happened?

He was across the street from the school. I saw him head toward Shawn. I stopped him.

Josefina's scowl lessened. *How?*

I projected an energy barrier, a shield, to keep him away from the school.

"Hey," said Shawn. "What's up with you two?"

Georgie said, "We'll fill you in later, somewhere more private."

GEORGIE PARKED her bike in the crowded rack at Javatea Novelty. Helmet off, she attempted to stuff loose hair into her pony tail, and calm herself. She opened the shop door to an explosion of coffee and spice. The place was packed with older kids. Accompanied by hisses of the espresso machine and shouts of "order ready," young women on a raised platform played a harp and stand-up bass. Georgie spotted Josefina at a table with a steaming mug. Georgie scanned the chalkboard menus. The counter displayed CDs by the harp and bass duo next to gift cards, mints, and chocolates. Ledges and other wall space exhibited local art with artists' names and prices.

Georgie picked up her chai tea and moved to a sideboard to add coconut creamer.

She joined Josefina at her tiny table.

"About before . . ." Georgie started. "We good?"

"I guess." *I guess I was just scared, for Shawn.*

I guess I could have communicated better. I was trying to keep tabs on both Shawn and Black Jacket Man. I didn't mean to knock Shawn down when I reinforced his shield.

It's okay, Georgie. You did what you had to. I understand now. Josefina blew into her hot tea. "I *was* going to ask what you're doing for Thanksgiving. But, now . . ."

"Thanksgiving? That's a ways off."

"I know. It's not even Halloween."

"We're going to my Grandma and Grandpa Ryan's. We'll be back by Saturday. Dad has a gig that night at the City of Mystic Creek's pre-holiday gala. The police, fire department, transportation, and rescue workers all get together before the season kicks into full swing."

"I think Mom's going with Mr. Luther this year. It's a fundraiser for charities."

"Let's text while I'm gone."

"Text?" Josefina asked and sipped through the foamy surface of her tea.

"Yeah, as a backup." Georgie leaned over her cup for a taste.

"Good idea. Texts will verify our telepathy."

"Maybe it won't matter, but we haven't communicated long distance yet. What are *you* doing for Thanksgiving?"

"Adolfo is going home with a friend of his, Chris, from college. Mom and I are going out to Mr. Luther's. I'm not sure who else will be there."

"Cool." Georgie set her cup down and stared off into space.

"Hey!" Josefina grabbed her hand. "Are you okay?"

"What?" She retrieved her hand. "Of course I am. Why?"

"I wanted to make sure you weren't, you know, like what happened when your dad played the piano the other night."

"No, I . . . Well, sort of." Georgie finished her tea, dabbed her mouth with the square napkin and reapplied her lip balm. *Hey, wouldn't it be great if you could see what I see, or somehow know what's going on?*

It would be. Josefina reached for her bag and helmet. *Another good idea would be if you were aware of your surroundings during the visions. I'm just saying, for safety's sake. Let's ask Mr. Luther about it today.*

"And," Georgie started, switching topics, "about that dream I had."

"Tell me." Josefina sat back and listened without interruption, her face especially wide-eyed and attentive. Once Georgie had finished, she suggested, "I'd say you can only wait to see if this Arthur person shows up again."

"Yeah, you're right, in a dream or otherwise." Georgie had many strange dreams. Maybe this was just another.

SUN PENETRATED their jackets through the clear, balmy air. Rasps and clicks of the bicycles punctuated their silence. They rode side by side until they were inside the gate on Luther's Lane. Georgie zoomed in wide circles around Josefina, who pretended to ignore it.

"So about Halloween?" Josefina asked. "Mom makes a big, but understated deal of it."

"Big, but understated?" Georgie asked, glad to be using her poking-fun voice again.

"It's important to her, but she doesn't go hog wild over the usual decorations. For her, Halloween, or Samhain, is about the season."

"Sour what?"

Josefina spelled it out. "S-a-m-h-a-i-n, but it's pronounced sow, like the pig—sow-in. It's an old Celtic holiday which marks the end of the harvest and beginning of winter. You know it's all about nature for Mom. We come out here to the lighthouse and it's usually pretty laid back. We don't get trick-or-treaters. Last year, after their meditation, I joined Mom and Luther for pizza and old movies." They coasted into the carriage house. "You think you can come?"

"Uh, let me think." She leaned over her handlebars. "There are invitations to crazy zombie costume parties to consider. You know, the ones I didn't get, or want?" She swung her leg around and tapped the kick stand with the toe of her boot. "It's Friday, right? I'm in!"

CARL, Maria Elena, and Luther were gathered around the kitchen worktable with a woman Georgie didn't know.

"Hello, girls," Maria Elena said. "Meet Penny Hanna. She's going to help out around here. Penny, these are our teenagers, Josefina and Georgie."

They lifted their right hands like they were pledging.

"Nice to meet you both." Penny's smile was authentic.

"Likewise." Georgie returned the smile and shook her hand. Younger than her sister Peggy—the waitress from Skipper's and anonymous famous writer—by a few years, she shared her sister's bright red pony tail and attentive green eyes, but with less mascara.

Josefina followed her lead, then directed to her mom, *What's this about?*

Luther responded aloud. "You remember Peggy Hanna? Penny here is Peggy's sister. She's moved back to Mystic Creek just as we needed help here at the Light."

Josefina threw Georgie a look. *I didn't know we needed help.*

Georgie raised a brow at Josefina's protective posture. Her friend was a balker, until she sorted out the intruding change. *Whoa, mama bear! Penny is Peggy Hanna's sister—which means she might be meta too! And might hear you?* The woman gave no sign she heard their telepathic banter. She was probably too polite.

Josefina stepped up. "Welcome, Penny. It's been busier around here, for sure."

"Penny brings many meta-normal talents, *mijas.*"

Georgie stifled her told-you-so, but couldn't resist a wink at Josefina who rewarded her with a narrowed eye glare.

The six of them crowded around the third floor drawing and Luther briefed the new construction progress. "The entire floor has been cleared for the workers. Girls, please use a guest house to change into your exercise gear." He looked up from the drawing. "We are also remodeling the second floor bathroom." He glanced fleetingly at Maria Elena.

Luther shoved the pencil he'd used as a pointer behind an ear. "The contractors, Cooks and MacIvers, siblings and cousins, have worked together for years. Their labor is a choreographed dance accompanied by music using improvised speakers—cell phones inside empty buckets."

"Their ancestors helped build this place," Carl added. He gave Georgie and Josefina a meaningful look.

"They're allies?" asked Georgie.

"Yes, for the most part," Luther answered.

"Miss Georgie," Carl said, "I've set up a weight station for you in a corner of the workshop."

"Oh?" Georgie arched her brows before realizing he meant weights as in lifting.

"Mr. Luther said it's to measure your progress."

"How fun." Josefina grinned.

Carl rose to leave. "Thanks for setting up the weight station, Carl," Georgie said.

"You're welcome, Miss Georgie." He threw on his cap. "I've got work outside. Thanks for the cider, Maria Elena."

Georgie seized the moment. "We had an 'almost incident' with Black Jacket Man."

Josefina added, "Georgie handled the situation. No metanormal abilities were exposed."

"Please tell." Luther briefly clasped Maria Elena's hand.

The girls, led by Georgie, related the experience.

Penny gave a silent whistle.

Maria Elena remained still.

"I applaud your use of telepathy, girls," praised Luther. "Georgie, you were able to employ one of your primary abilities to diffuse the threat *and* maintain your anonymity. Josefina, your spontaneity as a team player protected your identities. We'll discuss the effects Georgie's shields had on this man and Shawn later."

Josefina moved on to Halloween. She asked her mom to expound on the topic.

"Gaelic and pagan folklore are credited with what is called Samhain or All Hallow's Eve," Maria Elena explained. "However, the day is recognized by peoples and ancient traditions around the world. In the northern hemisphere, the holiday marks the end of harvest season and longer nights. Samhain seems like any other during the light of day, but many believe the veil between this world and others becomes thinnest at night, allowing seers, *curanderos*, shamans, and other sensitive souls to span the threshold and do their work."

"I've never heard anyone talk about this." The faces around the worktable told Georgie this was just another normal, everyday conversation.

Luther rolled up the drawing and slid it into its long tube. "Maria Elena finds clearer communications with the plant world, or to be more specific, their spirits."

"Okay," Georgie said, relieved the communication was with plant spirits and not ghosts.

"I cook and walk the grounds a good deal of my day," said Maria Elena. "Communing with the plants is an integral part of my yearly planning. After Luther's global meditation and the harvest dinner—he was selected by Oma to conduct it this year—I will dedicate the remainder of my evening to the plants."

"Global meditation?" asked Georgie. Josefina widened her mouth into a straight line and shrugged her shoulders.

Luther replied, "We will simultaneously webcast from the great hall to regions around the world. Many make it their annual harvest celebration. While most, even those with telepathic abilities, will watch via our intranet, some may teleport in. A few from Mystic Creek will attend in person, like Penny who will set up the network communications."

Teleport in? "Teleport in, what do . . . ?" Georgie threw a questioning look at Josefina who responded with her perfected one-shoulder shrug.

Luther explained, "Some may join us *sine corpore*—without their physical bodies. Given the aforementioned ethereal effects of the evening, you will likely detect their nonphysical projections."

Georgie visualized people shimmering in and out like with the transporter of the *U.S.S. Enterprise.*

"Others, for whom the Halloween holiday is traditionally busy, will not join us at all." He grinned. "Imagine the shenanigans Chief Ganzhorn's likely to discover this All Hallow's Eve."

A long view of downtown Mystic Creek artfully draped in two-ply popped into Georgie's mind. Her unshielded image generated laughter around the table and a knee knock from Josefina underneath. "What will Josefina and I do?"

"You may assist Penny and me with the evening's preparations," Maria Elena suggested.

Luther added, "We encourage you to join us for the entire evening—introductions from regions around the world, the meditation, and, of course, the harvest dinner."

Josefina asked, "Will we meet others shielding Shawn?"

"Perhaps during introductions, though they will not be identified as such."

"Still, it's exciting. Right, Josefina?" Georgie grew more in awe at this world with each new peek into it. It was vaster and more connected than she'd imagined. How far reaching was the meta realm?

THE MOAN of a foghorn reached the kitchen. Penny excused herself and rose to gather her things. Luther, flanked by the others, grinned as he opened the door to the always vibrant Peggy. The women exclaimed delight at her exaggerated autumn colors of intense plum, orange, yellow, red, and green before the sisters climbed into Peggy's red Prius, drove around *Peaceful Seas,* and out Luther's Lane.

CHAPTER THIRTY-FOUR

METANALYSIS

Six sets of meta-normal eyes locked onto Luther as he spoke during Tuesday's meeting of adult meta-normals in the great hall. "We believe Don Pingue and his people are behind the Shawn Green kidnap attempt."

"Who's this Don Pingue?" Nancy Blackeagle asked.

"He is the leader of a crime organization headquartered in Mexico," Luther replied. "Our associates in the Western North American and Central American Caribbean regions with ears to the ethers, including some of you here, report both meta-normal and human telepathic, clairvoyant, and empathic communications. Penny Hanna, whom we welcomed earlier, along with her cyber counterparts—meta-normals and allies within international regions and government agencies—have verified information linking the gunmen at the high school with known Pingue provincial networks."

Penny nodded in acknowledgement.

Maria Elena said, "As you may remember, my brother Alejandro is in Mexico."

"Alejandro is working with meta-normals and others in the

region," elucidated Luther. "Chatter about a portal has surfaced in their communications analyses. Their interest piqued at indications the portal was a human device, not meta-normal activity."

"Whose chatter?" Melanie's brows poised in query.

"The traffic came primarily from individuals known to be involved in criminal activity, whom we now know are Pingue's people."

"I see."

Luther said, "Their communications increased, which drew attention of both meta-normals and allies in the Central American Caribbean region, and both east and west regions of North America. Analysis of social media, email, text, voice, and thought traffic revealed communication trails from Don Pingue's organization in reaction to the blog written by Derrick Green's receptionist."

"There is a human transmission device capable of transporting something besides data, a pseudo portal?" Peggy asked, her tone incredulous.

"No, nor is the Greens' device capable." Luther elaborated, "I will say it looks typical of its kind—sleek casing, digital display, and status lights—yet between us, its potential may one day spearhead human data transfer toward the more etheric.

"Meanwhile, the blogger's original verbiage mentioned transporting sea life out of harm's way. The reference was removed, but by then Pingue's underworld had construed a connection between the Greens' device and the *curandero*."

Chief Ganzhorn said, "We believe Pingue connected what he had heard from the blogosphere with the old man's alleged portal. My human investigations have identified one of the intruders as a first cousin of one of the blogger's friends."

"That young receptionist certainly ignited a chain of events from her wishful thinking," Peggy surmised.

Nancy asked, "So where are we now?"

"There is no evidence of physical movement by Pingue," said the chief, "but comms by his people are at an all-time high. The fictional portal is practically a meme. Interest in the Greens' Project Hermes has intensified and security has been elevated."

Luther said, "Penny has extended protection of Shawn and his family to the web. Government personal security agents . . ."

Nancy interrupted, "Body guards?"

Chief Ganzhorn answered, "Yes. One agent is covering each family member, casually and from a distance. In other words, Shawn is not being walked to school."

"Georgie, Josefina, and Shawn witnessed a man loitering across the street from the high school," Luther said. "They believe he's been watching Shawn. Georgie thwarted the man's attempt to cross the street toward Shawn yesterday. He is likely Pingue's man versus the government's. I ask everyone here to continue energetic shielding of the entire Green family." He added, "And, I'd like to know why Mr. Pingue believed the *curandero* knew about a portal."

CHAPTER THIRTY-FIVE

SAFETY FIRST

T he teenagers darted up the tower's staircase behind Luther. They craned their necks as they passed the second and third floor construction, filled water glasses in the gallery's kitchenette, and took their seats.

"Welcome to our meta mind-sharing session."

Luther unfurled what the girls had dubbed his newfangled whiteboard. "That just never gets old," Georgie remarked. She scanned notes from previous classes still visible on the opaque screen. Colored highlights, circles, and arrows jogged her memory. A new bullet had been added: Visions.

"We have things to add to the list," said Josefina.

Georgie gasped internally. *Oh no!* Arthur's hazel eyes flew into her mind.

"Yes, Ms. Garcia?" asked Luther.

"One is lucid dreams, and the other is being lucid during a vision, or whatever we're calling what Georgie does. It's about safety."

Luther set his water glass on the bar. "Great questions, Josefina. We must incorporate smart safety with every developing ability, and manage ourselves so as not to allow the vision or the circumstances within it to control us. A living, breathing, mental vision checklist will help you maintain awareness on all levels." He glanced to their left for a fraction of a second.

Georgie held her sigh of relief. Maybe they would skip over dreams. Her attention moved toward the soft whoosh of the elevator.

Luther continued, "This session's primary focus is on passive visions, the less voluntary variety. Will you please differentiate an active vision from passive?"

"I've never had an active vision," Georgie said, "if it means doing it on purpose."

"I don't know if I've had either kind," Josefina said.

Luther spread an arm in invitation to Maria Elena. "Would you care to share?"

"My vision in which the men searched for Shawn at the homecoming dance was initially passive. It came unbidden. An active vision is intentional, as when I later reinserted myself into the space of the vision in order to glean more information. That night, Luther directed questions to me during the vision for specific descriptions of what I was saw."

"What do you mean by 'space of the vision'?" Georgie asked.

"Think of when you dream. There is a feeling with it, a sense of place, specific emotions. People, activities, and conversations are within the dream. Have you ever begun to wake but wanted to stay with the dream? Perhaps you zeroed in on your primary emotion or on an individual to remain within the dream."

Huh? Where was she going with this? Georgie shifted in her chair. "You switched from passive to active while in the vision?"

"Yes. I knew where I was, which is key. The vision took me inside the high school but I was physically with Luther at the picnic table on the beach." Maria Elena moved to a chair. "I am able to be here where my body is while my inner focus is with the vision. You will be, too."

The young women absorbed Maria Elena's process. Luther sensed a subtle shift as their affection grew into deeper respect. The warmth in his abdomen and heart spread to his throat before the feeling edged its way into his face. He savored the moment in silence.

Maria Elena's eyes flickered to him before she resumed. "I'll now share prudent practices for visions. First, be in a safe place physically. Survey your surroundings. Are you away from physical hazards, like stairs, a busy street, or cliff's edge? Are you with friends? In public? Can you move to a secluded place? Do you have sunglasses to disguise an unfocused stare?"

"That's a heap of questions," Georgie remarked.

Luther offered, "They are perfect questions for your check list."

"It may not seem like it now," Maria Elena said, "but when you survey your surroundings, questions like these will blend into each other in a flash and you will have an instant sense of your first priority, your physical safety."

"I don't see how you can control it if a vision comes upon you, like it has for Georgie," Josefina remarked.

Luther replied, "We use normal and meta-normal senses to be cognizant of our surroundings at all times. Maria Elena's questions are good examples of how to stay conscious of your physical environment and remain in the vision. Call it situational awareness. With practice, the process becomes automatic. You won't need to stop what you are doing to gauge your physical environs."

Josefina leaned forward in her chair. "We can begin working on situational awareness right away."

"Good idea." Georgie shared Josefina's enthusiasm.

"Excellent," Luther said. "Document your progress for the next three days. You may present your experiences Thursday afternoon."

Maria Elena said, "Passive visions, whether it is one you suddenly find yourself in, or an unscheduled response to a request, you will . . ."

"Unscheduled response?" questioned Georgie.

"Imagine you transmit to ask Josefina what she's wearing to school on Friday. You receive her reply later, when you're not thinking about it. Unlike your verbal telepathic messages, you receive an image of her dancing in an outfit to a favorite tune. Along with the visual, you may also perceive her thoughts, how she feels, and hear the music."

Luther added, "What you receive depends on your own receptivity as well as what she transmits. It could be an abbreviated mental response—from which you merely receive the words—or a full sensory experience."

Josefina asked, "Like this: black t-shirt, jacket and jeans, black boots, and orange scarf?"

"If that is what you send, *mija*. However, if you send more, she will get more. This is something you can practice, but I suggest you start slow, with minimal amount of sensory information. Remember your first priority."

Josefina hesitated. "Safety first?"

"Right." Maria Elena's smile crinkled her eyes.

Georgie asked, "So how do we go from being bombarded with a vision to asking questions to knowing our surroundings?"

"Be present—centered where and when you are, not reliving what happened yesterday or worrying about tomorrow. Know who and what is around you. Differentiate your personal thoughts from those of others you hear or feel. Ascertain whether the wind has picked up or changed direction. Gauge the emotional climate. Be centered and present. This is your anchor, your seat of control, so to speak." She waited, quiet.

"That's a tall order," said Georgie. "Who doesn't think about yesterday or tomorrow?"

"It is one thing to think of them, yet another to be so lost in thought about them you live in them emotionally, mentally, and every way," explained Luther. "Your body, existing in this space and time, reacts to the thoughts and emotions of your else-when focus."

Josefina said, "So it's like planning for Christmas. We are excited with the anticipation, but we know what day in October this is."

"Yes, *mija*. You are not so engulfed in the future that your center shifts from today. You may immerse yourself in the upcoming event in every way—smell the pine, feel the cold air, imagine a person opening your gift—yet you know you are here, now."

Georgie said, "I can see how it would be easy to have your center of focus taken to an event in the past, especially if it's an intense one." She tried not to think about Starkton.

Luther leaned forward and spoke in a slow, measured pace. "A memory which evokes strong emotions can take over a person so she feels she is actually back in that time and place. However, when the center of focus shifts, so does the power we gain from the present."

"Power from the present . . . ," Georgie repeated.

Luther ushered the women to the windows facing the port of Mystic Creek. Wind buffeted against the glass. "A simple look back in time can be like boarding a yacht moored in its harbor slip. Mentally, you see where everything is, you smell the water, hear it lap against the side of the boat, feel and hear your steps as you walk around the deck and descend into the cabin. Cold air hits you as you open the refrigerator for a cool drink. Cushions support your body as you rest to the undulating rock and slosh of the boat. But you know you are here, in this lighthouse, listening to me." He motioned them to their chairs.

"When your yacht is not moored, when you are not centered in your awareness, you can believe you really are on the boat drinking that cool drink, lulled by the waves, seemingly tether-free." Luther moved his hands to mimic the motion of waves.

He placed one hand on his heart, the other on his solar plexus, and inhaled deeply. "But when centered in the here and now, it is like you're the anchor and ropes that keep the yacht in place. You board it without a moment's hesitation, confident the yacht is secured. Yet the power of centered awareness is even stronger than the moorings of our hypothetical yacht. Over time and with practice your awareness will grow in strength, meta-normal strength."

"What about storms or sabotage?" Georgie flushed red at Josefina's quizzical reaction.

"Your centeredness keenly sharpens your awareness. You will be alert to a severed rope, the vibrations of interlopers, impending danger, or tumultuous weather."

"I will?"

"Yes, just like you did today when you saw the man in the black jacket across the street from the school. You will detect warning signals using all your senses and notice something or someone out of place. As Maria Elena said, gauge your emotions. Are they yours, do they warrant the situation, or are you out of sorts for no particular reason—irritable, short tempered, easily saddened, suspicious, or fearful?"

"Sounds like PMS," blurted Josefina.

Georgie laughed, grateful for the humor.

Maria Elena grinned. "Okay, girls. Time for a break."

"Meet back in ten?" Luther suggested.

They refreshed their glasses with water and orange slices, and munched on Maria Elena's pumpkin bars with crumble tops.

"Definitely a keeper," Luther said after his first taste.

"It's the raspberry bar recipe updated for pumpkin season."

"More, please!" The girls each grabbed another.

"Slow down, *mijas*." Her grin dimpled a cheek. "Let us summarize situational awareness." She wrote "Safety First" neatly on the whiteboard. Maria Elena spoke as she scribed. "1. Be Here and Now (Focused Awareness/Centered in the Present Moment). This helps us 2. Assess Our Surroundings." She asked, "What are some questions about your immediate environment which will become as automatic as breathing?"

"Where am I?" suggested Josefina.

"Am I close to a cliff?" Georgie asked.

Maria Elena wrote their responses on the board.

"Who is around me? Oh, and what thoughts, other than my own, do I hear?"

"What is the weather?" Georgie submitted.

"What am I wearing?" Josefina drew snickers from Georgie.

"Am I in public? Is Josefina with me?"

Luther observed the session. The board filled up with their responses. He quietly analyzed their levels of understanding and pressed a button on his remote control. The whiteboard's screen cleared amid gasps. "Not to worry," he assured them, "it is saved digitally."

Maria Elena's smile was sweeter than usual. Georgie peeked over at Luther, whose appreciation looked more than generous. Josefina bestowed her deliberately blank face.

"Visions," Maria Elena said and printed the word. She looked over her shoulder.

"Active," Georgie said.

"Passive," Josefina said.

Maria Elena held the stylus midair and fired off questions without waiting for responses. "What minimizes your chance of being bombarded? What must you be before you can guide a vision with questions and gather information? What prevents you from getting lost within a vision? How do you move from a passive vision to an active one? How do you determine your true location? What gives you your seat of power? How do you establish your personal safety?"

"Being anchored in the present moment, plus maintaining it," Josefina answered.

Georgie waved a hand toward her friend. "Yeah, what she said."

"You're off to a good start," Maria Elena declared.

Luther joined her at the whiteboard. "Good work, everyone. I leave you with a question before you go downstairs to work on your Mystic Creek High homework. How would you shield yourself to maintain your first priority and remain open to visions?" He held his hands up as if to ward off questions and pressed a button. The newfangled whiteboard folded into itself and disappeared into the pole next to his bar stool. "You are right, Georgie. That never gets old."

GEORGIE LAID flat on her back in bed and stared toward the dark ceiling. It had been a long, jam-packed Monday: the strangest dream she'd ever had, breakfast with Dad, shielding Shawn's thoughts, the school assembly, Black Jacket Man, Javatea Novelty, and Penny. The vision lesson was timely. She and Josefina rode home, worn out and sandwiched in between the front seat's recipe chat by Dad and Maria Elena, and the clank and rattle of bicycles in the back. The day's memories, like smoke from Luther's sage and cedar logs, drifted through her mind until they fell away and the last thing she remembered was Arthur's face.

CHAPTER THIRTY-SIX

META-GEEK

I t was Thursday, the day before Halloween. Georgie had kept track of the situational awareness homework exercise on her phone. There were in fact three lists: hers, hers, and theirs. Josefina oversaw all the lists but Georgie's which, no surprise, were practically identical since they asked the same questions over and over. Plus there were drill down questions for when the first set yielded curious answers. Georgie could now rattle off who was late to the bus, names of every person in every class, each day's topic of discussion, which way the sun came in the windows, or how the clouds moved, what outfits Josefina, Shawn, Harvey, Ruby, and several others wore, some of their thoughts, and endless other mundane things, including which class period the seat was hardest on her butt.

She and Josefina squeezed through the exit doors in the teenage swarm that scattered toward the long yellow line of buses. The breeze was pleasant but the same could not be said for the assault of chaotic sound. Lively chatter about costumes, party plans, and mischievous doings competed with multiple sources of music, including several marching band members who enthusiastically accompanied the exodus.

An onslaught of thoughts and high emotions had hit her early. Though she'd activated a full-on shield by the end of first period, she still buzzed from the collective energy. Glad for the contrast of cool air on her warm face, she slalomed through crowds, lesser clumps, and single stragglers to the Nancy Blackeagle finish line with Josefina glued on her six.

Nancy's neon green scarf starkly mismatched her P.E. uniform, a gray long-sleeved jersey with crimson sport pants. Georgie relaxed her self-shield. She followed Nancy's gaze. Shawn trudged toward them, weighed down with a heavier than normal backpack, and a hefty, boxy black case in each hand.

"Hey, Shawn."

"Hey." Slightly out of breath, he lowered the cases carefully to the ground and blew on his angry, red palms.

"What's up, Shawn?" Josefina inspected the cases.

"I'm going out to Mr. Luther's with you. He asked me to help him set up some networking and video stuff."

"This is Nancy," Georgie said.

"Oh, hey," he said. "I've seen you around school. I'm Shawn Green."

She shook his extended hand. "I'm Nancy Blackeagle. You're Derrick's son?"

"Uh, yeah." He looked confused.

Josefina took a step closer to him. "She's . . ."

"Oh!" He took a closer look at Nancy. "You're a, uh . . ."

"Yes." She cut him off, glanced around, and gestured to the open bus door. "Shall we?"

"Hey, Shawn, can I help you carry something?" Georgie grabbed both cases and jumped up the stairs before he could answer. Josefina scrambled up behind her. Shawn heaved himself up the steps, the heavy pack strapped on his back. They deposited bags and cases, and took seats on the opposite side to monitor jostle.

Georgie caught Josefina studying Shawn. *She must wonder why she can't hear his thoughts about her.* Georgie hadn't considered this effect of her shielding.

Shawn peeked at his phone and shoved it into a pocket. "I guess Mr. Luther is having some big meeting or class Friday night. He asked if I'd like to come, but I already promised Aunt Darlene I'd help her at the Botanical Gardens with their annual Harvest Celebration."

Georgie asked, "You notice any strange men following you?" He was quiet. She didn't hear his thoughts, which wasn't too unusual— she still didn't always hear people's thoughts, unlike Josefina.

"Other than that one guy we saw? I thought I had, but changed my mind. At first I was paranoid and always looking over my shoulder, which is crazy-making. I lock the doors. What else can I do?"

"Always be with someone or in public?" suggested Josefina.

"I try. If you think about it, it was a crowded dance where they showed up the last time." He shrugged. "The best I can do at this point is not be stupid."

"That should be . . . " Josefina held midsentence, " . . . easy."

He grinned and shook his head.

Nancy slowed the bus and pulled to the side of the road. "Luther's Lane to Andersen Light!" She switched off the engine. "Looks like you've got company today." Georgie and Josefina rushed to the roadside windows. Luther and Carl waved from grounds carts, Carl's with an attached utility wagon.

Nancy shook Carl's hand then stepped aside to speak with Luther.

Shawn sized up the wagon and introduced himself to Carl. "What a relief. I wondered how I was going to get all this to the main house."

Georgie slung her bag over her shoulder and grabbed the two cases. "With our help of course." She loaded the cases into the compact wagon behind Carl's back bench seat.

Nancy waved and the stubby yellow school bus departed. Georgie and Josefina climbed into the utility cart behind Carl, and faced Shawn and Luther as the carts rolled along the lane toward the house.

"This is a nice surprise," Georgie said.

Josefina's expression and thought relayed, *Really?*

You knew they'd meet us here?

I heard Carl's thoughts. Luther had shielded his, as usual.

How long before we got here?

I started hearing Carl once we turned onto Lighthouse Way.

"Why there? What if distance doesn't matter?" Georgie asked aloud.

"Good question. It's when I thought about the bus stop."

"Distance doesn't matter," Luther said, loud enough to be heard over the breeze, carts, and wagon wheels. "Josefina focused on the bus stop. Carl was here, thinking, like people are wont to do. His thoughts were available and she heard them." He shrugged to emphasize the simplicity as the girls chewed on his words.

"See, it's just that easy." Shawn mimicked Luther's shrug. The palms up and exaggerated crazy smile were his own. Everyone laughed but Carl, his eyes on the lane ahead.

Luther relieved Shawn of his weighted backpack and Georgie carried the heavy cases into the great hall. Maria Elena and Penny ushered them into the kitchen for a fresh batch of chocolate zucchini bread squares and steaming apple cider.

Luther observed their individual energies around the kitchen worktable. Together they created a powerful center of potentiality and creativity. Pleased with how far the girls had come in less than two months, he savored this pivotal place in time. He acknowledged the changes and embraced the anticipation for those still manifesting. Shawn's emotional elasticity gratified Luther and he prayed the young man would continue to grow and stretch. The boy's enthusiasm and open mind would serve him well. Luther's eyes met Maria Elena's. Her gaze warmed him foot to head.

He drained his mug. "The order of this afternoon's events are switched around. Shawn, Penny, Carl, and I have some network and video setup to do."

"Wait!" Unable to contain his excitement, Shawn asked, "Is Penny the meta-geek?"

Penny's blush was imperceptible, but Georgie saw it. Penny was a shy geek. It fit her.

"I've never been called that before," she said, "but, yes, I guess I am."

"Penny understates her talents as you will soon witness, Shawn. Carl and I will get the hardware in place while the two of you set up the network software and security for tomorrow night. Afterward, we'll run through an operational test."

Carl placed his napkin in the basket, mug and plate to one side of the sink, caught Shawn's eye, and cocked his head toward the door. Shawn and Penny followed suit. The three dodged through the double doors with thank yous and see you laters.

"I'll be right with you," Luther said after them, then turned his full attention to Georgie and Josefina. "How did you do with your lists?" Josephina brought the app up and gave him her phone. He peered at it with such intent seriousness he almost laughed at himself. Instead, he scrolled through the three days, handed it back, and thanked her. He repeated the process with Georgie's phone. "Very good. There are duplicate entries, which is to be expected, plus a few unique ones. Good work, you two. I trust you will persist in your situational and environmental awareness.

"Now, I suggest vision practice. First, send visions in the forms of thoughts, feelings, and images for the other to receive, then switch off. Lastly, discuss the differences between receiving a vision and reading the other's thoughts." He waited for questions but none came. "Very well." Luther stood to leave, but swung back around. "Consider shielding during your vision practice."

"Okay, thanks," Georgie said.

"Thanks, Mr. Luther."

His lips widened as Maria Elena approached, lovely as ever after a day of work in the kitchen and gardens in preparation for tomorrow. She colored only slightly, but he caught it.

"Okay, girls," she said too quickly. "Go on up. I'll be here if you have any questions."

Georgie made a beeline up the spiral staircase to the chairs Luther used for one-on-ones. She dropped her bag on the floor and made herself comfortable.

"So, Penny's the meta-geek." Josefina slouched across from her.

"Looks that way."

"She's actually pretty awesome."

"Oh?"

Didn't see that coming. Josefina had hedged her bets when they first met Penny, though Georgie had liked her straight away. Had Penny passed a Josefina empathic litmus test?

"I know I was iffy about her at first, but she has a good feel. And, let's face it, it can be no easy task to keep this place clean, except maybe for her."

"What are you talking about? Penny's the new cleaner-sprucer *and* lighthouse systems geek?"

"Apparently she has super speed, among other abilities."

"Okay." Georgie made a mental note to get speed tips from Penny.

"Mom told me she used to work for some big-name defense contractor as a hotshot cyber security expert. She moved back here to live with Peggy when her husband, an Air Force helicopter pilot, was killed in the line of duty."

"How sad." It was hard enough to move, even to a familiar place, but losing your husband? Georgie couldn't imagine Penny's grief, or having a husband for that matter. "No wonder she's so quiet." She added, "I'm glad she has Peggy."

"Me, too. So, Luther asked her to work with him on the Andersen Light and classroom network stuff. She said yes and also volunteered to help him, Mom, and Carl with the rest."

Georgie said, "It seems an odd fit but it's also perfect. Keeping everything here up to speed, pardon the pun, will be even harder with the construction."

"And there's the whole 'what she can teach you about super speed' thing."

"With bad guys hacking into school networks and whatever else, the timing is right on. I'm not discounting the mad skills of Luther and Shawn, but it doesn't hurt to have a pro, right? I mean, if somebody hacked the Halloween teleconference it would sure put a kink in things. But I imagine protection of Andersen Light also extends to its web presence."

Josefina sprouted up from her lounging posture. "Mom's coming."

They sat up straight as Maria Elena pivoted off the last stair and dragged Luther's desk chair over. "How goes the visioning work?"

"We haven't gotten very far," Josefina said.

"We've been distracted," Georgie offered, self-conscious.

"Sometimes we need to take a moment to digest, and it's been a constant flutter of ordered chaos around here lately."

"We were discussing Penny and web protection," Georgie said.

"I heard the last part on my way up. Let me see if I can describe Penny's tasking correctly. She will do what she calls 'hardening the network' and push secure solutions as far as she can legally to nodes and systems beyond the boundary of our regional network. She'll offer those on the intranet ways to enhance their network security. Penny can also extend metaphysical protection to computers and their far reaching connectivity. She can feel weakened spots and sense trouble, perhaps the way I do with plants."

"Wow," said Georgie, "I bet her company was sorry to lose her."

"I doubt they knew all of what she was capable."

"Their loss is our gain," Josefina said.

"I don't mean to sound stupid, but how does Luther pay for

everything?" Georgie asked. "I mean, there are the salaries and the renovations, and . . ."

"Curiosity does not equal stupidity, *mija*," Maria Elena corrected. "Meta-normals tend to accumulate wealth by virtue of living long lives in harmony with universal laws, and Luther descends from ancient meta-normal lines. His teaching is a source of revenue as are the many patents and royalties from his ongoing work with Carl." She rose. "If you have no more questions I will leave you to your vision work. We're having extra guests for dinner tonight. Shawn and Penny are staying, and Peggy and William are joining us."

"Do you need help, Mom?"

"Thank you, but William and Peggy are coming early." She patted them each on the closest knee and slid Luther's desk chair back into place. "Enjoy your practice." She disappeared noiselessly down the staircase.

CHAPTER THIRTY-SEVEN

RASPBERRIES, BURGERS, AND SOCKS

Ocean wind knocked at the lighthouse windows. Josefina wriggled into the chair and tossed back her braid. "Start easy and work up? I'll imagine a piece of fruit and transmit it to you. Let me know when you've got it."

Georgie closed her eyes and imagined a blank chalkboard. An orange appeared. *Maybe this wouldn't be so hard.* "An orange."

"Yes. Now send me something."

"Okay, I'll stick with your fruity theme." She conjured red raspberries overflowing a white bowl and pushed the image.

"Got it. Raspberries, right? In a white bowl." Josefina said, "Let's try a scene between people. The stronger the emotion . . . "

" . . . the easier to receive. I'll go first. Let me think. . . ." Her mind flew to Starkton and her stomach twisted. She shook her head. Images of Harvey and the dodgeball replaced Starkton. *Okay, I can work with this.* Georgie moved into the memory. The sight of Harvey ignoring pleas to stop pummeling Shawn slammed her gut. She clamped her jaw to silence a feral growl. It left her breath shallow and measured. Her stomach churned. Hot spikes shot into her extremities. Her body screamed for action, and justice. *The jackass! Who did he think he was?* She wrenched the ball away, and threw. She pulled her attention back to Josefina, and pushed.

Josefina slammed back and gripped the chair's arms, her body straight and rigid, her eyes closed tight and face pinched. Georgie scrambled to her. "Josefina, are you okay?" No response. Her friend's facial muscles fell slack. *No! What have I done?* She blurred to the kitchenette, grabbed a glass of water and flew back, sloshing. "Josefina! What's going on?" Georgie looked up at Maria Elena's arrival.

Maria Elena knelt down and took Josefina's hand. "*Mija,* open your eyes and tell us."

Josefina's lashes fluttered and she shifted slightly. *I'm okay.*

"Out loud, *mija,* and open your eyes," her mother demanded.

Josefina's eyes opened. Unfocused, they searched for her mom, then Georgie. She took a deep breath. "I got the wind knocked out of me, literally—physically *and* emotionally. But I'm okay." She took the water. "I get meta emotions are strong, but those were off the chart. Why was I affected physically?"

Luther appeared from nowhere. "Hello, young Josefina."

Some color returned to her face.

He patted Georgie's shoulder. "Tell us what happened."

Georgie said, "We started our vision experiments with a fruit image test. Next we opted for transmitting a scene to each other, and I pushed first." She described the rest.

"You *pushed?*" asked Luther.

"Yes, you know, sent, like pushing or throwing it over to her."

"It appears your burgeoning telekinetic abilities have resurfaced, Georgie."

"What?"

"When you *pushed* to Josefina," he emphasized the word, "you literally shoved the emotionally charged scene with your meta-normal strength—using focused intent. I expect you will find you can move things around without using your hands, but we shall save that for another day. Your emotions, amplified by reliving the dodgeball experience, supercharged your transmission of the vision and bombarded Josefina with your meta-normally strong emotions."

Georgie shook her head. "A double whammy."

Josefina spoke up. "We decided it would be easier to receive a full vision if there was more emotion." She tipped her head at Georgie. "I'd say we checked that box."

"Now we know for certain," remarked Maria Elena, "Georgie's meta-normal strength is emotional as well as physical. Did you shield yourself, Josefina?"

"No," Josefina admitted.

Georgie's face contorted. "We didn't shield ourselves or each other. I feel terrible. I never meant to hurt you. I'm so . . . I so apologize, Josefina."

"I'm okay. It wasn't your fault," Josefina emphasized. "It seemed like a good idea."

"It *was* a good idea," Maria Elena said. "We've all learned something here. I'm glad you're okay, *mija*." She appraised Georgie. "You are teaching us new things."

Georgie crossed her arms. *It doesn't feel like a good thing.* "I did the same thing Monday when I pushed the reinforcing shield at Shawn and knocked him down."

Luther said, "Again, that was partially telekinetic."

"We all have budding meta-normal ability stories." Maria Elena smiled. " I'll tell you girls one of mine someday."

Georgie's interest piqued, but Josefina said, "I literally just now experienced Georgie's emotions from Dodgeball Day. I mean, they were volcanic! I know we were both blown away, and it triggered my empathy and stuff—but wow!"

"Volcanic?" Georgie arched a brow. *Really? Volcanic's what you're going with?*

I could have said explosive.

"Your approach to vision practice was sound," Luther said, "except for not shielding yourselves. You may continue your practice, but with Maria Elena or me in attendance for the next few sessions. Let's all be alert to developing abilities." He turned to leave.

Josefina protested, "But I didn't get to transmit to Georgie."

"If you feel up to it," Luther said, and left by the spiral staircase.

Georgie received a clear vision of their Halloween costume.

Maria Elena leaned in to inspect Josefina. "I suggest you break for regular homework."

"Yes, ma'am." Josefina rose, wobbly. Georgie clasped her elbow, extra slow and gentle.

"We'll take the elevator, girls." Maria Elena took her daughter's other arm.

An antique oak table covered with laptops, other high-tech equipment, and coils of cable sat next to their sofa. They sipped warm ciders while Luther and Carl lowered the enormous video screen from the ceiling. It covered the face of the huge fireplace clock. Georgie peeked at Josefina. Her aura colors wiggled. *Hmm.*

Stop worrying. We don't worry, remember? Josefina placed her cup on a coaster. *I admit it was intense.*

More like you were bowled over.

Okay, it was very intense. Seriously, I don't know how you walk around in that skin of yours. You must constantly squelch yourself or I'd feel more of your daily angst.

I don't have daily angst.

If you say so. Josefina retrieved her tablet from her bag. "We better read our history assignment. You know, the one from a more distant past."

"I don't have angst."

"Okay."

Maybe I do now, after what just happened.

Josefina rolled her eyes.

Georgie tapped her chapter open. Thoughts of her earlier vision session distracted her from the homework's gothic architecture. She reread the names of different parts of the old churches and continually glanced back at the diagrams. Finally in a groove, she looked up as Shawn and Penny entered the great hall, laughing and gesturing in shared geek code. Josefina's brow wrinkled, probably from not hearing Shawn's thoughts, as the pair neared the sofa. Georgie reaffirmed how his privacy justified her extra shielding.

"Hey," greeted Shawn.

"Hey," echoed Georgie and Josefina. "Hi, Penny."

"Penny is one awesome meta-geek. I've learned more this afternoon than I have in two years." He brandished a notebook and gaping smile. He glanced at Penny. "Most of it I can only admire from the sidelines. The concepts are amazing and there are loads of practical things I can use." He slunk into one of the armchairs.

Penny took a chair closer to the homework sofa. "You've had an exciting afternoon."

How could she know? "Yes, we . . ."

"How could you know that?" challenged Josefina.

"A trace of residue lingers in the air, so to speak. Are you okay?" Her eyes were kind. Georgie instantly knew—*Luther called it claircognizance?*—Penny had had a similar event.

"I'm okay, but Georgie is still experiencing angst," Josefina said against Georgie's head-shaking protests. "We were sending and receiving and I received the equivalent of a full-on fire hose when I was expecting a latte. Georgie also has meta-strength in the transmitting department, but no one knew until today."

Shawn's quizzical expression lingered while his gawping mouth shut when the doorbell moaned. Carl and Luther welcomed Dad and Peggy, who were loaded with canvas food bags, then spirited Penny and Shawn away.

Josefina resumed reading. Georgie didn't blame her for telling what happened, not like it was a secret, but she needed time to process these changes within her. She'd have to be careful with everything she did. Not only did she need to regulate her walking, gripping, throwing, and touching, now she would have to monitor her telepathy. How was she going to learn how to use it? She returned to the world of spires and gargoyles but minutes later pulled her eyes away to sniff at drifting kitchen aromas. Georgie looked over to Josefina staring at her. "We're good?"

"Of course. I can only imagine what you're going through."

She could almost see Josefina's empathy antennae oscillating. "You more than imagine."

"What are friends for? We'll figure this out. It'll be exciting!"

Georgie laughed. "You're right. This could be fun—as long as I don't hurt anyone."

LUTHER THANKED God and all the realms for the meal the eight of them were about to eat. Georgie didn't know about the realms, but there were three types of veggie burgers and as many kinds of "fries." She chose the crunchy quinoa patty and baked sweet potato fries. To her relief, the topic of her and Josefina's vision work did not come up. There were heaps of laughter and banter around Dad and Peggy's high school and marching band escapades. Penny feigned shock that the two of them had pulled off so many of Mystic High's more notorious shenanigans, including bath bubbles in someone's tuba during one season's final game.

Luther revealed he had rationalized a few of their capers with Chief Ganzhorn. "I had to pull the meta-normal card to deflect Peggy's true identity more than once, particularly the time in which dozens of life rafts were 'borrowed' from the harbor and hung decorously from around the roof of Mystic High."

Georgie, Josefina, and Shawn exchanged wide-eyed looks.

"You were pranking with meta-normal abilities? I never noticed a thing," William said.

"That was the idea," Peggy replied.

"Hey, I remember that!" Carl stabbed the air with a french fry. "The photo made the front page. Life rafts were hanging from everywhere. That was you two?"

"We had help, didn't we, Will?" Peggy nudged her sister.

Penny's face flashed red. "Lots of kids wanted in on that one."

Dad's face brightened. "It was our senior year, the night before senior skip day. Penny was a freshman." Her shade faded to pink. "It was an amazing night. Kids from every year helped." He sobered suddenly at meeting three pairs of teenaged eyes. "Of course, it was all highly dangerous and not to be repeated by the current generation."

Laughter resounded around the great hall.

"It's okay, Dad, it's not really our thing."

"Yet," Josefina said.

"Josefina Ana Maria Martín Garcia!" her mother exclaimed.

"Don't worry, Ms. G. She's joking. Right, Jo?" Shawn's question raised the mirth level.

Luther held the door as everyone shuffled out for the night. He waited until Carl's pickup, Peggy's Prius, and William's crossover vehicle drove around *Peaceful Seas*. The delicate scent of beach flower signified his mother's presence. "I agree. This was a good day. I shall commune with a cup and my intuitive self, then retire." His thoughts gently seesawed between today and tomorrow, All Hallows Eve. *Centering tea and quiet time is just what I need, and a good night's sleep.*

"GOODNIGHT, DAD!" Georgie beelined to her bedroom and dropped her bag. Outfit rejects lay strewn across the end of her bed. Book piles spilled onto flat surfaces of the dresser, night stand, and floor. What could she move? She'd considered it all the way home. Luther had mentioned telekinesis again. It was time she did it on purpose, this time no pushing.

She pointed her finger at a stray sock fallen short of the wicker laundry basket. *Should I point? Would that be showing your cards or telegraphing your moves?* She'd fling the sock through the open closet door and into the basket. Hand lowered, Georgie focused and imagined picking it up by the toe. *Okay!* The sock hopped, but like a half-hearted frog. She tried again. Nothing happened. A point and wave won her another hop.

Okay. Let me think. She sat on her bed and stared the sock down. What if she imagined placing a hand under the sock and picking it up? *It worked!* The sock dropped, but the next time it moved through the air, hit the closet door, and slid to the floor like a defeated cartoon. Encouraged, she scooped it up with her energetic hand and tossed it into the basket. *She shoots, she scores!* Georgie high-fived the air. The hamper smashed against the back wall of the closet, ricocheted forward and dumped its clothes to the floor. *Oops! Okay. No breakage, no foul.* This time she pictured both hands right the basket and scoop the clothes inside. The basket tilted up but only half of the clothes went in. *That's cool. I choose to see the basket half full anyway.*

Was her school bag too heavy to move with telekinesis? She envisioned raising the two energetic hands to lift the bag up from the bottom. It barely moved. Should she use the imaginary hands to push energy at the bag? She took a breath and let go. The bag shot to the ceiling and crashed at an angle onto the bed. *Whoa!*

Dad yelled, "Georgie, everything okay in there?"

"Yep, just dropping things," she called out and checked the ceiling for marks. Again, no foul. The angle thing was weird. *How did it fall that way?* She'd planned to move it there, but later, after the experiment. She sat on the floor, leaned against the door, and stared at the bag. *Did pushing the energy carry my desire for the bag's ultimate destination? Did it infuse the energy of the act with intention? Seriously? Could thoughts have that kind of focus?*

Georgie collected the morning's rejects and placed them on hangers, careful not to touch her school bag so as not to dilute its mystique or discourage it from giving up its secrets. Distracted by the bag, she sent a blouse to hover its way to the closet clothes rod. It fell to the floor. She kept her eyes on the next one until it settled. Half her clothes hung on the rod, half piled on the floor. With hands on hips, she stood at the side of the bed and studied bag and clothes for the why and how. *Ah ha! It's focused attention. Or is it focused intention, like when I run?* She thought about what she could have done differently with Black Jacket Man yesterday.

Don't forget your costume. It was Josefina.

Hey! I heard you all the way from your house! Georgie pulled tomorrow's outfit forward.

CHAPTER THIRTY-EIGHT

HALLOWEEN

Dressed and ready to head for the bus stop, Mom and the sibling units occupied Georgie's mind. Being the oldest, she'd always been their shepherd and trick-or-treat escort. It was a role she wouldn't have tonight. She checked her phone for the time, and called.

"Hi, Georgie. You okay, honey?"

"Yeah. What are you doing for Halloween?"

"We're leaving today after school and driving down to Grandma and Grandpa Ryan's. They're having a party tonight with your cousins, aunts, and uncles. Rose and Bill made decorations last weekend while I was there in Mystic Creek. Everyone's excited. How about you, dear? Are you and Josefina up to something fun?"

"We'll be at Andersen Light for a meditation and dinner. It should be cool."

"I'm glad, Georgie. Talk later? Love you!"

"Love you too. Send pictures!"

. . .

THE BLUE SKY with its clear, crisp, electric air promised a perfect day. She self-shielded before she left the house, but maybe she'd overdone it. Distances between her body and the bus's interior were distorted, like she saw and heard through a soap bubble.

"Better safe than sorry," Josefina said when she telepathied her.

Was her shielding meta-powered too? She abandoned her self-searching as Josefina adjusted Maria Elena's borrowed cape around her shoulders. Their matching black capes with red satin lining contrasted sharply to their all-white turtlenecks, jeans, and training shoes, but not their Ruby Lee-worthy makeup.

Josefina hung a heavy chain necklace identical to her own over Georgie's head. "They didn't have pentagrams."

Georgie clasped the peace sign pendant. "I heart this."

Shawn sank into his seat. The patch on one sleeve of his official looking khaki uniform depicted a tree. He bent toward them for a closer look. "What are you, Florence Nightingales?"

"I told you we should wear the hats," Georgie said.

"Real white witches wear flowers or something, not pointed hats." Josefina unzipped an outside pocket of her bag to retrieve two wide headbands adorned with sprigs of wheat, lavender, rosemary, twigs, and tiny pinecones.

Georgie reached for one. "Nice."

Josefina slipped hers on. "There. What do you think, Shawn?"

"Better. More pagan, less Nightingale."

"Take a picture?" She handed him her phone and leaned into Georgie.

"Take one for me too?" Georgie produced hers. "What are you wearing, Shawn? May I take a picture?"

"Sure." He straightened to face her. "It's my Botanical Gardens uniform. In case anyone asks, I'm going with safari guide."

Josefina asked, "Where's your pith helmet?"

Shawn patted the side of his pack. "Right here." He crossed his arms over the seatback and hung his head. "Between us, I'd rather be out there with you tonight. I'll be surrounded by forest, borrowed farm animals, vegetables, and scarecrows at tonight's Botanical Gardens' Harvest Celebration."

School was a madhouse. Everyone was in costume. Teachers dressed to reflect their class subjects. Ruby came as a fashionista in ridiculously high heels. *How does she not fall and hurt herself, or anyone else?* Harvey's neon orange tie matched most of his hair. It stole Georgie's attention, as did the orange and black striped socks which peeked out from his baggy, black pinstriped zoot suit and black wing tips. Ruby flitted around him while she feigned indifference. His amused glances at her cracked his own aloof facade.

The cafeteria lunch was like an autopsy. Meatloaf forms in tomato sauce masqueraded as body parts floating in blood. Dinner rolls were shaped like bones. Eyeballs peered up from a nest of worms, but a closer look revealed mini mozzarella balls with black olive pupils in a bed of buttered spaghetti. Carved watermelon, cantaloupe, and pears posed as tongues, lips, and ears suspended in green gelatin. Tasty crumble cake disguised as cat litter and Tootsie Roll deposits tempted from stainless steel pans. Georgie inadvertently stuck a finger in the red jelly heart of a shortbread cookie corpse as she bit its head off.

The P.A. system crackled, followed by mike thumps and Ms. Storey's booming voice. "This is your principal speaking." An eardrum-piercing sound squealed into their ears but cut off. Lower decibels accompanied the next mike thumps. "Students, as you know, it is Halloween and many of you plan to celebrate this day into the evening. I remind you that we here at Mystic Creek High very recently experienced an intrusion that could have been far worse in terms of casualties. I, along with the rest of the staff here, and local Mystic Creek police urge you to be careful tonight in your revelries, and report any trouble immediately." She inhaled too close to the microphone. "Have fun and be safe. School will let out one hour early." The cafeteria exploded in cheers, applause, banging trays, and shrieking whistles.

Outside, Georgie, Josefina, and Shawn cracked up at the toilet paper wrapped around the trunk of the otherwise stately old tree in front of school. Armed more than decorated, its branches held an arsenal of black and orange water balloons, one of which drenched a fellow first-year dressed as a pirate. Georgie glanced across the street. All clear.

"Have fun tonight, Shawn," said Josefina.

Was Shawn lingering? Georgie edged off as he moved to Josefina.

"Yeah, you too, Jo," he said, but abruptly walked away.

Was it just her or was Shawn going to say something to Josefina? She glanced at her friend. Josefina's eyebrows narrowed in her usual analytical expression. One brow cocked up. The moment passed and they moved on without a word.

Nancy Blackeagle leaned against the yellow bus dressed all in white, from sport shoes to an odd ballcap and in between—trousers, shirt, cable sweater vest, and long pads that covered her legs from ankles to knees.

"Hi, Nancy," they said.

"Cricket?" asked Georgie.

"Correct! Maybe I'll introduce it to Mystic High. You're totally ripping the witch thing."

The noiseless ride, a dramatic contrast from the school day, allowed Georgie's mind to wander to Mom and the sibs. What were their costumes this year? She attached the morning's photo with Josefina and texted her mom, "Pls send pics?" The edges of her eyes prickled. The weekend party at her grandparents' house would be fun.

Josefina was quiet as they walked up Luther's Lane. Neither mentioned her near-encounter with Shawn.

"Check him out," Georgie said. A scarecrow atop a bale of hay surrounded by gourds, pumpkins, and giant sunflowers met them at the front door. Unlit candles in Mason jars created a path up the steps. Distracted, Georgie accidentally bumped into Josefina and sent her staggering ahead. She reached out to steady her friend. "Sorry. You okay?"

"No problem," she said, as if interrupted from a daydream. She restored her bag onto a caped shoulder. "I guarantee there'll be more candles. Mom's been working her magic."

Penny opened the door. "Good magic, white witches, right? Welcome to Samhain Central. Maria Elena is making her rounds of the gardens and said she'll be in after she connects with the fruit tree spirits. Luther is up in his office. Carl and I are working on finishing touches." She took a breath. "Want to help?"

Carl, plaid shirt half-escaped from his work pants, stood in the grand sitting room. He held one end of a sofa. "You're just in time, Miss Georgie. You mind grabbing the south end of this couch?"

Georgie dropped her bag and blurred across to him. "This end?" She lifted.

Carl grinned. "Yep. We're expanding the fireplace area for tonight. If you'll . . ."

She raised the entire sofa onto one shoulder.

"Okie dokie, then," he said. "Wait up and I'll show you where to park it." She eased the sofa down where his index finger directed. "That'll do nicely." He swirled his finger in the air and scratched his head. "This area needs fixing up so the camera will see everyone. Maria Elena says to make a place for drinks and have plenty of footstools."

Georgie perused the U-shaped area with its three sofas and three chairs around Luther's glass-topped table. "How many are we expecting?"

Penny counted fingers. "Peggy, Nancy, Melanie, you two, Maria Elena, Luther, and me."

"That makes eight," said Josefina.

Penny added, "Plus teleporters. They don't require seats but they do need spaces within camera range." She indicated an impressive webcam near the fireplace mantle.

Autumn foliage in pottery vases flanked the fireplace, river rocks, crystals, and gourds at their bases. *Nice.* Georgie refocused on seating and tapped the sofa she'd carried over. "Let's add this one in case we get stragglers." For fun, she used telekinesis and her physical hands to realign the furniture into a relaxed C shape, but couldn't tell which did the moving.

Carl directed Georgie, Josefina, and Penny to pose for the camera from various seats. He verified each space from the webcam's view and dipped his head in salute. "Looks good. Thanks."

Luther entered the great hall in light-weight, wool navy trousers, a sky blue turtleneck and navy blazer. His blue eyes sparkled as he removed a microphone from his blazer pocket and held it up. "To capture introductions from this end." He winked and placed it in the center of the table's glass top. "If anyone snores during the meditation the whole world will hear."

Carl said, "I'll run a sound check of Mr. Luther's microphone before I run off and leave you to it." He asked them to speak in conversational levels from various seats. Their voices rang out from unobtrusive speakers throughout the sitting area.

Samhain Central was nearly ready. The dining room table was set and decorated. The meditation zone held seats and ottomans for those physically attending, plus designated spaces for teleporters, should they appear. And, sumptuous smells teased from kitchen warming ovens.

"Hello, everyone." Maria Elena entered via the terrace door in a chocolate brown pants suit and forest green, patterned blouse. Carved wooden jewelry embedded with gem stones and comfy, yet stylish, brown shoes completed her ensemble. If her outfit was any indication, communing with the plant spirits was a success.

Georgie's gaze swung to the two identical jackets Maria Elena held. Emerald green satin lining peeked out from the black velvet embroidered in silver and iridescent thread. She handed her one and the other to Josefina. The material was exquisite, soft and tailored with attention to detail.

"Thank you, Maria Elena," said Georgie. "This is beautiful." Electricity tingled the tip of her finger as she traced the smooth embroidery.

"Hang your capes there on the coat tree." She pointed toward the front door. "Penny, Peggy has something for you to wear."

Carl cleared his throat. "I'll leave Penny and Luther to ping the distant ends of your intranet. Luther, I'll wait by the gate in case of stragglers. Goodnight and good luck to you." He ducked out through a shower of thank yous, good nights and happy Halloweens.

Georgie estimated she and Josefina lit over a hundred candles around the great hall and the front steps. They assumed positions in the foyer to begin their official greeter duties of escorting the metas to the C-shaped seating area. It was a hard job, but somebody had to do it. To keep from fidgeting, she and Josefina played a game of intuiting the identity of each next arrival.

Peggy Hanna arrived first. She resembled a blue corn maiden draped in cobalt and indigo accented by maize earrings fashioned out of variegated blue beads and bits of white corn husk. She carried an insulated case she claimed held a delicious, healthy dessert. She also held a blazer so colorful Georgie questioned to herself whether Penny would wear it. Penny did, and grinned as she slipped it on.

Melanie Ball floated in ethereal pastels of sienna, turquoise, lavender, blue, and copper. Dramatic drapery made it difficult to tell where blouse, cover, or skirt began or ended. She lugged a lidded bowl by the long handles of a macramé bag possibly meant for a potted plant. At Georgie's glance, she laughed. "It's one of my new creations. I call it my potluck holder."

Tie score so far. Georgie high-fived Josefina. Nancy Blackeagle arrived on a motorcycle still sporting her cricket uniform, minus the leg pads. She removed her helmet, stuck her gloves inside, ran her fingers through her short black hair, and shrugged on a lavender blazer.

"Hi Nancy, long time no see." Georgie admired her silver post earrings. "Labyrinths?"

"Medicine wheels."

Josefina asked, "What's in the bag?"

"Seedy, hearty, sprouted harvest bread for Maria Elena. As requested."

An RV drove around *Peaceful Seas* and parked behind Peggy's car and Nancy's bike. Two couples got out with covered dishes. They introduced themselves as Lori and Kurt from British Columbia, and two friends they'd collected from Washington, Tommy Yamada, the conference translator, and his partner, Bobby. Maria Elena and Peggy scurried to the kitchen with their dishes, probably to create more fish and loaves. Chief Ganzhorn, the only local meta missing, wasn't expected tonight. With half credit for the stragglers, and not counting potential teleporters, Georgie won by two points.

The evening progressed with technological and metaphysical magic. The giant screen displayed the world's meta regions in separate frames, with Luther's in the bottom right corner. Each frame captioned the geographic location and displayed people gathered, some in traditional garb. She squinted to make out the t-shirt messages in English—Namaste, I Am the Rainbow, No GMO, Love-Meditate-Peace, and Lightworker. Shirts worn over orange robes by the Southern Asia region read *"Luther Rocks!"* Georgie elbowed Josefina and pointed.

Luther announced, "During the introductions, a live view of one location at a time will fill the screen. We will see our friends as they say their names." He nodded to Penny.

She said, "This process will be employed at each of the thirteen regions."

Thirteen regions of metamazing-normals! Georgie had committed them to memory moving east from Mystic Creek—Western North America, Eastern North America, Central America Caribbean, South America, Africa and Western Asia, Northern

Europe, Southern Europe, Western Europe, Eastern Europe, Central and Eastern Asia, Southern Asia, Southeastern Asia, and AuZea Pacific. She watched, fascinated, as each window populated. Penny set up a rotating view so that first one region then the next took up the larger, overlay window.

Something moved to her left, a shimmering light-shadow, there and not there. Like pixels in a gradual, developing focus, a person formed. She tapped Josefina's arm, who, with everyone else, stared at the spot.

"Welcome, Herman," Luther greeted.

The flickering image placed his hands together, bowed his head to those present and the webcam, then winked directly at Georgie. She managed her shock into a polite smile and forced her eyes back to the display after Josefina's elbow nudge.

The window remained for thirty seconds then cycled to the next region's metas. A few teenagers interspersed the regions and Georgie silently guessed at their meta-abilities. The camera captured Herman so well he almost looked solid. Luther's metas made for a good-looking lot. She was oddly pleased Penny had rearranged their pagan headbands of flowers and twigs. Her hair no longer sported the bouquet-meets-socket look.

A second shimmering alerted them to another arrival. Brian Olson apparated as a smallish man, with a bushy mustache and short hair thinner on top than around the sides. Georgie glimpsed inquisitive intelligence behind his round, gold spectacles. *Or was it humor?* He dipped his head to Peggy and winked.

The huge display refreshed. People on screen flashed the peace sign. *That's cool.*

It might have something to do with our necklaces. Josefina held up her pendant.

Oh right, we're wearing peace signs. Still, it's . . .

She froze. Western Europe was on. Arthur held up his hand in the peace gesture, and, with a wide smile, looked right at her! *Arthur!* She fought for control. She willed her hands not to fist and clenched her jaws to keep from gaping. Something zinged from her brain to her guts. Everything in between felt like jelly. *He was real?* Since the dream, time had battered and fried her certainty. The view changed to South America. Did he wave before the switch? She might have been glad she hadn't imagined him, but the emotional stun threatened to engulf her body.

Josefina elbowed her. *Are you okay?*

Georgie twisted enough to share a wooden half-smile before facing the display.

Well anyway, your breathing is all over the map and you look like you've seen a ghost.

Tell you later. Saved by the bell—Penny tapped her tablet to activate the microphone.

Luther rose. "Hello, everyone, I am Luther Andersen, mentor for the Western North American region, and honored to be your host for this year's annual global Samhain meditation."

Applause erupted at a volume their speakers weren't meant to manage.

Georgie caught Josefina's eye. *Luther is some kind of meta superstar!*

Right?

Luther pressed his hands together then lowered his right palm. "Thank you." The noise subsided. "Welcome all, with a special greeting to the newly acknowledged young meta-normals, and anyone joining the meditation for the first time. When your region is announced, please stand and give us your name and primary meta-normal ability or abilities. Please ensure your microphones are powered on. Let us commence introductions." Laughs and twitters reached through the sound system. He nodded to Herman.

"My name is Herman Groesbeck. I am an empath, clair-intuitive, and your meta-normal global historian." Sounds of ohs floated through the surrounding speakers.

"I am Maria Elena Magdalena Martín Garcia, empath and seer."

"Hello, I go by Peggy Hanna, intuitive and agile."

"Penny Hanna here." She raised her hand. "Speed, empath, cyberpath."

"Hi, Nancy Blackeagle, and I'm a protector-shield." She stole a glance at Georgie and Josefina and took her seat.

"I'm Brian Olson, apparating from the Western North American region. I am an empath and inducer-influencer."

Luther gestured to Georgie to stand. "Hi. My name is Georgie, er, uh, Georgia Rae Jones. I'm . . ." Applause blasted through the air. Startled, she looked to Luther. He lowered his hands, palms down, three times in quick succession and nodded for her to continue. The applause lessened. "My abilities are speed," she paused, "and strength in most everything I've tried so far." More applause followed, with laughter. Her face burned, stinging at the edges. She landed hard in her seat between Josefina and Penny and squirmed inside as if to hide from camera and people. Her feet itched to run. Arthur popped into her head. *Was he transmitting?* *"Keep" what?*

Luther stilled the excitement she didn't understand and introductions resumed.

"Hello, I am Josefina Ana Maria Martín Garcia, empath, telepath, and shield." The screen split to show all regions. Metas held up peace signs.

Georgie gingerly shoulder-bumped Josefina as she sat. Introductions continued, often accompanied by Tommy Yamada, who mimicked the voice of the speaker—no matter the gender, nationality, or accent—through his English translations. Luther leaned forward a fraction when Eastern Europe appeared. Georgie cast a sideways glance so as not to draw attention. His left eyebrow's arch and stone-like stillness was almost imperceptible as a James something from Eastern North America introduced himself. *An old friend visiting the Eastern European region?*

The next meta called herself a persuader. *Same as an inducer-influencer?* It spurred Georgie's imagination, but soon the faces and abilities blended in and out of her mind. A rhythm developed after several regions, lulling her, and she fought to stay alert—until Western Europe commandeered the full screen. Their regional mentor, Nora Emma Smith, introduced key representatives from her region. Next she heard, "My name is Arthur William McCabe —empath, telepath, agile, strength, and," he looked directly at her, "traveler."

Is that . . . ? Josefina started.

Shh . . . , later!

The handsome boy brandished the peace sign. "Here's a shout out to welcome Ms. Jones and all you other newbies." He took his seat—hastily, she thought. Georgie's face, which had cooled near to her normal complexion, again flamed.

"Yes, thank you for that, Mr. McCabe." Mentor Smith's brows briefly narrowed. "Now we'll hear from our esteemed representative from Wales."

The Welshman stood to speak, but Georgie didn't hear him. She was numb from too many feelings—a contradiction, but there it was. Until a strange, mixed sensation—like the thrill of walking on Grandma Ryan's frozen pond but the fear of not knowing the thickness of the ice—grew in her belly and expanded into the rest of her. *Fear and uncertainty? Anticipation?* These and more accompanied her confused thoughts and emotions, fuzzy and unnamed. She no longer doubted her earlier impression of Arthur's telepathic and metaphorical tap on the shoulder to "keep calm." *But what was the clapping about, and the laughter?* The familiar, disorienting sense of not knowing who she really was haunted her. *I'm just a girl.*

Georgie . . . It was Luther . . . *there is no such thing as just a girl. The expanse of possibilities—worlds within worlds, lifetimes of experiences—in one single girl is absolutely limitless. You have never been just a girl. As for the applause, the other metas know of the prophecy and welcome you. They laughed when you made reference to things you'd "tried so far" because they recognize you are young and at the beginning of who you will ultimately be. They anticipate you will achieve many great things, and what you described are your first stepping stones. Their perspectives come with much time and knowledge, and, as evidenced, a meta-normally developed sense of humor. Okay?*

Okay. I guess that makes sense. Thank you. She grasped, even through her protective bubble, that her improved sense of well being was aided by any number of empath-healers, like Melanie. Georgie stole a glance, but Melanie's eyes were on the Southern European metas. Finally, the last meta stood, Lucia Zerilli, a beautiful Italian woman who identified herself as an empath-healer and telepath.

As the big screen again cycled through the regions, Luther announced a short break to be followed by the global meditation. Georgie stared blindly as people, on screen and off, stood, stretched, and moved in and out of camera range.

"Hey, are you getting up?" Josefina stood in front of her.

"Yeah." She looked up. "Bathroom break?"

"Are you okay? Did all that clapping surprise you too?"

"Yeah. Weird, right?"

LUTHER RETURNED Georgie and Josefina's tandem hug with a squeeze and waited for folks to settle in, some in cross-legged positions, like his teleporting guests. Andersen Light's great hall, glowing in candlelight, displayed on the widescreen. He shielded the newest meta-normals from unknowingly transmitting open thoughts and feelings during the meditation and, after a silent prayer for divine guidance, proceeded in a moderate, soothing voice.

"Let us begin by inviting the Divine Presence to surround us with loving and infinite protection, wisdom, and compassion. Allow the healing light energy to move through and around you. Relax and receive. Picture and feel this light encircle your feet and gradually enfold you. Expand the light to fill the room and all those within. Imagine this healing, loving, peace encompassing your loved ones, your region, and the entire world. Relax. View our planet as if from space and witness the healing light grow, pulse, and do its work." He paused to bask in the light as it played, swirled, and shifted.

"Slowly bring your focus back to your body and remain relaxed. The primary purpose of this gathering is to give thanks—first for the bountiful harvests in our lives, individually and collectively, then for the lessons, even those we might have not consciously chosen. Please take a moment to consider and appreciate your personal, bountiful harvests." He again paused.

Georgie's mind went to Jackass. He turned out to be mentally ill. *What do they say about mean creatures, like scorpions? Don't hate them, but you don't have to invite them for tea?* He and the pain he'd caused her family were lessons she would not have consciously chosen. But everything that had happened so far had led her to here. Back then, there was no way she could have made up this kind of life. She really did have plenty to be thankful for. Her parents were talking again and her mom had her dream job. She had awesome new BFFs, plus Luther and Maria Elena. She'd grown closer to Dad. She could go on and on, but Luther was talking again.

Her fingertips tingled as if her hands were asleep, like tiny bubbles, not prickly needles. The sensation grew more intense until her fingers trembled. Georgie tried holding them still, but the sensation overcame her literally, as bubbles moved from her hands up her arms, and spread throughout her entire body. *Was she vibrating on the outside? She couldn't control it! What was happening?*

Her heart raced and banged. Luther's serene voice was in her head. *Relax and allow. Your body is recalibrating your new normal.* The bubbles fizzed from her feet through the top of her head as if she was a shaken soda pop. Like a pilot desperately gripping a shaking wheel, she held course until the effervescence slowed and dissipated. Far from relaxed, she was invigorated—jazzed, energized, ready to run and jump, until a floating sensation took over. From a distance, hands pressed down on her arms and thighs. She took in a deep, calming breath as Luther spoke aloud.

"Now, allow the gratitude to fill you until all you feel is love. Sense it with every cell of your being and extend it deep within you and out in every direction, geographically in space, and in time—to your past, present, and future, your everyplace, everywhere, and anytime self."

Breath ebbed and flowed through the room and surrounding speakers like ocean waves. Georgie's hyper energy subsided and her breathing fell into rhythm. The idea of sending love to her past self was sort of like being her own ghost of Christmas past. It was like the book by that English guy, Dickens, but she was doing the sending and not some ghost. Here she was, bathed in gratitude and love. She sent it to herself, no matter where and when she was, and surrounded that self, too. "Hi, I don't care what you're doing, or what you did, or whatever. I am sending you love. So it's okay. You're okay." *This is so cool.* Somehow, she knew her every-when self had received the message.

Luther resumed. "Bring your attention to your breath. Take this moment to release anything in your consciousness which no longer serves you. As we accept and celebrate the harvests of our year, we clear away our fields, plow them under, and prepare the soil for new seeds to take hold. " He waited. "Immediately plant your thought seeds into your fertile imagination. May they grow strong and abundant now and in seasons yet to come. We extend the love and protection we have experienced here tonight forward along our paths to better accomplish our tasks as individuals and as lightworkers." Luther reinforced the circle and redirected their attention to the present. "Great blessings, everyone." Hands together, he bowed.

Luther gestured, "Penny will remain available for a short

period to assist those who wish to converse with friends or family in other regions."

Josefina had disappeared. Georgie glanced up from the sofa to the screen. Lori, one of the British Columbia RVers, spoke with her friend Anthea in the AuZea Pacific region. Georgie edged closer to Penny as the women waved their goodbyes.

"Georgie," Penny asked, "shall we call up Western Europe?"

"What?" Her meta-normal heart resumed its pounding.

"Perhaps that young Mr. McCabe is standing near the camera. It was nice of him to acknowledge you," Penny said by way of explanation.

"Uh, sure." Why did she feel as if she walked on thin ice in unknown territory? Where was her confidence? *It's run off, and I should too.* But she couldn't. Whatever caused her to resist also propelled her forward.

"No need to be nervous. You're just saying thank you, right?"

Penny was an empath, and who knew what else. Georgie said, "You're right. No need to be nervous." She willed her heart to normalize, whatever normal was, while Penny tapped away at her tablet. The view opened into a huge library crowded with cozy chairs and clumps of people milling about. Her stomach flopped. A solitary figure facing a grand fireplace, turned. He walked toward the camera, and, presumably, their display screen, which enlarged Arthur and the intensity in his searching eyes.

"Stand there," Penny whispered to her and pointed to a spot near the glass-topped table.

"Right, there you are, Georgie." He brightened. "Good to see you again."

"Yeah, hi, Arthur," she said, significantly more shy than their first meeting. "Thanks for the shout out earlier. It was . . . unexpected." *But not as unexpected as finding out you're real.*

"You're most welcome. You okay? Tonight must have been pretty intense for you."

"Yeah, I'm good. I wasn't ready for the whole applause bit." She didn't mention the recalibration episode and instead stared at the a halo of red and gold in his chestnut hair created by the light behind him. She refocused.

"You were brilliant."

His smile hit her and her throat constricted. Her neck and face prickled hot. She struggled to relax her throat. *Was her face red?* He must be close to the camera. How else could his blue-green eyes resemble miniature earths? Their expression, a jumble of kindness and happiness, scanned her face as if to memorize it. How weird, she'd done the same thing.

He spoke telepathically. *Yeah, I'm real. And you, I'm very pleased to see, are as well. Shall we meet again sometime?*

But that was just a fluke! You said I invited you, but I don't remember doing it and have no idea how. And how can I hear you all the way from the UK?

Perhaps there's no distance factor for us. As for meeting up again, I've been practicing. . . . He glanced off camera and looked back. *Look, I have to go. They're calling us for the Harvest Breakfast. I'll visit again.*

She said aloud, "Thanks again, Arthur." *See you later.*

"Have a nice evening, Georgie Jones. I hope to see you again sometime." *Soon.* He waved his hand in the peace sign and the screen blanked.

Penny returned. "Everything went well?" Her eyes were kind, not judgy.

"Yeah, thanks, Penny." Tommy and Bobby lined up to talk with a friend. "Hey, you've got new customers." Georgie dashed off to find Josefina.

Clanking sounds and delicious aromas spilled from kitchen to dining room. Georgie moved toward the long, ornately-set table where Josefina was halfway into lighting candles. Josefina's body was there, but her blank expression said her mind wasn't. She dropped the lighter as Georgie approached.

"Hey, you okay? Where are you? You look like you were

abducted by aliens, only your body was left behind." She picked up the lighter.

"I'm scanning for Shawn."

"He's probably teaching junior harvest badgers how to bob for apples."

"Yes, it's still early. I'll try again later." She focused and straightened her shoulders. "How are *you*? I thought you might float off to the ceiling during the meditation."

"That really happened?"

"Yes, and you were shaking. Penny and I had to hold you down to the sofa. Don't worry. I doubt anyone else noticed your attempt at levitation."

"I definitely want to talk to Luther about it."

"As long as you're okay. Finish lighting the candles while I fetch the drink pitchers?"

"No problem." She skipped the subject of Arthur.

White candles and chandeliers illuminated the dining room in a soft, bright glow. Place settings at the table's end held spaces for Chief Ganzhorn and the teleporters. Before their forms dissipated, the latter transmitted telepathically how everything looked so delectable it made them too hungry to stay. Georgie lit the last candle as the kitchen doors burst open with tray toting meta-normals. She rushed to unburden Josefina from a heavy tray loaded with pitchers of iced drinks and Peggy from her pots of hot teas. Georgie relegated them to the side board. Nancy whisked by with baskets of warm harvest bread and asked Georgie to carefully carry in the heavy soup tureen. Others who had lingered in quiet conversation in the sitting room seated themselves at the table as she set the soup down on the space in front of Luther and Maria Elena.

"Thank you for tonight, Luther," Georgie whispered. "I'll never forget it." His response was a crinkled, twinkly-eyed nod.

The expectant circle gazed through the tureen's escaping steam to Luther. Every hand at the table now held, eleven faces beamed at him. He was reminded how, for a man with no living relatives, he was indeed blessed with family. "In our joining together tonight we honor our source and hail our deep and ancestral bonds. We give thanks for this meal—a symbol of our appreciation for the harvest of our seasons—prepared with love and laughter, and our ever-expanding knowledge of ourselves, each other, and the world around us. May it nourish our every cell, thought, word, and action, and ready us for our next adventures." He raised his hands, and those of Lori and Maria Elena. "Let us eat!"

He filled bowls with butternut squash soup. Maria Elena sprinkled fresh sage and handed bowls along until everyone spooned, slurped, and dunked harvest bread. Seasonal harvest fare accented earnest conversations—fresh salads, squash overstuffed with southern style cornbread-quinoa dressing, pumpkin seed and herb-encrusted sweet potato chunks, and Georgie's favorite, tasty baked veggie pockets.

Georgie and Josefina made a game of naming off the abilities proclaimed during regional introductions, during which adult metas provided hints.

Peggy asked, "What ability was like a persuader and what meta-normal proclaimed it?"

Josefina answered, "Inducer. It was Brian Olson, from . . . "

" . . . teleporting from the Western North American region," finished Georgie.

"Who identified theirself as our meta-normal global historian?" Tommy asked.

After a short pause, Georgie and Josefina declared simultaneously, "Herman Groesbeck!"

"From . . . ?" At their silence, Bobby said, "Mr. Groesbeck didn't say, did he?"

Josefina clapped her hands. "You're right, he didn't."

Kurt, quiet until then, said, "Herman Groesbeck lives in the countryside near Toronto."

Luther stroked his goatee. "Who was the only meta-normal to

self-identify as a traveler, though teleporters were on camera and interspersed throughout the regions?"

"Oh, I know," Nancy said, "but you're asking the teenagers."

Georgie said nothing. Arthur William McCabe was one subject she wanted private.

Josefina elbowed her. Her look was quizzical. "You remember, right?"

Crapola . . . now what? "Uh," she stalled and reinforced her thought shield.

"Arthur McCabe from Western Europe," Penny said and squeezed Georgie's hand under the table. "Did you know that bi-locator is another term used for traveler?" She shrugged the shoulders of her boldly colored blazer. "I came across a few in Virginia Beach."

Melanie winked at the teenagers. "Which region claimed team status with what meta-normal superstar?"

Georgie exclaimed, "The Southern Asia region for Team Luther!"

Laughter rippled around the table. She grinned. *Metas sure like to wink and laugh.*

CHAPTER THIRTY-NINE

WHERE'S SHAWN?

J osefina's screams ripped Georgie out of deep sleep. Georgie jumped out of bed, her heart pounding, her eyes wide. She scanned the bedroom of the guest house. It was quiet. What time was it, before dawn? Outside, moonlight beamed at an angle through a circle of trees onto dew-drenched grass, and into the guest house window.

Josefina's screams must have been silent. The girl paced in the pale light and alternately rubbed her red, blotchy face, moist with tears, and jammed fingers into her hair creating a tangled mess.

Georgie blocked her friend's pacing, held her shoulders, and willed a gentle flow of calm energy into her. She maintained the stance until Josefina looked at her. "What is it, Josefina?"

"I can't see Shawn. Well, I did see him, but in my vision he was being carried. That can't be good, right? And now I can't see him anywhere." Her voice squeaked.

"Being carried? Who?"

"I don't know! I just saw him and two people, but not their faces."

"Okay." Georgie forced an even tone. "We'll get dressed and go up to the house. We'll check with your mom and Luther to see what they can see. We'll find him, okay?"

"I don't understand. Everyone's been shielding him."

Georgie ducked into the bathroom, splashed her face, speed-brushed her teeth, and pulled her hair into a pony tail. Josefina, still in her long white t-shirt, stood stiffly at the window. This was not like her. Georgie felt cold fingers of panic slide into her throat and stomach. She shook it off, kicked into big sister mode, and coaxed Josefina into a chair. Bent into a crouch, she looked up into her friend's face. "Let's get dressed, Josefina. As nice as your sleep shirt is, I doubt you'll want it on all day."

LUTHER DESCENDED the spiral stairs from his rooms. It was early. Watery rays of light dawned through the high windows of the tower. He entered the great hall and lit a small fire in the fireplace as Maria Elena entered from the kitchen. They sat in meditative silence at the end of the dining table accompanied by the flicker of a votive candle she'd brought with the tea. They gazed through the windows toward the sea's horizon where the tower's light shined through dissipating fog.

Disquiet hung on their stillness. Luther broke their companionable silence to mention it to Maria Elena. "I feel it, too," she said. They again entered quiet contemplation—until two wild-haired teenagers raced across the veranda. They skidded, yanked open the glass door, and spilled into the dining room.

"Something's happened to Shawn!" Josefina cried through quick intakes of breath. Maria Elena rushed to her side.

"She saw him being carted off," Georgie explained.

Georgie wasn't out of breath, but Luther detected her shared panic. He stood, gathered up the tea tray, and gestured with his head. "This way." They trailed him to the kitchen. Georgie helped him prepare hot chocolate. Maria Elena sat with Josefina at the worktable.

"I don't understand. Everyone's been shielding him," Josefina repeated herself.

Luther selected two good-sized mugs while Georgie heated up the coconut milk. He refreshed the teacups from the cozied teapot and took his seat. Maria Elena deftly worked Josefina's hair into a braid to comfort the girl. He said, "The Samhain activities took varying amounts of attention from all of us. However, it is unlikely they distracted anyone from shielding Shawn."

Georgie slid Josefina's mug of steaming chocolate to her. She shifted on her stool and quietly turned her own hot mug in slow rotations.

Luther observed Georgie's face through her fallen lengths of dark curls. She argued with herself. He waited.

Maria Elena finished Josefina's braid, reached for her tea, and studied Georgie.

Georgie mulled over Shawn's protection. How could anyone penetrate all of that meta shielding? Unless the shielding was being affected somehow. But by what? She saw Shawn in her mind's eye on the bus, his face the reddish color he had when he worried Josefina read his thoughts. But Georgie had given him extra shielding. Oh, crap. Could that have affected his overall protection? Her blood drained toward her feet. *What if . . . ?* She was suddenly light-headed and sick to her stomach. Bent over the table, she held her head with one hand and her stomach with the other, and blurted out, "What if it's my fault?"

Luther requested, "Please explain."

Georgie looked up, everywhere but at Josefina.

"Yes?" he encouraged.

She tucked a curl behind her ear, but it fell back. "Well, ever since Shawn learned that Josefina's an empath he's been squirmy and embarrassed, and I felt sorry for him." Josefina sat her mug down with a heavy thud. Georgie paused. When no one said anything, she continued, "So, I decided to shield his thoughts, just the ones about Josefina."

"What? I can't believe you did that! It was none . . . " Josefina's eyes flashed in anger.

" . . . of my business. I know. I messed up. I see that now." She forced her eyes to Josefina. "I felt bad for him. I knew you weren't trying to listen in. It just happens. I was trying to help. It's only been since Monday. I'm so sor . . . I apologize. I didn't think it would affect his overall shielding." Her hands flew to her face.

"Your superpowers obviously overshot their mark! Again!" Josefina shouted. Maria Elena patted her arm. Josefina's anger appeared to cool a fraction of a degree.

Georgie lifted her head. "I know! I feel terrible. What if my attempt to protect Shawn from embarrassment somehow altered everyone's shielding of him? Or I messed up his shielding when I pushed the protection at him that day with Black Jacket Man? I mean, what if . . . ?"

Luther stepped in. "Playing the 'what if' game helps no one, least of all Shawn. We do not know what impact, if any, your targeted shielding has had on the situation." He glanced pointedly around the room. "I am confident Josefina will come to see how Georgie endeavored to remedy an awkward situation between her best friends. I am equally optimistic that Georgie will consider possible effects her actions may have before she employs them."

Josefina's scowl softened but remained.

Maria Elena rose with her teacup. "Mr. Luther is right."

"Please tell us what you saw, Josefina," invited Luther.

"Shawn looked barely conscious." She held her mug in a death grip.

"Think of your situational awareness. What details do you remember?"

She closed her eyes. "One man wore a chocolate brown corduroy jacket." Her eyes looked toward Luther. "The other wore a black leather jacket. They both had on dark blue jeans and black boots." She looked over their heads. "They threw him into the back of an SUV." Abruptly, she stared at Georgie. "It's Shawn's driveway."

Maria Elena turned to Luther. "Derrick mentioned a carriage house workshop?"

"We need to go!" Josefina slid off her stool.

Georgie turned to follow, but Luther interceded, his palm up. "We need more data. Ask yourselves—where is Shawn now? Is he in the carriage house lab? Is he alone?"

Josefina huffed back in her seat.

"We don't doubt your vision," he said. "We need more details."

Maria Elena cautioned, "You can't go charging into Mr. Green's not knowing if Shawn is even there. Or if those men are there. Or if they've booby trapped the place. Go back into your vision, *mija*, and see what you can see, and I will do the same. Then we plan what we do next."

Luther stroked his goatee and mentally transmitted a heads-up to Chief Ganzhorn.

No further vision-sourced information was received by Josefina or Maria Elena. Georgie, however, did see water lapping at a dock. Luther mentally saved her image from being lost in the space between mug slurpings and the quiet of clairvoyant scans.

He said, "It's time we had a look around the Greens' place."

They climbed into Woody and drove off under the morning's overcast November sky. The girls grudgingly nibbled on the dried fruit and nuts Maria Elena insisted they eat. A red and white soft-sided cooler sat between the teenaged passengers.

Josefina replied to Georgie's unasked question. *It's Mom's personal emergency kit of homemade tinctures, poultices, balms, sprays, and bandages—which I hope Shawn doesn't need.*

Georgie ignored Josefina's dig. The ride was quiet except for muffled sounds of glass bottles and jars clinking inside the cooler and Josefina nervously twisting and turning in her seat.

They turned down Birch Street and made a right up Elm. Shawn's street leveled out into a well-established neighborhood where privacy walls protected large homes. Georgie gulped at the sight of lights flashing on parked police cars and an ambulance pulling through the gaping gate to his house.

"Oh, my God!" Josefina cried.

"*Mija*, remember who you are," Maria Elena warned. "Don't add to the chaotic energy."

Josefina was quiet, but she strained against her seatbelt for a better view.

I feel you, Josefina. And she did. Anxiety wrapped around Georgie's internal organs and squeezed. She made herself breathe and the grip lessened a micrometer. Across the street, a couple of older dad-types took video with their phones. *Rude.* Her fingers drummed her thighs until she spotted Chief Ganzhorn's trench coat. She scarcely waited until Luther pulled in behind a police car to bolt out of Woody with Josefina at her heels. They leapt up to the porch where the chief stood speaking with uniformed officers.

"Good morning, Georgie, Josefina," he said.

They answered with, "Where's Shawn?"

"I'm afraid I can't answer that, but. . . . Oh, there you are, Luther. We found Ms. Green inside the home, tied to a chair in the dining room. She's shaken, but the EMTs say she's okay physically." He dipped his head in greeting to Maria Elena. "Good morning, ma'am. They have her in the living room, if you'd like to go on through."

Georgie clasped Josefina's arm. *Let's go!* The two flew down the steps, dodging uniformed police officers. Georgie stopped short. *Look.* She tilted her head to where Harvey rode his bike toward the front gate. *He can help us.* The area had not yet been cordoned and the police were focused in front and inside of the house. The girls headed his way.

Harvey rode right toward them and barely stopped in time, for what Georgie knew was effect. He leaned over the handlebars and squinted his green eyes at them to look mean. His animated red hair spiked out and away from the blonde. "What's going on?"

"Break in." Georgie measured him.

Harvey's eyes narrowed. "What's up?"

They'd come some distance since the dodgeball incident, to a place where Georgie could sort of befriend him, though at arm's length, and nod from yards away. Their uneasy and infrequent association mainly consisted of Georgie asking him about his favorite subject, Harvey. It had been Luther's idea, probably designed to teach her humility and patience, but she had come to see that Harvey was learning something too. She didn't know what.

"Look, Harvey." Georgie worked to keep her tone even. "This is your big chance. You can do some good here. Think of it as balancing your karma."

"What are you friggin' talking about, Jones?"

"How would you like to take down some real bad guys?"

His mouth moved to smile, but aborted. "Oh, yeah? What's the deal?"

"Shawn's been kidnapped. We'll explain later. Come on!" Josefina demanded.

"Whoa there, you two. What do you mean? Wait a minute. I'm not sure. . . ."

"Come on, Harvey," Georgie said. "You're a tall guy, a big guy and we need your, uh, talents to find Shawn and rescue him."

"Well, when you say it like that. I'm in."

Georgie threw a glance to Josefina.

"Thanks, Harvey." Josefina's charming, almost cooing voice was one Georgie had never witnessed. Harvey's mouth gaped and pink tinged his freckled face. Georgie caught the periphery of the warm surge of energy Josefina shot at him, and raised a brow.

Josefina returned a faux innocent look. *What?*

Georgie pointed. "There's the old carriage house Shawn's dad uses for a workshop."

"Carriage house?" Harvey dropped his bike on the grass outside the open gate.

"Garage," she translated. "Let's go!" Georgie regulated her

pace with difficulty. The other two trailed behind. The morning conspired to hold her back. Slowed to a near stop, the others caught up and she whispered, "Silence your phones." There were no windows in the wide double entry doors. A tug told her the doors wouldn't budge without breaking off the handles. They ran to the side. The single, high window was either very dirty or frosted around the edges with a thin coat of dust at its center. She looked up at Harvey.

"Yeah, I got it," he mumbled.

"Do you see anyone?" Georgie questioned softly.

Harvey put his hands around his face to block out the light and peeked in.

"Well?"

He whispered back, "No one, but the place is trashed."

"Are you sure?" Josefina's voice rose an octave.

"Well, no. I can't see every corner or under every table. Maybe we should go in. I see a door on the other side."

They scrambled around back, and mostly dodged a large black-berry bush on which Harvey snagged his jeans. They held position at the corner of the building and checked for company. The three then quietly darted alongside the carriage house to a door situated in the center. A large tree stood between them and the main house. Its autumnal canopy provided sketchy privacy. Georgie pushed at the door. It moved, but barely.

"Is it locked?" asked Josefina.

"No," Georgie whispered, "but it feels like something's blocking it, something very heavy and solid." *I can probably move it, but . . .*

"Here, let me try," Harvey said. Georgie stood aside.

Harvey leaned and shoved against the door. It didn't budge. He took a breath, pressed his shoulder into the door and pushed with his legs. The door opened a smidge. "There is definitely something heavy on the other side of this door." His back against the door, he heaved until his face reddened.

"Stop, Harv," Georgie warned. "I heard something, like scraping."

"Maybe it's Shawn!" Urgency edged out the last of Josefina's composure.

"We can't be sure," cautioned Georgie.

Josefina's face pinched inward. "I wish there was a window on this side of the building."

Georgie squeezed Josefina's arm in support, and said to Harvey, "Go ahead."

Harvey leaned his whole body into the door and pushed with his feet and legs. Georgie mentally calculated how much of her own strength she could use before provoking unwanted questions, then lent her shoulder to his effort.

"Look!" Georgie said in a loud whisper. The door had opened enough to squeeze through. Harvey wiped his forehead with his sleeve, twisted his body, and slipped inside. The girls knocked into each other to follow and nearly ran into Harvey. He'd stopped at an enormous, upturned shelf blocking the door. As slowly and quietly as they could, they stepped around the shelf, still loaded with most of its books, binders, and equipment.

Georgie scanned the large open room. It resembled a more sophisticated version of the electronics lab at Mystic High, minus the overturned tables, smashed equipment, and cables and wires jerked out of component racks. The contents of file drawers spilled onto the floor. A small safe stood open and empty, as empty as the room was of Shawn. What was the scraping sound she'd heard earlier?

It was an echo of what happened here.

Whoa! That thought wasn't hers. It had slid into her mind uninvited, but from where, from Arthur? Before she could answer herself she spied a piece of fabric wedged between several power strips under a worktable. She dove under the table. One side of his shirttail had been ripped from Shawn's Botanical Gardens uniform. She held it up. "He's been here!"

"Where is he now?" Josefina cried.

Georgie checked over her shoulder. Harvey searched behind storage cabinets. She gingerly grasped Josefina's shoulders. *You've got to get it together so you can see* him. *Take a breath. I saw a dock this morning. We need to find where that is. He knows you're telepathic. Maybe he's transmitting but can't get through your panic.*

Okay. Josefina closed her eyes. They popped open. *The front of a building—I know it! It's the old cannery! We have to go there, now!* She started for the door.

Georgie, whisper-shouted, "Wait!"

Josefina glowered.

Harvey watched them like a rubbernecker at an accident.

Georgie asked, "How are we going to get there?"

"What's up?" Harvey asked. "Is this a chick fight?"

"No!" they whisper-yelled.

"Okay. . . ."

Josefina said, "We'll take Shawn's bike, and his brother's."

"Okay," Harvey repeated.

"They're on the back porch."

Georgie and Harvey followed her out and up Shawn's backyard before Georgie could question that they had no real plan. Two police officers stood on the back porch talking but said nothing as she and Josefina grabbed the bicycles and headed down the side steps. They pushed them up the drive. Harvey picked his bike up off the grass.

"We should let somebody know, somebody like the chief or Luther." Georgie glanced back at the front porch. "They must have gone inside."

"I'm not waiting around for them to decide if we're credible," Josefina quipped. She straddled Shawn's bike and peddled into the street before Georgie could respond.

Georgie totally got what Josefina meant about kids being credible. She swung her leg over the high bar of Earl's large mountain bike.

Harvey grinned. "You two are weird, but I'm good with that."

They turned the corner from Birch Street and sped toward Old Mystic Creek Bridge, bounced up, and caught air. It was a straight shot to the docks, downhill Union Avenue all the way, flanked by a streetcar line running along its center.

Josefina, Georgie, and Harvey zoomed down the hill, dodged cars, and ignored stop signs at cross streets. They slowed only at red light intersections. Union Avenue ended in a split where streetcar lines merged from either direction. Street signs declared Bay Road to the left, Dockside Way to the right. Ahead, railroad tracks ran between them and Mystic Creek Bay. On their left, high rises on Bay Road boasted lofts and office buildings. An official blue sign announced the Mystic Creek Port Authority and names of other government offices. Saturday traffic traveled left toward trendy businesses and restaurants.

Georgie and Harvey followed Josefina right, past functioning docks and warehouses. The buildings, ships, and boats appeared older and more neglected the further they went. Georgie could almost hear the last gasps of abandoned buildings, echoes of the forgotten and forlorn across the years. Graffiti was absent here, which oddly made the area more dubious. Angel bumps crept up her arms and tingled over the back of her head. Naturally, this was where Josefina stopped. Just in case, she shot to Luther, *We're at the old cannery!*

Josefina stared across the wide lot, her leg stretched up and over the bicycle's bar in an exaggerated angle, her knee an apex. "He's in there."

Faded, old-fashioned script in smooth waves and curls scrolled across the side of the huge brick, wood, and tin structure: Cannery of Mystic Creek, from Sea to Fine Dining Tables around the World. An expansive shipping and receiving area ran its length. Huge corrugated roll-up doors hung along the cannery's warehouse docks, anchored to the concrete with over-sized and corroded padlocks. Heavy, rusting chains dangled alongside the doors, unmoved by the light breeze reaching from the bay across the silent railroad tracks behind them. Out of place and time, a tan car, the kind her dad would call a land barge, parked at one end. Alongside it sat a white, windowless van. Nearby, cracked concrete steps led to the docks' wide platform.

"Now what?" Harvey's voice took the same pitch Josefina's had. Of course they were nervous. Georgie was too.

"There." Josefina pointed to the single entry door near the steps at the far right. They pedaled over and hid their bikes around the end of the building.

Georgie turned to the others with a finger to her lips, rounded the corner, and stepped up to the loading dock. They scampered across the platform. The door opened into a spacious office, its inner walls windowed and opaque, waist to ceiling. She crouched in place. The room was filled with remnants of the past—spindled receipts, two-hole punches, wooden boxes with metal "In" and "Out" tags. Cupped pencils stood near manual typewriters, old-fashioned telephones, and dirty coffee cups powdered with time. She took in the file cabinets. Yellowed paper poked out of brittle folders from gaping drawers. Upended desk chairs, a wooden coat tree, and a moth-eaten umbrella lay beneath a schedule table neatly drawn on a black chalkboard, but partially obliterated by the years. The place reminded her of favorite black and white movies. The relics held a loneliness and she briefly wondered how such collectibles could be left behind.

"Duck down," she said to the others, her voice hushed. Fresh scuffs and street grime led through the dust to another door. It was ajar. She heard nothing aside from their breathing and cautiously moved to the door to peek out onto a massive factory floor. Greenish windows situated high above were cracked and filmed over by decades of dirt. Catwalks created a mezzanine over old processing areas and assembly lines. Haphazard piles of pallets in front of the roll-up doors partitioned off a broad, open section from the rest of the bay. Georgie scanned the cavernous room with every sense and zeroed in on the set of huge double doors at the far end.

"We need to go there, through those doors," Josefina whispered. Harvey sneezed.

"Shh!" both girls warned.

"Whatev . . ." He stifled another sneeze.

Georgie studied the floor. The trail through the dust led directly to those double doors. No footprints veered off into other areas of the cannery. With a calm she didn't feel, she said, "Follow me on the path as quietly as you can." She reached inside, pulled courage over her fear, and ran as fast as she could with Harvey present. Though glad for her rubber soles, she felt exposed as they passed through the enormous space. Their steps echoed faintly against the walls and windows. This was a good time to reinforce—not push—force fields. Protective shields instantly pulsed around the three of them.

The double doors were the swinging type. Georgie prayed they weren't the squeaking type. She pushed open one side to get a peek, and winced when it creaked. It opened into a hallway. On the left, a metal plate labeled Supply Room perched over a door with wire-embedded glass windows. A padlock hung open through a hasp above the single door handle.

Josefina was in her head. *Shawn's in there.*

That open padlock means whoever wants that room locked is in there now. We can't risk it. We're here to rescue Shawn, not get him hurt. Josefina's face fell, brows furrowed. *Sorry, Josefina.*

You're not sorry, you're right.

Georgie waited a long minute for resolve to overshadow Josefina's anxiety, and glanced at Harvey. Freckles stood in sharp relief on a face drained of its usual color and surliness. She briefly clasped their forearms then gestured, palms down, and mouthed, "Stay." She took a deep breath, ignored her clammy sweat, and slipped through the swinging doors.

Grime wiped from one of the windows left a circular viewing

area. She tiptoed up to it and peered inside. The sight slugged her in her solar plexus. Oh my God! Kids! One man leaned against a wall while another man paced in front of the group of at least eight girls. Black cowboy boots with long, dangerous points jarred the floor—bang, bang, repeat. The girls, anywhere from twelve to sixteen, visibly shook with each pounding boot step.

Crap! Georgie spied a handgun shoved into Pointed Toe's pants at the small of his back. Neither man spoke, but they could have been in between speeches. She searched the faces for Shawn. He looked right at her! Still in his khaki uniform, the aura of his protection vibrated around him. She winced at the bruises and swollen lip mere hours old, the hours before she and Luther corrected her earlier shielding efforts. Georgie promptly placed shields around the girls, ducked, and scurried back to Josefina and Harvey.

"We have to go," she whispered. At Josefina's hesitation, she emphasized, "Now!" She beelined for the office door at the far end, careful to stay in the dust-free trail, her friends close behind. The sound of a door slamming stuttered their pace, but they ran faster to the front office. Once inside, Georgie peeped through a crack in the door to see the double doors open. "Out! Hurry!" she commanded in a forced whisper. She followed them out onto the concrete dock and carefully closed the outside door. "Go to the end of the building where they can't see us."

"What the . . . ?" Harvey started.

"I'll explain when we get down to the bikes. Run!"

They skidded around the corner at the cannery's end and rested against the brick wall. Georgie sent a visual to Josefina. She quietly described the scene she'd witnessed to Harvey and Josefina. Hard boot steps echoed along the concrete dock. They peeked around the corner of the bricks. Pointed Toe clomped down the steps and got into the land barge. Was he Black Jacket Man? Georgie ducked her head back and mashed herself against the building. She commanded in a whisper, "Up against the wall."

"How often do you get to say that in real life?" Harvey joked, but flattened himself.

Josefina ignored him. "Maybe we can distract the other man and get them all out."

"Yeah, Garcia," Harvey whispered sarcastically, "maybe one of us can get shot while the rest of us save the day."

"You have a better idea?" snapped Josephina. Snarl met snarl.

"Shh!" Under other circumstances, Georgie would have been impressed.

The land barge's engine started. Georgie peered around the corner to see the sedan pull out of the huge parking lot and onto Dockside Way.

"Look, you both have good points," Georgie assured them. "Harvey, call 911." She turned to Josefina while he fished in his baggy pants pockets for his phone. *Meanwhile, I'll transmit the situation to Luther and the chief while you do the same to your mom.*

I can distract the man still in there. You can overpower him.

That just might work. Georgie smiled to her friend. Aloud, she said to Harvey, "Wait by the street for the cops?"

"What?" Harvey was between questions with the dispatcher. He swung his head between the multiple demands on his attention. "Okay." Georgie made to leave with Josefina. "Wait," he said. "Where do you think you're . . . ? Uh, yes, ma'am. No. Dockside Way. Some old cannery. Yes, two friends and . . ." They left him with the dispatcher and bicycles.

CHAPTER FORTY

RESCUE

S tooped inside the office, Georgie cracked the door open and scanned the factory floor. Heavy chains hung still against the frames of aluminum rollup doors. She caught Josefina's eye. *Ready?* With no Harvey to witness, she flew across the open cannery floor. When Josefina caught up Georgie opened the double doors and pointed. *It's there, the first door on the left, the supply room.* She heard Josefina's heart racing. Georgie bumped shoulders. *You'll be great. I'll wait outside the door while you charm him.* She surrounded her friend with a force field.

All right. Josefina took a breath, assumed a subdued and servile posture, and slipped through the supply room door. Georgie crowded up against the door jamb to listen and peek through the window's cloudy circle.

The man started and pulled away from the wall. His growl did not hide his surprise. "Where have you been?"

"I was in the bathroom," she answered meekly.

"Get over there," he barked and shoved her toward the others. "Sit down."

He stood in front of the door. A hand gun nestled in the small of his back meant Georgie couldn't "push" him. She wiped her moist hands on her pants. It was time. She turned the knob, burst through the door in a blur, tucked the gun into the back of her pants, and had him prone on the cold, concrete floor—all before he knew she was in the room. Georgie put one knee in his back and yanked the man's arms behind him. Her one-handed vicelock grip held his wrists while she smashed his face to the floor with the other. He cried out in pain. She checked her hold but held her grip.

Luther had said in class that metas don't use guns. But Shawn wasn't a meta. Georgie shoved the gun across the floor to him.

Shawn scrambled out of his position, grabbed the gun, and, wobbly at first, trained it on the man. "It sure is good to see you two."

"Same here, Shawn," Georgie said.

Josefina jumped up and gave him a full-on hug.

The other girls slowly stood, creeping toward the door.

"Wait!" Georgie shouted. They flinched and stopped. Younger ones whimpered. "Oh," she said, more gently. "I apologize for scaring you, but we can't leave yet." She needed time to regroup. Luther's face flew into her mind's eye: *Leave that place now.* But there wasn't time. Partly to Luther and to the group before her, she said, "We don't know if the other guy is on his way back, and he has a gun."

"He is," hissed the prisoner.

"Shut up," Josefina ordered.

"Everyone, move over against that wall," Georgie pointed with an elbow, "on this side of the door, out of view of the window. Be very quiet."

"You're one hot *mamacita*. Why don't I just turn over to get a better . . . ?"

"Shut up, you weasely rat." She caught Shawn's eye then dragged the scoundrel against the wall. Shawn followed outside the man's reach, the gun trained on him. Georgie re-straddled the prisoner and tightened her grip. The rat moaned. She held his face to the floor. An older girl handed her a wadded ball of clothing and gestured to her mouth. "Good idea," Georgie whispered. Careful to steer clear of his teeth, she stuffed the wad into the rat's mouth, and thrust a shield of silence around his entire body.

Josefina put a finger to her lips and guided the rest of the girls to flatten against the wall. She opened the door an inch, and turned her head to listen. Josefina's posture tightened and her aura radiated out like an electrocuted cartoon character. *I hear something.*

So did Georgie. Shuffling and scuffling preceded a boom through the hallway's double doors. A woman's muffled voice said, "Get up." More shuffling and another command, "Move!" Familiar hard boot steps stumbled closer. The door crashed open. It barely missed Josefina. Everyone gasped except the gagged rat. The booted man lurched into the room, bound with a bright orange ziptie, followed by the point of a rifle.

Several uniformed and heavily armed officers pushed into the supply room, S.W.A.T. emblazoned across their bullet proof vests. An officer stepped forward, pushed her face shield up, and relieved Shawn of the hand gun. She grinned down at Georgie's knee in the rat's back and hand holding his head to the floor. "Thank you, miss. We'll take it from here."

Georgie stepped away while another S.W.A.T. team member pulled Weasely Rat to his feet. "Good job," the first officer said to Georgie, then to Shawn, who reddened beneath cuts and bruises.

Chief Ganzhorn entered the room. Georgie's face fell. She was in trouble. He tipped his head toward the rat and his partner. "Get them out of here," his tone disgusted. Georgie took a step. "Not you," he said. His concerned eyes held no sign of their usual twinkle.

Shuffling replaced the ominous clomp of Pointed Toe and his exaggerated boot tips. His ungagged cohort spat, "Crazy bitch." Officers marched the prisoners out. An involuntary grin formed until her eyes met the chief's. Her stomach flopped, for the umpteenth time that day.

The chief took stock of the rest of them and gestured to the remaining S.W.A.T. team to wait in place. "I see we needn't have worried, what with the situation under control by Miss Jones and Mr. Green here, along with you, Miss Garcia. However, you will all share my concern when I tell you that we only apprehended the second gunman on his way back here, right before he got to you." Before they could reply he waved to the other girls. "Who are your friends, Shawn?"

The older girl who had helped Georgie earlier spoke up. "My name is Brittney. We were brought here—Yvonne, Paula, Liliana, and I were taken from my cousin's *quinceañera* party. The other girls were taken from a mall parking lot. The men wouldn't tell us why." The blood around Brittney's mouth said she'd asked.

Georgie took her first close look at the girls. Huddled together, hands held, bruised arms draped around younger shoulders, their faces were streaked with tears, makeup smeared or gone completely. Some wore wilted princess dresses with torn lace, rips, and streaks of dirt. Their up-dos had long fallen and heeled sandals or shoes were scuffed or missing. Holes in tights revealed skinned knees. Elbows of colorful jean jackets or sweaters were either dirty, ripped, or both. Ankle boots and canvas flats showed signs of battles waged. Hair once braided, straightened or curled now hung in ropes or clumps of tangles. It hit too close to home. Josefina's eyes were on her. They'd teared up too.

Chief Ganzhorn cleared his throat. "Thank you, Brittney. You're a brave girl." He glanced at Georgie but said nothing.

Did he think she was careless, a risk taker, a thrill seeker? No, but she could have gotten them all killed.

But you didn't, Georgie. She looked up at the chief. *I'm proud of what you did here today, but we'll have a long talk about roles and responsibilities. The conversation will include your friends there, too.* He tilted his head toward Josefina and Shawn.

Yes, sir.

Shawn raised an eyebrow. He must have caught her silent exchange with the chief.

The chief addressed Brittney, "Paramedics are here to check you over and administer medical attention. We will speak with each of you and get your statements later."

"When can we see our families?" asked Brittney.

Georgie didn't hear his answer. Luther walked in the room and her heart leapt. Bravery was the last thing on her mind when she rushed to the man wearing a fisher's cap.

OUTSIDE, salty sea air charged the crisp afternoon. An unchoreographed light show from law enforcement and emergency vehicles flashed across the cannery's parking lot. EMTs intercepted the supply room crew, minus the prisoners. Georgie declared herself injury-free but acquiesced when the kind EMTs asserted, "Chief's orders." She was immediately cleared but remained on a makeshift bench. Luther left to gather bicycles and greet her dad. Fidgety, she tapped her foot absently—until Josephina warned her telepathically that her foot blurred—and stole a peek at Mom's Insty. Bill and Rose happy in Halloween costumes yanked at her heart. She shoved her phone inside her back pocket and observed the scene around her.

Maria Elena and Shawn's Aunt Darlene arrived in a squad car and were dispatched to the triage area near her bench. Maria Elena leaned over Josefina with an EMT, one of her herbalist students. Josefina protested she was okay, would they please look at Shawn? Josefina rewarded Georgie's stares with a benign scowl.

Though an EMT, a police guard, and Aunt Darlene already surrounded Shawn, Maria Elena and her mentee found a way in.

Harvey had made a dash to leave, but got caught up in the business of giving his statement to a detective. Georgie's gut told her Harvey was trying to get home before his dad knew he wasn't there, maybe before his dad lost his temper.

Brittney waved to Georgie from the girls' check-out and patch-up area.

Chief Ganzhorn cleared a hole in the uniformed defensive line and lifted the yellow tape for Dad and Luther. Georgie jumped up from her observation post. In her excitement she hugged Dad too hard. He groaned but said nothing, being too busy hugging her back.

AT THE POLICE STATION, the kidnapped girls were asked to describe how they'd been taken. Georgie imagined the interviews ahead of them—there'd be many more questions—and passed their waiting family members in the hall on her way to Chief Ganzhorn's office.

She slowed her roll when she spotted Harvey and his dad. An officer congratulated Harvey's dad on his son's heroism. Harvey was nervous. Georgie hoped his dad would stay happily distracted by all the attention. Maybe this time there would be no hell to pay. The officer cautioned the two against responding to news media or posting on social media details about an ongoing investigation. *Right.*

She and Josefina faced Chief Ganzhorn's enormous desk from one end of a semi-circle of chairs. Next to Josefina sat Shawn, rounded out by Aunt Darlene, Maria Elena, Luther, and Dad.

The chief closed his office door, moved an old fashioned photo and sat on his desk between two phones. "Ms. Green, please pass along my apologies to Derrick and Earl. I'm happy to recap our meeting when they return to shore." He turned toward Georgie's side of the room. "When you teenagers arrived at the Greens' house and did not find Shawn, you decided to find him on your own."

"We . . ." Georgie stopped at the chief's raised palm.

"We will go over the events that took place as part of our investigation, and . . ."

Josefina interrupted him. "Frankly sir, it was kind of my fault. I didn't want to wait around trying to convince adults, er, the authorities my idea was credible. Meanwhile, who knew what was happening to Shawn. I was the one who insisted we head to the cannery."

Georgie added, "It's good we didn't wait."

Luther intervened. "We will subsequently analyze each moment of critical thinking and intuitive decision-making as part of our lessons-learned process." His glance volleyed the conversation back to Chief Ganzhorn.

"Yes, and as I started to say," the twinkle back in his eyes, "though your families are rightly concerned, as are Luther and I, we are also proud of you." Georgie stole a glance at Dad, whose expression morphed from observant to pleased. Her attention snapped back to the chief.

"Georgie, your telepathic communication guided us there—just in time. The second gunman had nearly returned to the supply room."

He addressed the room. "Maria Elena recognized the two from the homecoming incident. We suspect they'd returned and were hiding out in old smuggler caves near the port, then moved to the old cannery. It looks like the plan was to again use Shawn to ransom the black box from Derrick, Earl, and their government counterparts. The girls, intended as guinea pigs, were to be 'teleported' with the black box, and later used as part of an existing human trafficking ring." Gasps erupted around the room. "Where to, by whom, and other details are being investigated. We need not speculate or visualize what would have happened when they discovered Project Hermes did not function as they presumed. Why they believed it would work is under meta-normal investigation."

Georgie said, "It'd be great if rescuing people paid more than trafficking them. It might put some of those jack . . . , er, uh, bad guys out of business."

The chief winked. "I like the way you think, kid."

He ordered pizza for the whole station. Police officers handed out water and lemonade. People hovered over pizza boxes and smiled around slices in the crammed squad room. Pizza had that kind of power. Georgie pictured the *quinceañera* and mall girls, wherever they were by now, and wished them pizza. She made a mental note to ask Luther about long distance healing.

This wasn't over. There'd be plenty more discussions, one-on-ones, and classroom conversations. Luther caught her eye. What was behind his look—concern, pride, or planning? Maybe all of the above. Georgie chowed down on a vegetarian slice.

CHAPTER FORTY-ONE

PRESEASON GALA

I*t's beautiful!* Georgie twirled a full 360 degrees. An explosion of diverse holidays decorated the enormous ballroom, from floor to crystal chandeliers. Native medicine shields, leaves, and cornucopias comingled autumn colors with shiny green holly, mistletoe, and ribbons in red, green, blue, and white. A gigantic blinged-out, live Christmas tree anchored one end of the ball room, opposite of the stage end where Dad and his band jammed. Tables loaded with fancy desserts and photos of honorees lined the edges of the ballroom. Her mouth gaped and her eyes popped at the ice sculptures of an EMT, firefighter, and police officer carved with magnificent wings. *Somebody pinch me.*

No problem. Josefina reached out.

"Hey!" She sidestepped.

"But you're right, it's beautiful. And magical. Look at Mom and Luther."

Georgie followed her glance. The two stood under mistletoe.

"It's hard to believe it's almost Christmas."

"Right?" Georgie said. "It feels like I only just got back from Thanksgiving break."

"That's because you just got back from Thanksgiving break," Shawn said.

"Good one, Green." Harvey's gelled spikes flamed in full glory. He and Shawn had assumed truce mode after the rescue.

"Can you believe we're even here?" Georgie asked of no one in particular.

"Pretty cool, right?" Shawn said.

Harvey quipped "Well, we did catch some bad guys." He clapped Shawn on the back. "And rescue the Green dude."

"Oh, Harvey." Josefina rolled her eyes. "Give the girl her moment of awe and wonder."

"Jo's right," Shawn said.

"Jo's right," Harvey mimicked. "The Green dude is scoring points."

"Let's go check out the band. I see Dad and Earl."

"Hey, Georgie, wait up!" Shawn called out. "We're trying to keep up here."

LUTHER ADMIRED the girls in their beautiful dresses and the boys in tuxedoes as they migrated across the ballroom floor. It would be years before they understood, if ever, the impact their recent actions made on individuals and families. The effect would ripple far into the future and remain in memories for generations.

Images of lighthouse renovations flashed across Luther's mind as Maria Elena moved closer to his side and took his elbow. Completion by Christmas would enable the moves before New Year's. He followed her gaze to the mistletoe suspended from the high ceiling on a length of green ribbon—and kissed her perfect red lips.

PHIL GANZHORN LEANED against the balcony railing next to Luther. They gazed down at the crowded dance floor and groups huddled in conversation around tables. Maria Elena, encircled by young adults Luther recognized as her herbalist students, looked up and raised her glass.

The chief asked, "Have you thought more about James Gray since Samhain?"

"Yes. His roll call from Russia could indicate trouble."

"Especially if the whispers hold truth."

"If so, he would be the first," Luther said.

"The first from Eastern North American Region, or Russia?"

"If true, he would be the first rogue meta-normal ever."

Phil Ganzhorn shook his head. "We went through initiation together."

Luther said nothing, but turned to see the faraway look in his friend's eyes.

"James was different, even then. A loner, he set himself aside from the rest of us. But I don't recall him being a jerk. He was polite enough, did okay in class. Frankly, he was unremarkable. I don't even remember his primary ability."

"Fascinating." Luther smoothed his perfect goatee. "My initial probe after the global meditation indicated he may be shield-projecting to obscure his auras. I sensed negative emanations."

"Why would he shield-project such an unflattering image of himself, or is that what he has become?" The chief sipped around the lime in his club soda.

"It is curious."

"True," Phil stretched his neck and shoulder muscles. "James may be in over his head. I have colleagues in Russia and Europe working gang task forces. These people he's befriended are not nice."

"Hmm. Meta-normal reports of extremely successful human gangs have also been linked to activity in the Central American Caribbean Region. What do you know about Gray's business?"

"Umbrac Enterprises, Inc. is an international trade company. It deals in everything from finance to shipping. From what I've found so far, it and its subsidiaries provide services rendered, both in terms of long-term, binding legal contracts and on-demand procurements. On the surface, everything passes muster. Their flagship endeavors are successful, squeaky clean businesses that support global and local community charities."

"Such as?"

"Fishing fleets, eco-friendly luxury condominiums, and software development, for example. However, what I've unearthed from below the surface is seedy—and illegal, if as I suspect, he is associating himself with Russian organized crime."

Luther exchanged eye contact with his companion. "His business dealings have surrounded him with the wrong sort. Could he himself be the wrong sort, his ego seduced to the extent he believes he is more important than our tenets?"

"Perhaps," the chief agreed. "His abilities may not be superior, but enough to convince himself of his own personal greatness."

"Sufficient to inspire the stroking admirations of sycophants? Mr. Gray may have mentally separated, and set himself above humanity and meta-normals alike." Luther leaned toward his friend. "Or, he's playing at a larger game, one in which he projects a negative image of himself to better convince and ensnare his targets?"

Phil Ganzhorn's eyes widened. "Rogue, or self-appointed undercover enforcer?" He shook his head as if it would jostle the notions into a neat line of logic.

"Either way, we must err on caution's side."

The chief straightened. "There's another thing. Gray may have links with Don Pingue."

"Ah, yes. What more have you learned about *Señor* Pingue?"

"Pingue's a notorious businessman living outside of Mexico City. He's well-known in law enforcement circles as a man for whom nothing stands in his way, no act is too depraved, and evidence of crime historically evaporates."

"What is his connection with James?" Luther asked.

"International organized crime intelligence agencies tie coordinated criminal activity between Russia and Mexico. The connection between Gray and Pingue may lie there."

"There's more?"

Ganzhorn drained his glass. "There's fresh meta-normal intel on Pingue's consultations with a gypsy woman who told him of a man who could appear from nowhere. The blogged cover story about the Greens' project reached him about the same time. Pingue immediately began searching for a portal, which included interrogating the *curandero*. You gotta ask, what is Gray's angle? Does he aim to provide teleportation service?"

"Though we thwarted Pingue's most recent actions and averted a full-on lightworker campaign, maligned energy grows around both him and James. We encountered its leading edge with the recent kidnappings." Luther returned his gaze from the ballroom floor to the chief. "James Gray's motives will be revealed. I will deep-scan him personally, Phil."

"He may have access to meta-normal intel." Ganzhorn's eyes darkened.

"Meta-normals, including Penny Hanna and her cohorts, will conduct gradual, persistent shielding of meta-normal and relevant human information in all regions from James—grassroots, cyber, etheric, and in between. You can expect regular, coordinated scans of both him and Pingue, and continued monitoring of their communications." Luther frowned. "It would be prudent to conduct subtle assessments of specific regional mentors before I call for aid."

"Communication scans should include the aliases Gato, Fat Cat, and Shadow."

"Will do. Let us meet again tomorrow night, my office?"

"I'll be there."

"It looks like you'll be on stage soon." Luther pushed away from the railing. "Shall we rejoin the festivities and celebrate our young heroes?"

. . .

THE LAVA LAMP GLOWED, swirled and bubbled in the dark. Georgie would miss that lamp when she moved to Andersen Light. She'd miss time with Dad. She sank into bed and stared at the ceiling. Happy images from the evening danced through her mind. A telepathic voice fast becoming familiar stepped in.

Good evening, Miss Jones. Big night, eh?

Arthur?

All the way from university. The accent give me away?

She laughed. *That's it. Yeah, big night. It was fantastic. You should have been there.*

Oh, I might've popped in to see you and your mates get your awards.

Nice of you. She meant it.

You sparkled in your lovely dress.

She colored in the dark of her room.

It's meant as a compliment.

Yeah, thanks. You know it's the middle of the night here, right?

Of course! My apologies.

No, Arthur. She teetered on yet another precipice of her new life—and leapt. *It's okay.*

I say, it must seem like the last few months have been jammed with strange new things.

You don't know the half of it, but you are definitely on the list.

Strange and *wonderful, I hope.*

She grinned as she imagined his blue-green eyes. *Goodnight, Arthur.*

Goodnight, Georgie.

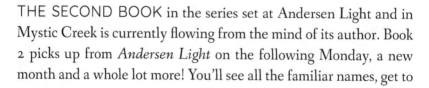

THE SECOND BOOK in the series set at Andersen Light and in Mystic Creek is currently flowing from the mind of its author. Book 2 picks up from *Andersen Light* on the following Monday, a new month and a whole lot more! You'll see all the familiar names, get to know them even better, and meet some new characters along the way.

Here are a few sneak peek questions: Is Mystic Creek High School really planning another dance after what happened at homecoming? What winter holidays hijinks are Luther and Maria Elena planning for the Andersen Lighthouse estate? On whose team is James Gray playing? How does Shawn surprise Georgie and Josefina? What's up between Nancy and Penny? Will Georgie meet Arthur IRL?

Look for the next installment of Mystic Creek coming soon from Empower Press!

ACKNOWLEDGMENTS

Whatever the collective noun for gobs of gobs is, I owe that many thanks and more to all of the people who have helped bring the light of this book into the world. Their support very often extended beyond grammar and story arc to helping me navigate the emotional, mental, physical, spiritual, and logistical terrain of the writing life.

A huge shout out of gratitude to everyone at **GracePoint Publishing**, especially cofounder Michelle Vandepas (who first *heard* me), Tascha Yoder (who got me, *Andersen* Light, *and* wrangled the green light), Mark Packard (wise beyond his years), the wizard Sheryl Babin (design, blurb, and marketing expert, and successful author in her own right), the cover designers, and my editor, Laurie Knight, who fell in love with my novel and characters and is a total joy to work with. I am so very grateful for her intuitive and critical skills!

To each of my **early readers and inevitable editors** (partial manuscript or complete), I pray you feel my love and gratitude: Kevin Anderson (accountability sponsor/coach & advocate), Zion Anderson, Paula Andra, Brad Bergland, Aunt Yvonne Beckner, June Berkey, Jo Casey, Steve Clark, Cassie Dawson, Gerry Otis, Dove Flowers, Mary L. Fritz, M.C.S.W, Jan Hampton (artist & author), Brittney Ingram, Randy Jiner, Kay Kepley (reader, editor, and inadvertent accountability coach), Val Kimball, Bambi Marion, Marlene Nagel, Kent Nelson, D.C., Mary Pearson, Jane Ray, Augustina Scardina, Heather Schollmeyer, Rev. Bonnie Smith, Barbara Villamez, Nancy Walczak, Ken Warner, Nordeen Warner (mother-in love), and Ed Williams.

Thank you, **subject matter experts**: Tobyn Ball and Jennifer Dawsen (young adult language), Mary L. Fritz, M.C.S.W, Adolfo Quezada, M.C.S.W., and Rev. Dalene Fuller Rogers (family psychology and dynamics), David Harper and Bobby Jakcsy (law enforcement), Susan Jennings and Ken Warner (cover letters, classified contracts, and special communications).

Good editors are also teachers. I was blessed with such **editors**: Kay Kepley, Rebecca Lotenero (K&N Literary), Laurie Knight (GracePoint Publishing), Margaret Loring, a.k.a. Rabbitt, and Mary Pearson.

Family, friends, and cheerleaders: I dare not name one without naming you all! Thank you, I love you.

Mentors, especially authors Adolfo Quezada and Lucia Zimmitti, thank for your long-time, unwavering love and support.

Thank you, **early endorsers**: authors Carmen Fox, Rev. Dalene Fuller Rogers, R.D. Petti, Adolfo Quezada, M.C.S.W., and Susan Mitchell, retired defense and intelligence executive. Your kind words carried me through days of flagging energy and hazy vision.

Thank you, Pam Hett (Hett Agency) for your kind and patient **marketing** education and support, and for introducing me to Bryan Sullivan, a.k.a Sully, (Sullivan Designs, LLC) who works his **web magic** for me still.

Las Cruces Writers group, thank you. I am forever grateful. See you at the next meeting.

Special thanks go to Kevin Anderson, Rev. David J. Miller, and Sarah B. Ruckdaschel. There are not enough words to convey my love and gratitude.

I must acknowledge and express gratitude to God, the **serendipity** of the universe, and three human earth angels—my dear friend, Val Kimball, and Alexa Bigwarfe through whose annual Women in Publishing conference I met Michelle Vandepas (cofounder, GracePoint Publishing, LLC). Thank you, serendipity players!

To all of **you I have not yet met**, readers, friends of family, friends of friends, bookstore managers, social media followers, book gift givers, lightworkers, and all the rest, I am grateful and honored for you reading and sharing *Andersen Light*.

Ken Warner, my dear, amazing husband, thank you for believing in me and supporting a dream, which, at times may have seemed more like a mirage than a reality. Thank you, for everything—not just the take-out dinners. I love you deeply. UBtheOne!

META-NORMAL PRIME TENETS

1. Anonymity
2. Take Light Where There Is Darkness
3. Support and Protect the Human Need for Self-Evolution
4. Restore, Nurture and Protect Nature's Balance
5. Cooperation Over Competition

NOTES & REFERENCES

The author wishes to extend her gratitude to Gene Roddenberry and the Star Trek Universe.

https://www.startrek.com/

Is there a "Jackass" in your life? Get help: https://www.childwelfare.gov/

Do you know about C.A.S.A.? Learn more: https://nationalcasagal.org/

Bullying is not okay. Get help: https://www.stopbullying.gov/resources/get-help-now

Cyberbullying is also not okay. Get help: https://www.stopbullying.gov/resources/get-help-now

Get help: National Suicide Prevention Lifeline: https://suicidepreventionlifeline.org

800-273-8255

Learn more about human trafficking and what you can do: https://www.a21.org/

Although Josefina's Uncle Alejandro is a fictional character, Mexico's CEDO, Intercultural Center for the study of Deserts and

Oceans/*Centro de Estudios de Desiertos y Océanos* is very real. Learn more: https://cedo.org/

Love lighthouses? Even if you have never seen one, you can read about their history and support their preservation. Become a pharologist and learn more:

- United States Lighthouse Society https://uslhs.org/
- United States Lighthouse Service
  https://en.wikipedia.org/wiki/
- American Lighthouse Foundation
  http://www.lighthousefoundation.org
- The Lighthouse Preservation Society
  https://lighthousepreservation.org
- World Lighthouses https://www.worldlighthouses.org
- National Park Service
  https://www.nps.gov/articles/lighthouse-keepers.htm

ABOUT THE AUTHOR

Tanya D. Dawson is a happy writer of fiction which she will tell you is "way more fun" than her previous work writing cybersecurity policies and documentation. She has emerged from a life-long career in defense and intelligence as a fresh voice with the intention to spearhead exciting, beyond-normal fiction for YA readers —*without* plummeting into the deep dark, and *with* a sparkling of light. Though fictional, her work is authentic, diverse and empowering.

Midwestern born, avid reader, and veteran of both the USAF and USAF Reserve, Tanya lives in the American Southwest with her amazing husband, a fellow Star Trek and Star Wars fan, surrounded by a forest of mesquite trees and creosotes.

Visit Tanya online at TanyaDDawson.com, read her blog, and sign-up for email updates. Plus, there's Instagram, Facebook, TikTok, and Twitter!

FROM THE PUBLISHER

For more great books, visit Empower Press online at https://
gracepointpublishing.com/empower-press/

EMPOWER
P   R   E   S   S

CPSIA information can be obtained
at www.ICGtesting.com
Printed in the USA
FSHW012304091121
85999FS